I'LL QUIT WHEN I'M DEAD

ALSO BY LUKE SMITHERD

The Physics of the Dead
The Stone Man: The Stone Man, Book One
The Empty Men: The Stone Man, Book Two
The Stone Giant: The Stone Man, Book Three
March of the Stone Men: The Stone Man, Book Four
In the Darkness
A Head Full of Knives
Weird. Dark.
How to Be a Vigilante: A Diary
Kill Someone
You See the Monster

NOVELLAS

The Man on Table Ten
Hold On Until Your Fingers Break
My Name Is Mister Grief
He Waits
Do Anything
The Man with All the Answers

I'LL QUIT WHEN I'M DEAD

LUKE SMITHERD

MULHOLLAND BOOKS
LITTLE, BROWN AND COMPANY
NEW YORK BOSTON LONDON

The characters and events in this book are fictitious. Any similarity to real persons, living or dead, is coincidental and not intended by the author.

Copyright © 2025 by Luke Smitherd

Hachette Book Group supports the right to free expression and the value of copyright. The purpose of copyright is to encourage writers and artists to produce the creative works that enrich our culture.

The scanning, uploading, and distribution of this book without permission is a theft of the author's intellectual property. If you would like permission to use material from the book (other than for review purposes), please contact permissions@hbgusa.com. Thank you for your support of the author's rights.

Mulholland Books / Little, Brown and Company
Hachette Book Group
1290 Avenue of the Americas, New York, NY 10104
mulhollandbooks.com

First Edition: October 2025

Mulholland Books is an imprint of Little, Brown and Company, a division of Hachette Book Group, Inc. The Mulholland Books name and logo are trademarks of Hachette Book Group, Inc.

The publisher is not responsible for websites (or their content) that are not owned by the publisher.

The Hachette Speakers Bureau provides a wide range of authors for speaking events. To find out more, go to hachettespeakersbureau.com or email hachettespeakers@hbgusa.com.

Little, Brown and Company books may be purchased in bulk for business, educational, or promotional use. For information, please contact your local bookseller or the Hachette Book Group Special Markets Department at special.markets@hbgusa.com.

Book interior design by Marie Mundaca

ISBN 9780316579568
LCCN 2025932206

Printing 1, 2025

LSC-C

Printed in the United States of America

For Erika...and all the Smithereens

PART ONE
Light

I always tell people that you can call me anything that you want. You can call me Arnold...you can call me Schwarzy...but don't ever, ever call me the self-made man...The whole concept of the self-made man or woman is a myth.

—Arnold Schwarzenegger

Chapter One: Johnny

Bringing Down the House

THREE THOUSAND PLUS people roar their approval as the final chord rings out. The crowd is fully warm now, four songs into Johnny Blake's set, loose and loud. Johnny holds up one hand, the other gripping the neck of his guitar, and tries to take in the screaming love. It's hard to absorb, but they are all here for him. Tonight, he is their king — they want him to be — and that means he has a responsibility. They want a fun show, and he has to deliver.

"How you feeling, Birmingham?"

Another roar. That one got through; the hairs on his arms stand up. Okay. He's here. He's trucking. "You know, last night, we were in..." Where were they last night? *Think. Jesus, that's weird.* "In, uh..." He blows air out of his nostrils, the mic picks it up, and immediately he can feel the audience tense.

Fix it.

Johnny lets out as genuine-sounding a chuckle as he can muster, and the audience relaxes a little, giving their own nervous laughter back to him. They want to. They want the King to be happy so they can be happy.

The air in the building is thick and sweaty, condensed in the packed town-hall-sized venue that is the Birmingham Academy. The smell of beer and the buzz of low-level conversation washing forward in a wave that rolls up onto the stage. It breaks and crashes over Johnny, and his heartbeat pulses strongly in his temple. It feels *close* in here tonight, even in a venue of this size, on a *stage* of this size. He shuffles his feet, avoiding the foot pedals at the base of his mic stand and wishing the stage lights weren't so fucking bright. He looks at them and blinks three times, as he's of course been doing all night.

"Jesus," he says into the mic, wiping his face, and the audience chooses to laugh louder, deciding to accept this as *rock 'n' roll, baby*. He's never, ever enjoyed playing live, never been comfortable as the center of attention in any space. He's a songwriter, not a performer. But the money is almost all in the touring now, or at least it is for someone operating at Johnny's level. He doesn't have much of a choice in the current streaming-industry climate. He's lucky that he's got enough of a following to make getting on the road almost worth it. But he isn't a showman. *The Guardian* called him "personally unengaging but vocally gifted" in their live review. "Come for the music, but don't expect a show."

He's been trying to turn it up lately, trying to learn from his musical heroes. Throw a wink in here, a bit of crowd work there. He can put on a show, right? He has to be the King, like it or not. Ivan told him that. "I think I'm as out of it," he says, "as you guys are. Hell..." The audience roars in delight. *You're fucked up, we're fucked up, and this is what we wanted; we wanted to go to a different place for a night.*

That'll do. What's next? He looks down at the setlist, his whole body feeling hot: "Please Don't Take Me Home." Perfect. An old, old song of his; he could play it with his eyes shut. He glances over to his right at Mark, his bassist—an older, skilled hired gun just like the rest of the backing band. Mark's brow is furrowed, noticing something is off; Johnny wonders if Mark realizes how close Johnny is to a full-blown panic attack. He's come close many times, but never—

He can fix this. He's already fixing it, it's fine, it's fine...

"You know," Johnny says quickly into the mic, jerking forward and just fucking *talking*, remembering *The Independent* calling him "robotic" and "distant." So he'll talk. "I wrote this next song when I was fourteen." If he can rattle off a quick, lucid intro, no one will know how bad he is right now. "I remember I had to do it *quietly*. You ever tried to write a song quietly?" Light chuckles. "My dad slept a lot in the evenings, as he worked nights, and if you woke him up, *woof.* Anyone here have a dad who worked nights?" Cheers. "You ever wake him up on the wrong fuckin' day?"

Open laughter. *That's better.* The King straightens up onstage. *They're here to see you.* "Yeah, yeah, you know what it's like." He gently forms the opening chord with his left hand as he talks: G minor. "The guy would just...light me up if I woke him." More laughter, but uncertain now. Johnny tries to correct it. "I'm talking, like...a fucking *belt.*" He forces another chuckle at the end, to make it clear that this is supposed to be funny, but he simultaneously realizes that (a) it isn't and (b) he doesn't think it's funny either. The room is deafeningly quiet. Now it's bad, *fuck,* okay, he can save it, he just has to make it *showtime,* he can do that, yes.

He quickly taps his thumb and forefinger together, *1-2-3,* the stress making another of his little rituals kick in. The ritual doesn't help, but then it never really does. He looks to his left, into the wings, and spots Ivan's short, wide form looking tense, the older man's shoulders set as he stands gripping a beer in each hand. Tonight is a rare night out for Ivan, Johnny insisting his friend and mentor come to a local gig while the show is in town, and the dude came to party. Ivan doesn't look as if he's in a party mood right now, though; he mouths something:

What's wrong?

Johnny looks back to the audience, the edges of his vision starting to gray as panic grips his throat. "But fuck that guy, eh?" Johnny cries, throwing up a hand as sweat runs down either side of his face. Now there is very little laughter, and that which does come is nervous.

Play the song. Just shut up, play the rest of the songs, and thank them, then go home.

But it's weird now, they all think he's crazy, and he needs this to be fun for them because now they surely think that he's some kind of fucking amateur.

He's not, and he has to fucking show them—

"Hey—"

And then he's throwing off his guitar, feeling lightheaded, and ignoring Mark as the bassist says whatever he's saying, because Johnny knows that if the audience have a choice between saying he was weird or saying he was wild they will pick the latter, they want to, so if he gives them something wild to talk about—

Fuck it—

There's a heavy and painfully loud clattering over the PA as Johnny's guitar hits the floor, followed by a feedback whine that makes the whole room wince, but Johnny is leaning into his decision. *This will work, I'm sorry you came to see me and I'm just not right, but I can make this fun, it can be chaotic fun that we all can—*

The sound engineer mercifully kills the channel and the feedback cuts out, but Johnny is already grabbing the mic and deliriously barking two words into it as his vision of the audience swims.

"Catch me."

He charges past the mic stand and runs up and over the monitor, pushing off it with his feet and catapulting himself into space as he flies off the stage.

His hang time in the air seems longer than he expected; he suddenly feels impossibly light and free, *glorious* even as he floats, completely and utterly present. He has time to see the upturned blank faces below him, briefly feeling as if he is taking off and will continue to rise higher as he hears three thousand people respond—more gasps than cheers, he will later remember, the audience's concern taking all the *fun* out of it—before he sees something terrible.

The people below him are parting like the Red Sea.

Johnny tries to turn in the air, to twist and buck like a salmon in order to right himself and at least stand a chance of landing on his feet, but all that does is flip him all the way over, exposing his back. He plummets spine first toward the concrete floor.

The sense of dropping beneath the level of the crowd's heads reminds him of that old trust game they used to play at school, the one where you fall backward and blindly let people catch you; the bigger kids would leave the save as late as possible to make the falling child believe they were going to hit the deck. Johnny remembers a flash of the exhilaration, the rush from the momentum of his then-child's body passing the point at which he thought he was going to be caught and feeling as if he were dropping into the depths.

Tonight, there are no bigger kids to catch him. He has the presence of mind to get his hands behind his skull just before impact. The floor of the Birmingham Academy hits him in the back, buttocks, and legs with an undeniability so dense and solid that it takes away all of his ability to move, to think. The faces of the people who moved away now crowd back in around and above him, staring down at him and making him feel as if he were looking up out of a grave, but just as the pain begins to break through, Johnny's vision starts to gray once more. He hears yelling over the PA system, but it sounds muffled; Johnny understands that he is falling into unconsciousness.

Thank God, he thinks, and lets the grayness take him.

Chapter Two: Madison

No Woman Would Ever Allow Herself to Be Put in This Situation

Madison can't do it.

There's copper in her breath, soup in her arms and legs where bones used to be, and a timing chip tied into her shoelaces that cannot be denied. Excuses are not an option. This irony is not lost on Madison as she stumbles into the final thousand meters, the home stretch.

Many other runners are keeping pace with her, all of them gasping and sweating in a spaced-out cluster. Beyond her temporary companions lie the roadside barriers, behind which a decent crowd stands two or even three people deep at certain points. They're cheering, clapping, waving. She has a weird feeling that her mother is somewhere nearby, but looking for her would of course be useless. The sky above is surprisingly gray for an August race. Through Madison's blurry, sweaty vision, the clouds blend in with the concrete of Coventry's streets. She tells herself *the* line, the one repeated so many times that the words are almost completely drained of their power, a cold steak chewed until all flavor is gone:

You can do it.

The phrase stirs nothing inside her now, as recognizable and instantly ignored as *Warning: Contents may be hot.* This is just too hard.

She curses herself for all those extra hits of the SNOOZE button, those *ten more minutes* of screen time that turned into an hour, those days when she did a light session instead of the heavy one. Those tiny capitulations all added up, whispering away her discipline until taking the easy way out became the norm all over again. How could she have forgotten how badly she needed this? The problem with motivation, she knows, is that it has amnesia.

She's furious with herself.

You didn't wanna do the work? Well, for this home stretch at least, you are gonna fucking hurt.

Madison cries out, her feet bite into the concrete, and the *other* words rage at the front of her mind, the ones that of course have more flavor and saltiness than ever:

How the fuck did I talk myself into this?

Three months earlier
PureGym, Coventry

Madison stares at the contents of the vending machine, seeing the wall of protein bars and £8 locker padlocks for sale behind its glass display. She's tried the bland, flavorless dough of the protein bars before. One of the padlocks, she thinks, might be the more enjoyable snack. Her brain unhelpfully conjures up a memory of the school vending machines of her youth: Twixes, Mars bars, KitKats. Then she's suddenly glad they aren't available. If they were, she knows she would be unable to resist. Imani is the one who can say no to chocolate.

"Hey, Madison." A voice from behind her.

"Hi," Madison mumbles, her response automatic and without recognition. She glances after the stranger who offered the greeting, and is suddenly struck for a moment by the incredible shape this woman is in. Her yellow spandex two-piece reveals a stomach so chiseled that she must surely be a professional athlete.

Of course many of the young women Madison sees at PureGym

are fit, but this woman is something else. Every muscle in her abdominal wall is clearly defined and sharp. Her shoulders are toned and rounded, her legs strong and smooth without a hint of cellulite. She walks tall, her posture upright and strong.

The stranger smiles and gives a little wave, seeing Madison—and now Imani too—looking, and Madison feels a flutter of what she knows is incorrect recognition. Madison turns back to the machine and presses the buttons for one of the dairy-free, carb-free, gluten-free (*and to quote Garfield,* Madison thinks, *flavor-free*) protein bars: E5. The vending machines are situated near the gym entrance, next to the small seating area where members can work or eat, or where staff sit with new signees and upsell as best they can. Away to the right is the gym floor proper, the sounds of clanging weights and thumping house music echoing off the gym's high ceiling. It's peak time and the place is packed, another reason Madison *really* doesn't like going to the gym.

"Is that Kelly?" Imani mutters behind Madison, not wanting her uncertainty overheard.

The woman's face *does* look a bit like Kelly's, Madison thinks, but then jerks her gaze away from the machine as she hears a surprised gasp. Imani is striding away with her hands on either side of her face.

"Jesus Christ, Kelly!" Imani cries. The stranger turns, pleased and shyly grinning—*Shucks, you got me, but I kinda wanted you to*—and Madison sees it *is* Kelly!

Madison's jaw drops.

"Oh my God," she breathes, openly looking Kelly up and down as she walks over, following Imani, who has wrapped Kelly up in a hug. "You look... Holy *shit*, Kelly." Now Madison and Kelly hug, and Madison briefly realizes they've never hugged before—they're only gym friends—but Madison is so delighted for Kelly that her reaction was instinctive. She remembers how Kelly used to try to cover her gymwear-exposed body with her arms as she talked.

"Is this where you've been?" Imani asks, gesturing at Kelly's abs. "Putting this together? You sneaky cow, you only went and turned yourself into a Bad Bitch!"

Madison smiles, rolling her eyes. Typical Imani.

"Yeah, I went away to grind for a bit," Kelly says sheepishly, red-faced again but now from *aw shucks* pride. The woman is glowing. "Thanks, guys! Nice to be appreciated."

"Well, how could we not?" Madison says, still dumbstruck. This is *not* how Kelly used to look. "I've never—"

"Seen a change like it," Imani says, shaking her head and speaking for Madison, which is one of Madison's pet peeves about their friendship. She lets it slide, though. She's been letting a lot of things slide lately, and she's finding that, in the short-term at least, it makes life a *lot* easier. The long-term can be dealt with another day.

"How did you do it, Kelly?" Madison asks. "Seriously, well done! I am so proud of you!!" She hears herself. Is she being patronizing? She switches to her usual rescue tactic: self-deprecation. "I can barely get myself to put on a sports bra and get over here."

"Don't be silly. You look great—you both do." Kelly smiles.

While the phrase is clearly meant to be kind, Madison also knows it's a lie; she glances at herself in one of the nearby floor-to-ceiling mirrors. As always, her brain tells her that she hates what she sees: chipmunk cheeks, pasty white skin, piggy brown eyes, brown hair too long and greasy. Two weeks ago she paid to have her body mass index measured. At five foot six and a BMI of 26, Madison has now officially tipped over into the realm of the overweight. The news didn't create any feeling of motivation, only resignation; she wasn't lying about what she can barely get herself to do. She has the list of well-intentioned remarks from Imani to prove it: "Just come to some classes with me. It'll be fun. Moving around will make you feel good." And Imani *does* look great—not Kelly great but still slim and without a single fold in her smooth skin... none of which would be a problem if Madison had anything else at all going for her right now. That way she could say, *None of that superficial bullshit matters; X is what matters,* and actually mean it.

Imani, at twenty-five, is only two years older than Madison, and already she has many, many things going on.

"I just had to make a lot of changes," Kelly is saying, "to my mindset, diet, training, everything. I can't lie; it's easily been the hardest thing I've ever done."

"I can imagine," Madison says. "Bloody *hell*. Like, how long did this take?"

"About six months," Kelly says, "although the hardest part by far was the first one. That was when I made all the changes. I did this course. It was a whole thing. Had to take a month off work."

"They let you do that?" Imani asks.

"Used all my annual leave," Kelly says. "I gave them plenty of notice."

"You still at..." Madison begins, and then doesn't have it. *Shit, what was the name of where Kelly worked?* "Barrington's," she finishes, making the save.

"Yeah, full manager now actually." Kelly grins. "You still at Gilligan's?"

Madison forces a well-practiced fake smile onto her face. "No, I left," she says.

"Ah, okay. Working a job and studying at the same time can be a lot—I get it."

Madison notices Imani stiffen a little at the statement. Madison reddens slightly. "No, I left university too, I'm afraid."

Her shame multiplies by a factor of ten, not just by being blasted by the security-floodlight-level shine of Kelly's transformation but also from having the aimlessness of her situation thrown into full relief. She wants to explain: *There was this relationship thing that became a bad breakup, and university had—*

"Oh!" Kelly says, embarrassed too. "Oh, I'm sorry. What's the plan now, then?"

"I don't know," Madison says. "I'm job hunting..." She trails off, desperate for something to add. *The book.* "Actually, I've been, like, writing a novel. Just for fun."

"Oh, that's so cool," Kelly says, grinning. "I always wanted to do that. Historical fiction, maybe. But you're actually doing it!"

Madison smiles. Kelly's nice.

"Meh," she says, shrugging comically. "It's not so impressive when that's all you have to do. And I've still got to finish it, I have a little money though for now, so I can focus on plot rather than rent, if you get me." Madison feels that little flutter of gratitude again for her mother's financial gift, and the companion thought follows straight on its heels as always: *At least the woman did* something.

Kelly puts a hand on Madison's shoulder and looks her in the eye. "You're going to figure it all out," she says, low and sincere. "And you're going to be okay."

Silence from the three women. Sounds of colliding and sliding metal all around them, behind all that the steady thud of house bass. Madison suddenly doesn't know what to say; the conversation was appreciative small talk, and now here is the moment of open concern and sincerity...but it's a bit odd. *Overly* sincere. Kelly isn't Madison's life coach, but she's talking like one. Even so, there's a warmth in Kelly's gaze.

"Yeah, I hope so, thanks, yeah," Madison says, scratching her ear and feeling awkward. "Hey," she adds quickly, changing the subject. "You said something about a course? What was that?"

Kelly's smile falters. She looks around the room and shifts uncomfortably for a moment. Madison glances at Imani; her friend is still smiling at Kelly in awe. She didn't see it.

"I'll have to get you the details," Kelly says, beginning to turn away. "Oh, one of the squat racks is finally free. I've got to go."

"Oh, no problem. Go, go!"

Kelly waves and hurries away onto and across the expansive gym floor, leaving Madison and Imani at the vending machines.

Imani whistles quietly. "Jesus," she says.

"I know," Madison agrees. The Twix, she remembers. It's still in the machine. She turns to retrieve it.

Then she stops.

"Hold on a sec, Ims," Madison says. She strides across the gym floor, trying not to think about what she's doing, her eyes searching for that bright yellow. She finds it; Kelly is loading plates onto the bar. "Kelly?"

Her acquaintance looks up, surprised, and then gives a confused smile.

"Oh, hey."

Whatever determination has propelled Madison over here suddenly vanishes. "Seriously. I just wanted to, like, say congratulations again," she lies. "You've obviously put in the work and you look incredible."

Kelly cocks her head, beaming and genuinely touched. "Thank you. You two have really made my day."

Ask her.

"No problem," Madison says, smiling herself. She is at least pleased that she made Kelly happy. But then she scurries away, the question unasked.

Loser.

Hey, forgive me for messaging you.

No, no, no. Too stalker-y.

Hey, sorry for chasing this but I simply had to ask!

That's better. More pally-pally, more work colleague-y. *If in doubt, add an exclamation point.* They might be Facebook friends, but Madison doesn't know Kelly well enough to send her a DM out of the blue. She never has before, certainly, and that makes this weird enough as it is.

Especially after I was really blown away today by the way you looked and just your overall energy. It was really impressive, but I noticed

Noticed what? How should she put it? She decides to just write the honest version for a first draft. She can always amend it before sending, if she sends it at all.

that when I asked how you did it you kinda ducked me?

If you'd rather not say what you did, I completely understand

Even if asking got her nowhere, she would have done something that made her uncomfortable; she could celebrate a small win. Maybe this could even be how she finally got back on track: picking smaller dragons to slay and chaining a few of those victories in a row.

...but I would love to know because I could use a win right now and I'd like to do whatever you did myself. NO JUDGEMENTS!

It wasn't just Kelly's weight loss or new muscle tone.

It was something in the woman's eyes.

She looked alive, as if Madison was simply drifting through reality and Kelly was now mainlining it.

But your journey is your own and if you want to keep it private, I TOTALLY understand. Love you lots either way and again, you look amazeballs.

She rereads it. It's not too bad as it is.

She hits SEND.

She waits for the sting of regret and shame to come—*Why the hell did you do that? She's going to think you're a weirdo stalker, asking her private questions*—but she manages to keep a lid on it. A little dragon slain. It felt unfamiliar, and good.

She even manages, over the rest of the evening in her tiny, messy apartment, to not keep checking for replies. She busies herself; she nearly goes to work on the mess, identifying a small dragon, but somehow ends up on the sofa with the TV on, staring at the ceiling. She can picture her dad standing over her now, criticizing, not getting after her for the mess itself but for the potential judgment of *visitors*, of *how passive* the mess is, asking if she *wants to go and live with the Wintermans down the road or even the Barstows if she wants to be like* those *kinds of people. Why can't you be more like your sister?* Then she pictures her mother walking in and her dad clamming up, not wanting to risk setting his constant powder keg of a wife off...

Bloody hell, Madison thinks, hearing her internal spiraling. *Relax.*

She tells herself that not checking her messages again will be the next tiny dragon she can surely slay, but by the time 9:13 rolls around, even that pathetic creature wins. She allows herself another check.

Kelly has replied.

Madison reads, not knowing why she's so excited by this but enjoying it anyway. It's nice to be excited again.

Sorry, Kelly has written. I didn't mean to. I guess I was a bit embarrassed because if I tell you what I did, you'll think I'm mental! Even if you were impressed with the results. It's personal development taken to the extreme. Physically intense with lots of mind games involved.

It's definitely not for the fainthearted.

Madison's heart sinks a little. She is definitely fainthearted. Previously that only meant failings such as not sticking with spin class. Nowadays she can barely bring herself to leave the fucking house.

I can tell you some of the basics here, Kelly says, but to really understand, it's probably better if you hear the pitch from Ellie herself.

Ellie who?

But if you go through with it, Kelly writes, to use Imani's phrase, you'll become a Bad Bitch in a way you never thought possible.

Bad Bitch. A buzz phrase that always gets under Madison's skin a little. She's seen it used far too many times online, along with the other mantras: *Rise and Grind. The 5 a.m. Club. Your Body is a Machine.* Such jargon always stirs jealousy, resentment, and irritation in her that gets worse each time she sees it. She's a person, not a robot. She wasn't put on Earth to *maximize productivity.*

But dammit...she needs a little of that at least. And hell, today the idea sends the briefest little thrill through her: Madison as a Bad Bitch.

The course I attended is called NO DAYS OFF, it's a females-only intake, it takes place in Vermont, USA, and it lasts a month. You won't find anything about it online. Here's my number if you don't already have it. We can chat first and then you can see if you want to speak to her. It'd be nice to talk outside of the gym anyway.

Madison feels that twist she always gets when someone wants to get closer, that strange tension of craving connection and yet instantly feeling overwhelmed by the prospect. She's trying to do better with it. She really is.

Vermont, she thinks. *Would I really go that far?*

She thinks of Kelly. Of her glow.

She types, and when she does, she manages to forget about her social anxiety and get excited for what she might become.

Hope. It's nice to feel that again too.

Sounds great! Madison writes. **When would you like to talk?**

Two weeks later
A Coventry Memorial Park bench

Madison expected some kind of densely built six-foot-tall Amazonian, but Ellie is quite a lot shorter than Madison. Petite almost, and while it is hard to tell through Ellie's jacket, it looks as if she carries the wiry frame of a long-distance runner. Her posture is perfect, her shoulders back, her lean neck proudly supporting a head covered in long black poodle curls scraped into a ponytail that rests upon Ellie's left shoulder. Madison doesn't know Ellie's exact age, but based on her CV, the woman must be at least fifty. She looks it, but a *good* fifty.

Kelly set up this rendezvous. It's a pleasant May afternoon. A gentle breeze buffets Madison's shoulder-length hair, carrying the distant yelps of young boys playing some sort of game that involves a lot of happy screaming. Madison ignores them and listens to her companion, feeling the warm coffee cup in her hand and the blood jumping in her veins.

"Ninety-nine percent of people wouldn't do it," Ellie is saying. "Ninety-nine point nine percent, really. It's a crazy idea, but some people need crazy solutions. And *those* are the people I'm here for. When I told my sister about my idea for the residential, digital detox version of No Days Off," Ellie continues with a smile, "she said no woman would ever put herself in that situation."

Madison understands. Kelly told her the premise of the No Days Off course, and it is crazy. "There are consequences for failure or refusal," Kelly said. "And you can always say no to them, but then you go home." She said a lot more than that, but the fire in her eyes sold Madison completely. Then *she* explained it to Imani, who told Madison in no uncertain terms that anyone would be utterly crazy for even considering attending this course.

Crazy solutions, Madison thinks.

"Like I say," Ellie says, "ninety-nine percent of the time? My sister was absolutely right about people not doing it. But ninety-nine percent of people wouldn't put themselves through a Navy SEALs Hell Week, and even the majority of those who do, drop out." She smiles and shrugs. It looks a little forced, but that's okay. Madison isn't here to make a friend. She's here to change her life. But she's sweating. It's warm out, too warm for the oversized coat she's chosen to wear. She feels stupid about it now, but before she left home, Madison decided she didn't want Ellie to see what kind of shape she's in. Not out of shame, even though that is a factor in everything, but because she was told Ellie had to accept you into the course. Is the woman looking for athletes, then? The question was skipped like most of the others; Kelly remained fairly coy when she and Madison spoke, explaining some things, but not many. "Talk to Ellie" was the insistent refrain.

Ellie, dressed in a stylish white jacket, black pants, and pumps, agreed to meet Madison in Coventry for her one-hour consultation. "It's equidistant for us both," Ellie said. They each have a coffee that Madison bought from the nearby stand. Madison's is a mocha with whipped cream, ordered out of habit. By the time she realized, changing it would have been weird.

Ellie's is black.

"So," Ellie says, giving the smile again that Madison finds a little unusual. It never quite reaches her eyes yet still manages to seem genuine and warm. Madison doesn't think she's ever seen a smile quite like it. "Light or Medium?"

Ah, now. This is something that Kelly divulged, and even Ellie mentioned it in her highly professional reply to Madison's email. Apparently there are two slightly different versions of the No Days Off course to choose from, if one is to be accepted. Ellie's email also mentioned what she called Hard Corrections: "the keystone of No Days Off." It is a frightening idea, and it is indeed—to use Kelly's word—extreme.

But Madison was intrigued.

"I'm nervous to say it," Madison says. "But I think I'm going to take Medium." She's trying to sound bright, energetic. The kind of person you *want* to have in a course like this. She reminds herself again to sit up straight. *Smile.*

"You sure?" Ellie asks, her California lilt working its way confidently and easily through the warm Coventry air, turning the heads of a mildly surprised English couple as they stroll past. Her voice is deep for a woman, loud without shouting. Madison has been extremely lucky in her timing; Ellie has come to the UK both to look at some investment property and to screen applicants wanting to take part in No Days Off. It is, apparently, the first time she has done such a thing. "As you probably know, the differences between Light and Medium are a lot more than just getting a cheat meal day on Light." Ellie sips at her coffee and picks at a piece of lint on her jacket; the gesture looks contrived.

Madison knows this. On Light, you may excuse yourself from three Hard Corrections. It sounds a lot more pleasant, but if there's one thing Madison knows about herself, it's that she will always take a back door if one is offered. That's the whole appeal of the course. She cannot choose Light.

"I'm sure."

"Kelly told you to do Medium, then?" Ellie asks.

"She did."

Ellie frowns for a second. "Remind me which Kelly," she says. "I've had a couple in the last few years. Was she on Medium?"

"You remember them all?"

"Oh yes," Ellie says earnestly. "I remember all my clients. It's a very personal course."

Madison says, forcing a joke, "Even when they, like, look totally different by the end of the month? All turned into skinny Minnies?" Ellie seems to understand it's meant to be lighthearted, but the way she smiles and looks at her cup makes clear this is a misconception she's a little tired of explaining.

"That's not the aim of what I do," Ellie says, "and we certainly don't want to be producing any size zeros by the end of the course."

"Oh, I know," Madison says quickly. "I was just being silly—"

"It's okay, Madison," Ellie says kindly, using Madison's name for the first time.

Madison is almost surprised, then remembers that Ellie will have of course read the extensive (and in Madison's opinion *way too personal*) application questionnaire Madison completed.

"You were just joking," Ellie says, "but it's brought up something I always like to make clear." She sets her cup on the bench. "I always tell people, you shouldn't come to me just because you want to lose weight, or to fit into a wedding dress, or to put another twenty pounds on your squat. There are a lot of great personal trainers for that. NDO is about something else. It's about making you better. Body, mind, and soul. The course is built to make you—not help you, *make you*—excel."

Ellie's eyes look alive. It's a look Madison has seen before. She has to concede that Ellie's appearance is actually intimidating as hell, not because she is beautiful in any kind of mainstream sense of the word—Madison doesn't like to think such things about anyone, though Ellie is almost inarguably plain—but because the woman just looks so damn *stylish*. Her olive-colored skin—perhaps Greek heritage, perhaps Spanish—would be flawless if not for the faintly visible scar that runs from under the edge of her jacket collar and up to a few inches below her ear. It is a thin track of white that looks somehow graceful and decorative, almost like jewelry.

"By the end of the course month," Ellie is saying, "you are not only going to be in the best shape of your life but you're also going to have undergone an entire mindset change. You'll feel like you've gone from being Pee-Wee Herman to a Golden Gloves champion in four weeks, and more importantly, you'll *stay* that way. It's no good to you *or* me if you walk out of there looking and feeling great and then are back to unhealthy ways by the end of the year. No Days Off is designed to drill the tools into you for *life*. That's why it's so effective, and that's why there's a two-year waiting list."

"Two *years?*" Madison is crestfallen.

"I'm afraid so," Ellie says. "The cancellation list is long too, but here's the good news: Someone dropped out of the September

Medium course, and it just so happens that's too soon or the wrong month or whatever for everyone else on the list. Potentially, that slot could be yours."

Excitement dances in Madison's chest, and for a moment she truly believes in the possibility of change. A different version of herself flashes before her.

"If you're going for Medium, that would keep the balance right," Ellie continues. "I have three Light people already on this intake. Any more than three, I find, tends to upset the dynamic." Madison knows that beyond Light and Medium lies Heavy, which is accessible only after you have done at least a week at Medium, and even then, the levels remain at Ellie's discretion. "It's hard for most people in regular jobs to get out of work for so long on short notice. But you're unemployed right now? And you're a novelist?"

Madison blushes. Ellie's language, like her it seems, is to the point.

"Yes and no," Madison says quietly. "I was studying, then I was working in the restaurant trade, and now I'm not. But as for being a novelist... I *want* to be a writer, and I've been working on a book. It's just harder than I thought since it's quite personal."

"Say no more," Ellie says, holding up a hand and smiling warmly. "Blocked artists are one of my specialties."

"I'm not blocked; I'm just slow. But, Ellie, you said someone cancelled." Madison is eager to get back to it. "It's so much money."

Ellie's eyebrows rise, but she's still smiling.

"Sorry," Madison adds quickly. "I don't mean the price; I mean I'm surprised someone gave that money up. I'm assuming the tuition is nonrefundable?"

The price of the one-month course, Madison knows, is just over ten thousand pounds. The price is another reason Imani was horrified by what Madison is planning. *That cash could go toward a house deposit.*

"No," Ellie says with no small hint of satisfaction. "There's usually someone to take their slot. I'd charge them if I couldn't fill it, or at least keep their deposit, but that's rare. Legally I could keep it all, but I don't. It *is* a lot of money. I'm not into creating more problems for people who are already looking for help."

Madison is pleasantly surprised, and pleased she can afford it. Even when she was working, there was no way she could cover this, but her inheritance finally came in. Liz got hers too, presumably, but Madison hasn't spoken to her sister in at least five years, so she can't know for sure.

"So," Ellie says. "Any questions so far?"

"Yes," Madison says, grinning. "How is the course organized?"

Ellie sits up suddenly and takes off her coat. Her white scar, Madison sees, continues all the way along the top of her trapezius muscle. Madison doesn't look away quickly enough. Ellie sees her staring.

"Goražde, Bosnia," Ellie says, shrugging.

"Sorry. I didn't mean to stare. I was just surprised."

"Happens all the time," Ellie says good-naturedly, gently folding her coat and placing it on top of her Gucci bag. "I think it looks kind of elegant, don't you?"

It does, this thin line of white that follows the olive-skinned curve of Ellie's neck. Exposed, Ellie's arms are slim but rock solid. The rest of her is equally lean, her otherwise flat chest filled out with noticeable muscle, her shoulders tapering down to a steel-belted waist. Madison catches herself staring this time and looks away, blaming Kelly for planting the seeds of fascination. Even the limited talk around Ellie and No Days Off has created great hype in Madison's mind.

"I never saw her eat anything outside of group meals."

"No matter what time we got up, she was up first. No matter what time we went to bed, we always heard her moving around afterward."

And then, said after a long pause with great seriousness: *"Frankly, I'm not sure the woman is fully human."*

"Tell me something," Ellie says. "What did Kelly tell you about the course?"

"Nothing," Madison says, slapping her hand on the bench. "Bloody *nothing*. You really do create perfect little followers." It's not quite true, but Madison suspects that if she says *almost* nothing, she'll have to recite what she does know, and she doesn't want to do that. Madison looked up Ellie Fellowes online; she has an internet presence, even if No Days Off doesn't. *Ellie Fellowes*. West Point graduate. Thirty-year military career. Served in Bosnia, Sierra Leone, and Afghanistan.

Recipient of the Medal of Honor.

Ellie grins. "That's good," she says. "I do tell my graduates not to divulge the key details to anyone they're recommending. General stuff is fine, just not specifics. It would defeat the nature of the course, and the idea is that they only recommend close friends whom they think will benefit. Why spoil it? Plus, the course structure is in constant flux. I try things out, keep what works, but never implement too drastic a change because people pay me to make them do things that I know work. So over time it turns into something new. Even so, a lot of people would think it's insane to sign up without specifics, I know."

Madison knows enough. *"A month-long course that makes an actual military boot camp look like a Swedish massage."* That's how Kelly put it. The results spoke for themselves. If Madison noticed whatever new sense of presence Kelly has, that same presence *radiates* out of Ellie.

"I'd think it was insane too," Madison says, "if I hadn't seen the changes in Kelly. I wouldn't be here."

Ellie spreads her hands as if to say *and there you are*. "It's the only reason anyone comes now," she says, pleased. "Because they've seen the changes in a graduate they know. Then I kept getting emails from people in the UK, and if I'm honest, applicants stateside have become a little frustrating. Too many *Real Housewives* applying and not enough real housewives, if you get my meaning. Too many fad applicants and not enough women who really need and want to change. Relying solely on word of mouth is a nice way to keep the whole thing low-key and hassle-free. It's exactly as big as I want it to get. If it was about the money, I'd be an idiot, because I'm always working. But it's damn meaningful work. Someone on my last course called me 'Ellie the Zellie,' as in *zealot*. I liked that one." She chuckles and then narrows her eyes a little. "But let me ask you: Why did you lie just now and say Kelly didn't tell you anything about the course?"

Madison freezes. "What do you mean?"

Ellie holds up a hand. "It's all right. It's not a deal-breaker. Everyone lies in response to that question. There's no way people's friends or loved ones recommend they do something extreme but then tell them nothing about it."

Madison reddens. "It really was *next* to nothing."

"I'll tell you what I tell all new applicants," Ellie says, folding her hands on her crossed legs, "and you tell me if Kelly told you any more than this, okay?"

"Okay."

"No Days Off," Ellie says, "is an extremely intense month-long mental and physical residential boot camp, and because you would be on a Medium course, there are punishments for not reaching the goals you set, and they hurt. Hard Corrections, as I call them. They don't break the skin, they don't do permanent damage, they don't leave you injured for any notable length of time. But they *will* cause discomfort. All the students are women," Ellie says, already moving on, but then she sees Madison's expression. She places her palms together. "Let me be clear with you, Madison: Nothing in this course happens without your permission. What people say or think they need and what they actually need are rarely the same. If I think your course needs adjusting, we discuss it first. You can walk away at any time, and—I *cannot* stress this enough—you don't have to accept the Corrections if you don't want to. You can leave whenever you wish, and I'll even pay for your cab to the airport. But know that to refuse a Correction is to quit the course." She pauses as if waiting for a question.

Madison remains silent.

"Your food is covered," Ellie continues, "since diet is a key element, and we work on that together—one-on-one and as a group. You have video calls several times a week with a contact of your choice, but other than that, it's digital detox. No internet." Ellie shrugs. "Did Kelly tell you more than that?"

Madison smiles. "That was pretty much it."

Ellie stares.

"Okay," Madison says, "she also said you were pretty intense. In a good way. You don't, like, mess around."

Ellie nods. "I don't. And I'd like to talk about both of your goals for a moment."

"For when I get accepted into the course?" Madison says, raising an eyebrow.

"For *if* you get accepted into the course."

"How am I doing?"

Ellie sips her coffee and smiles. "We haven't finished talking, have we?"

Madison laughs. "Go on, then."

"You want to lose fifteen pounds," Ellie says, "and cut five to ten thousand words from your novel. Both in a month."

"Yes. The book needs tightening. I've really been putting it off, though."

"Well, on the weight-loss side of things," Ellie says, "if you follow the program, you'll lose more than fifteen pounds of body fat, but you'll add muscle mass. Overall, you'll still clear fifteen. I'll make sure of it." Ellie leans forward, interlacing her fingers over her bent knee. "What I want to know is *why* you want to do this. The goals are the intended outcome, yes, but they're not the *reason*. What's yours?"

Madison shifts on her seat. She notices a jogger approaching. He isn't wearing headphones. "I'm just..." The jogger is only a few feet away, coming on fast. Madison waits until he passes out of earshot, but even when he's gone, she still can't say it. She's being asked to verbalize the screaming thoughts that rattle around in her head at night until only the soothing voice of her constant companion—Señor Cuervo, over ice—can drown them out. *Fat. Lazy. Boring. Piece of shit.*

"I dropped out of uni," she says at last. "Or out of *college*, as you would say. I'm drifting. I even left my service job. I want to become a more productive person." The words come out as if she were physically pulling them from her stomach and up her throat. "I can do better."

Ellie stares at Madison for a moment and then seems to realize Madison is done talking.

"That's the reason?"

"Yeah. Pretty much."

Ellie considers Madison for another moment, then stands and picks up her jacket. "Thank you for your time, Madison. It was nice meeting you."

"Did I say something wrong?"

"It's all right," Ellie says kindly, straightening. "Some people aren't ready to be open with me, and that's completely understandable. You don't know me. But this course is only a month long. If your barriers are up now, I won't have time to break them down."

"I don't see a future," Madison blurts.

Ellie pauses, waiting. Madison feels blood rush to her face as she realizes this is it; she keeps going or this is over before it starts. This has instantly become a humiliation, the truth she has managed to hide even from herself now crudely exposed. "I thought university would be a fresh start. I was going to create this new version of myself." She talks quickly, letting it out before she steel-clamps everything down tight again. Ellie wants honesty, so Madison must go against her instincts. "Away from home." *Away from the tomb of my parents' home. Away from ever-explosive Patricia and Faded Rugby League Wannabe of the Year Gordon... and of course their Golden Child, Lizzie.* "I was studying economics, Ellie, not because I wanted to go into finance but because I wanted to change the fucking world. I didn't know how, but I thought I should know how the world works so I could figure it out. And it was exciting at first, a rush! New friends, going out all the time, just being on my own." She pauses, briefly reliving the feeling for a second before it vanishes like always. "But there was this sadness on top of my chest. It just kept growing. And I couldn't focus, couldn't stick with anything. I just wanted to sleep all the time. And I met this good-time guy who was nice and all, but it didn't work. He had a lot of issues too, so even though it was fun, I knew I had to end it. But once I broke up with him, everything seemed even *worse*. Do you know much Shakespeare, Ellie?"

"I've read some, but I'm not hugely familiar."

"Well, I'm not normally a theater buff," Madison says, "but my writer side loves Shakespeare's work. Always has, ever since we did *Much Ado About Nothing* in secondary school. He wrote this line in *Macbeth*. I think about it a lot. It sums up how I feel perfectly, how looking at the future feels."

"Which one?" Ellie asks, sitting back down on the bench.

"'Tomorrow, and tomorrow, and tomorrow,'" Madison says, wincing. She sighs. "I couldn't think straight, so I dropped out. Got a waitressing job to pay the bills, did my shifts, but I still couldn't stop the spiral and didn't have the energy to do anything about it. They made me manager regardless! And eventually, I quit that too." She pauses, dizzy. She looks to Ellie for encouragement, but none is forthcoming. About fifty feet beyond her, a man is walking a beautiful golden retriever. The dog is ecstatic, joy embodied in animal form. "This wasn't how things were supposed to be," she says quietly. She wants to look at Ellie, but to do so would be to meet her battering gaze. Does the woman ever fucking *blink*? "I look around me and everyone is *grinding*. They have jobs and side hustles and kids. I'm fucking sick of what I see in the mirror, and I'm sick of what I hear in my head, and I'm sick of being..." The next word dovetails with something from the rancid rag bundle of memories she's pulling apart, thoughts of how she left the good-time guy in the absolute worst way. Of the awful, awful words she spat at him at the end, seeing them land on his crestfallen face, words dripping with venom because they were really aimed at herself:

The only reason you're in the mess you're in is because you're so fucking—

"Weak," Madison says, the word creaking under the weight of shame and self-loathing. "I really tried my best, Ellie. No, that's bullshit. I rarely manage to do my best. It's easier to focus on other people than myself, as that takes less work. That's why I end up in crappy relationships. I pick fixer-uppers and then blame *them* when they remain who I knew they were in the first place. I guess it's my time for some of the tough love I'm such a big believer in." She tuts bitterly and leans back, folding her arms. "There's a line in one of David Goggins's books about being addicted to comfort. It was like a slap in the face. That's me. I'm utterly addicted to comfort, and I don't know when it happened. How disgusting is that?"

"Do you genuinely consider yourself an addict, then?" Ellie asks.

"Yeah, I do."

"You didn't say it, though."

Madison sighs. "I guess I'm—"

"Not *you guess*, Madison. Are you?"

"I'm an addict."

"What is the truth, Madison? Sum it up."

She knows what to say, but the question tightens up the flow like a plumber's wrench. "It's not actually that I have zero faith in the *future*," she says slowly, looking Ellie dead in the eye now. "But the person responsible for fixing my shit is *me*, and I have absolutely zero faith in myself. And I honestly think I'd rather die than allow myself to chicken out on something ever again. That sounds brave, until you realize I *always* chicken out." She shrugs. "You know what I mean."

"Thank you very much for sharing all that Madison," Ellie says softly. "Can you stand up for me a moment, please?"

Madison hesitates, confused, then does as she's asked. She now feels a little lighter on her feet, a little smoother in her movement. That's good. Ellie stands too, her eye level several inches lower than Madison's. The trees lining the wide path behind her rustle gently in the breeze, sounding like a hushing audience.

"With your permission," Ellie says, "I'm going to slap you in the face."

"What?" Madison asks, thinking she's misheard. Ellie's face betrays no excitement, no anger.

"I want to slap you in the face," Ellie repeats. "Hard. With your permission."

"Are you serious?"

"I'm told it's rare that I'm not."

"You want to slap me because I wasn't honest?"

"No," Ellie says firmly. "We don't do Corrections at the interview, Madison, and we don't do abuse *anywhere*. The slap is something I always do so I know that people are serious about No Days Off. And, just as with the course itself, if you don't want me to do it, I won't, but then you can't do the course. It's completely up to you."

Madison blinks, looking around. The nearest people are a good thirty meters away, the dog walker long gone. A family of five have arrived—two parents, two kids, and a grandparent—and have emptied the contents of a cooler onto a blanket for a picnic. They probably won't notice even if they hear the blow. The jogger has long since passed, but Madison can see a couple approaching in the near distance.

"That couple will see," Madison says, pointing at them as her pulse races. Is she really about to be slapped in the fucking face?

Ellie turns and looks where Madison points. "You're right," she says. "One second." Ellie immediately jogs over to the approaching couple, her shoes lightly pounding the pavement.

Madison watches through a filter of unreality as Ellie reaches the people in seconds, raising a hand in greeting. The couple stop; Madison can't hear the resulting conversation as Ellie points back Madison's way. The couple look at Madison, who raises a hand uncertainly in greeting. The couple return the gesture, smiling. Ellie says something else and the three of them laugh, and then Ellie quickly jogs back to where Madison is standing.

The couple turn around and begin to walk back the way they came.

"Okay," she says. "I told them we're about to practice a scene and that I'm going to slap you. I didn't expect them to turn around, though. I think it made them a bit uncomfortable. Let's do this quickly before anyone else comes. Do I have your permission?"

This isn't a joke. Ellie wants to slap her in the face. Madison tries to remember the last time anyone hit her, an occurrence that has happened so rarely in her life. Her older sister drunkenly pulled her hair when Madison visited during her university Freshers' Week. While that was the straw that broke the camel's back of their long-strained relationship — leading Madison to cut the only remaining family tie she had — that act of violence was brief and, she could admit, mild. Lizzie hadn't pulled that hard.

This is going to be a *slap*.

"You said hard?" Madison asks.

"Hard enough to hurt," Ellie says, "not hard enough to leave a bruise. Remember, I never leave lasting marks, and I never do actual damage. That's key to the ethos. They're Corrections, deterrents, not punishments." She raises her palm. "Quickly, now. Do I have your permission?"

The sun is shining. There's a *family* nearby.

"Yes, but — " Madison's sentence is cut short as there is a whip of movement and she now finds herself looking in the direction of the family picnic. It takes a millisecond for her to realize that there was a sharp crack too—immediately after her saying yes—and that the family must have heard it after all; they are now staring at her. Madison stares back as the rapidly growing warmth in her cheek turns into a stinging, scratching pain. Her eyes start to water, not from emotion or pain but from shock.

Look back at Ellie, she thinks, *before this looks weird to that family.* She does. Ellie's hands are now back at her sides, her expression blank. Madison breathes in through her nose as the pain reaches a crescendo... and then begins to disappear back into the blooming heat.

"Very good, very good," Ellie says. "Just breathe."

Madison blinks away the water in her eyes and tries to calm the hitching breaths that are pumping their way into her chest.

"Are you okay?" Ellie asks.

"Yes," Madison croaks, nodding, and realizes that she is. She looks back at the family and sees that they are eating and talking again. She feels more than okay, doesn't she?

Ellie is smiling. "You feel it, don't you?"

"I think so," Madison says. "What... what is that?"

"You stood up and took it," Ellie says, "and now you've moved past it. The knowledge of that..." She shrugs. "It's hard to put into words. Madison, I'll give it to you straight: There's potentially a place for you in the course under one condition. If your baseline fitness isn't at a certain level, then there isn't a chance in hell that you'll complete the month." The rising fire in Madison's soul immediately starts to subside, unlike the lingering one in her face. "Not just that," Ellie continues, "but I need to see that you can commit to something. I know that sounds self-defeating when your issue is discipline, but of course there has to be a small element of self-motivation. It'll come easier when you have a clear goal, though, and I'm going to give you one right now."

Madison listens, the world around her now in high definition.

"In three months," Ellie says, "there's a half-marathon, right here in Coventry. I know someone who knows the organizers, and that person owes me some major favors, so I know I can get you a slot in it. A decent time to complete a half-marathon is two hours and ten minutes. I need you to complete the Coventry half-marathon in not a millisecond more than that. If you do that, you can have the spot on the September intake. That's my offer. Have you ever run a half-marathon?"

Madison almost—*almost*—lies on instinct.

"No," she says. "Never."

Ellie nods. "Start small. Make incremental changes in your training or you'll burn out, lose confidence. Build up from there. That's all the advice I'm going to give you. I'll send you a link to the entry form. Fill it in and send it back to *me*. I'll get it to the right people." She offers her hand. "Good luck."

"That's it?"

"That's it. If you make it, you're in—cash on arrival, of course."

They shake hands for a second time, Ellie's grip again small but tight, immovable like that of a wiry old man. Ellie releases her grasp and then opens her arms for a hug, smiling. Madison accepts it, Ellie's shoulders and neck slim and hard under Madison's hands.

"You can do it," Ellie says. "If you want it."

Three months later
Half-marathon hell

The final five hundred meters. Madison, breathless, hurting, the stitch in her side feeling like a broken rib. She looks to her right; an old man in loose-fitting running gear looks like he's suffering even more than she is. He catches her eye, and to her amazement he breaks into a smile.

"Come...on!" he gasps, and Madison gives a wheezing laugh, and with that she finds she is suddenly able to answer the pain's stabbing question of *Isn't this too much?* with *Yes, but...* She and the old man accelerate. They move together, faster, a final burst. The finish line appears on the horizon, the noise of the cheering crowd metallic and tinny in her ears. Madison looks at her watch: 2:09:02.

Holy shit.

The white banner grows larger, the blessed, blessed word FINISH ringed by the logos of various event sponsors, and Madison realizes she's going to make it. As she and the old man cross the finish line, she puts her arm around his neck and he, laughing, puts his around hers and *This is joy, oh blessed joy, this is what it feels like — I remember.*

Her hitching chest feels as if it might burst, her body craving oxygen, but she looks at her watch again: 2:09:49.

A full eleven seconds inside the target goal! That late second wind — that was what pushed her to succeed...

The sounds around her are instantly quieter; the colors are darker; all the good feeling of only the previous moment has vanished. Her brain runs through the automatic processes of ridicule that have held her back for so long:

If it wasn't for the old man's help, you wouldn't have made it.

If you *managed to run a half-marathon in less than two-ten, it can't be that hard.*

It's an all-too-familiar process, this self-sapping of joy, but for once — and to her great surprise — Madison has a response:

Yeah? Well, I still did it. I might just be a Bad Bitch after all.

She doesn't believe it, but the idea isn't quite as laughable as it was yesterday.

She walks, sucking in ragged air, and spots the old man hugging three women who are leaning over the barrier. They're all about Ellie's age — granddaughters, surely. She's delighted he has someone there for him. But then he spots Madison too and laughs, beckoning her over. Madison staggers toward the foursome, trying to say hi in hitching breaths, but reaching hands are already pulling her in, and suddenly she is engulfed in the biggest hug of her entire life.

She stands in the center of it, the crowd now muted, and tries to disguise her flood of tears as post-race breathing.

I'll Quit When I'm Dead

Months later
A field somewhere in Vermont

This particular field lies only a pleasant morning walk away from the house of early retiree Reg Eccles. Reg is enjoying that walk right now, in fact, and thinking—as he does most days—that he should really get a dog. He'd love to take a dog with him in the mornings. His mood is upbeat, and he has no idea this morning that the events of his life are about to connect with those of a young woman all the way from the other side of the Atlantic Ocean.

It's very early, the sun still undecided about whether it's time to get up, and that's exactly the way Reg likes it. The fields and gentle hills roll away on either side of him under the vague, hazy light, Reg hiking the narrow strip of untilled, rocky land between the low, wooden-rail fences that divide this part of the landscape. This is the last leg of his circular five-mile walk that will deposit him back at the house to make coffee and wise remarks about the time Sally *finally decides to join us for breakfast*. She always rolls her eyes, but she smiles; she's glad he's still there to say it. The daily walks were originally done at the doctor's insistence—along with cutting out the cigarettes and, much to Sally's relief, most of the booze—and once he got over all that particular misery, he discovered he liked walking. The start time of the walks slowly shifted earlier and earlier as Reg's health grew better and better, so much so that, after discussing it with Sally, he took early retirement at sixty-one, sold the house, and moved to the middle of nowhere. Vermont air, Vermont scenery, and Vermont Reg thinks that he has possibly never been happier. Vermont Sally too.

This is the part of the walk he likes best, the one stage that leads up a decent incline. As he draws alongside the gate in the field's north fence, he turns to look beyond it, sees two sets of tire tracks in the grass, one small, one large. A car and a tractor, perhaps. He follows them with his eyes and notices that the tracks enter the field from the west gate in the distance. Then he spots the *other* set of tracks, the ones that entered from the east gate. The car that made them is still parked at the end of the brown swath cut through the grass.

It's a police car.

Police tape encircles several thin metal posts staked into the ground in a hundred-foot diameter near the top of the rise. A few officers in high-vis jackets move about inside it, working at something Reg can't see. A backhoe is parked nearby; not a tractor, then.

Standing maybe twenty feet from the crime scene, his elderly dog, Emma, lying at his feet, is Reg's neighbor, Brandon Maple. Like Reg, Brandon is a city transplant. It's one of the reasons they became friends.

Brandon is talking with a police officer who looks as if he's trying to wrap things up. Brandon doesn't own the land; he must have been passing and the cops called him over to talk, Reg assumes.

Brandon sees Reg and raises a hand. The cop turns back toward the tape circle, saying something over his shoulder that Brandon nods at before he turns toward Reg. As the older man draws close to Reg's gate, Reg sees his bridge club friend's face is ashen. This is surprising; in the few years of knowing Brandon, Reg has never been greeted with anything other than the broadest of grins. Brandon has been retired a lot longer than Reg, and it's suited him well.

"Reg," Brandon mutters.

"Brandon," Reg says, bending to reach between the gate's slats and give the gently huffing Emma a pat. "What's happened?"

"I called it in," Brandon says, sighing. "Found it while I was walking Emma. She doesn't hold her water too well at night these days, and I couldn't really sleep anyway, so I took her out pretty early this morning." His brow furrows as he seems to consider whatever he found. "The goddamn shovel was even still nearby."

"Called what in?" Reg asks, already guessing the answer. Brandon's face combined with the mention of a shovel makes it obvious. "It's not... it's not a dead body, is it?"

To his great surprise, Brandon lets out a darkly amused snort.

"Yeah, it is," the old man says. "Even a goddamn *coffin* too."

Reg blinks, amazed. The sun finally peeks through the clouds, as if deciding to throw the busy crime scene into full relief. Reg wonders what the hell he's going to tell Sally. She's always half joked about country folks all being secret inbred murderers. He asks Brandon the question without looking at his friend, watching the busy police and feeling his stomach sink.

"Is it... is it anyone we know?"

Chapter Three: Johnny

David and His Stupid Pictures

"YEAH?" SAYS THE elderly, pale-skinned man upon opening the door, his tone flat.

"Hi," Johnny says, uncertain. He's been confused ever since he followed the short garden path to the front door, seeing the lights on inside the house and hearing the muffled classical music playing.

The place should be empty.

Johnny tries to spread his legs wider in a pointless attempt to hide the suitcase behind him. "I'm Johnny," he says. "Johnny Blake? I didn't, uh... I thought there wouldn't be anyone here. Ivan gave me the spare keys..."

"You're moving in," the old man says, his blank face breaking into a slow-witted-looking smile.

"Yes," Johnny says, returning the smile. But who is this guy? "Are you..." He doesn't want to ask *Are you the cleaner?* It feels presumptuous.

"We live here," the man says, smiling. "I'm David. Sandy is my wife."

"Oh, nice to meet you," Johnny says, understanding now that something is not quite regular with David. He immediately tries to push back his rising frustration. The roadworks going on across Coventry made the journey here — the last part of a particularly long and trying day — into an ordeal he didn't need, but he doesn't want to take it out on a stranger. "I'm sorry, David. I think I might have screwed up somehow. I didn't expect anyone to be here today." He doesn't ask what he wants to ask: *Why are you two still here?* The date. Did he have the date wrong? "Wait, it's the third today, isn't it?"

"It is!" David says cheerfully, hitching up the waistband of his dungarees. His thick brown wool sweater looks hot and uncomfortable. "We're moving today, you know." Now Johnny can see the boxes in the hallway behind the old man. *Ah.* That's at least part of the mystery solved, but Johnny had just wanted to get into the house and into bed. That's looking highly unlikely anytime soon. His mood sinks further. He already felt metaphorically lost before coming here; now it feels literal.

A woman of similar-looking age to David emerges from a doorway in the hall, her mass of still-thick gray hair barely contained by a paisley headscarf. Her face is sweaty and flushed, but she looks bright and alive.

"Hello," she says, looking confused, but her tone is polite. "You are...?"

"I'm Johnny," he says. "Uh...I'm supposed to be moving in today? I think I might have screwed up, though. You're obviously packing to leave. I can come back another day."

"I'm Sandy," the woman says, offering her hand, "and I think you might have, Johnny. I was told you were coming tomorrow, the fourth?"

Her tone is kind, but Johnny knows she's wrong. His move-in date was today. He checked the paperwork this morning. The landlord, Ivan, is a close friend who always does things by the book. "Do business well," Ivan said, "especially when you do it with friends, man." The last word, as always, pronounced *mahn*. Ivan's Midlands-infused Bosnian accent made the word sound Jamaican. Johnny wants to handle this nicely. The pair seem kind.

"It doesn't really matter either way," Sandy says, gesturing to the boxes, "as this is actually the last of it. Obviously, the beds and the sofa are staying; they're the landlord's."

Johnny nods. He knows this already. The house is partly

furnished, which is perfect. He owns a couple of properties, but they're rented out; he's lived out of a suitcase for the last few years. Even the more semi-permanent places he's rented have been partly furnished, with only things like his TV and precious hi-fi equipment moving with him.

"The removal people should be here in about an hour," Sandy continues. "You're more than welcome to drop your luggage and wait here if you like, perhaps take a seat in the garden while we pack up the rest of this?"

"Packing," David says quietly as he turns and shuffles away into the house.

"Oh, uh, no," Johnny says. "I don't think—"

"It's fine. Come in," Sandy says, turning quickly to follow David and leaving Johnny without much choice. He hesitates, not wanting to follow, but then steps over the threshold into a narrow hallway covered in red wallpaper. Once inside, Johnny parks his suitcase against the wall—his carry-on is still in the car. Seeing his long-haired reflection looming back at him in the hallway mirror, he looks away, not liking how thin he is now.

There isn't much natural light inside the house, but the artificial lighting is warm. To a visitor who was actually expected, it might feel cozy, welcoming. Johnny's discomfort makes him touch the nearest wall as he moves farther inside, and then the one opposite, counting to three in his head as he does so. Sandy suddenly reappears, her gaze looking down the hallway.

"Sorry," she whispers. "I have to keep an eye on him. He's just a bit absent. Quite happily in his own little world. We're moving nearer the kids so I can have some help keeping an eye on the silly old fool." The affection in her voice is so strong that it makes something ache inside Johnny. "We'll miss the place for sure, though," Sandy adds. "This is a special house. Good energy. This whole area, really."

"That's good. Well, I can just..." Johnny begins, having no intention of waiting around while these two finish packing, but Sandy is already heading down the short hallway once more. Johnny follows, trying to think of the best way to get out of this. In the kitchen, two elderly dogs lie curled up together in a large basket bed on the floor. One is a Jack Russell, the other a black spaniel. Their eyes are locked on Johnny as they rise with difficulty, joints stiff, tails thumping lightly. He bends down to stroke their heads. A radio plays the classical music Johnny heard outside.

The room is only just beginning to look dated. One end has a large wooden dining table surrounded by chairs. Two drink coasters sit neatly in each of the table's corners; part of a set of four, the other two lie nearby, loosely piled on top of each other. Just Sandy and David here, then. Beyond them stands a door that leads out to what looks like a surprisingly dark conservatory. Shouldn't a room made of glass be all light?

David picks up a remote control from the counter and aims it at the TV on the wall, standing nearby and changing rapidly through channels as Sandy places an old-fashioned teapot near the stove.

"Do you want us to leave that here, by the way?" Sandy says, pointing at the table. "The chairs too? They're some of the few bits of furniture here that are ours, believe it or not." Johnny notices the table's unusual centerpiece — a glass pyramid atop a wooden box. In front of that sits a tea candle in a flat round glass holder, and in front of that, an open bag of Werther's Originals. The bag has fallen on its side, and some of the candies have spilled across the table.

"You don't want it?" Johnny asks, surprised. The table is nice.

"Not really. We were only going to take it if you didn't. The dining room in the new place is small."

"I'd love it," Johnny says, pleased. "You sure?"

"Done." Sandy grins broadly.

"Wow, thank you." Johnny smiles. It's a small win, but he's needed one for a while. This could be a good start to a new home.

It's not good, though, a voice in his head whispers. *Nothing is or ever will be again. You know that. Why are we still here?*

"We have a guest," David tells Sandy airily, his eyes on the chattering TV.

"Yep," Sandy says, crouching and beginning to pull random objects from a lower cupboard before placing them on the counter. "Why don't you ask him what brings him here?"

"What brings you here?" David repeats, eyes still on the TV.

"It's only a temporary rental," Johnny says, unsure of whom he is talking to. "Six months with the option to extend if I like it. Are you retired?"

"Former teachers, both," Sandy says. "I don't miss it, and David doesn't really remember it. Are you local?"

"Yes," Johnny says. "Not to Waterton specifically, but I've lived in Coventry off and on for years."

"Then why are you moving?"

The question sounds a little odd, a touch barbed, but Sandy seems engrossed in what she's doing.

"I guess...uh, I needed a change," Johnny says, keeping things surface level. "Good to get somewhere a little more private, pleasant." He was relieved, upon arrival, to see that the house was as he had hoped. He agreed to take the place based on Ivan's word alone, although the price didn't hurt; Ivan sweetened the deal to get Johnny to agree to move here, knowing Johnny's finances had taken a hit and really wanting to help his friend. A detached bungalow sitting just off a street, set back from the road via a narrow hedge-lined alleyway that leads to three other near-identical houses. The four of them frame the alley in a little green keyhole shape with this house at the top of the circle. Enclosed front garden, totally private back garden, all bills included in the rent. It would do for Johnny's current, limited needs, and would be—according to Ivan—a fresh start at the same time.

"What's your name?" David asks pleasantly.

"Johnny," Johnny says, smiling. "What's yours?"

Sandy nods at Johnny gratefully.

"David," David says. "What's your job?"

"I'm a musician."

"Oh," Sandy says, impressed, pausing to look at him. "Full time?" This is the usual response.

"Taking a break from it for a little bit."

"But you're so young," Sandy says.

Johnny shrugs. "It got a bit much," he says. "Burnt out a little."

"Important to look after yourself," Sandy says. "Have you recorded anything, or do you only do live stuff?"

"I kind of broke out on social media, and then I did this album. It pays the bills. I've toured small venues since it came out. Well, small to medium. It was pretty nonstop."

"Anything we'd know?"

Johnny reddens a little bit. He isn't sure he wants to bring this up. They're nice people, though, and they probably won't have heard of it anyway.

"The album was called *Mister Caravaggio*," he says.

Sandy pauses. "You're Johnny *Blake*," she says, smiling slowly. "I didn't make the connection. Wow."

"Wow," David mutters happily, clearly not knowing what Sandy is talking about and totally cool with that.

Johnny shrugs, embarrassed. "It pays the bills," he repeats. He's always surprised when anyone over forty knows who the hell he is, let alone people of Sandy and David's age, despite it happening many times in the two years since *Mister Caravaggio* was released. It was only in the top ten on Spotify for a few weeks. Johnny is deeply thankful for his just-right level of fame; enough for people to often recognize his name when they hear it, but he's rarely recognized by sight in the street.

"Well, well," Sandy says. "We have a celebrity in our midst."

"Very minor," Johnny says.

"*Ah*," Sandy says, wagging a finger. "I think I can guess why you're here and not on a beach in Barbados or something. You had a little trouble, didn't you? I heard about that. Everything okay now?"

Johnny flushes bright red. The *Daily Mail* had run a minor exposé on his personal issues; a roadie had sold them the story. It didn't get a huge amount of traction—the response was mostly sympathetic—and quickly died, but it was mortifying to Johnny all the same. Sandy sees the awkward expression on his face and puts her hand to her mouth. "Oh goodness, I'm so sorry. I speak without thinking sometimes. Forget I asked that. It's none of my business. I'm not used to having famous people around."

"No, that's okay," Johnny says, appreciating her words. "And I'm doing okay, thanks. Ticking away."

He quickly blinks five times.

It's a gesture so automatic and so often repeated, literally millions of times throughout his life, that he is more than a little surprised when Sandy seems to notice, her eyes squinting slightly.

"Do you have many other things like that?" Sandy asks, her voice quiet. She looks very serious. "Little things?"

"Sorry?"

"Little OCD things," Sandy says, her expression blank. "The kind of thing you just did with your eyes, the blinking. Do you have many of them?"

That's kind of personal again. But—for the next hour at least—this is still their house, and Johnny is beginning to understand that perhaps Sandy is a little eccentric. Her demeanor and conversation are unguarded, which is oddly refreshing.

"Actually...yes," he says. "Nothing debilitating, but, you know, counting and things. It's not a huge problem."

Sandy continues to stare at him for what seems like a long time before nodding.

"It's all right," she says finally. "Sorry. I didn't mean to sound rude. David always had a lot of things like that, little routines he has to do, even before he, you know, was this way."

"Oh, sure, yeah."

"I ask because..." Sandy takes a deep breath, looking as if she is choosing her words carefully. "Ah, I'm sorry to bring this up again, but it might be important. Your, you know, your trouble. How major was it?"

Now Johnny *really* doesn't know what to say, but then David speaks first.

"Major," David mutters, not looking away from the TV. "Very major. Had a big fall from high up and hurt his back. Pain. Needs relief, all the time, even after his back was fixed and the pain ended. Got so bad that he had enough. Ran a deep bath, nice and deep—"

"All right, David," Sandy interrupts loudly, but Johnny is gaping at David as the older man stares at the TV, oblivious to the enormity of what he just said.

There is no way that David could know the information he just divulged.

"Don't worry about David," Sandy says, turning to a stunned Johnny. "He picks up on things from people sometimes since he... you know. And you have nothing to be embarrassed about," she adds, flapping a hand dismissively. "Pain, though? You need pain relief? Do you smoke cannabis? It can really help."

It wouldn't be too surprising a question—Sandy looks like the old hippie type—but Johnny is still so surprised by David that he simply says, "I mean... sometimes."

"Ah, okay," Sandy says. "I wasn't sure you would be allowed if you're trying to get clean. You went to rehab, right?"

"No," Johnny says. He has not gone, and will not go, to rehab, the mere mention of it stiffening his spine, and *how the hell did David know about the bath?* "Wait. Sandy, how—"

"I ask," Sandy says, pointing at a row of cabinets, "because there's a box of pre-rolls in the second drawer down, over there. I don't like to travel with them. Police are highly unlikely to pull over a couple of septuagenarians on the motorway, but you just never know your luck. I'd hate for them to go to waste. They're really good. Might help inspire your music too."

This conversation has to end, right now.

"*Okay*," Johnny says. "I think—"

"Who told you about this house?" Sandy asks in that same quick-but-kind tone, but Johnny is already standing up from the table.

"I should let you finish packing," he says. *This is getting way too personal.* "You've both been extremely kind and welcoming, but this conversation is getting a little odd. I don't mean to disrespect you in your own—"

"I don't mean any of this to offend *you* either," Sandy says. "I honestly don't. I'm asking out of concern. I thought you might have been told the truth about this place—Waterton as a whole, but these few streets in particular—if you came here for a reason. If you have a touch of OCD, which it looks like you do, and you're coming in blind, then it might potentially be a little dangerous."

"This was a last-minute thing. Ivan's..." Johnny begins, but then his brain catches up to Sandy's last word. "What do you mean, dangerous?"

"Well," Sandy says, shrugging, "dangerous could be a matter of opinion, and some of us have strongly differing opinions about all that—it depends how you were raised, if you ask me. Different families believe in different things. We didn't always call it OCD, but I couldn't leave here in good conscience without checking."

Now Johnny *can't* leave. "*Dangerous* is a very serious word," he says.

"And it came with several modifiers," Sandy says. "I said, 'might potentially be a little.' Don't get all worried—you don't have to be."

"Dangerous how?"

"People with OCD," Sandy says, "in a place like this... they *stand out,* shall we say. OCD is an attempt to control the sheer unpredictability of the world around us, after all, according to the psychologists. The idea being that if there are rules that need to be followed, then following those rules means we will be kept safe. But the truth is that such secret, unseen rules *do* exist. They are part of the way the world truly works." Sandy pauses and sighs, looking embarrassed by what she's saying, hearing herself. "OCD manifests when someone senses those rules—when a person has a natural sensitivity to them—and misunderstands them, lets them get all twisted up in their brain, and ends up washing their hands endlessly, for example. They end up controlled *by* their attempts to control."

Johnny reddens, embarrassed.

"The irony is," Sandy continues, "that those people are putting themselves in far more danger. Such actions—handwashing, counting, touching objects in order—are demonstrating not only a sensitivity to the secret processes of the world but also an unassuming *intention* to control it. There is power in intention, always. But the person doing these things stands out like a light in the darkness to the moths that lie outside our perception."

"I'm not... sure I'm following," Johnny says, feeling lightheaded.

"Don't go into the Shallows if you're not ready," David mutters. "*That's* dangerous."

"Who told you about this house?" Sandy repeats, ignoring her husband. "Wait, did you say Ivan?"

"Yes," Johnny says. "I'm renting it from him. He's my friend."

Sandy completely relaxes.

"Oh, that's okay, then," she says, looking relieved. "I wouldn't have bothered saying anything. I'm sure he'll have checked everything."

"You know him personally?" Johnny asks. "Not just as a landlord?"

"Of course, of course," Sandy says. "Daris and Merjem, his parents, they had this place before us. We had them here for dinner many times after they moved in with Ivan. They taught us a lot—"

"What are the Shallows?" Johnny asks, frustrated by Sandy's meandering. His temper has become shorter in the equally short time since he got clean.

Sandy winces. "Johnny, you're here for more than a change, aren't you? Ivan *told* you to come here, yes? Let me guess: He said he'd explain more once you moved in but that you should just trust him and do it?"

Johnny doesn't answer. He hasn't been in a state to have much of a conversation with anybody; he didn't care when Ivan skimped on the details. Ivan said Johnny could move in right away, the area was green and nourishing, and more importantly, Ivan lived nearby and could keep an eye on what Johnny was up to. What more was there to explain?

"I'd bet a thousand," Sandy says, "that Ivan is planning to take you to the Shallows himself. He's going to be your guide, and he'll want to prepare you, in his own way. If that's the case, then I shouldn't really say anything." She sighs. "It's all right, Johnny. I'm so sorry I made you uncomfortable. You're here for a good reason, and it's all going to be okay. I was just checking. The OCD thing...it can be—"

"Boggart," David grunts.

Johnny's head jerks up. Hearing that word was like a mild static shock. *Boggart.* Two murky syllables, sounding like *jogger* but harsher, much less pleasant.

"What did you say, David?" Johnny asks.

"Boggart," David says, louder this time, cocking his head as he looks at the TV.

"He never shuts up about *that,* or doesn't nowadays at least. Silly old sod. Look at this — he's obsessed." She walks out through the door at the back of the kitchen, smiling broadly.

Johnny follows on autopilot, leaving David to his TV, and finds Sandy standing in the conservatory beyond. Immediately, Johnny understands the darkness. Pieces of paper are taped to the conservatory's transparent roof.

Each contains a near-identical black squiggle that Johnny can't make out.

"He used to be an artist," Sandy sighs. "He can't do it anymore since he started to diminish. This" — she gestures at the images taped above — "is all he draws now."

Each picture is a rough black circle with angular lines jutting from it; a zigzag slashes through the center of each circle.

"What is..." Johnny begins, but then he sees it.

The circle looks like a round body. The angular lines are many legs. The zigzag looks like a jagged mouth.

His back prickles.

"The Boggart," Sandy says, shaking her head. "Or at least his drawing of it."

Johnny turns on the spot, somehow simultaneously fascinated and repulsed as he takes in all the jagged black drawings around him. *A Boggart.* It doesn't look or sound good at all.

"David used the Boggart to scare the kids before they grew to love the idea. Scary stories, you know? He didn't even come up with the name. I think it's a Celtic thing, some kind of monster myth, but the stories themselves were his. At least according to him. Ever since he started to..." Sandy does a finger twirl around her ear that strikes Johnny as surprisingly cruel. But then, he reasons, perhaps gallows humor is simply how one must deal with the diminishment of someone you love deeply. "He's begun to remember it all. I know we've been talking about some weird things, but trust me: David really is mixing up the good weirdness with the stuff he used to imagine. He can't tell the difference anymore; he used to come up with stories about it, little picture books for the kids."

"No," David calls from the other room. "Seen it. At night. It's around here now."

"The picture-book illustrations were obviously a lot better than these," Sandy continues, ignoring David. "But drawing them seems to bring him peace. Maybe he's remembering an easier time—"

"It's true. I asked around about it."

"Uh-huh," Sandy calls back. "Who did you ask, exactly, David Marlborough?"

"I asked at night. Listened to the answers. It has *rules*."

"Sure. Makes total sense. Watch your bloody TV, you."

But Johnny is too busy looking at the jagged, zigzagging lines at the center of every single picture, the ones that look like mouths. Some have additional triangles inside that look like the notches of a saw.

"It's always hungry," David says in a singsong voice. "Just don't make any deals with it."

"Ignore him," Sandy says kindly. "Yes, this place is different—the whole of Waterton, I think—but it's a good energy we're talking about, despite what David might draw."

"Oh yeah," David calls. "Don't be scared. Boggart can't just get you if it wants to. Not allowed. It can't just *get* you."

"*Thank you, David.* I think you've told him now," Sandy calls back, rolling her eyes for Johnny's sake. "Seriously," she says to Johnny, "when David knows someone's...struggling, shall we say, he talks about monsters. It's his way—speaking in metaphor. You're here to heal, aren't you, Johnny?"

"Yes."

Sandy nods. "And you will. This is a good house—let me be very clear about that."

Johnny suddenly laughs, shaking his head and throwing up his hands.

"Good, sure, that's good," he says, utterly bemused. "Whatever you say."

Sandy smiles.

"Glad to hear it," she says, and Johnny laughs again. *Screw it.* Ivan will be round in a few hours and Johnny hasn't unpacked his suitcases yet, hasn't even fetched the carry-on from the car. He can talk this over with Ivan later and figure out if he's going to stay. He doesn't need to go back and forth with Sandy before she and David leave, and if Ivan has some weird, secret spiritual reason for Johnny to stay, it will be for Johnny's own good. He knows his friend, and by this point, Johnny is ready to try anything.

"Go on, then, I'll bite," Johnny says. "What *are* the Shallows?"

Sandy surprises him by wincing, an expression Johnny has seen on the faces of many customer-service reps over the years: *I'd love to help you, but I don't make the rules, sir.*

"I really can't tell you since it might be important later, if Ivan does take you to the Shallows. It's probably irrelevant, but I don't want to throw anything off. *Seriously,* don't worry. If you're going, he'll go with you, and it'll be fine. Just take all this as the rambling of a bat-shit crazy old lady."

Johnny laughs, startled by this old lady dropping curse words of her own, and decides he will take her advice. Once these two are gone, they're gone.

"There's a deck chair in the garden," Sandy says. "Park yourself in it and I'll bring you some tea, then I can finish packing." She opens the conservatory door to the outside; Johnny hears the clicking of claws in the kitchen as the dogs stand and walk over to take advantage of this opening.

"No offense," Johnny says, "but I'm going to try to ignore everything you just said and assume you *are* crazy. But, you know. Nice crazy." He smiles, and Sandy returns it.

"Good," she says, watching the dogs quietly slink past her and out into the garden. "Mary and Wilson," she says, pointing at her pets in turn. "They're angels now, but you wouldn't have liked either of them when we first got them. Rescues. Badly messed up, poor things."

"That's awful." Johnny smiles, watching Wilson flop down onto his side on the grass, tail gently whapping against the earth.

"Yep. We coaxed them out of their shells once we figured out what their temperaments were and worked *with* them. Mary here, the bitch, needed a very strict, no-nonsense approach." She points at the Jack Russell. "And the gelding needed the opposite. Softly-softly, firm but compassionate. Now they're both happy as Larry. Aren't you, trouble?" Sandy coos, and now both tails slap in response.

Gelding, Johnny thinks, knowing the word but unable to remember its meaning. Maybe a term for an old dog? He smiles, struck by the scene: this kind, gentle, weird old couple and their two devoted dogs. It's cozy and warm, and despite the oddness, Johnny feels that he is, in fact, home. He moves outside, finds the deck chair against the wall, and opens it as Sandy heads back indoors. Johnny sits in the garden, bathed in gentle sunlight, and to his great surprise he finds himself relaxing.

A short while later, Sandy emerges to tell Johnny they're done. They make small talk for a few minutes until the moving people arrive, and Johnny helps with the carrying of boxes. The dogs have to be crated due to constant snuffling of everyone's legs, and eventually they go in the car too.

Finally, all Sandy and David's things are gone, and Sandy stands before Johnny in the hallway, holding out the house keys. The door is open behind her, and the pleasant summer light shining through the archway is beginning to turn to dusk. Clouds on the horizon mean it might rain a little, and soon.

"All yours," Sandy says. "Lovely to meet you, Johnny. I hope you find what you're looking for."

"I think just staying still for a while will help achieve most of that," Johnny replies, even though he's lying. Constantly moving isn't his biggest problem. Even the painkillers aren't. After all, they didn't drive him to run that bath, to try to end his suffering.

If Ivan hadn't shown up, Johnny would be dead.

He takes the keys.

"Try one of those joints tonight," Sandy says, her voice low. "Might give you some insight. A good start."

Johnny hears the toilet flush, followed by a blasting tap, and then David emerges from the bathroom.

"Present and correct," he says quietly. His brow furrows a little as he sees Johnny. "Hello," he adds.

"Hello," Johnny says, smiling. "I'm Johnny."

"Don't make any deals with the Boggart," David mutters, and then heads toward the door before pausing. "There's one living around here, you know. He's always looking for an opportunity." Sandy does her loving eye roll again, but David's eyes don't roll at all. They look straight into Johnny's. "I saw this one in a dream. It's horrible. It told me about itself. It wanted me to know. But I said we were leaving soon. It said it wou—"

"Goodbye, Johnny," Sandy says.

"Goodbye." Johnny hesitates and then gives Sandy a hug.

She receives it and then steps back, taking one last look at the hallway. She smiles softly, raising a hand to affectionately pat the front doorframe. Then she nods, turns, and steps out of the house, following David as he shuffles away along the garden path.

Johnny watches them go and then closes the front door.

He wanders about the quiet and stripped place, checking out the rooms and trying to imagine what he would do with the space if he stayed here long enough to make it his. Eventually he comes back to the conservatory.

They haven't taken down David's drawings. The crude black-and-white pictures still hang from the transparent ceiling, horror film posters drawn by a toddler.

"Well, *that* shit's going right now," Johnny mutters. He takes them down and puts them in the bin.

The *outside* bin.

Back inside, he registers the deafening silence and remembers the Bluetooth speaker in his bag. He looks at the kitchen table and the surprisingly comfortable seats all around it, noticing that Sandy and David forgot not only the little glass pyramid centerpiece and the tea-candle holder in front of it but the open bag of Werther's Originals too. More have spilled out onto the table, bumped perhaps by one of the movers. Johnny suddenly has an image of himself lighting it, sitting in his new kitchen, listening to music on his speaker, and smoking one of Sandy's joints.

Wouldn't that be a nice way to spend his first solo night here?

Johnny closes his eyes.

Get used to it, he thinks. *You have to stand on your own two feet if you want to be strong.* Yes, he is living here by himself, but to his surprise—and for the first time in a long time—he feels a sense of hope. His friends will come here, and soon. Johnny does not even slightly believe any of David's talk about a Boggart. There's a good energy here. As he looks for the pre-rolls, his thoughts of the day suddenly catch something in passing, recalling the unusual word: *gelding.* He remembers what it means.

It's not a term for an old dog. It's a term for a castrated male.

Chapter Four: Madison

"You're going to make the rest of us look bad"

THE LITTLE ELECTRONIC key safe whirs as it accepts the four-digit PIN of Madison's choosing. Cogs turn and barrels move, and with that Madison's phone is locked away until she either graduates or chooses to leave. She's swapped her device for the set of house keys inside the tiny little storage locker. Nine other identical key safes are mounted to the left of the building's front door, before which sits Madison's suitcase. She has arrived at No Days Off.

Ellie's house, or at least the house she uses for her residential course, is far bigger than Madison expected. She has parked her car to the building's left because she is a considerate parker, leaving the easy front spaces for the others. It also hides her piece-of-shit rental car at the same time. She got a sense of the house's depth while she was at it.

The place isn't quite a mansion at two stories high, but the building is still large, sitting snugly at the end of a short lane that runs off the main country road. The surrounding gardens are flat and expansive, grass rolling away to the east and west with the occasional large tree dotted here and there. Ellie's property sits high in the landscape; Madison thinks there may be quite the view from the rear of the house. The building sports new-looking gutters and fascia boards. Several modern dormer windows are set into a sloped slate roof, managing to blend old with new in a way Madison likes. A stone single-story barn sits to the right of the main building, connected by a walkway that looks — despite someone's failed efforts to merge it seamlessly into the original masonry — to be a recent addition. The barn conceals the rear of Ellie's grounds from view, and Madison finds herself excited to see what landscape they're going to be working in. This second building has also been updated; the flat rubber roof looks fairly new. It appears to have been divided into halves, with a pair of evenly spaced (and locked) glass doors marked by two signs.

One says SQUASH COURT. The other says DOJO.

Madison is wearing her running gear; she lives in yoga pants anyway, so the only change to her regular clothing is a sports bra under a long-sleeved T-shirt. She came ready to fulfill a promise to herself: that she would start the work as soon as she arrived, not waiting for the course itself to begin. She wants to make a statement to herself. Kelly said doing so was a great start for a positive mindset when she was here. It's probably stupid to get a run in when the course starts later tonight, but it'll only be a short jog, and intention is important. Plus, it's only two o'clock, and Ellie won't be here until five.

Madison goes inside. She hopes she's the first one; she doesn't want to walk into an already established group. She feels enough of an impostor as it is.

No one's in. She's the first. She breathes a sigh of relief and looks around. Oak beams run across the ceiling and down the walls of an expansive entranceway. The original wooden floorboards are a pleasant contrast to the minimalist, open-sided staircase that leads up to a mezzanine. Large colorful artworks that Madison doesn't recognize adorn the walls, abstract and colorful.

It's abundantly obvious that No Days Off is a successful business. Madison isn't surprised; the maximum intake, Ellie told her, was ten students per one-month course, and Ellie prefers to keep it smaller than that. Ten grand per student isn't chump change, and certainly not as far as Madison is concerned. If it weren't for the not-inconsiderable inheritance from her mother, she wouldn't be here. She wouldn't have been able to earn that amount of cash herself, she knows, any more than her mother would have, another inheritance baby. Her mother's temper would have stopped her from holding down a job long enough, for starters.

She catches her reflection in the floor-to-ceiling hallway mirror. She can't say she's unrecognizable from the way she looked several months ago, but the difference from consistent cardio is certainly noticeable. Ten pounds noticeable. She's no "Slender Lizzie" yet, the ostensibly playful nickname for her sister that her father used overly loudly whenever Madison was eating a snack, but she's getting there. That feels good, but it's fragile. One undisciplined day and she worries she'll slip back into her old ways.

Well, that's why we're here, isn't it? she thinks.

Yes. She did well to get this far. She's proud of herself. But she's ready to be pushed now. She turns back and forth, looking at the pudge of her belly and slight overhang of her hips. She may have lost ten pounds, but her No Days Off goal remains the same: She wants to lose another fifteen while she's here. At only twenty-three, she's surprised the race training didn't take more weight off. It would have just a few short years ago.

It doesn't have to anyway, she tells herself. *It looks just fine. You look good.*

She nearly believes it, although she's glad she decided to cut her hair to just below her jawline. She likes it.

She's also surprisingly nervous. *Really* nervous. What if she's the worst one?

So nervous, in fact, that she starts a little as the door opens behind her. Another woman walks in.

"Oh!" Madison says, surprised. "Hello!"

"Oh! Gosh," the woman says merrily, putting her bag down. "Thought I was the first to arrive. Hello!"

Madison isn't great at placing accents, but this woman is definitely American. A grin lights up the woman's eyes, strikingly hazel against her blond hair. She's several inches taller than Madison's five feet six, and while it's hard to tell — the newcomer is wearing sweatpants and a hoodie—she seems to have the build of a real athlete. She looks older than Madison, perhaps in her early thirties.

Damn. This was exactly what Madison was worried about. This *is* going to be the standard, a league into which Madison has not yet entered. Since the half-marathon, Madison still works out five days a week, but she'd be in *great* shape if she quit drinking and laid off the pizza. She is not yet good enough, she knows. The remaining evidence around her waist is more subtle now, yes, but still undeniable.

"Ha, nice to meet you," Madison says.

"Oh, you're a Brit!" the blonde exclaims. "Welcome, my *limey* friend!" She immediately looks mortified, putting her hand to her mouth. "Oh shit. Is that word offensive? Sorry, I was trying to be funny. I'm such an asshole."

"No offense at all, Yank." Madison chuckles, holding out her hand.

The blonde laughs and spreads her arms, inviting a hug instead of a handshake. "Shall we?" Her voice is deep but rich and pleasant. "Going to be a long month. We should start right."

"Good idea." Madison laughs nervously, stepping forward. They hug. "I'm Madison."

"Jennifer." The blonde steps back, still grinning. "Excited?"

"Nervous!" Madison laughs. She nearly doesn't voice what she's thinking, but something about Jennifer's infectious smile puts her at ease. Madison turns her insecurity into an honest compliment. "If everyone here is going to be built like you, I think I'm going to end up being the frickin' cheerleader."

"Nooo, no, no," Jennifer says earnestly, slapping Madison lightly on the arm with one hand, waving the comment away with the other. "It's not a competition, remember. This is about *everyone* being *everyone's* cheerleaders, even though I can't dance a routine to save my life! Look." To Madison's complete surprise, Jennifer starts tapping each foot on the floor twice, one at a time, carefully watching Madison's face as she does so. Madison watches, amused but bewildered, and then gets it. Jennifer's rhythm is slowly going off, one foot moving out of time with the other. The dance move is *terrible*.

Madison raises her eyebrows.

"Yep," Jennifer says, still clumping away. "And I promise you, this is me trying as hard as I can." She stops. "With rhythm like mine, the thing *I'm* worried about is if they make us do aerobics. I'll die of embarrassment." Jennifer laughs at her own joke and Madison can't help joining in, her feelings of intimidation disappearing at the sound.

"Did you come far?" Madison asks, expecting the answer to be yes. The limited intake is international.

"From Seattle," Jennifer says.

"Oh wow," Madison says. "You've come a long way."

"Not as far as crossing the freakin' Atlantic, my British chum," Jennifer says, smiling. "Hey, did you see the tarp behind the big side building, the barn or whatever?"

"No."

"There's some tarped-off area back there," Jennifer says, "like a section of ground covered up for something. It's really long. It sticks out from the left side of the building. I'm surprised you didn't see it. Got to be well over a hundred feet long. I'm nosy, yes. I wonder what it is." She shakes her head, grins. "Sorry, I'm just excited."

"Me too," Madison says. "Maybe it's a rain cover for a running track or something. I'll look on the way out."

"The way out?" Jennifer asks, but the penny drops as she takes in Madison's outfit. "You're going for a run *now*? Before we even start this afternoon?"

"Just a little one," Madison says, flushing. She's impressed the athlete, it seems. "More of a light jog. Wanted to start off right."

"Oof. You're going to make the rest of us look bad."

Madison feels a faint thud of satisfaction; *she's* going for a run when the athlete isn't. It isn't a competition, no, but if it were, Madison would already be winning. Jennifer takes in the foyer spreading out onto the open-plan-ish lower floor and points at a nearby doorway.

"Did you pick a room yet?" Jennifer asks.

"No," Madison says. "I just walked through the door about two minutes before you did."

"Ugh, I'm in a world of my own sometimes," Jennifer chuckles, arching an eyebrow as she walks toward the nearest door, a solid-looking oak affair with a brass number 5 screwed onto it. "I should have spotted you going in, but I'm so unobservant. D'you know, a bird once pooped on my hair at a wedding, and I didn't notice for *four hours*. My partner at the time didn't say a word either. Idiot probably thought it was some kind of postmodern fascinator." She opens the door and glances inside before closing it again.

Madison looks toward the kitchen, noting the long table with eleven chairs, six on one side, five on the other. Ellie said they'd all be eating together.

"Any notes left for us from the boss?" Jennifer asks. "Maybe a plan for the first week?"

"I think I probably got the same email you did," Madison says.

"Ellie not being very forthcoming?" Jennifer snorts. "That's not been my experience of her at *all*, goodness no."

Madison smirks and heads up the stairs. Jennifer follows.

"Not just me, then," Madison says. "That makes me feel better."

They reach the mezzanine. Its glass-panel railing looks over the living area below. Three doors are set into the right-hand wall, labeled BEDROOM 3, STORAGE, and CONSULTING ROOM. Directly in front of Madison a floor-to-ceiling window allows her a beautiful view of the rear gardens and the rolling fields around the house. A rectangle of sunlight shines through, blessing the carpet. Sitting perfectly within it are a sofa, two armchairs, and a coffee table. Upon the table is a pile of books.

"Five of your British pounds says there's at least one copy of *Can't Hurt Me* in there," Jennifer says.

"I'm a fan." Madison walks over to the table and spreads the pile out. Jennifer is wrong about that particular title, but Madison recognizes a lot of the others: *The Power of Now. The 7 Habits of Highly Effective People. The Art of War. Tuesdays with Morrie.* There are a few she hasn't heard of: *Die Empty. Atomic Habits. Cracker Juice.*

"I'd get into taxis and start talking to the drivers about Goggins's book," Jennifer says, "although I did the audiobook, not a print copy."

I can't tell if the man is a genius or a lunatic, but I really got a lot out of it. I need to get back into fiction again, though. You know, I haven't read a good *story* story for a while."

Madison nearly mentions the book she's writing but doesn't. There might be questions, and she doesn't have all the answers yet. She's finished the first draft and isn't sure she's happy with it. She printed a physical copy to reread and make notes on. She crosses to the window and looks down at the expansive back garden. A high fence separates the garden's far end from the fields behind it. The only way to see over would be to stand on the wooden dais that has been constructed in front of the fence.

This dais is big enough to hold several people, but there is an obscured object that might have the shape of a chair. Madison can't tell for certain because it's wrapped in what looks like a plastic overnight cover for a motorbike, presumably to keep it dry. If it isn't a chair, then the whole platform is odd. What would it be used for other than as a lookout point? There is a second, higher fence to the right. It takes her a moment to figure out what it's for: The main road, though far away, curves back around in that direction. The higher fence is a privacy screen so that anyone on the platform would be out of sight from the road.

"What's that for, do you think?" she asks, pointing at the scene below.

Jennifer joins Madison at the window. "Some sort of stage. I bet there's some kind of graduation ceremony at the end of all this." She opens one of the doors, then the other. "Looks like these two are both bedrooms. If you don't mind, I'm going to take this one here."

"Go for it," Madison says, thinking she'll take an upper-floor room too. Farther away from any potential kitchen noise.

"I'll get my bag." Jennifer heads for the stairs. "I'll sling it in my room, and then do you want to help me find the coffee? Or tea bags for you?"

"I promised myself I'd start with that run, and I don't want to…" Madison feels that awkwardness shiver over her, the feeling she gets whenever she has to say no to a friendly request. She can hear Imani grumbling now, the same thing she said ever since Madison started training: "Missing one isn't going to hurt."

Jennifer finishes the sentence for her. "You don't want to miss it. No, totally get that—my fault." She taps her finger on her temple as she reaches the banister. "I forgot. Don't let me derail you. We'll have tea when you get back. Maybe some of the others will have arrived by then."

Madison feels a rush of happiness. This is going to be *great*. Jennifer seems cool, and she's glad it won't all be people her own age. She has always felt more comfortable around older women for some reason.

Jennifer reaches the ground floor and scoops her bag onto her shoulder. Madison can tell by the way the bag hangs that it's heavy, but Jennifer lifts it easily.

"How long do you think you'll be?" Jennifer asks. "I'll try and have the tea ready when you get back."

"Only going up the lane to the main road and back," Madison says. "At a slow jogging pace, that's twenty, twenty-five minutes."

"Okay. This is going to be fun. Which are you, by the way?"

"Huh?"

"Light or Medium?"

Madison mimes running on the spot, grinning. "Which do you think?"

"You're on Medium too?" Jennifer asks, surprised. "And you're still going for a run now?"

"Yep." Madison shrugs, delighted that Jennifer is in the same bracket... while also enjoying the Head Girl feeling that is coming with going on this run while Jennifer makes tea.

"Wow," Jennifer says. "See you in twenty. Thirty if you're smart. Milk and sugar?"

"I'll actually have a black coffee," Madison says, opening the heavy wooden front door. Sunlight streams into the hallway. "Do you think she even *has* sugar here?"

"Probably not," Jennifer says, heading back up the stairs with her bag. "See you in a bit."

"See you," Madison says, and nearly calls after her to add, *So what are your goals?* She's curious, but she doesn't ask, remembering they were instructed not to discuss their goals with their course mates until orientation. What the hell could Jennifer be here to do? She looks practically Olympian already. By the time Madison is ten steps out of the house, she's already jogging. That's sensible. This is the smart thing to do. But it feels like cheating.

By the time she's reached the end of the long driveway, Madison is running. As she turns onto the country lane she hears distant hooves.

She sees a woman on a sturdy white horse heading toward her. This road only leads to the house, so either she's here for the course or...

Ellie waves, pulling the reins. The horse whickers, chewing on its bridle. The beautiful gray speckle on its nose forms a crescent.

Madison pulls up alongside and jogs in place. Ellie takes her sunglasses off and gives Madison a weak smile. Despite her assured posture, the woman looks tired. Stressed, perhaps.

"Hi, Madison," Ellie says.

"Hi!" Madison says. "You're early!"

"I am. I finished some business items quicker than expected, so I thought I'd take Winter here out for a ride. She needs it."

"She's beautiful," Madison says, reaching up and stroking the horse's thick neck.

"She absolutely is." Ellie runs her hand over the horse's mane, and the first undeniably genuine smile Madison has witnessed lights up Ellie's face. "She's my girl. Had her eighteen years now. She's getting up there. Aren't you, girl?"

Winter doesn't reply, instead continuing to chew gently on her bridle.

"She lives here?" Madison asks.

"Stables are around back. I take care of her myself, no stable hands. I enjoy it."

"You take care of the whole place by yourself?"

"I have grounds people who manage and tidy the place up between courses, but never when students are here."

The grounds. Madison remembers the tarp Jennifer mentioned. She forgot to look. She will on the return leg.

"Did you bring your photo?" Ellie asks. "That's important."

"Of course." Madison was told to bring a photo of someone she admires. In Madison's bag is a photo of tennis legend Serena Williams.

"Good." Ellie takes in Madison's outfit, her movements. She smiles. "You came to play."

"I did."

Ellie nods, then turns her head to the west and looks into the distance. Madison waits for her to speak again, but when Ellie's brow furrows a little, Madison understands that Ellie is trying to think of something to say, unable to do so. Ellie doesn't look anxious or particularly concerned by the awkwardness of the silence between two relative strangers. She looks like a woman trying to figure out a jigsaw puzzle.

Madison feels awkward even if Ellie doesn't; she begins to speak and then Ellie suddenly dismounts, her face brightening as if she's just had an idea. She removes Winter's bridle, lays it on the ground, and gently pats the horse's flank. Winter ambles up the lane.

"Stable's open," Ellie says, "and she wants a feed. Anyway... catch me."

Suddenly Ellie is sprinting up the lane. She's wearing sandals, jeans, and a thick roll-neck sweater. The sun is still warm and high in the sky. Madison watches her for a moment, dumbfounded. Is Ellie serious?

"*Catch me!*" Ellie yells, still running.

It doesn't sound like she's playing.

Madison dashes after her, still shocked, but after a few more strides she starts to laugh. This *is* going to be great.

Ellie — in her riding clothes and sandals — has almost doubled the gap between them.

"Ladies," Ellie says. "I think we can officially get things started."

All of the students are now seated on the dais Madison saw from the mezzanine window. The object under the plastic was revealed to be a heavy, ornately carved wooden armchair. It faces the folding chairs the students now occupy, and to its right sits a wooden plinth with a metal bucket on top. A lovely cool breeze blows across Madison's skin, the smells of grass and nature within it, the heat of the day still thick and heavy around her. It's a beautiful evening to be outside in the last of the sun. "I like to perform the last part of the Sunset Ceremony right as the sun is dipping below the horizon," Ellie continues. "I say that, but I don't think I've ever actually managed it." She grins. The students chuckle, Madison included, but it's a nervous laughter. Of course it is; the meet-and-greet stage is about to officially end.

Madison returned from her run to discover Frankie—from Wisconsin—unloading her bags in the driveway. Madison didn't warm to the lean, petite, chic-pixie Frankie as easily as she did to Jennifer. Frankie's body language when she saw a sweaty, post-run Madison walking through the front door with Ellie, the boss, said it all. Frankie was jealous. She offered Madison a handshake and a smile that could most generously be described as frosty. Madison attempted to keep the good vibes going by turning it into a hug, and Frankie complied, but barely. Her hands rested on Madison's shoulders, and she chuckled as if Madison were a provincial idiot for attempting anything as gauche as a hug. Frankie hugged like a disapproving mother. Madison recognized it all too well.

Soon after, however, Frankie started to relax a little, even complimenting Madison on her voice, of all things. Madison thinks perhaps Frankie's just not comfortable around new people, maybe anxious and defensive, which Madison can't wrap her head around. She'd kill to have Frankie's job—interior designer—and the woman is straight-up, flat-out *beautiful*. Running her own successful business and only five years older than Madison to boot.

The others arrived soon after, all clearly having the same idea to arrive early. As it turns out, there are only six of them on this particular course: Madison, Jennifer, and Frankie on Medium, and the other three—Namrah (New Jersey), Cameron (Illinois), and Sarah (Idaho)—on Light.

After showering and changing, Madison returned to the kitchen to find the five other women seated at the center of the room. They were enjoying tea and coffee around the large rustic dining table. Ellie's taste — or her designer's — was excellent, the colors and new-world stylings of the space blending perfectly with the white ceiling and wooden beams above.

Madison felt a stab of anxiety again — here everyone else was, getting to know one another, and she was the newcomer, the outsider already — but that feeling was quickly put to rest as more hugs were exchanged. The chatter was super positive, all of them upbeat. Madison found out she is the youngest by at least five years — something she was concerned about. But she also found out that Cameron, too, is unemployed — a former paralegal and currently job hunting. Madison feels a little better thanks to this — not superior in any way, but she was worried about being an out-of-work waitress. The kind-faced brunette reminds Madison of a leaner, late-twenties Melissa McCarthy.

To her surprise, Madison enjoys their company much more than she thought she would. She struggled in the past to be her true self in all-female groups.

Namrah, taller even than Jennifer, perhaps clearing six feet, is quiet, with long limbs like a basketball player. Madison is surprised Namrah is only on Light. So far, Namrah has asked polite questions and been friendly, but Madison hasn't gotten much out of her other than what she does for a living; she's a police interpreter for Urdu speakers. Sarah, on the other hand — a stocky, smiling elementary school teacher with flaming red hair — is forthcoming in the extreme. If you asked her what time it is, she'd tell you that as well as the story of how she got her watch and the way it was made. She's nice, though, positive and energetic, and a passionate biker. The roar of her Yamaha was audible long before she arrived. Madison thinks it's nice that Sarah seems genuinely interested in the others.

Jennifer and maybe Namrah are way beyond you, Madison told herself, *but perhaps you can outdo Frankie. Sarah and Cameron look beatable, but being on Light gives them an advantage.* She adds another, familiar mental note to the assessment: *Not that it's a competition.*

The chatting and excitement continued until Ellie appeared to invite them into the garden for the Sunset Ceremony.

Jennifer sits to Madison's left, Frankie to her right.

Ellie looks to the horizon and then moves around behind the large chair. As she does, Frankie leans over and whispers in Madison's ear.

"Are you getting Mayan-human-sacrifice vibes from all this or is it just me?"

Madison chuckles. "Of course," she whispers back, mock serious. "Didn't you read the brochure? You *are* a virgin like the rest of us, aren't you?"

Frankie snorts and puts her hand to her mouth.

Yeah, Frankie's all right.

Ellie produces a leather bag from behind the chair and removes six notepads and pencils. She takes another look at the position of the setting sun and then hands the notepads out to her students.

"This ceremony," Ellie says, "is what I like to think of as a little rite of passage."

Madison sneaks a glance at the others and sees echoes of her nerves etched across their faces.

"It also serves as a small taste of the kind of thing you may experience should you fail to complete — or worse, quit — any of the modules: Hard Corrections. Short but unpleasant." She grins, and everyone forces a chuckle. "Much like yours truly." No chuckles. Ellie has screwed up the timing of the punch line but seems not to notice. "Before we get to that, I need you to write down on your notepads what you are here for. You don't have to let the others see if you don't want to, but I *don't* mean write down your goals. You already know what they are. I mean write down what *will happen* by the end of this course. Your intention. It's important, but at the same time, it's only a starting point. Most people come to NDO because they don't know what they *need*. Then there are the people coming here thinking they *know* what they need." She shrugs. "At their core? They both need the same thing. But your mission statements will be something to aim for and may even *be* your ending point. That's rarely the case, but it's a good way to start all the same."

"You understand a word of that?" Jennifer mutters.

Madison doesn't answer, not wanting to admit that it sounded like contradictory mumbo jumbo. She believes in Ellie.

"Have a think," Ellie says. "Take a moment, then write your note and place it in the bucket here." Ellie grabs a notepad for herself, writes on it. "Here's mine," she says, turning the notepad to show **I WILL HELP MY STUDENTS TO SUCCEED** written in neat block letters. She then tears off the piece of paper, folds it, and places it in the bucket. She looks at her watch. "You have three minutes."

Madison looks at her blank page as the others all hunch over their notepads. What is she here to do? The answer comes quickly, though. She jots it down:

I WILL BECOME STRONG

She stands—the first to do so—and crosses to the bucket, dropping the note in and catching Ellie giving her an encouraging smile. Madison is embarrassed by the way she reddens a little with happiness. She returns to her seat and waits. One by one, the others drop their notes into the bucket. As she watches Jennifer, it occurs to Madison that she still doesn't know what Jennifer does for a living. She makes a mental note to ask.

Once everyone is seated, Ellie speaks.

"Very good, ladies. Now we send them into the universe." She produces a kitchen lighter from the leather bag, the kind with a long barrel, and ignites it before lowering it into the bucket. Small flames quickly poke their dancing heads above the bucket's rim, black smoke rising into the yellowing sky. "Some of you," Ellie says, "might consider this kind of thing pointless. I can assure you it is not. Ritual and process are extremely important to facilitate change, whether you believe that from a spiritual or purely psychological perspective. Personally, I believe it's a matter of both. Discovering what I call your True Strength—your ability to unlock your power—during your time on this Earth...This is the most important thing anyone can achieve in their lifetime." Her gaze becomes intense, and her smile disappears. "When my students understand this—truly absorb the message—it is the greatest thing I see. It is unquestionably my calling. Yours begins here."

She moves behind the wooden chair once more and comes back with a large cooler. She carries it in one hand, but it appears to be full, the slender muscles in Ellie's forearm tight, the tendons standing out. "If you complete this course," Ellie says, "you will be new women by the end of it. I hope you truly understand that." She looks to each of the Light women in turn. "The ladies on Light—Cameron, Sarah, Namrah—each have three passes to use throughout the month to skip exercises of their choosing, Hard Correction–free. But they will still go through this rite of passage."

Madison looks around at the Light ladies, surprised, but they look like they already knew about this.

"This may seem a little silly when you first see what it involves," Ellie says, opening the cooler, "but it isn't."

She reaches into the box and pulls out a one-liter bottle of Pepsi.

"I'll go first," Ellie says, looking again at the sun's position. "Jennifer, could you come up here?"

"You're going to do it with us?" Namrah asks, her soft voice surprised.

"Of course," Ellie says. "I've stated my intention, and I am on this journey with you." She hands the bottle of cola to Jennifer and sits in the chair, facing her charges.

Madison, confused, wonders if Ellie is going to drink the whole thing in one go or something, watching as Ellie breathes heavily through her nose a few times with her eyes closed.

"Jennifer, take the lid off and, with your thumb stuck in the top, I'd like you to shake up that bottle as much as you can, please."

Jennifer looks as confused as Madison feels but does as she's told, giving the bottle a few token shakes. The foam inside rises fast and leaks out from around Jennifer's thumb.

Ellie hears the trickle and opens her eyes, brow furrowed. "Jen," she says, her tone lightly exasperated, "I picked you because you're physically strong. Give it some *oomph*, if you will. Quickly now."

Jennifer glances at Madison, uncertainty written across her face, then gives the bottle a thunderous shake. The bottle hisses violently now, small jets of high-pressure fizz launching into the air where they escape around her thumb.

"Come close, *quick*," Ellie says, and when Jennifer moves the hissing bottle in front of Ellie's chest, Ellie grabs it with one hand. She holds Jennifer's wrist with the other.

Ellie angles the top of the bottle toward her own face.

"Thumb out," she commands, and before Jennifer can respond, Ellie is gripping the bottle and pulling Jennifer's wrist up. Her thumb pops free.

A cannon blast of fizzing, high-pressure cola fires straight up Ellie's nose.

All the women gasp.

Ellie's free hand slaps against the other side of the plastic bottle, then crushes it as her whole body tenses. Her face disappears behind a foaming jet of brown and cream, and her foot stamps repeatedly on the ground as she takes the powerful jet directly into her sinuses. Now her face is visible again as the riot hose of cola quickly reduces to a rapid overspill, the pressure finally spent. Ellie's teeth are gritted, the skin around her eyes and nose a bright red. She drops the bottle, gasping as she rocks back and forth, pushing her palms against her eye sockets. Her foot slowly stops stamping, and Ellie stills.

Madison is stunned. She looks at the others: Some hold their hands over their mouths; some stare blankly at Ellie. Jennifer gawks, clutching her chest. Cameron's face, Madison notices, is as white as the fizz that is running down Ellie's vest.

Ellie opens her eyes. They are red and heavily bloodshot. Then she smiles.

"Phew," she says finally, blowing out her cheeks and standing. "Okay. First thing to know: I'm fine." Her breathing is already slowing. "What you've just witnessed is an interrogation technique used by the Colombian police. As you know, none of the punishments here will leave wounds, break the skin, mark you in any way, nothing like that. But they *are* a brief, intense deterrent. You have to know this: Almost everyone earns at least one Hard Correction during the course. No one gets serious until they've had their first because they need to know what they're avoiding in order for the system to work. Once you've been through one, you won't want a second." She gestures around herself. "What we're about to do is one of the lesser ones, so it won't have quite the same effect, but this is where you set your intention for the month, ladies." She points at the group, and Madison flinches a little, thinking that she is being singled out to go next. "You are all—*all*—capable of completing this course. You wouldn't be here if I didn't know this." Ellie points at the chair. "This is to let you know that you can bear anything I dish out." She pauses, scanning the group. Behind her, the sky is beginning to turn a beautiful shade of orange.

"Who's going first?" she asks.

No one speaks.

Ellie nods. "I understand. I'll pick, then. Cameron?"

Everyone turns to Cameron, who looks as if she's about to throw up.

"I'm..." she begins. She stops. Thinks. "I don't think I can do this."

"You definitely can," Ellie says, her voice firm. "It's short, and it hurts a lot, but then it's over."

"Yeah, but..." Cameron's round face suddenly reddens to a shade almost as dark as her hair. She shrugs petulantly. "Just... what's the point? I know this is supposed to be some we're-all-in-this-together thing, but we're not. I'm on Light. They're on Medium. Our sessions aren't going to be as long as the others' anyway." She brightens. "Can I use one of my passes for this?"

"I'm afraid not."

Cameron chews her lip.

"Cameron," Ellie says kindly, "all change requires ritual. And the changes on this course—even on Light—will be painful. The *workouts* are going to be worse than this because those will involve suffering that goes on for a long time. This is just—" She snaps her fingers. The sound rings clear in the evening air on that elevated platform. "And you are going to feel so glad you did it. What you're listening

I'll Quit When I'm Dead

to right now is the inner voice that has kept you *exactly where you are.*" She slaps the chair, her face darkening. "This is a *statement,* a rebellion against yourself that means you aren't going to be held back *by* yourself anymore." She holds out a hand to Cameron. "Come on," she says. "You want this. You need this."

Cameron's terrified eyes dart from Ellie's hand to the empty bottle on the floor. Madison thinks she sees tears beginning to form. Madison doesn't speak. Everyone is staring at Cameron, still in mild, lingering shock and not saying a word.

Then someone breaks the silence. It's her own voice.

"I'll go first," Madison says.

Ellie looks at Madison, face blank. Then she turns back to Cameron.

"Take a moment, Cameron," she says, a smile creeping onto her features. "Breathe slowly, calm your mind, and prepare." She holds her hand out to Madison. "Come on up, Madison. Jennifer, please return to your seat." None of the other students say a word, but Madison can feel them seize the air around her. Madison stands. Jennifer passes by and raises her eyebrows. *Good luck,* her expression says.

Madison forces a smile, an odd sense of calm taking over. She volunteered. She went *first*. That thud of satisfaction comes again. This is so unlike her that it's absolutely exhilarating. It's immediately different, however, when she sits down in the chair and sees five faces staring back at her; her tension shoots up. She doesn't know what to expect in terms of sensation or pain. Behind her audience, Madison sees the house and barn looming large in the distance, their walls cast in rich, colorful, September-evening light. A pair of goldfinches flitter across the darkening sky that hangs above the old buildings, including the stable where Winter has been shut up for the evening.

Ellie pulls another bottle out of the cooler, removes the cap, and begins to shake it up with her own thumb inside the bottle's neck. Madison can hear the hissing pressure inside the bottle more clearly, can more easily see the sharp press of those jets of gas around Ellie's thumb, *smell* the cola as its vapor pushes out into the air. Something about that sets Madison's heart racing.

This is going to *hurt*.

It's too late to back out now. The neck of the bottle is moving down and toward her face.

"Push your neck forward," Ellie says gently, "and tip your head back a little."

Madison does as she's told, her now-rapid breathing drowned out by the hissing bottle. Ellie's thumb pops free—

Madison's ears are suddenly full of a crackling roar, and she has a nanosecond view of the other women's faces before they vanish, not because she has closed her eyes against the high-pressure blast but because cola has fired through her sinuses and out into her tear ducts.

The pain is instant. It feels as if she has been simultaneously head-butted in the nose while someone has ignited a flamethrower inside her skull. The sheer physical force stuns all her thoughts into silence. She opens her mouth to unleash an agonized scream but almost immediately begins to drown instead as she swallows the endless tsunami of cola detonating inside her face and throat. It *burns*, the fizzing electric and painful in its volume. She bucks in her seat, blind. The liquid *just keeps hitting her* as a sense of tortured unreality washes over Madison's mind.

The punching, physical force of the jet is starting to abate, but the burning doesn't. Ellie's hands leave Madison's body, and as that awful crackling in Madison's ears begins to subside, she can hear Ellie talking to her. Madison leaps to her feet, her breath coming in wet moans as she turns on the spot, her hands gripping helplessly at her hair. It feels as if something sore and hot is wedged in the back of her throat.

"Walk it off, Madison," Ellie says encouragingly.

Madison feels something pressed into her hand. It's a towel, and she thrusts it against her eyes, grunting as she begins walking in a tight, blind, and unsteady circle... but now the burning is subsiding too, and Madison starts to understand that she is already coming out the other side of this.

She's done it.

She's begun her journey... in the weirdest, stupidest way possible, perhaps, but she's *done it*. She pulls the towel away from her face, opening her blurry eyes, and sees Ellie with her arms spread wide for a hug.

"Well done," Ellie says, grinning that strange grin of hers, but her eyes shine with approval.

Madison immediately walks into the embrace, but whatever truth Ellie's eyes might show, the action of the hug is angular and robotic. Madison's eyes still leak a little, though, and not with cola. She's overcome by the moment. As bad as Ellie is at giving hugs, Madison knows Ellie is proud of her already, and the hug therefore beats any of the hugs received in her family home. Those had either been given by her father with half the enthusiasm of those given to Slender Lizzie or had been a rote gesture from her mother that never became warm no matter how hard Madison squeezed back—

Madison catches herself. Where had that come from?

That's the process at work, she thinks. *You took a step and it's already happening. You're already releasing. My God. And Ellie came up with this.*

She looks over Ellie's shoulder to the audience behind her. The discomfort there has turned into uncertain smiles; they've seen that Madison has come through it and that she appears okay. Maybe it's not that bad... but they've also seen the pain involved.

And they're next.

Jennifer's big hands start applauding, and the others join in immediately. She is smiling. "Maddy!" she cheers.

Madison gives Jennifer a thumbs-up with a wobbly grin, sniffing back her tears and hoping they look like leftover cola to her fellow students. She wants them to think she walked it.

Cameron isn't applauding. She stands, shaking her head. "I can't do it," she says quietly.

Ellie breaks away from the hug. "You *can* do it," she says.

The used-up phrase nearly spoils Madison's buzz—her *fizz*—but she's feeling too good to let it.

"No," Cameron says.

Ellie stares for a moment, as if reading the other woman. "Okay," she says, her voice solemn. "Okay. You know that means you can't do the course?"

"... Yeah." Cameron's voice sounds like a child's.

"And you'll lose your deposit."

Cameron looks surprised. "Only the deposit? You'll refund the rest?"

"It's okay," Ellie says, nodding. "Means maybe you think about it and come back another time. I'm running a business, but I'd rather you have the money to return if you decide to." She shrugs. "I think — well, sadly, I *know* — that you'll regret walking away." She gestures to the chair. "Last chance."

Cameron looks at the chair for what feels to Madison like a full thirty seconds. No one speaks.

Jennifer breaks the silence. "You can do it, Cameron."

Madison wants to repeat it too, but she doesn't.

"I'll hold your hand," Frankie says kindly, standing with her arm outstretched.

Cameron stares at Frankie's hand.

"Sorry, no," Ellie says, eyes lowered. "She has to do it alone."

Frankie looks at Ellie, chastened, then back to Cameron, embarrassed. Frankie sits. Cameron just stands there awkwardly, waiting to be told what to do.

"I just can't," she says finally.

"I understand," Ellie says. "You'll have to go back to the house while we complete the ceremony, okay? I'll come see you when we're done."

Cameron nods and turns away, avoiding the others' gazes as she walks down the steps from the dais.

"Good luck, Cameron," Sarah calls after her, her voice trailing off, sounding uncertain for once — a rarity, Madison would guess — about what she should say or perhaps if she should speak at all.

"Take your seat, Madison," Ellie says quietly. "Frankie? You next? By the way," she adds as Frankie stands, "you'll all get to rinse out with saline after this, so don't worry about any residue."

As Madison reaches her seat, Frankie passes her going the other way. Madison holds up a hand for a high five. Frankie gives it to her, looking nervous, and as Madison sits down, Sarah gives her a slap on the back. The others follow suit, and Madison suddenly feels even taller than Namrah. She's *glowing,* and she knows it's not from the liquid sugar that has just been blasted into her face.

This level of intensity—she now knows for certain—is exactly what she needed.

She turns to look down into the garden, watching the now-distant form of Cameron make her way back to the house, her shadow cast long by the low sun. Madison feels a mix of pity and, to her great surprise, shame... and something else.

Disgust.

From behind her comes the loud sound of a fizzing jet mixed with Frankie's choked-off screams.

This time the applause comes right away.

Chapter Five: Johnny

The Boggart Are Always Listening

THE STARS ARE so clear that Johnny swears he can see them twinkling. That might just be the joint doing its thing; it's been a while since he smoked one, and Sandy's stuff is *good*.

He watches the distant points of light above, enjoying the cool twilight air and the smells after the brief spell of rain: chlorophyll in the high and overgrown hedges, the unkempt grass. What was he thinking, sitting inside while *this* was on the other side of the door? Isn't this exactly what he's come here for, to be refreshed by nature's bounty, even if said nature is badly in need of a trim? He smiles lazily, feeling good. It's been a while.

His mind wanders aimlessly, his awareness returning only when some small animal in the undergrowth moves and makes a noise. The weed is making it hard to think straight. A painkiller fix is different from this. Less of a head high. What was he doing? Oh yeah, he was *taking in nature.*

He went out there, into the green, opening the kitchen door and crossing through the conservatory beyond to step out onto the grass and into dusk. He walked the boundary of the private garden, culminating in a tiny lap around the small apple tree at the far end.

He straightens now, neck protesting as he tips his head forward—he's been standing stargazing for some time—and looks back at the house from the other end of the garden.

Every window on this side of the bungalow is open.

He might have opened them earlier, but the evening isn't that warm, even for early September. He wouldn't have needed to close the windows for security reasons; there is no outside access to the garden, thanks to the hedges on all three sides, and there are only bungalows to the left and right, so the garden isn't overlooked. A safe, leafy space.

A faint sound comes from inside the house.

Foreboding suddenly creeps up Johnny's back, leaking upward from his feet as if growing into him out of the moist earth. Something is wrong here. A word lurches to the front of his mind as he stares at the exposed house.

Boggart.

That stupid picture, *David* and his stupid pictures, putting the idea in his head. The fucking joint too, the cannabis in his bloodstream making it impossible to push away the idea worming eagerly and hungrily into his brain.

There is a Boggart inside this house.

"Stop it," he says out loud. Where the hell is Ivan? What was he doing before coming here? The thought flutters—it's so fucking hard to think—but Johnny snags it. Ivan was *packing*, if gathering the handful of items that constituted Johnny's stuff could be called packing. Johnny sees this as a massive, massive favor. He hadn't wanted to ask, but Ivan, in his usual quiet way, understood what Johnny needed. He insisted Johnny not set even one foot back in the old place again. Johnny's emotional gratitude only brought Ivan's usual response: "There is no such thing as a self-made man, Johnny."

Bailey, Johnny thinks. Is she coming here with Ivan? Yes, his girlfriend is currently helping Ivan, they're packing together, and he thinks Ivan said they'd arrive today. Is that right? He pulls out his phone, makes several unsuccessful attempts to unlock it, and then manages to call Ivan. The call goes to voicemail, but that's not surprising. Ivan's phone is always off. He tries Bailey. The same. No text from Ivan to explain his lateness either, but that is also normal.

The joint has also given him bad dry mouth; he wants water. He will go back into the house; enough of this stupidity. He staggers across the garden, enters the conservatory, and walks through to the kitchen. He's surprised to see how dim it is inside before remembering Sandy explaining that all the lights are on timed dimmers. The long room looks like a cave. He forces himself to walk to the sink and put his mouth under the faucet.

Why are you trying to convince yourself you don't believe in the supernatural? his stoned brain whispers as he drinks. *Sandy offered to burn some sage around the place before she left, and you let her. Even before coming here, you've been lighting a candle every day.*

The every-day candle lighting was something he decided to do a few months ago, a decision made with a sober mind and a practical intent. Johnny had been told that, according to quantum physics, the vibrations we put out shape the world. He wasn't sure if that was true, but he felt that lighting a candle while thinking *Please give me strength today* could only be a good thing. If nothing else, the intent would mean something to him psychologically.

He switches the tap off, turns around, and sees that he has unintentionally laid out a shape on top of the dining room table.

At one end, the end nearest Johnny, two drink coasters mark each corner; Sandy left them loosely placed in the middle of the table, and Johnny's OCD couldn't leave them so disorganized. He placed them opposite each other, and his brain accepted this mirrored placement as just fine. This, he now sees, means that the tea-candle holder in the middle of the table — the candle set into it now lit — sits at the top point of a triangle of objects. Slap bang in the center of this triangle — almost perfect in its placement — is a crumpled scrap of paper towel.

The words **I WILL GET CLEAN** are written on it.

He vaguely remembers writing it, four words pencil-scrawled onto a hastily snatched Bounty Select-a-Size. Like his daily candle lighting, the note was meant to be a kind of mission statement to start him off right in his new home. Johnny is a big believer in such things these days.

Between the note and the candle sits a pile of nine or ten Werther's Originals.

Right now — sitting as they are, set before the note and the burning flame — they look like an offering.

"Take a breath," Johnny says aloud. He talks to himself a lot these days. "If you were somehow going to summon" — *a Boggart*, he thinks — "*something*, then surely you would need to be way more... *specific* to have a successful spell or whatever. Relax. Turn your music back on."

He realizes that he didn't actually turn it off, but it is now off. He doesn't turn it back on after all; he feels too exposed. Now there is only a silence that feels like it is listening to him.

The house no longer feels safe.

You know something is wrong, he thinks, *and this place is supposed to be good. You are doing something wrong.*

"Check the rest of the house," he says aloud. "Do not be a bitch. Stop with the bullshit."

What Johnny doesn't know is that it most definitely is not bullshit.

If it hadn't been for the note, he could have done anything he liked in the garden and it wouldn't have made any difference.

As it was, every step he took — the weaving, stoned ones that staggered around the circle of weeds surrounding the apple tree farthest from the bungalow — was another unknowing stumble down a road infinitely less traveled. He even made a pledge. He had enough passing knowledge of pagan ideology to know that one does not write something tantamount to a mission statement — albeit brief — and then go out and do weirdly ritualistic stuff in nature, however mild. *Walking in circles around trees*, he will later think. *At dusk? Everyone knows, if they truly listen to themselves, that means something. It's asking for trouble.*

Something moves across the other end of the ceiling.

He lets out a shocked bark — *hoh!* — and staggers backward a few steps. He didn't imagine that. This is real. *This is real shit* —

Squirrels. Sandy said they got into the attic sometimes...

Another sound in the ceiling, away to his right, and this time Johnny hears it more clearly.

Pok...pok...pok-pok.

Harsh but muffled sounds, like the heavy ends of four pool cues several feet apart being jabbed into the ceiling. This isn't a squirrel. He listens. Holds his breath.

Nothing.

Then his body freezes—so hard that a stab of pain dances across his back—as he hears a rush of pool-cue sounds go *pok*-ing quickly away across the attic. He hears them move off along the hallway; it would now be above the master bedroom, the attic running the length of the whole house.

There *is* something in the attic. Something big.

The understanding is instant: The distance between the *pok*s means that if they are the sounds of feet, then whatever is walking above Johnny has very long legs indeed.

"You have to go up there."

He asks himself why he must.

"Because you have nowhere else to go," he says, his voice trembling. "Because you are high as fuck, and you are freaking out. If you do not go up there now and find out what it is, you cannot stay here, because you will be terrified for the rest of your time here, and then you will not be able to write any music, and *then* what the fuck will you do?"

He catches a glimpse of movement in the room with him, and his fists fly up. Then he sees that the movement is the shadow of the bushes and trees in the front garden. Their dark silhouettes dance on the wall as their leaves move in the light of the streetlamp standing in the hedge alley leading to the house. It's a light that Johnny is extremely grateful for, because in the next moment he hears the distant snap of a breaker firing, and all the lights in the house go out.

The circuit box is in the attic.

"*Get up there*," he says aloud, trying to bully himself. It works. Johnny strides out of the kitchen before he has time to think.

He enters the hallway that leads to the three bedrooms and the bathroom. The streetlamp shines through the glass panels on either side of the front door, but he leaves this light behind as he grabs the attic-hatch pole and reaches up to unhook the catch. The wooden panel falls back on its hinge to reveal the feet of the metal ladder above. Johnny freezes with the pole's hook on the ladder's bottom step as he hears the sound again.

Pok. Pok-pok-pok.

It's much louder now that the hatch is open. It is inarguable that there is something very strange and very big in the attic—

Stoned Johnny finally realizes *what the fuck he's doing*.

"Jesus," he gasps, and then he turns and darts to the front door, flinging it open and rushing headlong down the hedge alley to the street and his car.

By the time the police arrive, it's an hour later, and Johnny is a lot more sober. He's even begun to doubt what he just heard, at least in terms of it being anything supernatural. There had to be some*one* in the attic. And that meant calling the cops. Ivan wouldn't pick up his phone, and there's no one else local Johnny can call for backup to go up there with him. It's a mark of how scared he is that he even considered asking for help; that isn't Johnny's way. The dispatch officer told him to wait outside the house, perhaps in a pub or somewhere nearby, but Johnny opted for his car, sitting with the engine on to warm the vehicle up against the cold and full dark outside. By this point, he almost feels stupid. Again: *almost*.

The cops are Tillsey, a tall, paunchy white man in his early fifties, by the looks of it, and Rinton, an Asian woman not much older than Johnny and about half his height. Johnny feels embarrassed. Not because she is a woman but because he's asking this tiny person to do his fighting for him, and Johnny doesn't like anyone to do his dirty work. He blinks three times in the nearest lamppost's light as the cops quietly ask Johnny a few questions about what he heard; he tells them it was footsteps. Their responses aren't snarky or patronizing. They listen carefully and take notes, and then Rinton suggests they head to the house.

"Okay," Johnny says. "I'll go up first." It's the least he can do. If someone *is* up there, he wants to be the one who gets attacked first.

Tillsey and Rinton exchange a look.

"Sir," Tillsey says politely. "You won't be going into the house until we've checked it out for you. What I'm going to need you to do is wait in your car until we come back, okay?"

"Oh. Yeah, okay. Be careful, though, yeah? Might be dangerous. If there's someone there, I mean," he adds. The pair exchange another look. Johnny can't read it.

"We'll be careful," Rinton says. Her voice is deep for such a small body. "Let's get it done. Can we have your house keys, please, sir?"

Johnny hands them over and gets back into his car, watching through his windshield as Tillsey and Rinton disappear into the hedge alley. Rinton turns to give him an encouraging thumbs-up just before they disappear.

Johnny waits ten minutes.

The cops don't come back.

Twenty minutes.

Johnny starts to get a horrible sinking feeling in his stomach. If there was nothing there, or even a person they had to deal with or restrain, they'd have been back long ago just to update him. He's getting that horrible ache again, that phantom pain that reminds him *exactly* what would make everything feel so much better right now. He tries to focus on his breathing instead.

Ten more minutes pass; Johnny's skin is covered in goose bumps. This is real. Something bad happened to the cops. They might be hurt.

Call more police! Go and get some neighbors!

"You cannot do that," he says to himself, rocking a little in his seat. "Then whoever else comes will get hurt too." He *knew* he shouldn't have involved other people; cowardice made him break his rule.

He has to go back into the house.

He gets out of the car, noticing that everything sounds unusually still. The constant, gentle rustling of the trees that stand around the hedge alley's keyhole shape is gone. The trees are now silent, unmoving watchers in the darkness, waiting to see what happens. He walks through his new home's tall garden gate and up the short path. Listens at the closed front door. Nothing. He turns the handle and enters.

The ladder is now pulled all the way down, leading up from the hallway floor to the dark open square of the attic hatch.

The lights in the house are back on.

"Hello?" he calls.

No one responds.

The cops might be up in that attic right now, needing—

He darts to the ladder as quietly as he can and begins to climb, hands trembling as they grip the rungs. He looks up and discovers that, from this new angle, he can see the feet and legs of two people standing just beyond the edge of the hatch.

They are facing away from the hole, and they aren't moving.

"Hello?" he says, almost relieved for a second, a moment that is instantly lost when the trousered legs of Tillsey and Rinton don't even twitch at the sound of Johnny's voice. "*Officers,*" he says, and there is terror in the sound. No response.

He continues to climb the ladder. He has to. Halfway up he reaches for the backs of their legs. He grips one of them, expecting it to be cold, the leg of a corpse, but it's warm and moves lazily under his grip. Not a sudden *Hey, whaddya think you're doing?* movement but the lackadaisical motion of someone who has been disturbed in their sleep.

"*Pfff…*"

What the hell was *that?*

"What are you doing?" Johnny whispers, hating the tremor in his voice. When there is no response, Johnny takes a shaky breath and ascends until his head is poking through the hatch. The attic is enormous, the high, pitched roof giving the space a sense of real size; Johnny could stand up under the roof's highest point and have several feet of clearance. A network of thin metal struts and stanchions crisscrosses the attic, looking to Johnny like the frame of a half-built barn, albeit much narrower. The attic feels even bigger because so much of it is empty. There are no windows, however, so the only illumination is from the now-functioning hallway lights below; their glow shines faintly up through the hatch and is almost instantly devoured by the darkness. The cops would have flashlights; why aren't they on? He can't see what the two cops are looking at because their legs are between Johnny's head poking through the hatch and whatever lies beyond; the cops' bodies are pressed together, shoulders to ribs. Johnny leans back, away from the ladder upon which he is standing, and peeks around Rinton's legs. The darkness means it takes Johnny a moment to figure out what they're staring at, but then he gets it: There's some old bedding there, a pile of black sheets sitting upon a stack of boxes, stuffed into the eaves of the attic maybe ten feet away. He turns quickly, peering into the deep shadows at the other, much-farther-away end of the attic and sees only a sea of yellow loft insulation... which is, he realizes, bulging up hugely in places.

Could something have burrowed in under there?

Something has happened to the cops. Johnny must help them now and get everyone out of the house. Sending them up here was a mistake.

He clambers up the last few steps of the ladder and pulls himself into the attic, moving around in front of Rinton and Tillsey as quietly as he can but still watching that loft insulation behind them. The floor on Rinton and Tillsey's side of the hatch is made of crudely laid boards.

"What hap—" Johnny begins in a whisper but immediately understands that he won't get any sense out of either officer.

Rinton and Tillsey look as if they have been shot full of Valium.

Their eyes squint vacantly, both taking slow, hazy nose breaths and looking as if they might fall asleep at any minute. Johnny remembers that both cops are standing above a ten-foot drop. If they pass out and fall through the hatch, they'll break their necks, and that would be such a stupid death.

He's starting to panic now because their faces mean *he hasn't imagined this*, something has happened to them, and that means that whatever he heard up here is fucking real. "Come on, come on, guys. We need to..." His trembling words trail off as Tillsey's mouth curls into a sleepy, pleasant smirk.

"*Yfff...,*" he slurs, and then his shoulder jerks a little as he snorts a tiny laugh and shakes his head, amused by his own inability to communicate.

Johnny assesses the ladder behind them; he can almost certainly carry Rinton down it over his shoulder if she lets him, but doing the same with Tillsey would be considerably more difficult.

One of the stanchions behind him creaks.

He whirls around, the darkness unyielding, and squints at the eaves where Rinton and Tillsey are gazing, desperate to know *what the fuck is in there*. His whole head seems to throb with his heartbeat, but there is only the black bedding and the boxes and *wait*—one of the blankets, he now sees, is tied around the nearest stanchion. A thin line, taut and straight, leads from the pile to the metal strut.

Another thin piece of blanket emerges from the pile, rising slowly and lazily into the air, and then wraps itself around a stanchion to the pile's left.

Johnny is not looking at a pile of black blankets.

A distant part of his mind quietly recognizes that the crisscrossing lattice of metal stanchions all around him look just like a web.

The smiling, near-catatonic cops are bait.

The black form of the Boggart uncoils itself, its slender arms grasping the metal as it rises into the air. The Boggart has almost no torso; the center of its form is a large, bulbous head. It is the creature's limbs that are extremely long. Two more extend now and step down from the boxes upon which the Boggart poured itself, thumping gently onto the floor with a familiar and more audible *pok-pok*, lithe and lean, looking like fluid versions of the stanchions they grip. Its mouth—for its head is mostly mouth—spreads in a wide grin.

Johnny hears Rinton and Tillsey give satisfied sighs. Tillsey's whole body convulses in a rapid shudder.

Johnny staggers backward, his lungs suddenly full of ice, and his heel catches the rim of the hatch. He begins to fall before his other foot pushes his body backward on instinct. He clears the hatch, falling onto his backside and hitting his head on a metal roof support. One of his legs dangles through the hole, but his eyes are only on the Boggart as it clambers eagerly toward him, grasping and releasing parts of the metal latticework. It pulls and heaves itself across the attic.

There are only two words in his mind. One of them is *monster*.

The other one is *no*.

Johnny sits up, hearing himself gibber as he does, and moves to jump through the hatch to hopefully land on the ladder, but the Boggart is already covering his exit, knocking Rinton and Tillsey to the floor, limp. All the Boggart's feet—or *are* they feet, for now Johnny sees that its limbs end in hairy hand-feet much like those of a gorilla— stop on either side of the hatch. Its knees (elbows?) are high in the air, its enormous, bulbous black head sitting low, filling the hatch and blocking Johnny's path. The teeth in its immense, wide mouth are immaculate blades—long, thin fangs that almost look like porcupine quills made of gray bone.

Its eyes are like a goat's. Just like a goat's.

Johnny can't expand his chest enough to scream.

"Say your name," the creature says. Its voice is unnervingly human. Quiet. Breathy. As Johnny feels it on his face, he expects to smell rotting meat. He doesn't. Its breath smells sweet like citrus. Its eyes look him over. The creature blinks. "Say your name," it commands.

Johnny tries to breathe in to answer it. He can't; he can only make choking sounds.

"Say your name."

"Jo...Jo...Jo..."

His stammering doesn't come only from terror. Something inside him knows that he should not tell this creature his name. He *must* not.

"Say your name."

Johnny can't say anything.

"Say your name. *I invoke it,* for we are meeting, yes."

He suddenly doesn't have a choice. His lungs compress, his mouth somehow moving of its own accord as if spider legs press into the muscles around his jaw and lips.

"*Juhnnuh.*"

"Johnny."

"Ye...yes."

"Want to consume you, Johnny," it says. "Want to gulp all that you are into my belly, yes."

"Don't...don't..."

Now Johnny screams, a full-throated bellow.

The Boggart smiles. Johnny thinks about trying to push past it, throwing himself out of the hatch, but his brain rejects that idea the same way it would reject attacking a tiger. It knows a doomed idea when it sees it. *The cops? What's happened to the cops?*

"*Humans,*" the Boggart calls, goat eyes on Johnny as it whips a hand into the air. There are shuffling sounds as Tillsey and Rinton get to their feet, but Johnny is stunned by the impossible and sudden speed with which that hand moved. "Leave," the Boggart says.

Rinton and Tillsey let out deeply satisfied sighs and turn toward the hatch. The Boggart *pok-pok*s around them until its slender but enormous bulk crouches even closer to Johnny. The dopey faces of Rinton and Tillsey disappear down the ladder, and Johnny thinks about leaping after them, but the Boggart is too close, and Johnny knows how fast it can move. It would easily get him. *Keep it talking,* he thinks, desperate. *If you can get it to move back a few feet, you might have a chance to get away.*

The Boggart watches Johnny, smiling, until Johnny hears the front door open and close. The Boggart retakes its previous position, its head now hovering over the attic hatch. It watches for a moment longer, still smiling.

"Are you...here...for *me*?" Johnny asks.

The Boggart's goat eyes narrow, pleased. "I am, Johnny."

"Why?"

The Boggart spreads its long arms wide. "The same reason the Boggart always come, Johnny," it says, and Johnny hears it say *the*

Boggart the same way humans would say *the Apache, the Inuit, the Maasai*. "You invited me, yes."

"I didn't!" The words come out in a panic, loud in the attic. Johnny finally thinks to look around for a weapon, but none are close by.

The Boggart sees this and looks amused. "You will remain alive while we speak this night, yes, for you must clearly understand why we are bound." It relishes this last word, delivered with the weight of rusty steel.

"Bound? Wait—there has to be a mistake. I didn't invite you—"

"You know you did, yes, even if you did not know that I would be the answer. Clearly made your altar. Clearly put your words before it. Your intention. Clearly knew what our deal was. What it is. Clearly knew why you came to this house. Felt my approach, yes, even if you did not know *what* I was."

"My intention—"

He understands immediately. Words before an altar. `I WILL GET CLEAN`. An offering. Sandy's weird glass pyramid centerpiece. The tea-light holder. The spilled sweets.

Oh my God. He lit a candle before it all.

"My intention to get clean?"

Johnny sits petrified. What the fuck is he supposed to do? If he says the wrong thing, it will—

"Tell me," the Boggart says in response, the words like thin blades held at his throat, "what our deal is, Johnny. Think. You know what it is, yes."

Johnny thinks he knows but is too scared to speak, to say anything.

"*Say it.*"

It isn't eating him, even though it says it wants to. It says there's some kind of deal in place to do with him getting clean. "You can only...*consume* me...," Johnny says, "if I ever take painkillers again?"

"Very good, yes. That is our deal."

"But—"

"Repeat it: *That is our deal.*" The Boggart flashes its teeth.

"That is our deal," Johnny says. Anger flutters briefly, memories of being bullied at school, at home.

"*That is our deal,*" the Boggart repeats.

Johnny's panic tells his eyes to look around for something bright to blink on, his OCD a foolish and pointless self-rebuke in the face of such a solid horror. His eyes glance through the hatch to find the glare of the hallway's light, blinking rapidly against it three times as the Boggart sniffs the air.

"Such *sadness* in this deal," it says, sounding almost disappointed. "All your kind...so unable to make yourselves do that which you wish, yes." It exhales, and Johnny tries not to breathe; the Boggart's breath may be like fruit-scented steam, but Johnny does not want to inhale it. "I must end our exchange with a warning, Johnny-Mine, for a deal must be understood in order to root, yes." The Boggart leans toward Johnny. "Time may pass," it says, "and you may doubt this meeting, yes. You may think that I am the result of a fevered mind, a metaphor for all you wish to resist."

The Boggart's awful eyes are cold and utterly without mercy.

"Johnny-Mine, you may think this, yes," it says, "and thus take your *painkillers*."

Its toes drum on the attic floor with a horrible eagerness, as if the creature can scarcely contain itself at the thought.

"If that day arrives," it says, "I will come for you that night."

Johnny can't help it: His mind flutters to that which he has in his suitcase. His stash. His *fuck-it, last-gasp, I-can't-do-it-I-quit* OxyContin.

"I am no metaphor," the Boggart says, its voice low and inarguable. "No figment of your imagination to be overcome by bravery. I cannot be outwitted, yes. There are no loopholes."

It takes a longer sniff, as if savoring the air above Johnny's head, and then turns away, its hand-feet *pok-pok*-ing on the floor. Johnny watches. Is it finished? A cold sweat breaks out over his entire body at the thought of a reprieve. The Boggart clambers toward the eaves, its eyes on Johnny as it lowers into place once more and curls its limbs back around itself.

"So," Johnny says, his voice a little steadier. The whys and hows and what-the-fucks can wait. If nothing else, it seems he has breathing room. He can get out of here and regroup. But he needs to know: "We're done? And you can't eat me now?"

"We are concluded, yes," the Boggart says, sweeping one long arm toward the hatch. "The deal has begun. Exercise your time as you see fit."

"Where will you be?"

The creature strokes the boards beneath itself.

"Shall remain here, yes. Shall sleep. But shall always be closely listening, wherever you are, yes, as you go about trying to find a way to be free." It chuckles, shaking its head as if at the futility of such action.

"You're going to be up here all the time?"

"Yes."

"Will you come down?" Johnny asks, noticing that he is already accepting the situation.

"Perhaps not," the Boggart says. "But if the deal is broken, then yes."

Johnny waits for the Boggart to continue speaking, but it says nothing else, its eyes content. They are harder to see at this distance, settled now amidst the darker gloom. They stand only out when their shine briefly disappears and returns. A blink in the blackness.

Johnny watches them carefully as he descends the ladder.

PART TWO
Medium

It's tough to get out of bed to do roadwork at 5 a.m. when you've been sleeping in silk pajamas.

—*Marvin Hagler*

Chapter Six: Madison

Bad Bitches

MADISON TIES HER running shoes and straightens, wincing as pain jabs her lower back and thighs. It's just delayed-onset muscle soreness, she knows, but she's never had it this bad. She sighs, realizing she has to bite the bullet; she's been trying to go without pain meds, seeing them as cheating somehow. But the aching has rooted itself all over her body, and she needs to dull it a little.

She unzips her toiletry bag, sees the blister pack of ibuprofen. She pulls it free, and another, smaller blister pack is revealed behind it. She pulls it out as well, curious. Then she sees what it is. These aren't hers. They must have been left at her place by mistake, and she scooped them up in her usual chaotic packing style. She scowls as she tucks them back into her bag; she'll keep them, but only for an emergency.

They're OxyContin. She knows the damage it can do to people. She's seen it, up close and personal. She zips the toiletry bag closed and sits quietly for a moment, then stands to get some water to wash down the ibuprofen.

Someone knocks on her bedroom door.

"Yeah," Madison says.

The door opens. It's Jennifer. "*Oose.*" She grins, pumping a fist as she enters. "Let's fucking do this."

"Oose," Madison says back, Ellie's chi-focusing word, but she hears how flat it came out.

So does Jennifer. "Now, now," she begins, raising her eyebrows in mock rebuke.

"*Oose!*" Madison interrupts loudly, rolling her eyes as she gets off the bed. "Fucking *oose!*"

"Better!" Jennifer laughs.

"How long do I have?" Madison says. "About another twenty minutes?"

"Yep," Jennifer says.

"Cool. I'm gonna do a bit more here and then I'll see you downstairs."

Jennifer spies the thick plastic-ring-bound pile of paper in Madison's hand. "Jesus," she says. "You're studying or something?"

Madison misses her MacBook, wishes she could type her notes rather than writing them on paper. All her handwritten edits will just need to be entered into the computer later. But due to the digital-detox nature of the course, a laptop is off-limits; only the course-provided iPad is loaned out for the scheduled Zoom calls, and that is tightly locked down.

"No," Madison says. "It's, like, this novel I wrote." She tries not to wince as she says it. "I'm just reading through it and making notes." She doesn't know if she'll be able to keep spending time on it later in the course—the book is just a hobby, after all, and sleep will surely be at a premium in the coming weeks—so she wants to get after it while she still can.

"Get out," Jennifer says, pleased. "How cool!"

Madison shrugs, wanting to kill the question but be nice at the same time. "I guess it's my way of processing some stuff. Inspired by, you know. Real life."

"Yeah? So what's it about?"

Madison doesn't know how much else to add, how honest to be.

"Um," she fumbles. "This person who's gone away to better themselves. To find themselves... to toughen up?" Madison begins to redden, about to add *it's kind of personal* but hoping Jennifer will spot

Madison's awkwardness on her own and get the message... and then she sees Jennifer nodding and smiling warmly, beaming at Madison with open pride.

"*Say no more,*" she says. "I hear you. But if you ever change your mind and want a... test reader, I guess? Is that the right term?"

"Beta reader. Although you know Ellie would probably insist you be an *alpha* reader."

Jennifer laughs as she heads for the door. As Madison turns back to the bed, her eye catches the picture of Serena Williams on her nightstand.

She finds herself giving it a thumbs-up.

"The secret behind all of this," Ellie is saying, her voice comfortable, her breathing easy, "is to make your body understand one key, important thing."

Close behind Ellie, Jennifer runs with an easy gait, even if her gaze is locked firmly on the country lane ahead. Jennifer's hoodie and joggers have come off to reveal a training vest and leggings, and Madison can see the solid muscles in her broad back as they run. Madison is a little embarrassed by her own workout outfit. Not that her sweat-soaked tights and sports bra are inappropriate or low-budget—they are neither of those things—but she's chosen outfits so much more fashion forward than the others. Theirs are more functional, workout gear purchased solely for working out. Frankie is close behind Jennifer, breathing hard but keeping pace. Unlike Ellie, both are shiny with sweat.

Madison runs in the center of the pack. She's ahead of Sarah and, to her surprise, Namrah, who is bringing up the rear. Madison's suspicion that the tall, lean, and rangy woman would be one of the stronger remaining members of the group is proving, so far, to be wrong. Madison tries to push down the mild feeling of superiority. Namrah needs encouragement to improve.

"You got this, Namrah," she calls back.

"Don't worry about me, ha ha," Namrah replies, but the laugh sounds forced and bitter, as if she didn't like Madison's comment. Did she think Madison was trying to embarrass—

"Your body has to learn," Ellie is saying, "that it doesn't have a choice. That your mind is stronger than the body's will to concede. The body is then left with no other option but to trigger its own sympathetic nervous system to carry out your will, to cross you over into another state of being."

Madison wonders when that happens, because right now she is very close to just dropping. Fear of a Hard Correction keeps her moving, yes, and that of course is the idea, but it's more than that; Madison believes what Ellie is describing *will* happen, it's just a matter of pushing herself to that point. Madison believes in No Days Off, believes in *Ellie*.

She'll push herself. She can do it. She knows it.

"When that happens," Ellie continues, legs and arms pumping confidently, "you experience euphoria. But the land you must cross to get there—to where the body becomes accustomed to this process—is barren and unforgiving. A howling wasteland of suffering."

No fruity motivational-quote language from Ellie. She prefers dramatic, dark phrases. Madison thinks this is Ellie's way of conditioning her charges to a new paradigm of thought. This is the difference Madison came here for, but right now, that version of herself—the person who wanted this—seems very far away.

They already hit the weights that morning. Sarah and Namrah, the two remaining Light women after Cameron's departure, were allowed a small snack during the rest period before this run. Jennifer, Frankie, and Madison were not.

After the Sunset Ceremony, Ellie followed Cameron to her room to talk, but no one saw Cameron after that. Madison doesn't blame her for not wanting to say goodbye. The woman quit at the very first hurdle. Madison can understand; she wouldn't have been able to look the others in the face afterward either.

"Euphoria can't be reached by pushing hard," Ellie is calling from the front of the pack. "Euphoria can't be reached by doing your best. It can only be reached by pushing past the point of collapse."

Madison feels like she is approaching that point right now. After her confirmation of a place on the course, Madison did longer runs than this daily during her training for No Days Off, but never at this pace, and certainly never after a weight-lifting session. And there's the rest of the day still to go.

You're thinking about the negative, Madison thinks. *This is the opposite of what you're being told.* Embrace *this. Lean into it. It's the only way to reach the other side.*

"Nice steady breathing, Frankie," Ellie says. "Good."

Frankie visibly flushes with pleasure, and Madison immediately speeds up—

Her ankle suddenly buckles; she stumbles and knows she is going to fall.

No!

She staggers out of it, ankle throbbing, and finds her rhythm again, now sporting a slight limp. The others pass her, but she catches the back of the pack, falling into pace with Namrah.

"You okay?" Namrah asks quietly, her voice and shallow breath bouncing with her steps. She's looking straight ahead, chin high.

"Yeah," Madison says, but with the ankle now, she worries she can't keep the pace Ellie is setting, which was made clear would be cause for a Hard Correction. The thought spurs Madison on, drawing her alongside Namrah for now, the pain in her foot starting to fade as she runs it off. She *was* getting ready to drop. Fear gave her wings.

The system works, she thinks, and then Namrah speaks again.

"You got this," she says, and then accelerates a few steps to run ahead of Madison. Madison stares after her and then—blessed, blessed relief—Ellie holds up a hand.

"Walking pace," she says as they draw alongside the head of a trail through the field beside them. "Over that fence, and then we're walking the rest of the way back. Good job, everyone. Take on fluids."

Everyone pulls on the water they carry. No one, Madison notices, drank any before now. Why? She's thirsty. All but Ellie are sweaty as hell. They had to be thirsty too. *No one wanted to be the first to drink,* she thinks. To impress teacher? Or just not wanting to lose face?

She of course knows the answer. It's the same reason she didn't previously drink any either.

She catches Namrah's eye as the tall woman swallows her water and tips Madison an unsmiling wink. *Okay,* Madison thinks. *Okay, then.* But to her surprise, she's smiling.

Ellie clambers nimbly over the fence first, and the others follow, their breathing loud and grateful. A red-faced Sarah sees Madison coming and steps back.

"After you," she says breathily. "How you doing?"

"I can't lie," Madison says. "That was tough. After this morning, I mean," she adds quickly.

"I hoped this wouldn't be as bad as I feared." Sarah chuckles as Madison climbs over the fence. "But this is day one, and it's worse than I imagined. I mean hell's bells..." She chuckles again, but there's no humor in it. Sarah sounds truly worried.

"You'll get through it just fine," Madison says, wincing at the nasty thought that follows straight on its heels: *You should. You're on fucking Light.* She neutralizes it with kindness. She holds out a hand to help Sarah over the fence, but Sarah pauses, looking at Madison's palm. She glances to see if Ellie is looking.

Come on, Sarah, Madison thinks. *You can accept help, right? I don't think it's that* strict.

Then she wonders if that's correct.

Sarah jumps down and turns the offered hand into a low five.

Madison smiles, oddly grateful. "Come on," she says.

They follow Ellie and the others. The early afternoon weather is cool and Madison's mind is at ease as they walk through the green, low-cut field. She likes this group, even Namrah; everyone seems warm and friendly for the most part, and she thinks Namrah is maybe just super competitive. Everyone's conversations are unguarded and honest, the kind Madison finds easy to navigate. Even if she's suffering, it feels a hell of a lot better when everyone has one another's back. She smiles, breathing slowly. If only her arms and legs weren't so heavy.

She realizes what's left: Unless this is some kind of shortcut, it's a good six-mile pre-exhausted walk back to the house, and hunger is fast approaching.

Ellie said she was going to ease them all in today. And there is more to do this afternoon.

Madison chooses to walk at the back of the pack.

⤚

"How was *that*, Mads?" Jennifer mutters, joining Madison at the kitchen sink.

Madison holds a glass under the filter tap. Even after her post-run shower, her hands are shaking and her face is red. She lifts one hand to Jennifer, palm flat, to show its tiny spastic vibrations.

"Damn," Jennifer says.

"Yep."

"Hope you can still hold a pen," Jennifer says.

"Hope so." Then Madison remembers to ask: "Jen, what do you do for a living?"

"I'm a life coach," Jennifer says, and Madison doesn't know what to say. Jennifer laughs, drops the straight face. "No. I just work in a fucking bank."

Now Madison laughs.

From the other side of the room, Ellie says, "Come on, team, food stations for meal prep."

"Yes, chef!" Jennifer calls back.

Everyone—including Ellie—laughs. It's a good time now, and it feels very, very earned.

Dinner is herbed-chicken salad, and it's good, better than good, even if Madison, under Ellie's close instruction, cooked it herself. That alone is a revelation. Madison hasn't made herself a meal from scratch since she finally moved out of her mother's house, although she doesn't think her mother ever made her one either; Madison would have dearly loved it if they'd cooked together, but Mum was never interested in that kind of thing.

The portion size is small yet filling, but not filling enough; healthy yet tasty, but not tasty enough. It is, of course, made up of perfectly balanced percentages of proteins, carbs, and fats to suit her fifteen-pound weight-loss goal. The conversation is bright if notably less so than the excited buzz that flew among everyone the day before. Madison wonders if this is due to Cameron's departure, exhaustion from the workout and twelve-mile round trip, or the presence of Ellie in their midst. Probably a combination of all three.

"I know we haven't finished the day yet," Sarah says, eating her sweet potato, "but can I propose a toast?"

"Be my guest," Ellie says.

Sarah raises her orange juice, as does Namrah. The others raise their waters.

"To becoming Bad Bitches," Sarah says, winking at Madison, because over the last twenty-four hours, the phrase has somehow been identified as Madison's.

All but Ellie laugh; Ellie smiles warmly, though.

"Bad Bitches!" Jennifer calls.

"Jennifer," Namrah says, smiling, "you're clearly already a Bad Bitch."

But Jennifer is shaking her head. "Never bad *enough*," she says. "I still don't have my manager's job."

"That'll change," Ellie says confidently.

"This is better food than I thought we'd be eating," Namrah says.

"Yeah," Sarah agrees. She's back to her talkative self, having been very quiet since the run. She tried to hide it, but she clearly struggled with the session. "I thought we'd be eating the same food as Winter." More laughter. "She's such a pretty horse. Pleased to see me too."

That sounds odd to Madison's ears. And did Ellie just shoot Sarah a glance? Sarah looks down at her plate.

"Speaking of changes," Frankie says with her mouth full. "I've been meaning to ask: Ellie, when did you strike out on your own? After you left the Army, obviously, but did you go straight into the life-coach game or did you, I don't know, wait tables or something for a bit first?"

Everyone looks at Ellie.

"Well," Ellie says, "I have to correct you in that I didn't leave; I was actually medically discharged." She points at the thin white scar on her neck.

"How'd it happen?" Sarah asks, completely oblivious to the discomfort around the table at the question.

Madison gets it then: Sarah just says things without thinking.

Ellie — a pro — doesn't bat an eye. "Roadside IED."

"Oh," Sarah says, and *now* she gets it. "Sorry, Ellie, I didn't mean—"

"No, no, no. Totally fine to ask, but I *will* say this." Ellie dabs her mouth with her napkin. "No, I didn't do anything else after the Army. I had money in the bank to support me for a while, but more importantly, I had a mission." She gestures to her scar again, this time with her thumb. "*This* gave me a mission. Don't worry, Sarah. This is something I usually go into anyway during the first week, but you've brought it up organically, so really, you've done me a favor. Thank you."

Sarah smiles uncertainly, straightening a little.

"I'd taken a lot of shrapnel," Ellie continues, "and was bleeding heavily. The blast threw me, and I landed very badly. I had broken ribs, a broken tibia, two broken fingers on my left hand, one on my right. But I also had a choice: get myself to someone who could help me, or die. And what got me moving was a revelation." She sits back in her chair, holding her palms up. "*No one is coming to save you.* You make it happen yourself or it doesn't happen. You live or you die."

"'Get busy living or get busy dying,'" Namrah mutters. "*Shawshank Redemption*, right?"

"I haven't seen a lot of films," Ellie says with a shrug. "If 'Get busy living' means going through hell in order to live, then yes. I was lying by that road alone. The rest of my unit was dead, and I was in hostile territory." Her eyes are focused on the center of the table now, looking down and through it. "My radio had taken a direct shrapnel hit. I couldn't call for help. No one was coming to save me. I couldn't feel anything at first. That was the scariest thing. I felt like I was alive and dead at the same time. I don't know how long I was there. A couple of hours, they think. And what got me moving was the pain. It was *bad*. I knew then that I was alive, and that I maybe *could* continue to live, but I couldn't think what to do." Ellie rests her elbows on the table.

Madison notices Jennifer looking concerned. All of a sudden, something is wrong here.

"When I tried to move, my bones..." Ellie shakes her head. "I wanted to live. I had to accept that I was going to *suffer*. I had to crawl."

She falls silent again and stays that way for a long time.

"Ellie?" Frankie asks nervously.

Ellie blinks, looks as if she's remembered where she is, and gives her head a little shake. "Phew," she says. "Sorry. Sometimes..."

The support is automatic and unanimous: "No, don't be silly." "Thank you for sharing."

But Madison feels how unsettled everyone is.

"My long-winded point is this," Ellie says. "The complete focus on that suffering, that *bone-deep* pain, gave me an inner strength that even I, an experienced veteran, didn't know I had. And once I was patched up, I knew I had to help people understand what they are capable of." She sits back and pokes the table a few times with her finger. "This course is extreme — crazy, even — but the results speak for themselves, even if we don't go as far as breaking bones, obviously. I'm proud of everyone who even makes the decision to attend, let alone the people who complete it."

"What does the HQB stand for?" Madison asks, changing the subject and pointing at the large framed poster on the kitchen wall. It displays the three big, simple capital letters on a white background. Madison assumes it's an acronym for one of Ellie's mottos, but the way Ellie's face darkens makes it clear that the question was a faux pas far worse than Sarah's.

"That's a reminder," Ellie says. "For me."

"Oh," Madison says, reddening a little herself. "Sure."

But Ellie's not done. "Those are initials. Hannah Quimby-Beck."

"A student?" Madison asks. "A graduate?"

"Not a graduate," Ellie says with a sudden smile so forced that Madison wants the ground beneath her to not only swallow her but spit her back out into space. "But she *was* a client back when I was first starting No Days Off."

"Oh, that's cool," Namrah says. "Was she your first success story?"

Ellie's forced smile fades. "No. Quite the opposite, in fact."

Now it's Namrah's turn to look chastened.

"The course," Ellie says, "in its current in-call residential form, with a group, didn't even exist then. In the early days, I did out-call residential—me staying with them—before I realized that wasn't the way to do it." She sips her water. No one speaks. "It was too personal, being in my clients' lives—their homes—that way." *Too personal*, Madison thinks. *I can't imagine Ellie being too personal with anyone. Personal, even.* "Their successes were incredible, but the few failures, Hannah included...just, no."

Madison doesn't dare look at Jennifer now. She wants to see her friend's expression, but she doesn't want to risk Ellie seeing them exchange a glance. In her peripheral vision, she can tell that Jennifer is staring at Ellie. Something doesn't feel right about this confession; Ellie suddenly doesn't seem present, as if talking about this has taken her away. Does Jennifer feel it too?

"After Hannah," Ellie says, "and before I made this a residential course, I made sure to use the questionnaires for psychological evaluations. I keep her initials on the wall to remind myself daily of the responsibility I have here. You see, *quitting*..." She emphasizes the word, softly chopping her hand on the table. "When the workouts make you feel like you're dying or the Hard Corrections seem too much, remember what quitting *means*. The statement you're putting into the universe. Believe me—*believe* me—the pain of quitting is far worse, and it's forever."

She suddenly seems to notice her salad and picks up her fork, scooping up a mouthful of leaves and meat. More than a mouthful, more than a normal bite. Everyone waits.

"Hannah knew," Ellie says eventually, "that working with me was probably her last chance. Then she had to accept—to live with—the fact that she *failed* in that last chance." She sniffs briskly. "Turns out she couldn't live with it."

She stands, pushing her chair back. "I need to prepare for this afternoon's training. Don't forget, feedback sessions tonight are with Sarah and Namrah. The rest of you can make home calls. I'll arrange your time slots for those." She looks at her watch. "Back here in an hour, everyone." She leaves the table without another word, striding across the common area.

Madison realizes she doesn't know where Ellie's room is.

"God," Sarah says quietly. "She's seen some shit."

"Did you think anyone who runs a course like this would be normal?" Frankie scoffs. "We came here to get a dose of crazy, or at least I did. I wasn't getting a life overhaul from going to spin class five days a week."

There are murmurs and nods of agreement, but Madison is watching Jennifer, who is staring off after Ellie. Jennifer looks thoughtful, serious, and Madison doesn't blame her. Even for Ellie, that felt off. The woman is the epitome of professionalism, but that was a glimpse of something else.

Or was it? The wheels start to turn in Madison's brain, remembering what Kelly said.

Mind games.

The others move on to other topics of conversation: how they feel after the work so far, how sore they're going to be tomorrow, how they can't believe there's even more to do that evening. Madison can't stop thinking about what just happened, her mind throwing up all kinds of theories, and watching Jennifer, who still isn't saying a word. Was Jennifer unsettled by that too?

Madison thinks they might need to talk.

She doesn't have to wait long. Madison is unlocking her bedroom door — she's going to put in a good forty-five minutes of editing her book — when she hears Jennifer approaching.

"Got a sec?" Madison asks.

"For you I have several, Madison Avenue," Jennifer says.

Madison beckons Jennifer into her bedroom and checks the hallway before closing the door.

"Who's after you?" Jennifer says, chuckling.

"What the fuck did you make of Ellie's little display there?"

"I think everyone felt awkward," Jennifer says. "It was...strange, wasn't it? Did it look to you like she spaced out there for a sec?"

"Uh-huh," Madison says. "And I'm totally not buying it."

"What?"

"She's very good—I'll give her that. Smart."

Jennifer furrows her brow. "You think she faked that?"

Madison hesitates. She really does believe in Ellie and her methods. Even if she thinks Ellie's actions at dinner were calculated, they have to be for the best. So it's okay to say:

"I do."

"Okay. Why would she?"

"Think about it," Madison says, stepping closer. "It's, like, for our benefit. Ultimately, we aren't in any real trouble here, right? With the punishments, I mean. We can walk away at any time, friends and family know where we are, we talk to them all the time, yada yada yada. Ellie's a real person, we're real people, and we all have to obey the laws of the land. Whatever punishment we get, it's never going to be that bad because there are witnesses here, and Ellie can't step over the line. Yes or no?"

"I guess so," Jennifer says, folding her arms and leaning against the bedroom door.

"Ellie knows we know that," Madison says. "So what better way to erase that sense of security, that knowledge that the punishments are restricted, by making us think that maybe—just maybe—she might snap in the middle of one?" She shrugs. "What's going to get us thinking that maybe it's a good idea to do that last push-up after all?"

Jennifer nods slowly, mulling it over. "Possibly. It's clever if it's fake. I don't know. Surely not?"

Madison holds up her hands. "Massive initials that just happen to be placed right over the dining table? Of course someone's going to ask about them. If that Hannah story was made up... I don't know. I think that's maybe a dirty tactic." *But Ellie knows what she's doing,* Madison thinks, *and she gets results, so what's actually the problem here?*

"Maybe the ends justify the means, if you're right," Jennifer says. "I mean, isn't that kind of the whole idea of this place? Besides, if you *are* right, then Ellie's tactics are still designed to make me benefit, and you just blew the effect by telling me your suspicions." Jennifer wags a finger, grinning. "Nice work, Madison Marple. Although now I'm showing my age. You're too young to know who the hell Miss Marple is." Madison puts on a smile and doesn't say that the only reason she read all the books is because her mother did. It's not a nice memory.

"Come on, I knew you were thinking the same thing," Madison says. "Back me up here and let me know I'm not, like, crazy. I saw your face at the table. I wanted to compare notes."

"I'll be honest," Jennifer says. "I actually came into the program expecting this sort of thing to happen. Mind games, you know?"

"Me too, and I guess I don't *really* mind. I just..." A thought strikes her. "Hold on. I'm too young? You're not much older than me, are you?"

"Thirty-five," Jennifer says. "My joints are aging before the face."

"Boo-hoo," Madison says, rolling her eyes. "You poor fresh-faced geriatric, however do you cope with such a burden?"

Jennifer laughs and gives a sarcastic curtsy.

"Thanks," she says, before adding—in what might be the worst attempt at a British accent Madison has ever heard—"It's because oi exfoliates me fayce with me chim-in-nee sweep brush, Mary Pop—"

A knock at the door makes them both jump. They exchange a glance.

"Mads," Sarah calls.

Madison and Jennifer let out a breath, relieved. Madison opens the door, and Sarah gives a jazz-hands wave.

"*Hel-looo,*" she trills. "Do you have any Deep Heat or something? I feel like I could do with..." She looks from Madison to Jennifer and smirks. "You two look guilty as hell. Oh shit, did you steal extra food at dinner?"

"We were just comparing notes on the structure so far, what we thought was the hardest session," Madison says. She deliberately doesn't catch Jennifer's eye. Madison has just impressed herself with the lie's combination of speed and sincerity. "Hey, Sarah, I'm glad you're here. Can I ask you something about the meal just now?"

Sarah reddens. "Sure," she says, but now she seems nervous.

"I just noticed something at dinner."

"Noticed something?"

Sarah isn't a good actor.

"What you said about Winter being pleased to see you," Madison says, trying to sound as nonthreatening as possible.

"Yeah, she...yeah." Sarah nods and fidgets. "She's such a nice animal."

"It sounded you'd you already met her at some point," Madison says.

Now Jennifer's gaze turns to Sarah.

"Yeah, yeah, I think, uh, yeah, she was familiar..." Sarah manages to turn an even darker shade of crimson. She isn't making sense and she knows it.

"Sarah, have you, like...done the course before?" Madison asks.

Sarah's mouth freezes open. She looks down, shifting uncomfortably on the spot.

Jennifer finally catches Madison's eye and raises her eyebrows. Madison cocks her head as if to say, *Yeah, dammit.*

"Guys, what I said at dinner...," Sarah mumbles. "Look, it was hard to get here, you know."

"We know. Hey, it's okay," Madison says.

Sarah's head comes up. Her eyes are shiny. "I can't blow this," she says. "I don't think I want to talk about this."

"I know," Madison says, and just like that, another lie comes. It makes her feel sick—lies always do—but part of her knows all too well she was once very good at it. "But being honest? Without going into my reasons, I'm thinking about quitting. I'm weighing my options."

Behind Sarah, Jennifer straightens.

Madison ignores her. "If this course isn't what I thought it was," she says, "then—"

"It is," Sarah says quickly. "Ellie is the real deal."

"But it seems like something's wrong."

"It's not like that." Sarah sighs heavily, sounding torn, then moves to the bedroom door and quietly closes it. "Look. *Look*. Please keep this secret. Okay?" Sarah's breathing speeds up a little as she steps closer to Madison. "It was a condition of my being allowed back in."

Back in. She *has* done this before.

Sarah's eyes dart back and forth between Jennifer and Madison. "Please don't tell Ellie?"

"Don't worry," Jennifer says, putting a hand on Sarah's shoulder before adding in a very sincere tone of voice: "We won't tellie."

Sarah looks confused but then bursts out laughing. Madison and Jennifer join in, but Madison isn't done with the questions.

"Did you quit?"

The smile vanishes from Sarah's face as quickly as it arrived. "No, God no. I got appendicitis. The pain got so bad so fast that I couldn't hide it. Ellie took me to the hospital, they confirmed it, and that was that."

"You tried to tough out *appendicitis pain*?" Jennifer asks, sounding amazed. Madison is too. The course apparently supercharges the mind even more than she thought.

"Only at first, and I didn't know what it was," Sarah says, reddening. "Until it got really bad. You have to realize, Ellie had just offered to move me up to Elite, and the thought of having to go home was too much."

"Offered to move up to what?" Madison asks. "Elite? You mean Heavy?"

"No," Sarah says, reddening another shade. "It's another level beyond Heavy. I was already *at* Heavy. I was doing so damn well. I was a week away from completing. Ellie offered me the option, and I was feeling so damn strong—seriously, this really is a great course, guys. I'm so glad to be back. Before I got sick, I wanted to push myself to the highest level. You won't be surprised to hear that you can't go back a level if the next one is too much." She looks nervous. "Don't ask me what happens at Elite because I don't know. Even if I knew and *did* tell you, there wouldn't be much point. Ellie probably told you herself: The course is always changing. Whatever Elite was back then might not even be the same now. But I can guarantee you that whatever she does do — if she even still offers it; she said she doesn't always — it'll be a head fuck."

Mind games, Madison thinks.

"This time," Sarah says, "I'm finishing this goddamn course. Imagine getting three weeks in and going through all that for nothing. This time, I'm sticking with it and *finishing this course*." But there's worry in Sarah's face. She doesn't believe it.

"What if you don't get up to the maximum level again?" Madison asks.

Sarah's eyes flash.

"Please just don't say anything." Her tone is pleading. "I've been as honest as I can be—"

"Of course we won't say anything!" Madison says quickly, regretting the question. "Sorry we rumbled you. We won't say a word."

Sarah looks uncertain but eventually nods. "Okay. Thanks. I'm going to go lie down. Did you say you do or don't have any Deep Heat?"

"Oh yeah." Madison roots around in her suitcase, feeling bad about the way Sarah's happy disposition vanished, but also feeling vindicated. She wasn't imagining things. She had to lie to *expose* a lie, so is that bad?

Yes. The thought is solid. *Always. You know that.* "Here you go." She hands the canister to Sarah.

"Thanks, guys." Sarah smiles before opening the bedroom door.

"See you later," Madison says.

The door closes, and Jennifer waits a full fifteen seconds before she moves close to Madison. "Well, *well*." She speaks in a conspiratorial and eager whisper. "And what was with your little bullshit act there?"

"Do you blame me?" Madison whispers back. "I *knew* something was up, figured I'd keep my cards close to my chest. A fucking secret returnee!"

"Yeah," Jennifer murmurs, shaking her head. "Jesus. I gotta say, if Ellie lied about that..." She shrugs. "Suddenly your Ellie theory sounds a lot more plausible."

"Especially if what Sarah just said is more bullshit," Madison adds.

"The suspicion deepens," Jennifer says. "Go on."

"Maybe Ellie told her to say that. Maybe Sarah's a plant."

"Plants? Come on."

"Who knows?" Madison says. "It's an expensive course. Ellie could comfortably have the money to be paying Sarah to go through this torture." Madison doesn't think she means what she's saying, but she's enjoying the game. In a strange kind of way it's only increasing her respect for Ellie. Who else would even think of implementing this kind of stuff?

"No crazier," Jennifer says with a wink, "than the fucking dickheads who actually *pay to come here* for the torture."

Madison laughs as Jennifer opens the bedroom door.

"Food for thought, Mads. Substantial food for thought. But all told, even if you're right, I'm still digging it so far." Madison's still digging it too. "See you in a bit."

Jennifer leaves. The door closes. Madison's gaze falls on her picture of Serena, who smiles back, committed, strong, confident. She's holding the Venus Rosewater women's trophy, delighted by her seventh Wimbledon victory.

Keep those eyes on the prize, girl, Madison tells herself.

That evening, Madison has her first Zoom call with her designated contact. She chose Imani not only because Imani is her best friend but also because Imani demanded it be so. "There is no way you are going to your salad-and-running cult and not making me your check-in."

The blue-patterned wallpaper of Imani's living room serves as her backdrop. It's a space Madison has seen countless times, but already the sight seems slightly alien, like a window into the regular world. Madison finishes telling a sleepy-eyed Imani — it's midnight in the UK — about the Sunset Ceremony. She asks if Imani would ever want to do the course. "Fuck no, darling" is her polite answer, and so Madison goes into some of the specifics. After all, Ellie said that students weren't allowed to talk about the details of the course to people who are considering doing it. Imani absolutely isn't going to apply for No Days Off, and so by Madison's thinking it's therefore okay to discuss it with Imani a little. Plus, the Sunset Ceremony isn't the actual *course*.

Imani says slowly, "You. Are. Fucking. Kidding. Me."

"I thought you'd say something like that," Madison says. "I'd say the same. But positive things are already happening."

Imani was skeptical about the course during the months leading up to Madison's departure, but constant reminders about the difference they both saw in Kelly brought Imani around.

"I knew the Corrections would be tough," Madison says. "But after that taste, I can tell you this: I am *not* going to quit *anything*. The system works."

"Wow. Just wow," Imani says, shaking her head and then throwing up her hands, a gesture Madison has seen many times in the buildup to No Days Off. *I'm just saying, I'm just saying.* "Well, don't forget you can leave anytime. No matter what Army Fitness Woman has to say."

"I know." She nearly tells Imani about Ellie's strange behavior at dinner, or about Sarah confessing she's a secret repeat attendee, but she decides not to. One of Ellie's strictest rules is that they never discuss other students on their Zoom calls to anyone, regardless of whether they think the person will later attend NDO or not—"the journey belongs to each student," Ellie said, "and is not yours to discuss"—so Sarah's business is Sarah's business. She also doesn't want to give Imani anything to grill her about. Plus, she's making this call with the course-sanctioned iPad. She doesn't know if Ellie can listen in or record any of this. It's unlikely, but it's not outside the realm of possibility.

The idea gives her pause. Would such surveillance be okay? Coming in, she expected that kind of thing. Presented with the concept now that she's here, she finds herself picturing Ellie in the next room, hunched over a listening device with headphones clamped on her head. *It's for your own good,* Ellie might say. But Ellie knows best, right? Isn't that what she came here for?

"But you feel good," Imani says tersely. "You like it. That's great."

Madison notices the look of slight concern on Imani's face and realizes her mind has wandered.

"Yes. It's been tough, and it's going to get a lot tougher, but I think I'm up to this."

"Mm," Imani murmurs.

Madison bristles. *You think I'm not as resilient as you. You always have. You might even have been right to think it too, but you've still always thought it.* "Hey, come on," she says. "I need you to support me, Imani. I'm here, and I'm doing this, and it's hard enough without you being all, like—"

"I just worry..."

"I *know*," Madison says, falling back on the bed and holding the iPad above her. From this angle she can see through her bedroom window as well. The sky outside is now almost fully black. "But you have to understand: I'm tired of trying to tell myself I'm enough while simultaneously knowing what I'm supposedly capable of—and what everyone else seems capable of—but not even coming close to it, all while having to show myself compassion—"

"Hey, now—"

"And I don't *want* to show myself compassion!" Madison snaps. "I'm tired of fucking babying myself. Of practicing self-care and keeping a journal and telling myself it's okay when I screw up for the millionth time in the exact same way. I'm always giving myself participation trophies, and *none of it's working.*"

Imani folds her arms. Her face is blank.

"I need a kick up the arse," Madison says, "and a major one. I need *this.*"

"I understand," Imani says, "but there's a difference between limiting beliefs and actual limits."

"There are no limits!" Madison cries. She hears Ellie in her voice.

"Yes, there fucking are," Imani says, rolling her eyes. "We can only survive three weeks without food, three days without water, three minutes without oxygen."

"Well, *duh*."

"You ever hear of the Milgram experiment?"

Madison hasn't, and in her moment of surprise at this response, she realizes how she's been talking to her friend. "No," she says quietly. "Look, I'm sorry for getting heated up. I know you're just worried."

"It's okay," Imani says kindly. "But listen. The Milgram experiment was this psychology experiment they did in the sixties, to see how much regular people obeyed orders from an authority figure, even when those orders were clearly harmful to others, right?"

"This isn't like that."

"So they took these participants," Imani continues, "and gave them a button that would deliver an electric shock to another person whenever the other person answered a question wrong. Thing is, the people answering questions were plants; they didn't actually get shocked, but they *pretended* to be in pain whenever the participant pressed the shock button, fake screaming and all that."

Madison is silent now. It's the second time today the word *plant* has come up.

"Turns out," Imani says, "many of the participants were willing to turn the fake 'power dial' up when told to do so, thinking they were giving increasingly intense zaps, even as the plant actor screamed louder and louder as the 'shocks' went up. The participants kept on shocking simply because they were told to do so by an authority figure. And they'd even been told beforehand that if they were to turn the dial all the way up, it would kill the subject. Guess what? When someone in a lab coat told them to give the maximum shock, *they did it*."

"What's your point?"

Imani thinks for a second. "Maybe that people can't be trusted to think properly in the face of authority."

"Oh. Nice — no offense taken this end..."

Imani grins and shrugs. "I don't mean you. Just... just keep your head on a swivel is all I'm saying, okay? I'm too tired to think about this shit."

"*You're* tired?"

"It's all relative, darling," Imani says.

Madison chuckles despite herself. "Regardless, the system is working for me. If there are shenanigans going on, I don't care. It's all to help *me*."

"The Milgram experiment was widely criticized for ethical issues, Mads."

"I don't give a shit, *Ims*."

Now Imani laughs.

"Just be careful. Please?"

"I will. I'll let you pass out. I know it's really late there."

"I love you, sweetheart. Be a Bad Bitch!"

"I love you too, and that's more like it. Good night."

"Good night."

Madison hangs up and locks the tablet's screen, staring at her reflection in its black mirror for a moment. *What will you be when all this is over?* It occurs to her that, in the grand scheme of things, this particular question is perhaps the biggest mystery of everyone's life.

No matter what, I won't be as much of a fuckup as I am now, that's for sure.

She stands, holding the iPad. She needs to return it to Ellie before bed.

Or, she thinks, heading for the door, *I'll at least be a lot faster.*

Chapter Seven: Johnny

Basking Shark. Tiger Shark. Reef Shark.

JOHNNY BOLTS OUT the front door the second his feet leave the attic ladder's steps; he hurtles down the hedge alley and back onto the dark road so fast it feels as if he's flown. He stands for a moment, shaking, seeing the reassuring lights in the windows of other houses — nearby, there are people, there is *life* — and then his legs buckle, and he has to sit on the curb. He rocks on the pavement and breathes. Tries pointlessly not to fall into the whys and hows.

He mentally retraces his steps. Where did he go before he went to the house? Before he met David and Sandy? *Sandy.* She left him her number in case he needed any help with things around the house.

He pulls out his phone and calls her.

"The number you have dialed is not recognized—"

"Fuck!" Johnny barks. He's saved it incorrectly in his phone. *Ivan* would have it, though; he was their bloody landlord, and hell, he needs to talk to Ivan about all this anyway, but of course he tries Bailey first. He gets her voicemail and manages to avoid yelling in frustration. He calls Ivan and gets a second voicemail; now he will bellow his frustration, but then he hears someone talking quietly.

He looks up. Across the street, a few houses to the right, Johnny sees a man in what looks like his fifties standing in his front garden.

His legs are obscured by the low brick wall. He wears a polo shirt, and Johnny vaguely recognizes him. They may have waved politely to each other earlier that day when Johnny first arrived. The man's pale arms are now by his sides, and he is staring at nothing in particular, talking steadily to no one, his thin hair slightly disheveled. He isn't wearing any earbuds that Johnny can see; it can't be a phone call.

Johnny crosses the street. He just desperately needs to talk to another human being face-to-face right now, to know he isn't crazy. As he draws closer, he hears the words the man is muttering.

"Poland. Paris. Quebec," the neighbor says. "Rome. Romania, Russia." He falls silent. When he resumes speaking, it's in a lower tone of voice: *"Grass. Greenhouse."*

Johnny moves closer, wondering if this man's verbal confusion might be the result of a stroke. Why is he outside this late anyway? Johnny tries to speak and finds he still has no voice. He coughs it into life.

"Hey," he croaks, and the stranger turns toward Johnny, eyes widening. The older man makes shooing gestures, waving Johnny away, yet he doesn't look angry. "No," he says, eyes still wide, but his voice is calm. "Not..." He frowns. His head twitches. "No," he says finally, before adding: "Fucking...leave me *alone*, will you? Prick."

Despite everything that's just happened, Johnny is shocked by the sudden aggression, but then the penny drops. This man clearly isn't in full control of his faculties.

"Uh...sure," Johnny says, backing away, his mind already leaping again to the horror that currently engulfs him. As he turns, his gaze falls upon the front window of the man's house, and he sees something odd.

The living room is completely empty of furniture.

Johnny can see this because the house doesn't have curtains, giving him a clear view through to the patio doors at the back. Before Johnny can say anything, the man cocks his head like a dog considering an unfamiliar sound. "Basking shark," he says. "Tiger shark. Reef shark."

The man continues to babble as Johnny takes a few steps sideways, trying to see through the other front window.

Also curtain-less, also empty.

An unpleasant feeling starts to pulse in Johnny's stomach. He walks the few feet to the front of the next house. Its lights are off, but it has no curtains either. Johnny hesitates and then walks to the next house's front gate. He opens it and heads up the path to the front window. There's a streetlight, so there's just enough illumination to see beyond the glass. Johnny doesn't need to lean closer to see that the room is also empty. He checks the kitchen window.

There is no sign inside that anyone lives there or ever has.

"Oh...," Johnny begins. He doesn't even know what to say to himself. "No."

The man's voice floats over to Johnny's ears. "Great white shark. Hammerhead shark."

"*Stay cool*," Johnny says aloud to himself. It's late now. Ivan and Bailey might be asleep. Ivan said they might stay at Johnny's old place tonight if they were late in finishing packing his things. Johnny types them a message in their WhatsApp group chat with a shaking finger:

EITHER OF YOU: PLEASE CALL ME AS SOON AS YOU GET THIS. URGENT.

He hesitates and then sends a second message, this one direct to Bailey:

BABY, PLEASE CALL ME. SOME INSANE STUFF HAS HAPPENED. I'M FREAKING OUT.

He hits SEND, puts his phone back in his pocket, and lifts his chin as he tries to slow his shaky breathing, thinking he is going to vomit. His mind automatically goes to one of his regular automatic-and-unwanted rituals—*1-2-3*—and then it becomes a loop: *1-2-3, 1-2-3, 1-2-3...*

He sees the air around him *shimmer*.

He blinks a few times, assuming it's something in his eyes like a floater, but it doesn't go away. He takes a few steps and finds that the haze stays with him as he moves, the light refracting through it and glistening as whatever it is rises.

Johnny moans softly, watching as the haze continues to move into the sky, rising from his body in an unending stream of impossibility. He stares at it, trying to understand, and then his sight of it glitches, cutting in and out a few times. Then it's gone completely, the air above him clear once more. He tries to concentrate to bring it back, but it doesn't work now. He looks without *trying* to look, and that works, but as it pops back into view, he has a moment of intense delirium. His vision splits—not into a twinned perception of the world around him but into a literal half-and-half double sight. One part of his brain sees the haze and the road in front of him, but the other half *looks down from above,* as if Johnny himself were inside the rising haze, his mind disembodied and watching his own face as it stares up at... well, himself.

Glitch. It's gone again, and the jerking out of sight is unpleasant, like his mind's eye just had sand blown into it, a sudden and sharp shift in perspective. *Glitch* is right, Johnny thinks, feeling as if something just went wrong in his brain, with his sight yanked out of frequency like someone slapped the top of an old rabbit-ears TV.

Jesus H. Christ, Johnny thinks, *you think coming back to reality is something* glitching*? Something going wrong? Seeing monsters is one thing, but if you can't even see straight, then you're done—*

He hears approaching footsteps.

He looks up, expecting to see the Boggart bearing down on him, and staggers back as he frantically fumbles for his keys in his pocket, the only weapon he has. Yes, there is a large shadow approaching from up the darkened street... but it's only an older man. He wears a wide-brimmed hat and a black three-piece suit under a thick overcoat. The clothing is out of place in this downscale neighborhood. Perhaps he's returning from a wedding reception at this late hour or some other special, formal occasion. He walks with an unusual, high-stepping gait.

"Are you all right?" the old man asks, sounding concerned.

His face reminds Johnny of an aged cowboy, someone who has

spent a lifetime in the wind and grit. Willie Nelson maybe, that old country singer Ivan likes, but it's the man's *gaze* that really gets Johnny's attention. His eyes are searching Johnny's face. But then the old man breaks into a nervous smile, an expression Johnny has seen many times—the amazement people feel when they see a celebrity in the flesh.

"Well," the old man says, shaking his head with cautious delight. "I heard you were here, but I didn't believe it. I have to say you were the last person I expected to run into."

Johnny forces a smile. He normally makes a point of being nice to people who spot him, but now is inconvenient, to put it mildly. He looks around again for the haze; it's gone, but his headache is persisting.

"Sorry, I'm having a bit of a..." He tries to think of an excuse. "A migraine. Cluster headache. Sometimes they get overwhelming."

"Oh, that's no fun," the old man says. "You don't have anyone with you? An entourage?" He grins. Again, Johnny is used to this kind of comment when he's recognized in small British towns: *I'd expect you to be in Hollywood. I'd expect you to be on a beach somewhere surrounded by blondes.* "I would expect you to—sorry, I haven't even told you my name." The old man—who is on the shorter side, maybe five foot five—moves closer, hand outstretched. "I'm Mister Kaleb," he says quietly.

"Johnny." He shakes the old man's hand. *Mister Kaleb.* The surname sounds Eastern European; he knows through Ivan that there is an extensive Bosnian community around Waterton. Johnny nearly asks how Kaleb heard he was around but remembers that this certainly isn't the first time the gossip train has unexpectedly brought people to see him. It only really happens here in Coventry, the city where his fan base began, but it happens.

"Technically, I live on the next street over," Kaleb says, trying to sound jovial but coming across as nervous, which is again common in Johnny's experience. "More accurately I have a place here, but I don't really *live* here. I'm just passing through as always, but I had to come and, uh..."

Kaleb is fumbling for the words, but talk of the streets around them makes Johnny blurt out: "These houses here are empty."

"Yes, it's sad, isn't it?" Kaleb says. "Especially when so many people in the world are without shelter. There are always people coming and going, though. It's quite transient. You'll have neighbors soon, I'm sure."

A memory suddenly tap dances across the front of Johnny's brain, a phrase—unwanted, unbidden, and inappropriate—leaping from Johnny's mental archive the way it often does when he meets a man notably shorter than him:

WHAT'S WRONG WITH THAT LITTLE MAN?

It is without malice or arrogance—quite the opposite, in fact; there is no relish here—but in Johnny's current state, the thought is so clear and awful that he winces. It's been a while since the deep unpleasantness of that memory made its way to the surface.

"I'm only thinking about moving in," Johnny lies. "Haven't decided yet."

Mister Kaleb hesitates, then nods sagely. "Very wise. You don't know me. I understand. Better to not give the details of your living situation to a stranger. But you don't have to worry about me either. I'm old, and you're young. Strong. Brave."

Brave? That's odd, but the word *odd* has taken on a new meaning for Johnny recently—so much so that he decides he doesn't have time to piss about.

"Look, I'll be honest with you, Mister Kaleb," Johnny says, pinching the bridge of his nose. "I've had a really weird and...bad day." *Ask him,* Johnny thinks. *You don't have the luxury of subtlety.* "Have you ever seen anything odd on this street?"

"What do you mean?" Kaleb says. His ignorance sounds utterly unconvincing.

"I think you might know, Mister Kaleb," Johnny says, lowering his voice. "You seem nervous, truth be told. Kind of like you might have a reason to be, and if I can be frank with you, I'm not really in a situation where I can afford to talk around things. Have you" — *say it* — "heard of a Boggart?"

Kaleb's face becomes instantly pale.

"I never get involved with anything like that," he whispers.

Johnny pauses. He expected denial or pleas of ignorance but not *that*.

"I...I just wanted to...say hello to you," Kaleb says, beginning to back up. The man is shaking. "I was allowed that, even this late in the day. Special dispensation. Everything's negotiable, to a point..." His trembling hand slaps at his coat pocket. "And this, I...I wanted to give you this, *this*..."

Kaleb fishes something from his pocket and holds it out to Johnny, his hand now shaking so badly that he drops the object, but Johnny catches it. It's thin, small, and rectangular. It's a tiepin.

"Wait," Johnny says. "You know about the Boggart?"

"Don't lose that," Kaleb says quickly, still backing up. His face looks like that of a corpse as he begins to look around himself. "It's... it's...it's been a long time since I was given it — doesn't work for me anymore. If you're going to stay around here, *keep it on you at all times*."

Johnny looks at the tiepin. Its surface is rough, clearly having been dropped or scraped more than a few times. It looks cheap and machine-made; a lot of the "silver" plating has rubbed off. There is a small hole in the middle where a tiny inset stone, presumably a fake one, has long since fallen out. There is a clip on the back, and the whole thing is dirty. It looks like something Kaleb found in a gutter.

"What do I...?" No. That can wait. More important is this: "What do you know about the Boggart?" Kaleb rubs at the back of his neck, looking torn.

"What did it say to you about the Shallows?" Kaleb asks.

"You know about those too?" Johnny asks. "What are they?"

"Did the *Boggart* tell you about the Shallows?"

"David and Sandy did," Johnny says. "They lived here until today. Did you know them?"

Kaleb stares at Johnny for a few moments. Then he shakes his head, removing his hat and pulling at his hair. "My ride," he mutters. "It...it's going to be here in a moment. I need to...think—"

"Think about what?" Johnny snaps, then holds up his hands. "I'm sorry, I'm just...Look, the fucking thing said it was going to eat me if I screw up. Do you understand?" He hears the desperation in his voice. "And shit, despite that threat, *there is a very good chance I will screw up because I have to...*" How can he explain it? How can he explain that, at its worst, his addiction makes him want to die rather than *not* take painkillers? That even the threat of death might not be enough? How does he make an old man understand that? "There were two cops here. It sent them away, but—"

"Were they affected?"

"Affected?"

"Like sleepwalkers. Dreamy, out of it."

"Yeah."

"Then it allowed them to see it fully," Kaleb hisses, his face dark. "If you remember talking to it, then it only allowed *you* to see its glamour. The Boggart have been around as long as humans. Part of us remembers what they are, deep down. We know how they work, even if we don't remember them consciously. We know there is only ever one of them in a territory. That's the rule, and the Boggart—no matter how they are manifested, no matter which characteristics they take on—exist at their core *because* of rules." A scowl flickers across his face, quickly replaced by a look of fear. "To truly see a Boggart the way those police did is to know that it is not here for you. The state of overwhelming bliss that realization induces..." Kaleb isn't even looking at Johnny now, his eyes darting to the shadows as he babbles, almost talking to himself.

"Can I kill it?" The question is out before Johnny even knew he was going to ask it.

"No."

Johnny's stomach turns over.

"I'm...I'm just a fan," Kaleb babbles. "This was unexpected, and I wasn't prepared. I just wanted to make sure you had the tiepin. I need to think. I need to *think*."

"About *what?*"

"Johnny...," Kaleb says. "*Johnny.* In a second my...my driver. My *driver.* He's going to come and collect me—"

"It said I was in a deal with it," Johnny says, stepping closer to Kaleb. "How long does that go on for?"

"Forever."

"*What?*"

"I don't make these rules!" Kaleb snaps.

"Who does? Who's in charge?"

"Who makes the rules of physics?" Kaleb says. He is red in the face now. "Who makes it so that an apple falls to the ground when it separates from a branch? Why do you think things would work differently for the Boggart? Why would they know more than we do about how atoms work? Listen, that *deep-down* part of you I mentioned? It knew you were summoning a monster, and if you weren't determined when you wrote down whatever you wrote down, then the whole thing wouldn't have worked. You didn't do it to get a Boggart to frighten you and then depart! The Boggart are often the last resort for those who can't help themselves, whose minds are naturally *attuned* enough to instinctively ask!"

The last resort, Johnny thinks. Johnny made it through the worst of it—his addiction, he thinks, was less severe than others', allowing him to avoid chemical interventions—but some days it was so bad that he couldn't get off the sofa.

"Those people who are ready to face death rather than fail themselves again. The worst kind of failure, Johnny! To knowingly fail when success was truly possible!" His face darkens. "Trust me. I know."

"I'm telling you I didn't ask for *any* of this!" Johnny yells, causing Kaleb to look around himself like a cornered animal searching for an exit. "It's all a big scam, and I'm the mark, Mister Kaleb! I've been suckered into this bullshit!"

"I didn't want...to have this conversation now," Kaleb stammers, "because I knew you'd react like this. I wanted to *think* about it all before we really discussed things. The...the tiepin was to keep you safe in the meantime. Stick to your deal as well and you'll be—"

"Will the tiepin protect me from the Boggart?" Johnny pleads.

Kaleb looks amazed. "Of *course* not," he says slowly. "Only your deal will do that. The tiepin is for... other things."

"You said there's only one Boggart in this territory!"

"Yes. Only one *Boggart*, Johnny."

The implication is an ice dagger in Johnny's spine. "What else is here?"

"*Other things.* Dangerous. I don't know if they will be dangerous for you, but they might. You'd be on their radar now, certainly, if not for the tiepin. Without it, if they decided to follow their awareness of you..."

Johnny quickly clips the scruffy tiepin onto the neckline of his T-shirt. "How do I—"

"No more questions," Kaleb says, suddenly stiffening his lower lip. "All right? You will shout and rage and ask me more things and I won't tell you anything. That's the way it happens with these things, isn't it?" Mister Kaleb's eyes bore into Johnny's. "You've read stories before, *seen* stories, no?"

"Please—"

"Johnny..." Kaleb pauses, blinking rapidly. "I...I *do* have to tell you this: The Shallows, if one can find the way in, will *always* take one where one needs to go, as terrible as that may be. They will always provide, at least, an opportunity. I'm not saying you should *take* that opportunity, but I do have to be...to be...*fair*, and I couldn't live with myself if I didn't tell you that."

Pok-pok.

Both men freeze at the sound.

It's distant and faint, coming from the other end of the hedge alley behind Johnny. Kaleb's reddened face immediately drains of all blood. Neither Johnny nor the old man says anything.

"It was inside the *house*?" Kaleb whispers, his eyes now seeming to bulge in his head.

The wind blows softly, and then Johnny understands it is not the wind at all.

"*Kaleb,*" the Boggart says, the grim glee of its voice all around them. "*You are abroad, yes, and the hour is foolishly late. Overconfident in the limits of your allowance, yes... How delightful to catch you in breach!*" A dark chuckle echoes around the street.

Pok. Pok. Pok. Pok.

The sound begins to grow steadily louder. Kaleb goggles at Johnny for a split second, then turns and flees down the road, sprinting with his strange hobbling gait toward the large black Mercedes that is now turning into the other end of the street.

"*Wait!*" Johnny screams after him, then realizes that he is standing still. *It said it would wait in the attic. Is it here for me or for Kaleb? Can it even do that? What does it mean about*—

None of that matters, he realizes, for the Boggart is coming—

The spell of confusion and panic breaks, and Johnny sprints toward his car, seeing Kaleb reach the Mercedes and fling the door open as Johnny does the same at his own vehicle. The key refuses to go into the ignition and then it blessedly does, Johnny starting the engine and screeching the car into the road as he drives away with his foot on the floor, not daring to look in the rearview mirror in case he sees what might be emerging from the hedge alleyway behind him.

He drives in terror, devoid of any destination, the only sound in the car his frantic breathing, as he desperately wonders what to do next. *Find Kaleb again?* The old man said his place was, what, the next street over? But there have to be two hundred houses on this estate. *Screw it.* He can knock on every door if he has to. But would there be any point? The Boggart sounded like it was coming for Kaleb. *You are abroad.* Did it mean the fact that Kaleb was out on the street? Did Kaleb hide somewhere the rest of the time, then?

Bailey. Ivan.

He tries phoning them both again. No answer. He rubs his eyes, and when he opens them, he sees that the haze is back. It's coming off him like magical steam. A stab of color catches in his peripheral vision, and he looks down to see that the haze is darker near the tiepin, but it turns back to its regular glassy clarity once it's a few inches away. The tiepin affects the haze?

Suddenly Johnny thinks he knows what the haze might be.

"*You'd be on their radar now,*" Kaleb said. "*If not for the tiepin. Without it, if they decided to follow their awareness of you...*"

Johnny watches how the haze rises toward the sky. How it looks just like a signal fire. Like a beacon pointing out where he is. If it's dark around the tiepin, then perhaps it really does have protective effects.

Either way, keep fucking moving. Get out of here, far away from here—

The idea gives him pause. Maybe even hope. The Boggart never said anything about having to be *here*. Look at what just happened: Some weird old guy came up to him in the street and knew about this shit? So this is obviously all something local, something to do with Waterton—hell, the *Shallows* has to be around here too, Waterton, water, shallows. Getting far, far away from here seems like an extremely good idea indeed. Ivan and Bailey will call him sooner or later.

But to where? His luggage is in the house, and he doesn't think he can go back in there.

No, not all his luggage, he realizes. His carry-on is still in his car.

His *passport* is in there. Johnny continues to drive, letting the idea grow.

Breathing space. Physical space.

An entire *ocean* of space.

Chapter Eight: Madison

Notes

MADISON SHIFTS ON the bed, the pages propped up on her knees, a twinge in her back breaking her concentration and returning her fully to her room. She checks her watch. She's been at this for only twenty minutes, but she wishes she could sit with her story for the rest of the day. No pain, shaking, or nausea; just making notes on her printed-out pages. The heaviest thing she has to lift here is her pen. While she could use this whole hour of allotted free time to nap — and she really could pass out instantly, something she usually can never do — she has vowed to spend it on the book instead. She's done with shortcuts. Another twenty minutes, then she'll go and see Jennifer. She's run out of dental floss, and Madison can't stand not flossing; she hopes her new friend will have some.

A thought strikes her. She quickly jots in the margin:

> DESTINATION? IT'S THE AIRPORT CHAPTER NEXT, BUT YOU DON'T ACTUALLY EVER SAY WHAT THE INTENDED COUNTRY IS. YOU SHOULD MENTION IT FOR REALISM EVEN IF IT'S NEVER REACHED.

She nods to herself, adjusting her still-damp top clinging to her back. The morning session was hot yoga followed by rehydration and a HIIT spin class; the yoga was challenging, but the ride afterward felt like cycling up Everest. She'll change her outfit before the next class. By now, showering in between such frequent sessions has been generally accepted by the group as pointless, and the fear of sweaty judgment is gone.

It's week two, day one. Madison has lost four pounds, and No Days Off is now down to four students.

An evening session of ab exercises on week one, day six, pushed them all to their absolute limits and, in Namrah's case, beyond them. She awoke on day seven and found herself unable to stand. A trip to the hospital was arranged, and Namrah was diagnosed with an abdominal hernia. She returned to the house to report the news, and she and Ellie agreed Namrah needed to withdraw. Namrah gave the others a tearful, heartfelt goodbye, and Madison was genuinely sad to see her go. She felt so close to all of them, even Frankie. Still, she'd be lying if she said she didn't envy Namrah's medical release.

The woman was leaving without the shame of capitulation.

Madison has desperately, desperately wanted to do the Q-word through all the countless session hours. Seemingly endless running, with her wheezing and nauseous. Planking that goes on until her abs are screaming at her, and continuing from there until she screams too. Weight lifting until her muscles are painfully pumped to what feels like a near-bursting point. Interminable meditating that feels like a secondary school punishment exercise. All performed on a progressively more spartan but apparently highly nutritious diet. Repetition after repetition, minute after agonizing minute, each seeming to stretch to four times its length, until she feels like she can't go another second. But she can't quit, because she *believes*. Plus—besides the unspeakable horror of having to say, *I quit,* having to look Ellie in the eye *as she says it*—there are the Hard Corrections.

No one has undergone one yet.

She can't be the first. The system, in Madison's case at least, absolutely works.

She's sore, but she still feels stronger and more capable than she did before she came here. There's no denying it. It's been only a week, but her stomach feels harder, looks flatter. She's standing up straight without thinking about it. How is that even possible?

Ellie. That's how.

Come on, she thinks. *Concentrate. You've only got a few more minutes if you wanna floss-check Jennifer before the next session.*

She rubs her eyes, refocuses on the page, and reads:

> His carry-on is still in his car.
> His *passport* is in there...

She pauses, needing to answer the question. Where would he actually be going? Bulgaria, maybe? Far enough to be out of a monster's reach, at least to his mind? Lots of regular short flights there too. Bulgaria it is. She returns to the page:

> Johnny continues to drive, letting the idea grow.
> Breathing space. Physical space.
> An entire *ocean* of space.

The chapter ends there, and Madison needs to get moving herself.

PART THREE

Heavy

If you bring forth what is within you, what you bring forth will save you. If you do not bring forth what is within you, what you do not bring forth will destroy you.

—*The Gospel of Thomas*

Chapter Nine: Madison

The First Hard Correction

"*DEE DEE DEE deee, TRY, POS-i-tive thinking, dee dee dee-dee-dee dee dee...*"

Madison knows only a handful of lines—she'd heard the song in the cab on the way to the airport and it had stuck—but she has sung these same snatches maybe a hundred times today, a particularly troublesome earworm.

The hallway glows with shafts of dust-mote-filled sunshine blazing through the Velux skylights. Madison reaches Jennifer's door and knocks. She's barefoot, the thick carpet soft and pleasant under her feet, a comforting sensation at odds with the aching in her muscles and joints. She's learning to deal with that—doing well with it, in fact; she's in a good mood—but here, she realizes, is a perfect example of how easily she slips into her old mindset: standing in front of Jennifer's door makes her think of *bedroom,* which makes her think of *bed,* which makes her think of *rest, oh yes, please,* and the idea is suddenly so appealing that she has to catch herself. There it is again. *Comfort,* her addiction. She's getting better and better at noticing it as it tries to worm its way into her desires.

"Yep," Jennifer calls from the other side of the door.

Madison opens it, continuing to happily burble, "*You got-ta look, onnnn the bright side...*"

She enters in time to see her friend striking a match. An incense stick stands in a holder on Jennifer's desk. Madison reflexively flinches and *really* hopes Jennifer didn't see.

The furrow in Jennifer's brow makes it clear that she did. "Whoa," Jennifer says, lighting the incense and blowing it out. The thin drizzle of smoke starts to rise. "Static shock or something?"

"No, no," Madison fake-chuckles, running a hand through her hair. "Just... nothing, nothing." She shakes her head, remembering what she came for. "I ran out of dental floss."

Jennifer is already crossing to her tiny en suite bathroom. "No worries. I was just going to meditate." She returns and hands some floss to Madison. She smiles, but Madison can see she is a touch unsettled.

Madison sighs. "See this?" She turns and lifts the shorts of her left leg.

"Is that a birthmark or something?" Jennifer asks, peering at the several-inches-long red scar at the top of Madison's thigh.

"It's a burn." Madison lowers her shorts again. "I got it when I was a kid. The rest were all first-degree and most of them faded away, but this one stayed. Open flames just make me a little nervous. I don't normally react, especially to a match, but when I walked in, I didn't expect it." She waves a hand, shakes her head. "Silly."

"Rest of them? You got burned all over? And no, not silly."

"Not *all* over, but I had plenty," Madison says. "I was playing in my dad's shed, and he had an old kerosene lamp in there. I went and got matches and lit it in the shed so my parents wouldn't see. In hindsight I could have probably, like, done it right in front of them and they wouldn't have said anything. Too busy arguing or being engrossed in some hobby to notice."

"Oof. Sorry."

"Thanks. So I managed to knock the lamp over, and the whole bloody shed went up."

"With you *in* it?"

"Yep." Madison shrugs, a little embarrassed. "And the door always stuck too, particularly bad if it rained and the wood swelled. Of course we'd had a downpour the night before. As it turns out, Dad was in the living room listening to music and didn't realize what happened until the neighbors heard me screaming. My parents were... They had their own lives and interests, shall we say. My mum especially." *Or Patricia,* Madison thinks. A day came when Madison accepted who—or what—her mother was. A devastating emancipation indeed.

"Jesus."

"It's okay," Madison says, smiling even as the memory of that tiny space dances like flames behind her eyes. "*I* was okay, in the end. The neighbors got me out quickly enough that most of the burns were first-degree, but the only patch that never fully healed was the one on my leg. The whole thing got into the local papers a bit. My parents didn't get in trouble; it was written up as a freak accident, which was a big relief for my dad. He was way more concerned about his reputation than anything else. My mum was too busy to really care, being blunt." Madison had often wondered if perhaps her desperate intention to be the exact opposite of her mother was the main reason Madison had no career to speak of. "Everyone at school knew and I got bullied a lot, but even when that ended, when I went up to secondary—sorry, high—school, the story followed. People would hear my name and be, like, 'Oh, you're the girl who nearly burned to death.' I fucking *hated*—" Fresh, mild panic suddenly flutters in her chest. She doesn't want Jennifer telling the others. "Hey, like, keep all this to yourself, please? Don't say anything to anyone."

Jennifer scoffs. "As if I would," she says, then starts to blink rapidly. "Shit," she says. "I've got to change my contacts; they've been bugging me all day." She crosses to her duffel bag, where it lies on top of the chest of drawers, and pulls out two boxes of disposable lenses. "But thank you for sharing, Mads. Of course I won't tell anyone. Why would I?"

"I didn't think you would, but now I know you won't, because I asked." Madison grins, fluttering her eyelashes. "I'm just a little self-conscious about it is all."

"I'm not one for gossip, Mads," Jennifer says, pulling out both lenses from her eyes. "Oh, that's better." She winks at Madison, slightly red-eyed. "And don't worry, I *especially* won't tell Frankie, eh?" She grins, and Madison reddens.

"I don't *dislike* her. I just can't figure her out. She's always asking very personal questions. 'Would you say you've had healthy relationships?' 'When was the moment you realized you needed to come here?' I just find her a bit...much." She sighs. "I'm being a bitch, aren't I? I'm just so fried. I probably have a short fuse right now. Frankie's okay, she's okay."

"Yeah," Jennifer says. "Did you talk about the shed thing on your questionnaire? In the part about fears and phobias and shit."

"No way," Madison says. "I wouldn't go to an extreme residential boot camp like this and give them that kind of ammo to use against me." The thought gives her pause. Now she's here and reaping the benefits, she wishes she'd been more honest. Perhaps Ellie could have used that truth to help her?

Jennifer looks worried. "Oh. I was pretty honest on mine. Maybe I shouldn't have been."

"Don't worry," Madison says. "You're only one of Ellie's plants, right? So it doesn't matter." She expects a laugh, but her joke is met with only a flicker of a smile. "Just kidding," Madison says, and again Jennifer only smiles. "Hey, *I'm kidding*." She laughs, but the laugh sounds fake. She needs to make things better. The only way to do it is to get things out in the open. "Hey, did that bother you? I honestly didn't mean it to."

"No, no, it's okay," Jennifer says. "I'm on edge too right now, and...Ah, hell. I guess this is a little woo-woo, but I feel like I'm closer with you than the others. After Sarah's confession about being a repeat attendee, I guess I just felt like I had a comment like that coming my way, even if you're only joking. Ugh. Now I feel stupid for even letting it bother me." She shakes her whole body. "Jesus, listen to us."

"It's intense here," Madison says, relaxing. "Nerves are going to fray. Let's you and I try to be aware of that."

"Yeah, you're right, one hundred percent," Jennifer says, turning her attention to her lenses and opening the two little packets.

The room is silent now as Jennifer goes about her ritual, and Madison stands still for a moment, watching. It's still not quite right, but then she realizes that, regardless, it's okay. *It'll be fine,* she thinks, *and if it's not, it doesn't matter. Completing the course is what matters.*

"See you in a bit, Jen," she says, turning and walking away.

"This," Ellie says, gesturing at the construction before her, "is called the Road to Heaven. The baby steps are over, I'm afraid."

They are standing outside by the huge tarp. Madison surveys the vast length of green tarp; it's covered in tiny pools of water from the rain that came in the night. The sky is currently cloudless, and the expansive, wet greenery of Ellie's estate smells fresh and reborn. It's a beautiful day. The sound of Winter's snort floats over from the nearby stable; Madison doesn't think the horse has been out yet today.

"As we head into week two," Ellie continues, "you will be well acclimated to the rigors of the course, and so we're taking things up a considerable notch." She's standing near one end of the tarp. Metal runners secure the tarp's edges, and the final foot of it passes under a metal crossbar, sealing it off before it disappears in an automated crank. Ellie inserts a key into the device and presses a button; the crank rattles into quiet life, and the tarp begins to retract.

Madison has gone from being mildly curious about what is underneath to fascinated. She's even tried to investigate in her free time when she's not editing her novel or napping—two activities in which she is delighted with her progress—but there's no way to see under the tarp without retracting it via the crank. Jennifer's guess that it's well over a hundred feet long looks correct to Madison, and it's about fifteen feet wide. Whenever Madison half jokingly asked Ellie to spill the beans over what was under the tarp, her request was met with a pause and then a somehow robotic-looking wink. "You'll see."

The far end of the tarp is now moving toward Madison. The water on the tarp splashes as it retracts into the machine.

"I had this built several years ago," Ellie says, raising her voice over the drone of the device, "after I was invited to observe training exercises of the Taiwanese Marine Corps. It cost a pretty penny, but as soon as I saw the Taiwanese using theirs, I knew this was something I had to have for No Days Off. This version, you'll be glad to know, isn't *quite* as extreme as theirs, but it is still a considerable challenge."

Madison is beginning to see literally and metaphorically what lies before her: a concrete-lined shallow trench, perhaps two feet deep.

The entire length of it is filled with rocks.

"We have to walk across it?" Frankie asks.

Ellie grins. A rarity.

"Before you," she says, "is a one-hundred-sixty-four-foot-long track of sharp rocks. The Taiwanese use coral, which is, believe me, far sharper. These won't cut you, but they will hurt. They will hurt because, while also performing a series of exercises designed to make your torso take most of your body weight, you will crawl along the entire length of this track on your stomach, pausing to form and hold a new pose when instructed."

Madison, stunned, looks at the impossibly long expanse of rock before her. *It can't be as bad as it looks,* she thinks. *It can't be.*

"I quit."

Madison startles and looks at Sarah.

Frankie and Jennifer are staring too. Sarah's round face — considerably less round here at the start of week two and currently flushed a bright shade of crimson — looks at each woman in turn, as if allowing them a moment to say something about her decision.

Jennifer and Madison immediately exchange a glance and look away from each other before Ellie sees.

"Sarah?" Madison says, unable to stop herself. Sarah is really going to quit? On her second attempt? "You can't be..." Madison checks herself, reddening. She can't let Ellie know she knows; she needs to ask carefully.

"I can't get it all *back*," Sarah mutters, lowering her head before immediately snapping it back up, realizing what she's confessed to. "I can't get back to being the person I became before, the person this *place* made me. I can't get the strength back, mental or physical... It's been so fucking *hard*."

"Even if you've been struggling," Jennifer says, stepping forward, "you can still—"

"If what we've been doing so far were the baby steps," Sarah says, beginning to tremble and looking like she's trying not to cry, "then even *they* made me feel like I was going to die, Ellie. I thought I was prepared for the whole thing. That I was strong enough. I'm..." She puts her hand to her mouth, then into her hairline. She bites her lip as if to keep in the words that have to come. "I'm not. I already *know* I don't have it." Ellie remains silent. Madison sees Jennifer take another step toward Sarah, but now the movement is uncertain, as if she's worried about contagion.

Madison is shocked. Sarah got further than this last time. Yes, she's been struggling, but she's quitting now? Did she get soft? Did Ellie make the first week harder? Madison can't believe it, even as that faint satisfied thud lands in a deep place inside her once more: *She's quitting and you're not.* She struggles to not let her thoughts show on her face. She doesn't look at Jennifer again.

"You're on Light," Ellie says calmly, "and you still have your passes to use. There's no Hard Correction for you if you try this and pull out. You might surprise yourself."

Sarah drops her head. "I know," she says to the ground, "but Light or not, after going through last week together, I couldn't let the rest of the girls do something I copped out of and then, you know, sit across from them at dinner or something. I thought..." She mutters something that might have been "*I was more prepared.*"

"Are you sure?" Ellie asks.

"Yeah." Sarah covers her face with her hands.

Madison watches with pity and a stirring of mild disgust. She pushes the latter away, latches on to her empathy, taking Sarah in, seeing the crushed woman in her fullness. The disgust fades. Madison moves to Sarah and puts her hands on her shoulders, glancing back at Ellie for permission. Ellie nods.

"Don't do this," she says. "Remember what you said."

Sarah's hands come away, showing her wide eyes.

"I can't get it *back*, Madison," Sarah whispers, so quietly that Madison can barely hear her. "I thought by now I would, but I can't get it back like before. I left and I can't fucking get it back."

Madison feels a cold shiver run up her spine.

Sarah covers her face again and Madison draws her in, gently holding her. She looks over her shoulder at Ellie, who nods solemnly and crosses to Sarah, switching places with Madison.

"Wait five minutes," Ellie says to the group.

"Sorry, guys," Sarah mumbles through her fingers. She sounds like a child. "I'm so *sorry*."

"No, Sarah," Jennifer says, earnest.

"It's okay. It's okay." Madison doesn't know what else to say. She, Jennifer, and Frankie stand awkwardly by the track of jagged rocks as they silently watch Ellie lead Sarah around the barn, back toward the house.

"And then there were three," Frankie mutters.

Madison shakes her head. *I couldn't get it back*, Sarah said, and Sarah was someone who was about to be moved up to fucking Elite before. Someone who excelled. Going home then meant Sarah didn't complete the course, and now, on her comeback, she can't even get past week two. *Fuck!*

You aren't quitting, she thinks. *Madison, you aren't quitting.*

Jennifer stares nervously at the track of rocks.

"Hey, it won't be that bad," Madison says. "Like she said, these aren't coral. We can do it. We got through everything else. Guys, we're the ones who are *still here*. Frankie, you were crying during that last flutter-kick session. How long did that go on for? How many did you do while *crying*?"

Frankie nods, still staring at the rocks.

"We can do this," Madison says. "We'll get one another through it. Strength together. Right?"

They hear the crunch of Ellie's returning footsteps on the gravel around the side of the house.

"Game faces on," Madison says. She holds up her hand, pinching her thumb and forefinger together, and raises her eyebrows.

Jennifer nods, Frankie rolls her eyes, but both reluctantly return Madison's "okay" sign.

Serena Williams fills Madison's mind. *Strong. Disciplined. Focused. Dedicated.* The version of Serena that Madison has summoned has another characteristic: *unbreakable.*

She finally discovered the reason she was told to bring a photo, the answer coming during a two-hour-long Visualization, Meditation, and Mental Fortification session: This is the Alter Ego technique, based, according to Ellie, on the work of Todd Herman. Ellie had them practice creating an image in their mind of a character they can summon when finding themselves in a "moment of impact." They spent an entire hour simply holding their photo and meditating upon their subjects, their thumbs and forefingers pinching their pictures tight. After several more sessions dedicated to topping up the mental connection, they were instructed to perform the same gesture to summon this alter ego into themselves. Once upon a time, Madison would have been highly skeptical of such a thing, but now she believes she can become her own version of Serena.

She wouldn't let Jennifer know, but she's secretly been calling herself *Serena* in her self-talk. It's very nice to have an alter ego.

"Okay," Ellie says, returning into the women's midst and, of course, already moving on. "If anyone has any feelings about what just happened, we can discuss them in your feedback sessions this week. Right now, I'm going to show you the exercises you'll be doing as you traverse the Road to Heaven. You'll perform them on command as I call them out. The only reason I'm not doing this exercise with you is that I need to be able to watch from the sides and make sure you're doing it properly. Any of you who fail to assume the position, pardon the phrase, within a few seconds..." She blows a raspberry and jerks her thumb over her shoulder, an uncommon gesture of levity from Ellie, but again, it looks rehearsed. "Hard Correction or exit. Those are the two options. All understood? Good. Here's the first position."

Ellie quickly gets on the ground and lies, of course, flat on her stomach, arms by her sides. Stiff and straight, Ellie lifts her chest and knees, curving her body into a U shape.

"You'll recognize this from the hot-yoga sessions," she says, her voice easy, her body effortlessly in position. "Locust pose."

Madison looks from Ellie to the trench of rocks, back at Ellie, and then one more time to the trench of rocks. She knows that, even on a soft yoga mat, she would be gasping and trembling, sweating and praying for the next position. She thinks about performing the same pose with rocks digging into her abdomen.

She can't even imagine it.

"Position two," Ellie begins.

Frankie speaks.

"Ellie, you're serious about us doing this? This isn't a test to see if we qui—"

"Of course," Ellie interrupts, her brow furrowing. "Wait, did you think you were *already* being pushed to your limits?"

Frankie turns from pink to deep crimson. "I guess not," she says.

Madison feels a real stab of pity for her.

Ellie says, "I've seen people conquer the Road to Heaven who haven't done half as well as any of you have at this point in the course. You need to trust me. You'll learn to do that. It's okay. Second position."

Oh my God, Madison thinks as the reality of what she is about to do sinks in. *We're really going to do this. I'm going to do this.*

This is it. This is where the real pain begins.

This is what you came here for. Isn't it?

As she watches Ellie—and without even knowing she's doing it—Madison's thumb and forefinger pinch together at her side.

Minutes later. Too few—*embarrassingly* few.

Ellie's voice rings out over the rocks.

"Are you saying you quit?"

The Road to Heaven is agony, making the endless runs and weight sessions and flutter kicks and hot-yoga sessions—the ones that make it seem as if there isn't enough oxygen in the entire room to stay alive—feel like a lovely afternoon nap by comparison.

"*Are you saying you quit?*" Ellie repeats. Throughout the exercise her voice has been thunderous and aggressive in a way Madison hasn't heard before.

"Yes!"

The first true challenge has ended in abject failure.

"Then say it. *Say it!*"

There it is again: the crack in Ellie's voice. It's unsettling somehow, but Madison's mind quickly moves beyond noticing it. She's in too much pain.

Silence now. Sweat pours down Madison's brow, but she can't break the pose.

She isn't the one quitting the exercise, after all.

"Say it or assume the position! Right now. One or the other!"

Ellie stands over Frankie, bellowing down at her. Frankie's limbs drop to the rocks, and the words leave her mouth in a half scream, half sob.

"*I quit! I quit!*"

"That's it!" Ellie roars. That crack in her voice again. It might just be from the volume, Ellie trying to yell as loud as possible, but there's an edge to it that makes Madison's body stiffen like she touched a live wire. "Get up! All of you!"

Everyone has to stop? That's confusing, but it doesn't matter. The physical torment is finally, blessedly over. Madison wants to weep with relief but absolutely will *not* in front of Ellie. For now, the relief of releasing the exercise will soon be replaced by the shame of incompletion.

But not as badly as it will for Frankie. Frankie has just quit.

Madison puts her shaking hands against the nearest rocks to slowly peel her burning stomach off the stone beneath her. Her still-intact skin lifts off them, making Madison think of pulling the adhesive backing off an envelope. A fresh, white-hot strip of pain lashes across her torso, leaving only the dull, throbbing sensation of the internal bruising in her abdomen. She gets to her feet, finding purchase on the rocks, and looks back down the trench. She was at the head of the line, Jennifer second, Frankie third. It is Frankie who is still face down against the stone. Madison can hear her quietly sobbing and doesn't know if it's from the pain or shame; she realizes it's almost certainly both.

Jennifer is sitting upright, breathing hard, her hands wrapped around her knees. "We're *all* stopping?" she asks, her voice hopeful.

Ellie ignores her and approaches Frankie, hopping gracefully from rock to rock until she squats next to her student. She bends and says something into Frankie's ear that Madison can't hear, and Frankie nods. Ellie takes Frankie's hand then and helps her to her feet. Ellie looks at Jennifer and Madison, silent for a moment, and that's when Madison notices Ellie *isn't* looking at her. Ellie is looking *through* her, expression vacant. Then Ellie comes back. The moment was only brief, but Madison noticed it. That vacancy again.

But if you thought it might be an act last time, she asks herself, *why do you believe it now?*

"You two," Ellie says solemnly to Jennifer and Madison. "Squash court. One hour."

They used the squash court interchangeably with the dojo for a lot of sessions in the first week—things like shuttle runs until Madison threw up (she kept going), countless laps, intense stretching, and of course no actual squash at all. Basically, anything that doesn't require mat work happens on the squash court.

Ellie puts Frankie's arm around her shoulders and helps her out of the trench without another word. Madison carefully crosses the rocks to offer Jennifer her hand; Jennifer takes it, and Madison pulls her to her feet. The two remaining women breathe heavily for a few minutes, quietly moaning and waiting for the pain to go away. It doesn't, and Madison decides that either Ellie's little bit of weirdness just now was all part of the act or she was just caught up in the intensity of the exercise. Again, pain makes other concerns so much smaller.

"Frankie didn't make it to heaven," Jennifer mutters through gritted teeth.

Madison thinks about how she used the finger-pinch technique, trying to conjure forth and *be* Serena. How it didn't even work a little bit. How surprised she was by that. *You're just not there yet,* she thinks. *This is a process—you know that.* Another thought occurs: "Do you think Ellie told us to meet at the squash court so we can... *watch* the Hard Correction?"

Jennifer considers the question as she begins to walk in a circle, grimacing and holding her aching abs. "Shit," she hisses. "I guess so. Yeah."

Silence. The pain in Madison's own stomach rolls over like an angry wave. "How close were you to quitting?"

Jennifer just raises her eyebrows in response, shaking her head. "That was...wow."

Madison nods. Jennifer didn't answer the question.

"I was pretty close myself," Madison says, giving Jennifer an easier route to confession.

But Jennifer pivots. "Why did we *all* have to stop, though? You and I should still be on our way to Heaven, shouldn't we? I didn't realize that one person quitting means the exercise ends for everyone. What's the benefit of that?"

"More mind games, probably," Madison says.

"What do you mean?"

"It's another reason to quit, isn't it?" Madison says. "Ellie's really got all this figured out." She hears herself, how her admiration makes her sound like Head Girl, but continues anyway. "Think about it. No one's done a true Hard Correction yet, right? Besides the cola thing at the Sunset Ceremony, and that was only supposed to be a tease. We don't know how bad the Hard Corrections are, and once we've all been through the unpleasantness of one, we'll be a lot less likely to quit because we don't want to go through another."

"That's my understanding."

"So we all have to quit an exercise at least once, in theory, in order for our, like, 'heightened punishment avoidance' or whatever Ellie the Zellie would call it to push us further. That's the idea, yeah?"

"Yeah."

"But now we know," Madison says, "that if *we* quit there's also an extra impact with that choice. If Frankie quitting ends the exercise for everyone, then it means no one else has to fail...but it also means no one can actually complete the task." She points at the rocks. "Imagine being Frankie and hearing that another student made it all the way to Heaven? She just stopped that from happening."

Jennifer shrugs as she walks. "But what would be the benefit of that?"

"Division," Madison says. "She's trying to break us down. For our overall benefit, of course," she adds quickly.

Jennifer stops but continues to breathe heavily. "Are you saying that Ellie *wants* to punish us?"

"No, that would make her a sadist," Madison says. "I wouldn't be here if I thought that was true." She sways on the spot, just talking to ride out the pain. "But I do think it's all part of the game. It's smart."

"I knew you were paranoid," Jennifer says.

Madison laughs even though she isn't sure that Jennifer is joking. "Gimme a better reason," she says, shrugging.

Jennifer shakes her head. "Can't." She grimaces and turns away, walking gingerly but already beginning to straighten up. "We have an hour. I'm going to take some ibuprofen and have a bath. I need to..." She shakes her head again. "Wow. Do you think it's going to get worse than this?"

"I don't see how it can," Madison replies. "None of the punishments are supposed to break the skin, remember, let alone the exercises. Hey," she adds, holding up her hand. "*We* didn't quit."

"We didn't," Jennifer sighs, turning and weakly completing the air high five.

"So how close *were* you?" Madison asks again.

But Jennifer has already turned away. "It was brutal," she calls, her voice flat.

Madison watches her go. Jennifer avoided the question, twice. Madison thinks a few days ago Jennifer would have answered. That's okay, though, even if it leaves Madison a little sad.

She didn't come here to make friends.

"Do I have permission to bind your hands?"

"What?" Frankie replies. She looks terrified.

Madison and Jennifer stand in the small timber-walled spectator room beside the squash court, watching through a plexiglass window. It's stuffy in that space, and hot, the rough, unfinished industrial wood seeming to somehow hold heat. To their right is the door that leads onto the court; it is the only way in or out. They were introduced to the squash court during week one. It is about the size of a primary-school classroom, with heavily rubber-marked white walls. Four strip lights hang from the ceiling, under which are Ellie and Frankie. The former stands; the latter is seated on a small plastic folding chair in the center of the court. Ellie asked Frankie if she minded the other two watching, and Frankie—to Madison's surprise—replied that she would like that. *For support,* she said.

"Your hands," Ellie says. "Do I have your permission to bind them?"

Madison and Jennifer exchange a glance. A small speaker in the ceiling carries the sound of their voices. Somewhere in the court there is a microphone.

Frankie looks to the spectator room as if asking what she should do.

"You can say no," Ellie says, "but you're on Medium. You'd be going home." Ellie's face is emotionless. There is no glee in what she's doing.

Frankie looks down at her hands in her lap. Her face is pale.

"I do need your hands out of the way, though. Do you trust me?"

"I do, Ellie," Frankie says quietly.

This time Madison doesn't look at Jennifer. She's thinking about Jennifer's comment from earlier. Paranoid? Madison isn't paranoid. She's a believer.

Frankie holds her hands out in front of her, but Ellie shakes her head.

"Behind your back, Frankie. Put your arms around the back of the chair."

Frankie nervously complies, and Ellie pulls two black zip ties out of her pocket. She secures Frankie's hands to the seat.

"It's very important that you remember," Ellie says as she works, "that this is not a punishment. You are a remarkable person for even agreeing to this, Frankie, and what is happening now is a step along your path." Ellie finishes binding Frankie's right wrist and moves on to her left. "This is just something you need to go through, and we are all with you. I told you, almost everyone fails at least once. Then their first Hard Correction changes things."

Almost everyone, Madison mentally notes.

Ellie refused to reveal what Frankie's Hard Correction would be when all four of them talked pre-Correction. She only repeated her usual Hard Correction mantra: "No damage, and brief." Frankie stayed silent, ashen faced. A few weeks ago, Madison would have been amazed that anyone would agree to a correction without knowing what it would entail. Now she knows differently. She knows because *she* would agree.

She feels stronger than she ever has in her life.

"Give me a second," Ellie says, exiting through the door on the far side of the court.

Frankie looks up at the pair in the spectator room. She is as white as a ghost.

"Good luck, Frankie," Jennifer calls, giving a double thumbs-up.

Frankie just nods and turns to stare directly in front of herself.

"You think she can hear us?" Jennifer mutters. The sound of her voice is heavily compressed in the close wooden space, as if they were in a recording studio.

"It's only plexiglass," Madison says. "The window's not, like, soundproofed or anything. It might be muffled, but I bet she can make us out."

"Yeah. Do you think that— *Oh my fucking God.*"

Ellie has reappeared in the doorway on the other side of the court. She wears what looks like gardening gloves. In one hand, she carries a metal bucket.

In the other, a glowing, smoking poker.

Frankie turns her head, trying to see what the women in the spectator room are looking at. Madison slaps her hands to her mouth in shock; Frankie catches the movement and does a double-take Madison's way. Ellie is only a few feet behind Frankie now and approaching fast.

"No fucking *way!*" Jennifer screams. She runs to the court door and pulls on it, but of course it's locked.

Madison darts forward and bangs on the plexiglass, the sight of that burning poker pulling up primal memories from the depths of her being. They tear and snap as they pull free, igniting their own fiery heat into her central nervous system. *Heat on flesh...*

"*Ellie! Ellie!*" Madison screams. "*No! No! You're not supposed to be doing this!*"

Jennifer starts kicking the door to the court, her strong legs delivering blows that sound like she's striking with a sledgehammer. It's pointless, Madison knows; the door opens inward, and the frame is dense.

Frankie is going to get burned, she thinks, *she's going to get burned—*

Frankie lurches about in her chair, trying to turn it to see what is happening, and then she doesn't need to as Ellie is now standing right behind her; the poker nearly brushes Frankie as Ellie bends down to place the bucket on the floor. Frankie flinches as she feels the unexpected and intensely radiating heat, and then Ellie's arm deliberately brings the poker into Frankie's field of vision.

Frankie starts to scream, terror lending her voice a shrieking pitch. It comes over the tinny speaker in the corner of the spectator room and sounds like a tormented chipmunk.

"*No!*" she squeaks. "*No! What? No!*"

"It'll be brief," Ellie says, breathing heavily now. "Accept this willingly and you will be *unstoppable*. Either way, here it comes."

Frankie lurches forward.

The chair folds, and Frankie is now pitching toward the hard floor, shrieking. She turns at the last minute so that her shoulder hits first, but it's an ugly landing. Her wind leaves her with a strangled *whouff,* her impact on the solid court heavy and concussive. Frankie tries to find her feet, making snorting, crying noises as her lungs struggle to refill, but her hands are bound behind her, and the chair on her back is making it difficult to rise.

Ellie closes in. She reaches between the slats of the chair's back. She lifts the bottom of Frankie's shirt to expose the skin.

Inside the spectator room, there is pandemonium.

"*Ellie!*" Jennifer screams, banging and banging on the plexiglass, trying to break it. "*Ellie!*"

Madison is paralyzed, seeing her childhood nightmare playing out in real time. She is back in that burning shed, the wooden walls of the spectator room suddenly turning into slats in her mind, but she can't look away as her skin begins to register the heat that will soon be inescapable no matter which way she turns, and then it will start to *burn her—*

"I'll make it quick," Ellie says to the screaming and helpless Frankie before reaching into the bucket and producing a frozen popsicle.

Madison and Frankie freeze too.

"What the fuck," Jennifer whispers.

Frankie continues to scream and plead; she hasn't seen the switch.

Ellie looks up and stares through the glass at Madison and Jennifer.

There is a brief pause, during which the only sound is Frankie's cries. Ellie continues to stare. Frankie, oblivious, continues to scream. Ellie raises her eyebrows, the question obvious.

Madison and Jennifer don't move.

Then Ellie nods and turns away, pressing the popsicle firmly against Frankie's exposed skin.

Frankie screams as if she is dying.

Now Madison and Jennifer look at each other.

"Very good, Frankie," Ellie says as Frankie's scream starts to taper off in confused distress. Ellie places the poker into the bucket, which emits a harsh, deafening hiss and a plume of steam. "You aren't burned. I didn't touch you with the poker. It was ice." She holds up the popsicle for Frankie to see.

But Frankie isn't listening. She's crying in ragged screams, pausing only to gulp in air.

"Frankie," Ellie repeats. *"Frankie."* She crouches down and holds the popsicle in front of Frankie's eyes. "Look. This is what I touched you with. I switched it with the poker. I touched you where your hands can reach, so feel your back. It doesn't hurt now, does it? It's only cold. The Correction's over."

Frankie's face immediately contorts with rage. *"What the fuck!"* she screams. *"What the fuck! Let me out! Let me out!"* She thrashes again, rocking from side to side, still face down on the floor like a helpless fish. Her movements make the chair clatter loudly against the squash court floor.

"I will," Ellie says, and then there is a sudden flash of light on metal as, from somewhere Madison can't see, Ellie produces a pocketknife with alarming speed. "Keep still, Frankie," she says. "I don't want to cut you."

But Frankie is too furious to hear her, still impotently rattling around.

"*Get me out of this!*" she bellows. "*Fucking get me out! Out! Out!*"

Ellie gently puts her knee in the small of Frankie's back, and Frankie stiffens for a moment, her rage turning into a brief, shrill grunt. Again the knife flashes, and Frankie's bonds are cut. Immediately Frankie scuttles out from under the chair, lurching to her feet. The cut zip ties still loosely hang from her wrists. Frankie yanks them off and throws them at Ellie.

"What the fuck was *that*?" she yells.

Ellie nods. "Get it out," she says calmly. "It's okay. Get all the words out. This is normal."

"That's too much!" Frankie screams. "That's *twisted*! You fucking *crazy bitch*!"

"Say it all," Ellie says solemnly. "Your adrenaline is sky high. You're frightened and angry. Use it. One hundred laps around the court to burn it off and finish. Take a breath, and off we go."

"Fuck off!"

Madison finally notices the pain in her cheeks. She realizes that her nails have dug into her face. She breathes out, coming back to herself, but begins to shake uncontrollably. She takes a staggering step backward, nearly falls, but keeps backpedaling until her spine presses against the rough wooden wall. It has been a long, long time since she had a panic attack like this. She's been a lifelong claustrophobic ever since the burning shed, and the panic threatens to turn the now-even-smaller spectator room into a tomb.

Jennifer hasn't seen Madison's distress; she remains standing against the plexiglass, her hands lightly resting upon it.

She was going to be burned, Madison's brain keeps hissing even when she knows the truth. *Ellie was going to burn her.*

"We're running," Ellie says, "in three...two..."

"Fuck off!" Frankie screams again, heading for the spectator room. "This is crazy, this whole thing is fucking crazy! This is *bullshit!*" She's crying again and tugging on the door, struggling with the lock. Then it opens, and the little ball of outraged fury that is Frankie barges inside, stopping in surprise as she sees Jennifer and Madison, remembering they were there all along. A moment of confusion flickers across her face as she sees Madison pressed against the wall, her hands folded across her chest. Then Frankie's rage steamrolls all her confusion aside.

"Did you see that?" she barks. "Did you see the *switch?*"

The question is simple. Madison can answer that. She nods, feeling terrible for Frankie, but she can't think straight—

"Why didn't you fucking tell me?" Frankie snarls.

Give me a minute, Madison thinks. *I'm sorry, Frankie. Please just give me a minute.*

"It was your Hard Correction, Frankie," Jennifer says, and there is a tremble in her voice. "Everything here is set up the way it is for a reason. If this is what Ellie thought you needed."

Yes, yes, that, Madison thinks, but suddenly she isn't so sure.

"Everything happens for a reason?" Frankie snaps, storming across the room and getting so close to Jennifer that she has to crane her neck to look up into the taller woman's face. "Have you heard yourself? 'Everything happens for a reason,' like Ellie is *God* or something? Can you actually kiss her ass any more than you do? Are you drinking anything *but* the Kool-Aid here or what?"

"Hey," Jennifer says, holding up her hands. "Calm down."

"Don't tell me to fucking calm down!" Frankie yells. "We're supposed to be in this together. Eating together, supporting each other, all that bullshit. Where were you?"

Frankie slaps Jennifer's shoulder.

The sound is short and harsh in the small wooden room, the audible *snick* of a line being crossed. The sheer reality of it snaps Madison back to herself as movement through the plexiglass catches her eye. Ellie is calmly picking up the various props on the squash court and heading to the door in the opposite wall. Ellie can surely hear this. Why isn't she doing anything about it?

"Frankie, stop," Madison croaks, pushing away from the wall and blinking herself back into the room. "We're on your side."

"Are you two in on this?" Frankie barks, but she's only looking at Jennifer, who takes a deep breath and gently pushes past Frankie to head to the outside exit.

"I can't let you talk to me like that," Jennifer says as she leaves. "I *am* your friend, but right now—"

Two things happen at once. Both, Madison later thinks, happen on instinct, creating a disaster no one wanted, the incredible touch-paper stress of the last week meeting the flame of the current situation.

Frankie grabs Jennifer's arm in fury, trying to stop her from reaching the door.

Jennifer pulls her arm away.

Frankie doesn't let go, foolishly trying to restrain the bigger woman, and so Frankie is pulled toward Jennifer. As she is dragged against Jennifer's body, Frankie lets out a furious yell and leans in. Her fight response in full force, she plunges her fists into Jennifer's hair and pulls, yanking Jennifer's head toward her.

"Stop!" Madison yells, grabbing Frankie's waist, trying to pull her away, but that only makes things worse, as it adds greater strength to Frankie's hair pulling.

Jennifer is bent at the waist now, but her hands find Frankie's wrists and expertly twist the smaller woman's hands inward toward her forearms.

Frankie grits her teeth, grunting in pain, and then she's releasing Jennifer's hair and Jennifer is turning Frankie's arms and pulling the smaller woman in toward her, turning her as she does. Jennifer wraps her thick forearms around Frankie's throat and the top of her head, hugging her into her chest and walking backward. Frankie's heels drag across the floor, her squinting eyes burning with impotent fury.

"Fucking calm down," Jennifer grunts, breathing hard.

Frankie doesn't respond, taking tight gasps of breath.

"Frankie, just wait a second, okay?" Madison babbles, not knowing what else to do. Jennifer is clearly trained in some kind of martial art, and Madison isn't surprised to see it.

"Fgfff!" Frankie spits, unable to speak clearly.

"I'm not letting you go," Jennifer gasps, "until you calm down. We're your friends here. We're on your side. Okay?"

Frankie doesn't say anything now. She just lets out those little hissy breaths, her raging eyes locked on Madison.

"Okay?" Jennifer tries again.

Frankie breathes for a few more seconds and then holds up her hands. Jennifer slowly lets the smaller woman go, and Frankie stands, her tearful gaze looking back and forth between the other two women.

"Screw you two," she says quietly. "I'm done with that crazy bitch, and I'm done with you. We were supposed to have each other's backs."

"We do," Madison says, but Jennifer is opening the exit door.

"Get lost," Frankie says, and it's spoken with a sob that carries hurt and betrayal. She storms out.

Jennifer lets out a shaky breath and moves back to the plexiglass. "Where the fuck was Ellie just now?" she asks.

"Cleaning up," Madison says. "The chair and the other stuff. What did you do there, when you grabbed—"

"Jiu-jitsu," Jennifer mutters, shaking her head as she stares through the plexiglass. "Done it since my teens." She lowers her head and exhales. "Did you see the way Frankie fell in there?" Jennifer mutters. "When she lunged forward in the chair? She couldn't get her hands down. If she hadn't turned at the last minute, she might have broken her neck. Or, at the very least, her face."

"Yeah. She was lucky."

"No, that's not what I mean," Jennifer says angrily. "Of course Frankie was going to go crazy and thrash about as soon as she saw the poker. But Ellie didn't account for that. The damn chair wasn't bolted down or anything, and Frankie's hands were tied to it behind her back. That shit's dangerous. Okay, she didn't get burned with the poker, *ha ha,* clever trick, she only got a really bad scare, and she was unhurt. But she could have been badly injured, and I don't think Ellie thought that through." Jennifer straightens, scowling. "And before you go on with your plant talk, that wasn't staged, unless Frankie's a stuntwoman who is very good at faking being basic." She shakes her head. "I didn't mean that."

But Madison isn't listening. The mention of the word *plant* has reminded her of their earlier conversation, which in turn has clicked another memory into place: She told Jennifer about her phobia of being burned, and only Jennifer. Madison deliberately didn't put that information on her intake questionnaire, yet the first Hard Correction just happened to be all about getting burned?

Jennifer is still talking. "I don't know," she says, turning away from the plexiglass and resting her back against it, her arms folded. "Ellie's whole vibe is being the consummate pro." She puts her hands in her hair and slowly turns on the spot. When she speaks next, it sounds as if she's talking to herself. "Cutting corners or just straight-up missing shit like that..."

Or, Madison thinks, *is this you trying to make me nervous?*

Jennifer looks up and perhaps sees something in Madison's face, because, for the first time, Jennifer scowls at her friend.

"What?" Jennifer snaps.

Then they both jump as the courtside door opens.

Ellie enters.

"Did you hear what happened?" Jennifer asks.

"The commotion?" Ellie asks. "Yes."

"And you let that happen?" Madison asks cautiously.

"It's quite common on this course, Madison," Ellie says. "There are always heightened emotions involved when you take people to extreme places. There has to be."

"So why didn't you step in?" Jennifer asks.

"You want me to run a course all about resilience," Ellie replies, "but you want me to step in like your mother when things get testy?"

"They nearly came to real blows, Ellie," Madison says. "It was kind of a fight."

"Was it, though?" Ellie asks.

"I restrained her," Jennifer says, "but it might have been much worse."

"But it wasn't, was it?" Ellie says.

"I could have knocked her out!"

"But you *didn't*," Ellie says. "You're a martial artist. You have self-control, and you also know what to do in these situations. Your questionnaire results were very clear about that. I knew it would be okay. I'm extremely careful about whom I group together."

"I'm not so sure," Jennifer says, reddening again, "that you have as good a grasp on what you're doing as you think, Ellie. Frankie had a bad fall out there."

Ellie's eyes flare for a moment, fastened on Jennifer...and then drop. "Yes," she says.

Madison sees it. Her stomach rolls over a little.

"You're right about that," Ellie continues. "That was a mistake. A lesson learned. The chair should have been secured. Look, I'm going to talk to Frankie, and then I think it'd be a good idea to do today's feedback sessions right after. You can get it all out to me then, and you can have some time to put your thoughts in order. We'll shift the feedback sessions forward to before tonight's workout."

"There's a workout tonight?" Madison says, her hand unconsciously going to the dull pain in her abs, still suffering from the Road to Heaven.

"Of course," Ellie says before heading for the door. "Jennifer, thirty minutes. Madison, you have ninety minutes to kill. Perhaps you could write down your thoughts on this afternoon's events." She pauses in the doorway. "It's better to write them by hand. The connection between the pen and the brain is proven to improve the fluidity of thought."

Ellie leaves.

Jennifer stares at the closing door. "I'll see you later," she quietly says to Madison.

She follows Ellie without a backward glance.

Chapter Ten: Johnny

And the Monster Begins to Squeeze

"Please remove all electronic items from your luggage and place them in the plastic trays provided."

Johnny hoists his carry-on onto the conveyor belt. His larger suitcase—the one he abandoned in the house—contains things he will happily learn to live without. His foot is tapping, tapping as both his item tray and suitcase trundle along the conveyor belt, and then he's stepping into the line for the X-ray booth. The airport is bright and bustling. He finds that soothing, the presence of so much light and humanity feeling like a wall of protection even if he knows it is no such thing.

He bought a ticket for the next cheap flight to Europe (his earnings aren't what they were), which in this case is to Sofia, Bulgaria. He needs to be as far away from that thing, that *street*, as possible. He certainly isn't going to stay in the same house. He's putting water between himself and the Boggart, with an Airbnb for the next few nights waiting for him on the other side.

He waited several hours until departure, sleeping in his car at the airport until it was time to check in. It's dark outside, but soon the sun will begin to rise. His phone is the only item he hasn't yet put in the tray. He still hasn't been able to reach Bailey or Ivan, and he's clinging to the device until the last second in case they wake up and call him.

His eyes find the nearest fluorescent ceiling light out of OCD habit. As he looks up, he watches that haze rising off him; during his journey to the airport, it flickered more regularly back into his vision, so much so that he is already used to it. He has found that he can will it into his perception, but it hurts his head if he stares at it for too long. Either the signal rising off him is getting stronger, or he's getting better at seeing it. He watches the haze move past the lights above until the glitch happens again; it always does, that skip, that involuntary twitch in his mind that flicks at his attention and stops him from seeing the phenomenon. This time, he doesn't try to bring the sight of the haze back. Is the haze a dinner bell for whatever entities Kaleb was warning him about? He wonders what kind of monsters would be watching if it wasn't for Kaleb's tiepin of alleged protection.

His phone rings. *Bailey's number.* Johnny answers it instantly. "Hello?"

"Johnny?" Bailey gasps. "We got all your messages! You sounded so freaked out. What's been going on? You're at the airport?"

"Yeah," Johnny says quickly, wincing in relief at the sound of Bailey's voice. He's not alone now. "Yeah, I am. Have you spoken to Ivan? I need to get hold of him too."

"I'm here, Johnny," Ivan's gruff voice says in the background. "You're on speakerphone."

Johnny exhales. His best friend is here as well. He has his whole team now.

Johnny was a student when they met, just another patron of the café bar that the older Ivan owned. Everyone on Johnny's course went there. Passing hellos turned into conversations that eventually became after-closing-time drinks with just the two of them. One night Ivan shared a bottle of vodka with Johnny, and after working their way through it together, the short, stocky fortysomething's face darkened. Ivan began to tell Johnny of the living nightmare that was the Bosnian civil war, stories as horrifying as they were astonishing in their account of the family unity that had enabled Ivan to survive.

Johnny was almost embarrassed to reciprocate with tales of his own upbringing; he could relate to Ivan's healthy family life about as much as he could to the idea of living through a civil war. Both were alien concepts to him, one a beautiful dream and one a hell too horrible to comprehend. But Johnny shared his past nonetheless. When he finished his story about his dad—a rare telling of his father's abuse—he looked up to see tears in Ivan's eyes.

"Johnny," Ivan said, slapping his sausage-fingered hand onto Johnny's back, "this is a tragic, tragic thing. When the father is not right, the boy does not become a man, and no man ever achieves anything alone."

It was a poetic statement of the kind only a drunk can make—even if Johnny didn't agree—and then Ivan went to the bar to get the *good* vodka. It was the first time Johnny ever saw someone as strong as Ivan Misic be emotional, vulnerable, yet utterly secure and sincere at the same time.

After that night, Ivan became something special to Johnny. The man worked harder than anyone Johnny ever knew, and he did it with a smile on his face, finding meaning in the work, his customers, their experiences, and the communities that came to his café bar. "The goal," Ivan loved to say, "is always secondary to the journey." Johnny loved that too.

He just wishes he wasn't so much *less than* his friend. Ivan is what Johnny's father have would called a "man's man"... but for once he would have been right in all the ways that are good.

"I'm sorry, baby," Bailey says. "The signal at your old place is so bad. By the time we were done, it was just easier to crash there. It took forever." Her voice, often so light, sounds like an innocent child's, totally at odds with the dockworker's sense of humor she possesses. It was the latter that drew him to her when they met at an after-party, Johnny's first time back on the scene since recovering from his injury. While he had long since healed physically, the pills now had him. No one knew about that at the time; Johnny, like a lot of addicts, was extremely good at hiding it. She was waitressing and, unlike everyone else there, completely uninterested in Johnny. She seemed sad, almost—Johnny hadn't been doing much better—and despite being struck by her high cheekbones, pale skin, shining dark brown eyes and hair, Johnny didn't want to bother her in that way. She was working, after all, and Johnny didn't want to be a sleaze. "Can I get a Bud, please?" he asked her. "We don't have them, sir," had been the reply. "How about a shot of Jack?" Bailey shook her head. "None of that either, I'm afraid." She gestured around herself at the room and looked as if she was trying to pick her words carefully. Then she gave up. "I mean," she said, sounding utterly over it all, "look around you. This is a douchey poser event. If you want booze for normal people, you're gonna have to get it from the place down the street." Johnny saw it then, even as she panicked, realizing the implication of what she'd said: how frazzled she was, how strained. "Oh, I didn't mean you," she said, but Johnny cut her off. "Don't worry," he said. "This is absolutely a douchey poser event."

She smiled, the sudden tension bleeding out of her shoulders.

"Oh," she said. "So you don't want to fucking be here either?"

A phone number turned into a first date turned into Johnny falling in love with her incisive intelligence, her incredible creativity. Her assertiveness where he was passive. A lot of women Johnny dated since becoming famous had dollar signs for eyes, but Bailey was down-to-earth, with her own life and future to build, and he loved her for that too.

"Tell him," Johnny hears Ivan say to Bailey.

"Tell me what?"

"Johnny," Bailey says, "something really weird happened, and we need to talk to you about it. We're pretty freaked out. It doesn't make any sense." She sighs. "Ivan and I can't remember anything that happened earlier today."

The temperature in the airport seems to drop several degrees.

"It sounds crazy," Bailey continues, "and it is, but we were trying to figure out how it took us so long to box up your things at the house. We can't remember most of the day, how we got to your old place, what we were doing for all that time. It might sound like I've gone mad, but we both can't remember, and we can't *both* be crazy, right?"

"Where are you?" Johnny murmurs.

"We're nearly at the new place," Bailey says. "Ivan has the key—"

"Don't go inside!" Johnny barks, causing all the people in the line around him to stare. He ignores them. "Listen, tell me quickly: What are the Shallows, Ivan? Sandy said you'd know. How do I find them?" He is drawing closer to the X-ray machine. Soon he will be made to put his phone in the tray. He can resume the conversation on the other side, but he doesn't want to lose his friends again now that he finally has them on the line.

"What are the what?" Ivan asks, making Johnny's heart sink. "The Shallows? I don't know this." After spending most of his life in the UK, Ivan's accent, grammar, and dialect normally sound British. He slips up only on certain phrases. *"What's happening,* Johnny? Are you okay?" The question makes a horrible realization settle into Johnny: He really, *really* needs his pills.

"Ivan," Johnny says. "Do you know a Mister Kaleb?"

"No."

"Johnny," Bailey says, *"why are you at the airport?"* Johnny looks up. He's four people away from entering the X-ray booth. "I'll call you back in a couple of minutes and explain," he says. "I have to go through security. But listen: I don't know if you'll believe what's happened to me when I tell you, but I think what's happened to me and you two losing your recent memories are connected. They must be."

"Sir?"

A short Black woman with a surprisingly friendly smile for airport security looks at him from the other side of the belt. To Johnny's right, his trays roll toward the mouth of the machine.

"Sure," Johnny says to her, hearing the shake in his voice and realizing how he must look: haunted eyes, pale face, trembling body. "I'll call you right back," he tells Bailey, before hanging up and tossing his phone into his miscellaneous-item tray with his keys, belt, spare change.

The security woman nods, still smiling, but taps the collar of her shirt with a long red fingernail.

"Sorry?" Johnny asks, confused. Is this some sort of *Come with me, sir* signal? Is he busted for something?

He then realizes the tiepin is still clipped to his T-shirt.

"Pop that in the tray for me, please, sir," the woman says good-naturedly.

Johnny freezes. If he doesn't take it off, he can't get on the plane. If he takes it off, he isn't protected.

Protected from *what*, though? It suddenly occurs to him that in all the fear and panic *he just took Kaleb's word for it*. How does he know Kaleb is even on his side? The tiepin could even be making his signal stronger.

"Is everything all right, sir?" She's looking at Johnny with an expression that might be turning from concern to suspicion. Maybe she recognizes him too. Shit. *Shit.* Should he take the pin off?

"Sorry. I haven't slept," he says, forcing a nervous chuckle. "I'm working on a deadline."

He unclips the tiepin.

"Been there," the woman says, giving a bitter little snort. "Economics dissertation. Oof."

Johnny looks at the scratched-up tiepin between his fingers. Tiny. Scruffy. He half expected to feel *something* when he took it off. But nothing. Only his nerves jangle as he leans over and tosses the tiepin into the slowly moving tray.

"*Please remove all electronic items from your luggage,*" the woman is already bellowing at the long line behind him.

Johnny turns back to face the X-ray booth and, out of the corner of his eye, sees another staff member joining the woman behind the conveyor belt. This person is short too, or perhaps standing a little hunched. He notices that they are wearing a different-colored uniform. This one is a dark red, an unusual enough shade of crimson that Johnny turns his head to take it in properly, but then realizes he's not looking at a member of the staff at all. For a moment, what Johnny sees under the fluorescent lights, among the jostling sea of reasonable reality going on all around him, doesn't seem possible. But it's there.

A human-shaped individual stands behind the security officer— human *shaped*, but clearly not human. What Johnny thought was a red uniform is skin that looks covered in sunburn cancers—strange, painful-looking blister-like things that create a moonscape of red, so dark in places it looks black. The creature is naked, without visible genitals, and it stands at what looks to be just over five and a half feet tall. As its head creaks slowly upward, Johnny sees that it doesn't have a face. Where a face should be is a slowly turning pool of red quicksand, disappearing *into* itself at its center. Johnny watches, frozen in shock, as the edges of this creature's red face pool crumble down into the quicksand a little, fractionally expanding the width of the churning surface. As its awful visage slowly collapses, its body shivers, and Johnny thinks he hears it moan—a vocalization from a throat that sounds clogged with wet sand.

It suddenly folds at the waist. Its hands—the thing has hands— find the conveyor belt.

Johnny screams.

He backs up a step, and he's aware of everyone in the line, everyone within earshot, turning to look his way, including the security guard, but Johnny's eyes are only on this creature.

It hops up onto the conveyor belt. Its feet—it has feet—perch on the thin metal frame as its head drops down again, watching the bags pass. Johnny looks around for men and women with guns, for protection, and realizes that no one around him is looking at the creature. Everyone is looking at Johnny. They can't see it. He wants to say, *Help,* but he can't get his mouth to move. It's like he's inside a soundproof glass box. He wants to take a step backward, to move away quietly, but he's still frozen. *He can't get his feet to move.* This isn't just fear; this is some kind of outside influence.

"Ah!" he yells again, this time to break whatever spell is on him, and it works a little too well. He yanks both feet up off the floor as if pulling them free of heavy glue.

"*Sir!*" That's the female security guard, coming around the conveyor belt now and completely oblivious to the monster squatting beside her.

Everyone cries out, and now Johnny sees security running toward him, but they won't be coming to help; they'll only hinder as they restrain him.

The creature's head snaps up and turns toward Johnny.

The edge of that horrible, turning quicksand pool in the center of its face collapses outward a little more, a bigger spread this time, and as that happens, the creature's whole body shudders again. Johnny looks for a weapon—there is zero doubt whom this creature is here for—but there is nothing, and then he remembers the tiepin, forgotten in his rush of adrenaline.

His protection. That's why this thing is here. He took the fucking tiepin off—

His trays are nearly inside the X-ray machine. In about two seconds he won't be able to reach them. He's already lunging forward and realizing that to reach the tray and the tiepin, he's going to have to get closer to the creature, but then it makes a guttural, hacking, choking noise like a dog trying to shift a throatful of steak and leaps off the conveyor belt. It scuttles toward Johnny and leaps onto him, its feet slamming into his stomach, its bubbled red-and-black fingers closing like iron claws on his shoulders. Its dense weight hoofs the air out of Johnny's lungs, and as Johnny drops to the floor, he hears the red sand in the creature's face moving, sounding like distant, sluggish waves. He hears running feet coming closer, several people screaming different things: *"Help him," "He's having a seizure," "He's having a fit," "He's having a heart attack," "That's Johnny whatshisname."* The creature's head drops, and its forehead cannons onto Johnny's chest, slapping its swirling, crumbling quicksand face onto Johnny's left pectoral muscle. Johnny feels something dig in, piercing.

Something inside that face is biting him. Johnny screams.

He punches the sides of the monster's head with everything he has, but the chest pain blooms into a spreading circle of agony as the thing grips tighter, and behind it all is the sensation of something wet and grainy moving around against Johnny's T-shirt. The fabric swishes against his chest as the monster bites down. It begins to pull its head back, trying to rip his pectoral muscle away from his rib cage as it tugs like a feasting wolf. Johnny screams louder and wraps his arms around the thing's head now, bellowing as he hugs the monster to him so it can't wrench his flesh away. Its bubbled red skin feels hard under

Johnny's forearms, like long-set epoxy resin. He feels something crumble against his chest, and the monster's head suddenly moves closer. It shifts slightly, and then the pain becomes tiny, barbed, white-hot pokers under his skin, and Johnny understands that the teeth under that red sand are gaining more purchase, that the thing is trying to close its jaws, that it is trying to snip the muscle off his chest. He gulps in air to scream as he begins to thrash and buck.

"*Aah! Aah! Help me! Help me!*"

Johnny clubs the monster's head, but now it is locked onto him like a barnacle. He feels hands on him, human hands, two on each limb, and then he hears the security guards yelling at him, but it doesn't matter because *oh, this hurts so much—please get this thing off me*. And then, horribly, the creature moves its feet off Johnny's stomach and its hands off his shoulders, and it wraps itself around his chest and waist, slowly tightening its grip. Johnny feels it lock its ankles at the base of his spine, feels its hands latch behind his back, and the monster begins to squeeze.

As the wind leaves him a second time, Johnny yanks his arm free of the security guard and wraps it around the creature, hugging it close to keep it from pulling its head back and ripping his pec off. He rolls and twists and his foot connects hard against someone's head, and now that limb is loose as well. Johnny's left arm tugs out of the grasp of a shocked guard too, and he tries to wheeze air into himself, his butt smacking against the ground as he feels a new, thin, hot sensation burrowing into the center of his chest. It's smaller than the teeth but going in deeper, almost like a long needle. Suddenly, words remembered all too well fill his mind, *deafeningly* loud now and perfectly recalled.

WHAT'S WRONG WITH THAT LITTLE MAN?

They repeat in his brain, reaching a crescendo, dragging other ugly things up with them, but Johnny is already lunging forward and sitting up, trying to focus and kicking his remaining still-held leg with everything he has because he might be about to die, and then that leg squeaks free as the guards try to grab him again, but now

Johnny is up and throwing himself forward, bending at the waist and gripping the monster to his chest like a war hero carrying a child out of a bombed building. He screams uselessly as his ribs start to bend from his passenger's constricting limbs, but he uses its added weight to barrel through the two approaching guards. The milliseconds drag through him like razor blades and the pain buckles him to his knees as he reaches the conveyor belt, but that's okay because he can still see into the trays even while kneeling...

The memory comes again from nowhere, recalled words spoken in an ugly, poisonous voice twisted into a high, wheedling, mocking tone:

WHAT'S WRONG WITH THAT LITTLE MAN—

The memory cuts off sharply as the back of the monster's head connects with the metal belt, hard, and Johnny is dimly aware that there is no resulting audible bang or thud as he looks for his tray. It's gone—*No*, it's disappearing into the machine.

Then he notices that the belt has stopped moving—he can still reach it; they must have hit some emergency protocol when the commotion kicked off—and now Johnny thrusts his arm out to grab the tray as four sets of hands grip his body tightly, and suddenly he can't breathe at all. His body protests from the indescribable pain in his chest and the limbs tightening around his torso and these hands he cannot escape and it feels like he's a fly trapped in amber, he's dying, he's dying, and as the security guards drag Johnny backward, yelling commands at him, he manages to pull the tray and it comes up and off the conveyor belt, but he's only got it with one hand and it drops. Coins and keys skitter away across the linoleum tiles, scattering between the feet of the astonished onlookers—of course several of them are filming this—and growing smaller in Johnny's sight as he is pulled away from them to wherever the guards are taking him, his remaining sense of hope shrinking in much the same way, but there are still things in the tray he's holding, a pooled mess of pocket crap and tangled headphones lying in the tray and then one of the security guards leans over Johnny to take the tray from him, his arms now firmly held, and he screams for his life—

"No!"

WHAT'S WRONG WITH—

As the tray leaves his grasping hand, Johnny realizes this will not be a quick or pleasant death, but when the tray passes by his other arm, he manages to thrust his hand into it despite the efforts of the guard. Johnny clutches a last-gasp fistful of whatever is left in there, too many coins, his phone, the edge of something angular—

—THAT LITTLE—

The tiepin. It's pressed against the back of his rubber phone case. But he's not *wearing* it. He flicks his hand and throws his phone toward his chest, not knowing what else to do. The phone clips the back of the monster's skull, flips over, changes trajectory, and lands on Johnny's neck just under his chin where it begins to fall sideways to the floor. Johnny presses his head forward and down, hard, trapping the phone between his chin and chest, and it stops moving. He's holding it in place, just, but he doesn't know if the tiepin is even stuck to it anymore.

—MAN?

Then he realizes from this chin-down viewpoint that the monster is gone.

It possibly was from the moment the tiepin collided with his body. The intensity of the pain masked the creature's disappearance, because there are, by the feel of it, still holes in his flesh underneath his T-shirt.

"Shit," he hears one of the security guards say. "Stop. Lower him down. Look!"

Johnny's back gently touches the floor, and even as he moans in pain—a sound strangled by his chin being tight against his collarbone—he is aware enough to stop resisting the guards now and go limp. He hears one of the guards speak into their shoulder radio: "Paramedic assistance required!"

Johnny knows why they're calling for paramedics. He can see blood seeping through his T-shirt. It forms two semicircles, each a mirror image of the other.

He feels something crumble a little against his neck and cries out, remembering that unspeakable, falling-away edge of the creature's red-quicksand-face-pool. It crawls onto Johnny's chest and stops as he realizes it's the tiepin falling free. The guards' grips have become loose in their surprise, enough for Johnny to put his hand to his chest as if to hold himself against the pain. Before they immobilize his arms again, Johnny's fingers scoop up the tiepin, and he rolls sideways a little, moaning; he flicks the scuffed metal object into his mouth as the phone clatters to the floor. Did they notice? He doesn't think so; the guards are rolling him onto his back once more but with more care now, the sight of the chest wound and Johnny's ceased struggles perhaps making them less aggressive. Johnny pushes the tiepin inside his cheek with his tongue, moaning in pain.

But he's alive.

Many people stand nearby, gawping. One in particular, a woman who looks about forty, plump and beautiful, speaks into her phone: "Wheat. Filter cannon. Flies. Balloon purple. Rich. Drum kit manual."

The creature, Johnny thinks, remembering the man standing in his garden talking about sharks. *It's affected her, the same way it made me feel like I couldn't move. It affects different people differently, then? Why? Kaleb said there were creatures other than the Boggart—*

The pain in his chest interrupts his thoughts, making him think of the Boggart's teeth.

He just notices the grayness racing into the edges of his vision before he passes out.

Chapter Eleven: Madison

Constructive Criticism

THE FEEDBACK SESSIONS always take place in the Consulting Room.

It's small. Its walls are clean and white, the beige carpet thick and lush, and the only furniture in the room are two of the comfiest armchairs that Madison has ever sat in and a table holding a water jug and two glasses. The large single window lets in a good amount of light, meaning the Consulting Room is bright but cozy, a hard trick to pull off. It smells of clean wool.

Madison, however, just feels cold. The day has been unsettling, and the debrief session isn't going well. She realizes she doesn't care, a state uncommon for her on this course. Ellie hasn't mentioned the Frankie elephant in the room, and Madison hasn't broached the subject.

"Can I give you an observation?" Ellie says. Her gaze is steady and relaxed, the exact opposite of how Madison is feeling.

"Sure."

"You aren't all that forthcoming today," Ellie says. "Even less so than normal; being frank, you haven't been hugely forthcoming in any of these sessions so far. I'd like to ask if there's a reason for that, and if you have something you'd like to get off your chest about Frankie's Hard Correction. This is a safe space to discuss it. I very much doubt you can say anything to offend me that I haven't heard before. I can't say I haven't deserved some of it either. But results are results."

"Results?" Madison scoffs. "Frankie's *gone*."

Ellie informed Madison of this at the start of the session; to her surprise, Madison felt sad that she didn't get to say goodbye. But then she remembered Frankie's parting shots and thought maybe it was for the best.

"My overall success rate," Ellie says calmly, "proves that the system works." She shrugs. "I grant you this, though: We've never had this many drop out so early."

Madison wonders how many completed the last course, or the course before that. *These successes,* she wants to ask. *How many have there been* lately, *Ellie? How long since you had a full complement of people at this stage? When did you start to get sloppy?*

But that's Jennifer in her head, Madison thinks. She isn't sure what *she* thinks. She's almost surprised by the venom she's now feeling toward Ellie. Madison has been quite the *zellie* herself so far.

"Tell that to Frankie," Madison says instead. "I'm sure that will make her feel better."

"I'm detecting a little hostility," Ellie says. "I'd really like it if you could just tell me why. Then we can move forward."

"I'm not sure how honest I want to be with you, Ellie," Madison says. "I don't know how much I want you knowing. I nearly didn't come to the feedback session tonight, and to answer your first question, I didn't come to this course for therapy. Call it feedback if you like, but we both know that's what these sessions are. I'm here to push my physical boundaries. I'm not here to see a shrink."

Silence for a moment. The old-fashioned clock on the wall ticks loudly, making the quiet feel extra charged.

"The feedback sessions aren't a mandatory part of the course, as you know," Ellie says, shrugging again. "And I'm not here to be your therapist. But why come to the session if you didn't want to talk?"

"I don't know," Madison replies. "I guess I just wanted to, like, see how you were behaving. How this affected *you*."

"This session isn't for my benefit, Madison."

"And I didn't want to see your behavior for your benefit," Madison says. "I wanted to see if you were *affected*. You haven't seemed bothered about anyone leaving. Not really. I guess I just wanted to see if I could get a read on whether your whole act is a front."

"I can assure you that it bothers me a great deal when someone leaves my course," Ellie says. "More than anyone could possibly understand. You think it doesn't bother me when someone leaves?"

"Does it?"

Ellie blinks. Her brow furrows.

"I can see why you might think that," she says, and there is great sadness in her voice. "But you would be greatly mistaken to do so. I'd really like to talk about that last thing you just said. You think this is a front? The way I carry myself?"

Madison looks out the window at the fields. It's bright but windy today. She tracks a small cloud as it moves across the sky.

"Okay," Madison says, taking a deep breath. "Ellie, it's not just a matter of whether you're the real deal. I think that very possibly some of the other women in this course have been plants. I think that maybe there's more, like, manipulation going on than I realize, which I'm finding I don't really mind, to my surprise, and trust me: I fucking *hate* lies. They're... a big deal to me. But if you're doing those kind of mind games *and* screwing up like you did today with Frankie and the chair, then that makes me nervous. People can get hurt."

"Plants?" Ellie asks. "Like actors?"

"Yes."

"I see." Ellie's expression is blank. She makes a note on her pad. "Before I respond to that, I'd like to ask: Do you think you have a problem trusting other women?"

Madison's gaze snaps back to Ellie. "What?"

Ellie shrugs. "I'm honestly not trying to goad you. I just wondered. I'm not making a statement."

"I trust women and men the same," Madison says. "I don't particularly trust anyone until they've given me enough reason to. If you think that makes me *mistrustful*, then feel free to make a note on your little pad there."

"What was your relationship like with your mother?"

Madison blinks, the question pulling her up with surprising efficiency. She lets out a loud laugh. Too loud. "Oh, okay. We're doing that, are we?"

"Doing what?"

Madison crosses her legs, causing the insanely comfortable armchair to creak. The noise is loud in the small, quiet room.

"I mention plants, and you ask about my mother? That's quite a big segue, isn't it? Just when I'm trying to get a little truth out of you. Okay, let me try a question for *you*: Did you know about my phobia about being burned? Did Jennifer tell you about that?"

Either Ellie is an excellent actor or she is genuinely surprised. "No. I almost always do the poker switch as the first Hard Correction. You have a fear of being burned?"

Madison doesn't believe her.

"Never mind," Madison says.

"Would you like to tell me about—"

"Never *mind*."

"As you wish. The poker switch is very effective," Ellie continues, "even though one of the cardinal rules is that the Corrections won't leave a mark. The reveal is a strong reminder that you should, in fact, always trust me."

"Mm."

"Why did you think Jennifer told me about your phobia?"

"Because I told her about it, and no one else, and soon after that there's suddenly this burning poker trick..." She pulls up, annoyed, wanting Ellie to understand. "It's not just a *phobia* either; it's what it meant. You have no idea how badly I was bullied over that! It *stuck*. For years kids would hear my name and say something about the kid who was *neglected* and got *burned*. When you're a kid, you think that story's going to follow you around for the rest of your life. It affected me for a long, long time."

"Sarah was a plant."

Even though Madison already knew Sarah was at least a returnee, she's shocked to hear Ellie admit it.

"Go on," Madison says.

"I'm telling you this," Ellie says, uncrossing and recrossing her legs, shifting her weight, "because I want your trust. Even if I'm working you. Everything I do here—everything—is so my students excel. Not to break you down or abuse you into success or trick you for no apparent reason. It's to ride with you, at your back. The truth is, I always have a plant in the course, I always have them pretend to struggle, and I always have them quit at the start of week two. It's to demonstrate the pain of quitting once you've made it that far into No Days Off, and also how NDO is possibly your only chance. The plant comes back and, oh no, they find it too hard and can't get that mojo back. They quit. That's a scary thing to witness. Wasn't it?"

Madison doesn't answer. Sarah's confession was fake? Her reaction today was fake? Madison had *comforted* her.

"Sarah completed the course some time ago, Madison," Ellie says. "I paid her to come back and work undercover, of course, but the main reason she agreed to come back is because she believes in what we do here. Cameron's quitting was unexpected. I could have used that had it not happened too early to be effective. But what Sarah's quitting demonstrated—the principle therein—was very real. The guilt, the damage. The horror of the quit. For many, when they sit with it afterward, it can be too much to bear. How did you feel when you saw Frankie quit today? Be honest."

"Sick."

"Exactly."

"Sarah told me she was a returnee. She slipped up and had to tell me, so I knew that already."

"That wasn't a slipup," Ellie says. "I told her to say what she said about Winter at dinner. Sarah said she told you and Jennifer at the same time, but Frankie and Namrah also asked her about it separately. Did you know that? If none of you had asked her about it, I'd have told Sarah to spill it somehow."

"But...why?"

"To demonstrate the *other* very true problem with quitting this course. You might not be able to get back to the level you were at when you left. Crossing over is extremely difficult, and while I may have sounded flippant about people coming back at a future date, the simple truth is that generally, you make it the first time or you never do. Don't ask me why that is; it just is. I've seen it time and time again."

Madison's blood somehow manages to boil and chill at the same time.

"Sarah's carefully staged quit is to make sure the students have all seen these realities play out before them," Ellie says.

Madison nearly doesn't ask the question, wanting to keep her cards close to her chest, but she can't help it. She wants to needle Ellie.

"What about Elite? She slipped up and told us about that too..." Madison stops. Of course. That wasn't a slipup either.

Ellie sees the understanding in Madison's face. "You're insightful, Madison. I hope it doesn't sound arrogant when I say that you remind me of a younger me. It's nice to see." Madison blushes, despite herself. Ellie is surely just playing her. She can't mean that. "Again, I wouldn't be telling you all of this if the Frankie situation hadn't necessitated me regaining your trust, but yes, that was intentional. It's only a small thing, but that's also my way of getting you to understand something not only about NDO but also about life." She cocks her head, her expression sad. "There is *always* another level of suffering to go to. Plus, didn't it make you want to work hard? The idea of going beyond Medium and even Heavy, that you could literally be Elite?"

Madison deliberately ignores the question, shifting in her seat.

"Like I said, Madison," Ellie says. "You're insightful. Some students go with the flow, others ask a lot of questions, and you're the latter. I *like* that you're second-guessing. It keeps you on your toes, and that's how I need you to be on this course."

Ellie's calm expression is maddening.

"There's a saying in Bosnia," Ellie continues. "*If you want to know what is in the tree, you shake it.* We're trying to change lives here. You think I want you relaxed and comfortable? I thought you said you were" — she checks her notes — "'addicted to comfort.'"

"You asked what my relationship was like with my mother," Madison says, quickly changing the subject out of frustration and realizing the subject she's chosen isn't good either. "Why? Where's that coming from?"

"We were talking about trust," Ellie replies. "Our parents should be where we first learn trust. Why don't we talk about her a little?"

Madison glares at Ellie.

"I'm not your enemy," Ellie says gently, "and I'm not trying to score points here either. Trust me: My favorite outcome is the one where *you* win."

Madison suddenly stands, then hesitates, opening her mouth to ask—

"It's okay to stand and talk," Ellie says. "Pace a little. Many students—"

"I wasn't going to ask for permission," Madison says, even though she was.

"Fair enough."

Madison crosses to the window and leans her hands on the sill. Outside the thick clouds make their endless way across the sky, casting their shadows on the rolling fields below. *Weightless*, Madison thinks—

Stop avoiding—

"My parents—my mother especially—were not *trustworthy people*, Ellie," she says. "They weren't safe. My dad was a borderline narcissist, and..." She hesitates. Even now, after everything that happened, she hesitates when she goes to truly speak ill of her mother. The first time she genuinely did that it was so final, so devastating—the rubber stamp upon her never, ever getting her mother's approval. The sting of that moment still holds her voice silent.

Madison can't have that. She forces the words out.

"My mother would go from utterly distant to exploding at the slightest provocation, and badly. My dad was scared to death of her. Worse, they *were both* fucking liars. I got out from under them as soon as I could. That good enough for you?"

"Not quite. Could you explain more?"

Madison suddenly feels something and now needs to get off this subject immediately. She turns and quickly returns to her seat, flopping down into it.

"Forget my mother. You say you want me to trust you, and if that means you want me to believe you have my best interests at heart, I believe you. But I can't trust you if you're letting your students get hurt because you're screwing up. Frankie was lucky she wasn't badly injured. She fell in the chair, strapped to it with no way to break her fall, because of your poorly planned mind games."

Ellie doesn't respond. She stares at Madison with her hands on her lap.

"I'm just being honest," Madison says.

Ellie nods, then looks down. "It's a fair criticism," she says eventually.

For the first time, Madison sees self-doubt in the older woman's expression. It's horrible to see.

"Today was a wake-up call, Madison. I usually weight the chair to stop something like this from happening, but today I just straight-up forgot." She looks up. "Can you keep a secret?"

"Sure," Madison says, her voice small.

"My partner and I," Ellie says, "we separated three days before this intake began. It was my choice for various reasons—a lack of love for her not being one of them—but it had to be done. I am usually a highly focused individual, but this last week has been as challenging for me as this course so far has been for you. My mind was elsewhere today when it absolutely should not have been. During a Hard Correction, even!" She scowls, shaking her head. "I got rid of the last of her things last night and didn't sleep. It made me sloppy today as a result. It's no excuse, but that's the reason. Madison, if you want to terminate your attendance—if you feel I've been compromised—you are more than welcome to return another time, totally free of charge. I'll even cover your travel. I don't believe I have been compromised, today's error aside, and such an error will *not* happen again, I promise you. But I understand your concern. It wouldn't be a quit either. Just a postponement. Return successes are rare, as I said, but I very much believe you could pull it off."

Madison can't meet Ellie's eyes. She somehow feels a dark camaraderie with her coach in this moment, so much so that she's rapidly flicking through her Rolodex of memories to check whether there is any way Ellie knows about her own recent breakup. Could Ellie be using that to manipulate her? No. Madison hasn't told anyone about what happened. She might have mentioned a breakup to Ellie, but if she did, she used the version she tells everyone: *Oh, this good-time guy, we had a thing, it ended, big whoop.*

But Ellie doesn't know how deeply Madison was in love. Ellie's story must be legit.

"How long were you two together?" Madison asks.

"Nearly seven years," Ellie says, smiling sadly.

Christ, Madison thinks. Her own relationship was only a matter of months. "I had to do something similar," Madison blurts. "Break up with someone. It was a big deal."

Why is she doing this? She doesn't trust Ellie! Why would she seize a chance to have a heart-to-heart??

Ellie is opening her pad, checking her notes. "You mentioned a breakup, but you said it was only—"

"I lied," Madison says, wincing. "And if we're talking, then no notes right now. This is Madison and Ellie just having a conversation."

Ellie looks up, considering. Madison knows she is encroaching beyond the provider-client relationship.

"Okay," Ellie says, tossing the pad gently to the floor. "Tell me why you lied."

"Because I loved him a lot," Madison says, rubbing her neck, "and I gave him a stupid nickname so I could minimize to myself what the hell I'd done. He..." The words freeze. She wants to open up—she gets to properly shoot the shit with Ellie as an equal, not as a student—but how does she say it?

He was infectious. Fun. She wanted to go and *do things* again, at least when she was with him. And then his own problems started to come out. He wasn't a bad guy; he just had a lot of issues, ones he was really working on, but then that one bad fucking night...

"I loved him a lot," she says. "But it wasn't right. He was a great guy with such a big, big heart...but he was this fucking *mess.* The thing was...Jesus, he still managed to function in the world in a way I couldn't. Like, he didn't have a job, he had a *career,* and I was just this *bum* by comparison; I always felt like I was embarrassing him when we went out together... but he was secretly even more fucked up than I am! Big time! You understand? He could still take care of business. But then our mutual messiness became too one-sided. It just... It had to end."

"Sounds all too familiar," Ellie says. "But you sound like you feel guilty, and I don't think you should. You have to have boundaries—"

"I don't feel guilty about ending it," Madison interrupts. Her eyes are screwed shut, suddenly overwhelmed by guilt. It was the *way* she did it: in public, drunk. A silly argument over nothing, and she snapped, attacking his weaknesses that only she knew... because they reflected her own. "I was cruel when I didn't need to be. Unforgivable. The damage that did, God, especially when... you know, after my mother... how fucking important it is to leave in the right way."

Madison catches herself babbling. What the fuck is she doing?

"No," she says, slapping her hands on her legs. "No. I'm done with that. I'm done navel-gazing."

"Okay," Ellie says.

Madison lets out an awkward laugh. "You're good. Really good."

Ellie smiles and shakes her head. "I'm not actually doing anything right now. But thank you for sharing."

"Yeah, well, I'm tired of whining. That's not what I'm here for. I'm here to *stop* being weak." She shivers as the memory passes through her: his face, distraught, as she spits those acid words into it:

BECAUSE YOU ARE SO. FUCKING. WEAK.

"You want to go all the way, then?" Ellie asks. "You're staying?"

"I think I am. Yes."

Ellie nods. "Then I have a question for you. I'd like to move you up to Heavy. Do you think you're ready?"

That's unexpected. "Do you?"

"Well, as you know," Ellie says, "starting the course on the Light or Medium levels is your choice. Heavy is only at my discretion, and I think you're more than ready to move up. Would you like to?"

Despite herself, Madison feels an electric tingle all over her body. *Ellie thinks I'm ready for Heavy.* A few months ago, Madison didn't even think herself capable of running a half-marathon. The thought of things becoming more difficult is frightening but exhilarating.

"I only ask at the start of the week," Ellie continues, "since the programs are laid out on a weekly basis. Obviously, today is the start of week two. You can stay on Medium and move up next week if you choose, but then you would lose a week on Heavy and the benefits that will bring."

FOMO. Always Madison's Achilles' heel.

Then Ellie swings the second part of her one-two: "Jennifer's already agreed."

Madison searches Ellie's face again. Nothing. *You sneaky bitch,* Madison thinks. It's not just her need to compete with Jennifer; the two of them have been in this together since day one. She doesn't want her friend to have to go it alone.

"Did you talk to her about what happened with Frankie?" Madison asks. "The Sarah stuff too?"

"Yes. We had a long and extremely frank discussion, and I was as honest with her as I have been with you. She seemed satisfied, and she wants to excel."

"Why do you want me to move up too?"

"Because there's still a big part of you holding back."

Madison opens her mouth to protest but stops. *Is* she holding back? She thought she was giving her all.

"Believe me, Madison," Ellie says, smiling. It looks more relaxed than normal. "I see how hard you're working. People understand the idea of NDO logically, but it's very rare I see eyes light up right at the start the way yours did when we met in Coventry. You truly grasped it. You came to me already *this* close to tipping over, didn't you? And if you don't make it, you're ready to 'get busy dying,' as the saying apparently goes. I've been there, Madison. I don't know if it's your mother or your ex or your whole life that's got you to that point, but *I've been there*, and I know it when I see it." There it is again: Ellie effectively saying, *You remind me of me.* "I know you're more than ready to work harder. We just have to find what you're avoiding." Ellie looks at Madison with pride, and as suspicious as Madison feels, she doesn't think Ellie is a good enough actor to be faking it. "If I wasn't thoroughly impressed, I wouldn't be offering you this option. But you came to me for a reason, and I *want* you to get what you want, dammit. You'll see no more screwups from me. I'm going to work harder on this intake than I ever have before. I want us to excel *together*."

That does it. The last sentence breaks Ellie's composure as she leans forward, clenching a fist. The woman *means* it.

"Sign me up," Madison says suddenly, the words unstoppable.

"Atta girl," Ellie says, and Madison feels warm all over.

Chapter Twelve: Johnny

Gray Areas

JOHNNY WAKES, STILL feeling hazy and dull from whatever they gave him—a sedative perhaps, to calm him down? Whatever it was, they administered it in the ambulance.

He looks around the strip-lit room for his things, taking in the office-style cupboards, the sink, the rails on either side of the bed in which he currently lies. It's a private hospital room. Johnny has private health care. He lifts a hazy hand to his chest, feeling the clinical texture of a hospital gown and the bandages and dressing beneath it. His wounds are sore but much less so than earlier. The sedative, the bandages, the dressing, and time all combining to dull the unbearable. He thinks he might have been here most of the day. *Yes*. The memory swims to the surface. He talked to the police. They came to question him earlier, which isn't surprising given that he caused a major scene involving blood at an airport. He remembers thinking they shouldn't be interviewing him while he's dosed up, but he was aware enough to concoct a vaguely convincing story. It was pretty good for an off-the-cuff piece of bullshit, fear bringing him focus. If he'd been taken into custody, he wouldn't have been able to find out *anything* about his situation. He also managed to appear relaxed and calm enough that both cops were prepared to believe him, so he was grateful for the sedative. Johnny thinks their inquiries were a procedural necessity rather than genuine interest.

He told them that his chest wound was a freshly healed bite from a friend's dog. That he had a panic attack about flying while standing at security, and that all his flailing around had reopened the injury—

The tiepin!

He frantically scans the room. It isn't in sight. It was in his mouth, tucked up in his cheek. He was lucky not to have swallowed it while unconscious. Or maybe he did? His keys are on the nightstand, the mini Swiss Army knife key ring attached. A pathetic weapon, but better than nothing. He grabs it and extends the single blade. No monsters here yet. Heart racing, he tries to blink away the ton of eye floaters he suddenly seems to have. He realizes they aren't eye floaters. It's whatever the glassy smoke haze is that's rising off him, still lifting into the ether and saying, *Come and get me.* Shit! He can see it effortlessly now, almost too easily. He has to squint to see past it to where his clothes lie folded on a chair, his carry-on suitcase parked nearby, his phone even plugged into a charger.

Bailey.

Ivan.

Johnny gingerly shifts in the bed, expecting a lot of pain but feeling blessedly dull. He picks up the phone and sees forty-seven missed calls and thirty-two text messages, all from Bailey and Ivan. He doesn't bother checking them; he calls Bailey right away. She picks up even before the first ring completes.

"Johnny!"

"I'm okay," Johnny whispers. *For now,* he thinks. "I'm in the hospital. I'm going to discharge myself as quickly as I can—"

"You're hurt? Why are you whispering—"

"I'm okay. Just listen. I just have to get my car, and then I'll come to you guys. I'll be maybe an hour and a half—"

"I've been scared to death. I didn't know if you were on a plane or, like, dead or—"

"I'm sorry."

He wants to keep this conversation short. Even his whisper sounds like a dinner bell. *Tenderized Johnny steak, pre-skewered.*

"We're at Ivan's house. We haven't been able to sleep! Johnny, what's been *happening?*" Johnny hears Ivan in the background asking, "Is it Johnny? Is it Johnny?" Bailey says, "First me and Ivan can't remember a whole day, then you're at the airport, then in a hospital bed. Just tell us the truth. I promise I'll believe you, John-John." Johnny's heart melts a little. He needed to hear her talk to him like that. "Johnny...," she adds, in a voice that's reluctant, awkward, "*are* you using again? I know you said you weren't, but maybe that was, like, just an automatic response. It's okay if you are."

"I'm not using—I promise," he says, his eyes darting around the room, his knuckles white around the tiny Swiss Army knife.

"I tried to call Sandy and David," Ivan says, his deep, gravelly, usually energetic voice sounding tired, and there is a darkness in it. "But neither of them answered. Strange things happen, Johnny. We don't remember most of yesterday, both of us, both unable. We both tried, both can't." Ivan's English is not as accurate as usual, his natural accent leaking into his speech. Johnny realizes that this is what Ivan feeling afraid sounds like.

"*Tell us what's been happening,*" Bailey says. "Start at the beginning."

Johnny does, starting with Sandy and David. When he gets to the part about David's drawings, he says: "Ivan, they said you would know about this kind of thing. Were they right?"

"I have no idea what they're talking about, Johnny."

Johnny curses inwardly, having believed Ivan would somehow know what to do, as always. But his faith in his friend remains unshaken. Ivan always comes through. Johnny just needs to make him remember. Johnny continues his story, hesitating once he gets to the attic.

"Keep going, Johnny," Bailey says.

"This is the part," Johnny says, "where I really, really doubt you're going to believe me."

But they do. Not effortlessly, not without great concern, and not without many, many questions, but he thinks they do. The weirdness of their last twenty-four hours makes them a lot more receptive than they would be otherwise. Johnny moves on to the empty houses, Mister Kaleb, and the attack at the airport. Once he's done, there is silence down the telephone line.

"Hello?" he asks, nervous.

"We're here, John-John," Bailey says, and the gentle tone of her voice tells Johnny that the statement is true in more than one way.

"This *haze* coming off you," Ivan says. "Can you still see it? Or was it only there when you were in Waterton?"

"It's still here," Johnny says. An idea strikes him: Was the attack at the airport because he was trying to leave the country? "I think I have it because I'm in a deal with the Boggart. I think if you two were, you'd each have the haze too."

"We already went to the street in Waterton, Johnny," Bailey says awkwardly. "When we didn't hear back from you. We needed to do *something*. We didn't go into the house like you said, but we had a look round the area. We didn't find anything, but...I mean, we saw the other houses there. They weren't empty."

"They fucking were."

"I'm not saying I don't believe you," Bailey adds quickly. "Losing a whole day tends to open the mind. But if those houses were empty then, they're full now. You said they had no curtains. These had curtains. And furniture. And lights on."

"The few houses near the bungalow?" Johnny asks defensively. "At the end of the alley?"

"Yes," Ivan says. "One guy was even outside his front door smoking in the middle of the bloody night."

"Did you talk to him?" Johnny asks, thinking of the neighbor spewing gibberish. "Did he make sense?"

"We described you and asked if he'd seen you," Bailey says. "He said he hadn't."

"Was he a middle-aged guy?"

"No."

"But—"

Suddenly Johnny has the connection. The middle-aged guy on the street repeating words to himself. The woman at the airport. Two people in one day.

It all collapses on him like an avalanche. It's bloody *obvious*, after all.

The gibberish people.

The empty-then-full houses.

The Needle Monster's attack.

The *Boggart*.

"Holy shit," Johnny whispers. "Guys, we don't need to find the Shallows." His hand finds the metal rail along the edge of his bed. It feels solid. Inarguable. Real. "We're already *in* the Shallows."

He waits.

"You're saying," Bailey says, "we don't remember what happened for a day because we, like, crossed over into... *into* the Shallows?"

"Maybe," Johnny says. "It would explain a lot, right?"

"It would," Ivan says, "if we knew what the Shallows were."

But Johnny is already entertaining a wild and crazy idea, one full of hope: If they *are* in the Shallows, and they can find a way *out* of the Shallows, then maybe he can escape the painkiller deal with the Boggart—

"*Ah!*" Johnny cries as he springs upright, two and two finally creating a terrifying four. He grimaces and moans, holding his chest. That movement was too much, too fast, but still his mind screams the terrible truth at him, one he was too hysterical to understand at the time and too doped up ever since to fully realize:

They didn't give him a sedative.

They gave him morphine.

"*Hello, Johnny-Mine,*" the Boggart's voice says, right behind Johnny's head.

Even before he turns to look, Johnny can tell it is smiling.

Chapter Thirteen: Madison

If You Can't Stand the Heat

Week three, day seven

THE TIPS OF Madison's thumbs and forefingers are almost completely white, so hard are they pressed together. Her hands are shaking—her knuckles have at least stopped oozing and are now sticky, painful, half-formed scabs—and her mind is going through the most intense doublethink she has ever experienced. One half is panicking and wanting to flee from the confines of her own skull, screaming, *Why are you allowing this to happen?* The other half is frantically telling her that's the old Madison talking, that after three weeks she is really Serena, that she is a *Bad Bitch,* that this is what she wants, that this is what she came for.

Madison is about to undergo her first Hard Correction.

It was so *stupid.* How could she have let herself—

"Are you ready, *Serena?*" Ellie asks. She does not say it sarcastically; she says it with kindness. She stands with her arms folded. Her gaze is calm, her face relaxed.

At her feet are two phone books and a short wooden billy club.

Madison opens her trembling lips to say yes, but all that comes out is a dry hiss. Her tongue darts out and slathers the outside of her mouth, and she swallows.

"Yes," she whispers.

She remembers what Ellie said at the Sunset Ceremony: No one gets truly serious until they've had their first Hard Correction. The Pepsi-up-the-nose was pitched as a *taste*. No one knows what they're working to avoid until it's happened. Jennifer and Madison have taken the course extremely seriously. *After this,* Madison tells herself, *you will reach new heights. It will be worth it.*

They're in the dojo. The locked spectator room at the squash court will not be necessary for this Correction; Ellie has told them both exactly what is about to happen. There will be no trickery here. Madison glances at Jennifer a few feet away, nervously shifting from foot to foot. Madison wants her to say something supportive, but Jennifer just nods, jaw muscles standing out as she bites down.

Jennifer still hasn't had a Hard Correction.

"We're both here with you, Madison," Ellie says softly. "We support you utterly."

Now Madison just nods.

"*Oose,*" Ellie hisses, forcing the air from her lungs.

"*Oose,*" Madison repeats, and her mind jumps back to this morning to marvel yet again at just how stupidly she managed to screw up. The change of place and time in her mind is good, though; it means she's anywhere but *here,* and maybe if she can stay *there,* she can endure what's about to happen.

Earlier that morning

"*Oose!*"

Smack.

The impact shoots all the way up Madison's left arm and into her shoulder for what is possibly the thousandth time. The pain hits a new high with this punch, darting all the way into the tip of her shoulder blade like some burrowing animal moving at lightning speed. She dreads the next one.

"*Oose!*"

Smack.

This one is worse, somehow much worse, and again she tells herself it's because she's resisting the pain rather than embracing it. But the words *I don't know how much longer I can do this* have been running through her head since they started. Jesus, how long have they been at this? An hour, two? She's almost crying with pain, frustration, *boredom*—that's what none of these exercise motherfuckers ever mention: the sheer relentless, staggering boredom of repetitive training.

"*Oose!*"

Smack.

Madison bites back a yelp as she thinks she feels something *chunk* out of place in her rear deltoid. Beside her, Jennifer grunts, a wet, through-the-lips sound that lets Madison know that her friend (colleague) is struggling too. That instantly brings a wash of bitter reassurance. *It's not just me. I might not be the first one to drop. Please let it be her.*

The guilt is immediate. She doesn't mean that. That's the pain talking.

"*Oose!*"

Smack.

They are training in the dojo, facing the wall, Madison wearing shorts and one of her many long-sleeved training tops. Both items of clothing are soaked several shades darker with sweat. In front of her, nailed to the wall at chest height, is a gray canvas bag about the size of a standard piece of paper and several inches thick. It is densely packed with sand.

Two clouds of tiny red spatters adorn the bag. Blood from Madison's knuckles, which split open, she thinks, perhaps twenty minutes ago.

"*Oose!*"

The bark of Ellie's command evokes a Pavlovian response in Madison, and her right fist cannons forward, bare-knuckled and bloody, into the bag of sand.

Smack.

The canvas takes another gritty nibble out of her wounds, and the lack of give in the bag makes punching it feel like punching the wall itself. Her muscles have been broken down by countless repetitions, and now it feels as if the *bones* of her arms are absorbing every impact.

"Embrace it." Ellie's voice passes behind Madison once more as she continues her circuitous pacing.

Madison can't see Ellie, but she knows the woman's hands are behind her back.

"You can't reach beyond the pain by waiting for the present to end! Commit!" she barks. "Lean into the here, the now!" The force of Ellie's language, tone, and rhetoric have ramped up since Madison and Jennifer made the switch to Heavy; that horrible, intense crack in her voice is a regular presence now.

We chose this, Madison thinks.

"*Oose!*"

Smack.

Her knuckles feel as if she is punching crunched-up glass. She's seen the movies, scenes in which people are being beaten black and blue and in *so much pain,* yet they manage to heroically keep getting back to their feet. She's always known she couldn't do that. She's always known she would just lie down and die, and now her moment of capitulation has come. Horribly, impossibly and—worse, she realizes—*inevitably,* the time has come to quit.

Not quit the *course.* But this exercise has beaten her.

She will take her Hard Correction.

"*Oose!*"

Smack.

Nothing is working. The finger-press thing, the alter-ego trick, is doing practically nothing. *Everything she has learned here* isn't working. She's trying to dig deep only to find her basement's basement has been picked bare. Her *gas tank,* as Jennifer would call it, is dry. She has no business being here.

"There is no ground floor in hell!" Ellie screams, and now she sounds like someone else entirely. "*Oose!*"

Smack.

Madison's fist is still against the bag, her arm held straight. Her other hand is at her hip, snapped back into pre-punching position, ready to strike again. Before Ellie can call out the command once more, Madison presses her thumb and forefinger together as hard as she can.

"Come on!" Jennifer screams.

Madison can hear the pain in her voice.

The image of Serena Williams suddenly blazes at the front of Madison's mind, powerful and capable and *goddamn Serena could do this shit all day*—

"*Come on,* Jennifer!" Madison screams back, and then realizes that the "Come on" from Jennifer was probably self-encouragement. Before the incident with Frankie, Madison would have *known* that Jennifer's "Come on" was yelled in support for her. Regardless, whether it's from the finger pinch or Jennifer's words, Madison begins to feel—

"*Oose!*"

Smack.

—good.

"Bahh!" Madison screams and then tenses her chest, her shoulders, trying to say to herself that this is what she came for, *this is good, this is good,* and maybe adrenaline continues to stir a little somewhere, and a cool feeling breaks out on her forehead.

"*Oose!*"

Smack.

She is becoming lightheaded, her mind wandering, but *oh my God*! Her mind just *wandered*! She actually went *elsewhere* for a moment, she endured a minute longer, and *yes,* her stance widens a little, just a little, her base becoming stronger and more solid, and *she's finding flow, holy shit, she's breaking through, it is really happening*—

"*Oose!*"

Smack.

"Aaah!" Madison bellows, and it's really a sob because no, it isn't happening, she can't maintain it, that hurt so fucking much, and she doesn't think she can—

"Time, ladies."

Madison's fist is already halfway to the bag before her brain understands what Ellie has just said. Her fist angles downward before it flops loosely to her side. She sways on the spot for a moment, feeling the ragged pain in her bloody knuckles and the sweat running down her back. They're done?

She held on? She made it?

She *is* one of those people after all?

The thought is so big that it's... it's...

Blinking, she looks at Jennifer. Her friend is standing much the same way as Madison: hands at her sides, head down, swaying as sweat drips from her forehead and chin and pools on the blue mats. Jennifer seems as if she doesn't know where she is. Madison sees Ellie fishing in the red cooler. She withdraws two large bottles of Gatorade and smiles broadly.

"Excellent." Ellie grins, unscrewing one cap and holding the bottle out to Jennifer, who takes it with an unsteady hand. Ellie unscrews the cap from the second bottle and turns to Madison. The smile on Ellie's face makes Madison feel as if she is being bathed in sunlight. As Jennifer tips her head back to drink, Ellie mouths an extra *excellent* just for Madison. Madison smiles, even as her face trembles, and takes the bottle before slumping against the wall. The delirium is alleviating the pain in her knuckles, triceps, forearms, shoulders, and lower back.

She did it. *She fucking did it.* Three weeks ago, she would have quit.

But what damage have you done to your body? She shushes that. She drinks the Gatorade as Ellie speaks.

"Take a moment," Ellie says. "And then we're going to walk laps around the room to cool down before we stretch. Then you're getting in the sauna for thirty minutes before dinner, followed by a whole ninety minutes of free time before tonight's fifteen-mile run."

"Fifteen miles?" Jennifer asks.

Madison can't see Jennifer because she has a buzzing feeling in her head now and needs to keep her eyes closed.

"Yes," Ellie says. "Take a minute. Drink."

Madison does as Jennifer is told, feeling the overly sweet liquid run down her throat as her pulse throbs in her forehead, neck, and chest. She's *hot*. She can't even think about the run. It's too much. *Wait—did Ellie just say thirty minutes in the sauna?*

"Steady yourselves," Ellie says. "You know what to do. In through the nose; try to slow down each exhale. Keep doing that as we start walking in five...four..."

Already? Madison tries to push off the wall with her elbows and discovers she can't. Her torso is too heavy. There's a metallic taste in her mouth. It takes a couple of tries, but she manages to take a staggering step forward and opens her eyes. She sways on the spot, and then Ellie's hands are on her shoulders.

"Look at me," Ellie says calmly, her stare soft but unblinking. "Focus. Steady." She lowers her voice so only Madison can hear. "You have this."

Madison nods. Ellie doesn't talk to Jennifer like that.

"Three...," Ellie continues. "We're walking in two..."

Madison blinks, straightens, and realizes how out of focus Ellie still is. She blinks a few more times. Ellie becomes clear.

"One," Ellie finishes, turning Madison's shoulders until she faces Jennifer's back.

Jennifer and Madison step forward as familiar music starts to play through the dojo's speakers, the same music Ellie plays for every cooldown because it sets the proper tempo: "Stayin' Alive" by the Bee Gees. It's a quick rhythm to walk to, and Madison stumbles a little as she obediently tries to lumber up to it.

"Stand up straight, Madison," Ellie says firmly.

Madison does, focusing on Jennifer, who is shaky but striding forward with her head still down. Madison's feet continue to find the padded floor in front of her, and while the pain is still sharp and glassy, the walking is, as always, helping her to breathe. She inhales so hard her nostrils close each time; she tries to focus on that rather than the lingering pain.

It was *happening* at the end there, wasn't it? For just a moment. She started to go beyond. *And she didn't drop.* The knowledge is life-changing. This is by far the hardest work they've done — something she never could have managed pre-course — *and she beat it.*

Ahead, Jennifer reaches the wall and takes a wavering turn to continue the circuit. Madison follows in her footsteps and notices Ellie in the center of the room, watching them walk. She stands upright, solid. Her back becomes straighter when she passes Ellie. Why does she want this woman's approval so much? She doesn't care. It's *working.* She's changing.

She spots Jennifer's sandbag on the wall and is so distracted by the sight that her exhausted body stumbles. Madison's bag was spattered with blood, but Jennifer's is soaked.

Stayin' aliiive...

The clouds of blood there are thicker, darker, and much larger in diameter. Madison's pride vanishes like mist in a wind tunnel. She thought she was a Bad Bitch? Jennifer went the same amount of time but clearly was punching far harder, working much more. Jennifer has *earned* the right to be exhausted. Madison stares at the blood on Jennifer's bag and knows that anything she felt during that exercise was a delusion.

It can't have been, Madison thinks. *You were Serena for a moment.*

The lights in the room are harsh and unpleasant, the high voices of the Bee Gees grating in her ears:

Well now, I get low and I get —

The music clicks off.

Madison snaps out of her reverie.

"Okay," Ellie says proudly. She is beaming. Madison doesn't think she's ever seen Ellie smile this much. Ellie produces a bottle of antiseptic out of her bag and two rolls of bandages. "Hands, ladies," she says.

Both hold out their split and bleeding hands for Ellie to rinse with the antiseptic liquid. It burns, but neither woman cries out. They are beyond that now. She begins to bind Jennifer's hands with the gauze.

"Before you hit the sauna, a quick word as we look at beginning week four. Final week, as you know."

Final week. Madison feels a stab of anxiety. This is ending soon. It's been absolute hell, but she's come so far.

"The last week will be considerably different," Ellie says, looking down as she works. "If you choose not to stay for it, you will be refunded twenty-five percent of your course fee."

Not to stay for it?

"But you will not graduate," Ellie continues. "I know this is a deviation from the original plan, but based on your progress—"

"Different how?" Jennifer interrupts. She looks annoyed, but Madison thinks Jennifer knows what's coming as much as Madison does, feeling the same fear and excitement. Ellie *has* to be talking about—

"I have a duty to you both," Ellie says. "It's rare I even offer this, but given that you two are possibly the best pair of students I've ever had, anything less than Elite for week four would be letting you down."

Silence apart from Madison's and Jennifer's labored breathing.

"As you both know, thanks to Sarah," Ellie says, giving a little smile, "Elite is a fourth level to the course, above even Heavy. The one key factor is this: Should you agree to stay and complete the course, there is no *leaving* the course once week four begins."

Whoa. *Whoa.* This is the part Sarah *didn't* mention.

"Naturally," Ellie continues, either ignoring or oblivious to the expressions on her students' faces, "agreement will be verbal, and the terms of your technical incarceration are not legally enforceable. The exercises will become more intense—"

"Wait," Madison says. "What do you mean, no leaving the course?"

"The building will be on lockdown," Ellie says. "No more outdoor exercises. Let me be clear: There will be no increase in the severity of any Hard Corrections, should they be required. But they will now be unavoidable. No quitting the course to avoid them."

Now Madison and Jennifer exchange a look.

"The same rules will apply to any Hard Correction," Ellie says. "No breaking of the skin, no permanent damage. Of course the nondisclosure agreement and the injury waiver still very much remain in place."

"What if we demand to leave?" Jennifer asks.

Ellie takes a deep breath. "If you agree to Elite and we start, you won't be allowed to. We will be locked inside this building for seven days."

"But you'll have the keys," Jennifer says flatly.

"I will," Ellie replies, and adds nothing more, quietly finishing Jennifer's hands and moving on to Madison's.

Jennifer says nothing, Ellie's implication hanging in the air. Madison doesn't know what she finds harder to believe: what she's hearing or the fact that she's considering agreeing to it.

"Why didn't you mention this before we signed up?" Madison asks. "I'm not saying no, but this is a big deal. Shouldn't this have been properly explained?"

"I told you," Ellie says, "the course is in a constant state of flux. I pride myself very much on its flexibility, how I can adapt on the fly to my clients' needs. Admittedly, this is a significantly larger adaptive change than normal. I do understand that this may not be something you are both comfortable with. But seeing what I've seen"—she looks between her two charges and nods approvingly—"I believe this is the only way to squeeze the most out of you both. You're doing so well already that if we don't go to Elite, anything we do will feel like a regression." She shrugs. "True Strength is the willingness to step into the unknown and remain committed *no matter the result.* You *will* unlock your strength. It will be the most important thing you do in your entire life." Ellie points at her ear. "Verbal agreement is all that's required. Once you say yes, you're in."

Jennifer furrows her brow. "I'll be honest, Ellie. Being locked in sounds pretty fucking cult-y."

It does, but Madison doesn't feel like she's in a cult. Cults lie about their benefits. Madison's mirror doesn't. She looks at Jennifer, noting how the taller woman's already impressive physique now looks as if it's been chiseled out of steel.

"I understand that," Ellie says, "which is why you have until the end of today to decide. If you aren't comfortable, I completely understand."

"Have you done this change before?" Madison asks.

"Yes," Ellie replies, "twice."

Was that the very slightest hesitation Madison noticed?

Jennifer looks skeptical to say the least, but the plate-sized patches of red on her bag and the blood seeping through her bandages let Madison know that Jennifer will be considering it.

Madison is considering it.

She felt something in that last exercise, that other state of being. If that was her feeling the edges of True Strength, she wants more of it. But agreeing to something like Elite and being *stuck* with it, trapped inside a deal of her own making...

Not being able to back out, you mean? Like you wanted? Like you realized you needed?

Madison thinks there's a very good chance she needs this. More than that, she wants it.

"Hit the sauna," Ellie says, stepping back. "Have a think. I can answer any questions you might have afterward. Hannah, you're all taped up. Head on out."

As Ellie turns away, Jennifer shoots Madison a questioning eyebrow behind her back. So she heard it too. But Ellie laughs softly. "Jennifer. My apologies."

"Don't worry about it," Jennifer mutters. "I'll leave you two to it." She heads for the door.

Leave you two to it? Was that Jennifer being catty again? She's made a few comments like that in the last week. Madison isn't really surprised anymore, but she is hurt. She didn't think Jennifer would be like this.

"I saw you," Ellie says as she works on Madison's hands. "At the end of the exercise. You felt it, didn't you?"

"Yes," Madison says immediately.

"I knew it," Ellie says softly. "If you'd been blown up by a roadside IED in the middle of a war zone, away from help, you would crawl to that help yourself. Wouldn't you?" She's nodding Madison's agreement for her, eager. Madison just smiles, but Ellie sees the hesitation. "Look in the mirror," she says, still focused on the bandages. "Look at yourself."

Madison turns toward the mirrored wall of the dojo. She sees a red-faced stranger, one with a flat stomach, toned arms, and pumped, clearly defined shoulders. How has she become this, a *Serena*, in just three weeks? Her whole body hurts, but she somehow still feels strong and lean.

"You're nearly a true warrior," Ellie says. "Did you ever think that would be possible?"

"No."

"Yet here you are. But you're not finished. Are you going to walk away this close to True Strength?"

"No."

"Good. I won't lie to you. It's going to be the hardest thing you've ever done in your life. But I believe in you, Madison."

How — *how* — could she walk away from this and not wonder, for the rest of her life, what she would have become? She has a choice, yet she has no choice.

"I'll do it."

Ellie looks up. "Is that verbal confirmation? I'll ask you properly — once you decide you're in, you're in — and we start Elite tomorrow." She holds up her hands. "Madison, do you want to go to Elite for your final week at No Days Off? Say it."

"I want to go to Elite for my final week at No Days Off."

Ellie grins. She even reaches up and ruffles Madison's sweaty hair. The gesture is too heavy, as if Ellie is repeating something she's seen other people do. But again, her eyes show she means it; she's proud. "Good."

Ellie finishes bandaging Madison's hands in silence. Madison glows.

"All done," Ellie says. "Go hit the sauna. Do your thirty minutes. I'll start the timer once the motion sensor registers movement, and I'll come get you when you're done. I'm going to mop up in here."

With that, Ellie turns away, already moving to the next item on her agenda, leaving Madison standing alone with her bandaged hands held out before her.

The sauna. Madison and Jennifer, sitting in silence.

Jennifer didn't even look up when Madison opened the glass floor-to-ceiling door. Now they've been sitting for ten minutes in the hottest sauna Madison has ever experienced—even though she's a little more conditioned to it after three brutal weeks—and neither has said a word. It's awkward but not *too* awkward. Even if they were on better terms, the sheer heat makes talking an effort.

Madison suddenly wants to say, *Hey, what happened with us?* She can't, though. She doesn't know why. Then Jennifer speaks.

"I nearly quit today."

Madison is stunned. "You?"

"It's not just because of my own limitations," Jennifer says, head down, her long blond hair tied up on top of her skull. "The course is rough, but I know I'm up to it. It's more about doing it with Ellie in charge."

"What—" Madison catches herself. Her tone was too defensive. "What about her?"

"I think she's sloppier than she realizes. She's either very good at covering it up or she genuinely doesn't notice."

"The thing with Frankie's chair?" That feels like a year ago.

"There have been other things."

Madison shifts in her seat. "Like what?"

"For starters, did you notice she called me Hannah?" Jennifer says. "She's called me that more than once. That's concerning." Madison understands, remembering Ellie talking about Hannah Quimby-Beck. The student who couldn't handle the quit. Calling Jennifer *Hannah*, given that Hannah apparently took her own life, is a more concerning slipup than if Ellie had called Jennifer, say, Cameron or even Madison.

"Teachers do that kind of thing," Madison says.

"And yes, there's the chair thing," Jennifer continues. "But on top of that... Well, I was in my bedroom during private time in the first week, and I saw Ellie bring Winter back into the courtyard after a ride. You've seen Ellie dismount before, right? *Whup,* straight off."

"Yeah."

"She gets off," Jennifer says, "and she just kind of staggers a bit. Then she does this." Jennifer sways gently back and forth for a second. "Then she leans on the horse like she has to get her balance back, and then she's okay. At the time, I thought she got lightheaded or maybe a little sick or something. I've thought about it more and more since I started noticing other things. I don't know, but if Ellie's head's not right, if she can't be fully focused, then I'm not sure I want to go into a more intense week with her."

Ellie's going through a very rough time, Madison nearly says, thinking of Ellie's breakup. Perhaps Jennifer saw Ellie in a moment of grief. But does Jennifer know about it? Either way, it's Ellie's secret, not Madison's to share, and saying it would only remind an already probably jealous Jennifer that Madison is close with the boss.

"Maybe the PTSD thing wasn't an act after all—I don't know," Jennifer says. "I guess what I'm saying is, I sometimes wonder if Ellie might be..." She raises her eyebrows and shrugs, looking away quickly.

Madison knows the word Jennifer isn't saying: *dangerous.* "Then why are you still here?" Madison asks.

Jennifer chuckles, the sound bitter. "Because, even now, I think about going home without graduating and I almost have a panic attack."

Madison gets it, even as the thought chills her: Ellie, dangerous to her students?

"Why didn't you say anything about it before?" Madison asks, but Jennifer makes a little *humpf* noise. "What?"

"Well, if I can be blunt, Mads," Jennifer says, "you and Ellie seem pretty chummy these days. I didn't want to find myself on the receiving end of an extra-harsh Hard Correction, when it inevitably happens, because Ellie thought I'd been bitching about her."

"You thought I'd snitch to Ellie if you told me you were concerned?"

Jennifer shrugs, looking away.

"Why even tell me now, then?" Madison snaps.

"I told you," Jennifer says. "I'm probably leaving."

"That's a little rich, don't you think?" Madison chuckles, her laugh the thinnest of attempts to mask her anger. She's glad her sweaty face is already reddened by the steaming heat of the sauna.

"What?"

"I tell you my fear about getting burned, one that no one knows. Then suddenly the same day we have a Hard Correction all about burning. Quite the coincidence, no? Ellie says you didn't tell her, but I think—"

"I thought it would be good for you," Jennifer says.

Madison's mouth drops. Jennifer's head does too, and she slumps a little, her back against the hot wooden wall.

"You... you were withholding the kind of information Ellie might need to get the most out of you." Jennifer sighs. "And I knew how badly you wanted to do your best. I felt bad. I felt fucking *awful*, Madison, I really am sorry, but I did it because I felt like we were friends, and I wanted to help you. I've felt like shit about it ever since, but I was too scared to come clean. I shouldn't have done it. You're on your own journey here, and I stuck my nose in—"

"Jesus *Christ*, Jennifer," Madison exclaims. "You *did* actually tell her? You know how much I gaslit myself into thinking I was paranoid? Ellie said you didn't, but I didn't believe her."

"You asked *Ellie*?"

"Of course!"

"Well... I mean, why even come here if you're only going to give half the necessary information?" Jennifer snaps, sitting forward, suddenly switching to defense. Already there is a dark ring of sweat on the wooden wall where she'd been leaning. "No, I shouldn't have said anything, but you were setting yourself up to fail. You're supposed to *fully buy in*."

"I haven't bought in?" Madison cries, holding up her bloodied and bandaged hands. "What the hell do you think this is?"

"Half a job," Jennifer says. "You weren't prepared to do what's necessary to break all the way through to the other side." She taps her head. "You know what I'm talking about. Look, I really *am* sorry I told Ellie. It was a mistake. I got swept up in the whole forcing-a-breakthrough thing here and involved myself when I shouldn't. And yes, I have concerns about Ellie too...but I'm still here because I believe in her principles. I've seen—I've felt—glimpses of what she's talking about. You must have too or *you* wouldn't still be here. It's the only reason I'm even considering staying."

"You're changing the subject," Madison spits. And then she suddenly understands. "Oh shit," she says. A bitter smile forms on her face. "Of course."

"Of course what?"

"Why would you be running to Ellie with my business unless—"

"Oh, *nice*," Jennifer says, scowling. "Are you at least gonna do me the courtesy of accusing me properly this time? I knew you were only half joking when you said it in my room."

"I was fully joking! But *now* I'm serious, so yeah, I'll ask straight out: Are you a paid actress? A plant?"

"You're really asking that?"

"Yes."

"Jesus, Madison. If nothing else, how many goddamn actresses are built like me?"

"So why are you even here, then?" Madison cries. "I've wondered that from the start!"

"Same reason as you, I think," Jennifer says. "To be punished."

"What?"

Jennifer leans back against the wooden wall once more. She looks at the ceiling and takes a deep breath before continuing.

"Nine years ago," she says, "I took my last drink and ended up in a drunk-driving accident. I waited at the scene of the crime, and I confessed. The other driver had been drinking too, as it turns out. I survived. He didn't. He was fifty-seven years old. I did five years for manslaughter."

"Jesus, Jennifer."

"I've never *stopped* punishing myself," Jennifer says.

Even through her surprise, the thought is clear in Madison's brain: *Did all that really happen, though, Jennifer?* She blinks, lightheaded as her sense of unreality mingles with the sauna's heat.

"I came here for more of it," Jennifer says, "to see how much further it can take me, because performance is all I have. How do you think I got into this shape? But when I don't trust the person running the show...I don't know." She looks at Madison's slack-jawed face. "And it takes one to know one, Madison."

It also takes a moment for the implication to land.

"I'm not here just for punishment," Madison says.

"Come on," Jennifer says. "No one puts themselves through something like this just for motivation. I don't know what you did, but I think you're really here because you think you deserve it. As long as you're suffering, the voices go quiet for a little while. I know how it works."

As if to confirm, one of those voices, directly from the past, speaks up right now. It's Madison's own:

BECAUSE YOU ARE SO. FUCKING. WEAK.

"Maybe we should both leave," Jennifer says. "Just get on your bike and ride it off into the sunset, right now." She sighs. "But you know what stops *me* from leaving? Even with Ellie being fucking sloppy?"

"What?" Madison asks, her voice quiet. Her heart rate is up. It's *hot* in here.

"The thought that maybe this is the only way to stop being the kind of person who had to come here in the first place. To stop being the kind of person who doesn't have any other choice."

Jennifer looks down again.

Silence.

"I'm staying," Madison says eventually. "I already told Ellie. Elite starts tomorrow."

Jennifer looks into Madison's eyes for a moment, squinting.

"Well, shit," she says. "I can't go home fucking having you one-up me like *that*."

Madison smiles. Jennifer does too.

"Plus," Jennifer adds, "I'd feel a lot more comfortable doing Elite if you're doing it too. Watch each other's backs, that kind of thing. We'll just keep an extra set of eyes on Ellie; not that it's necessarily needed... but that'd make me feel a lot more confident about the whole thing."

"Yeah," Madison says, repelled by her strong instinct to be a *helper* again, knowing she needs to be wary of it, but also intrigued by the offer to *be helped* by someone. By the *right* person for once.

"I really am sorry, Mads," Jennifer says. "Telling Ellie about your phobia was dumb. But I swear, there was no ill intent."

"I believe you," Madison says. "And I forgive you. But listen: No more catty bollocks, okay? We watch out for each other, and if Ellie *is* being sloppy, then fuck yeah, we keep an eye on it. Hell, we help each other through this full stop. Maybe we even help *her* stay focused. She's taken us this far."

Jennifer snorts gently. "'Catty bollocks.' Fucking Brit." She smiles and raises a sweaty fist for a bump.

Madison returns it and feels such a rush of *everything's okay* that her sight seems to waver. Is that a heat haze or something?

Suddenly she is looking *up* at Jennifer, the ceiling of the room *outside* the sauna framing Jennifer's head. There are shockingly cold tiles against Madison's back. She blinks, seeing the painfully bright ceiling lights. They illuminate the clouds of steam behind Jennifer's head, the ones generated by the sauna heat billowing out of the open glass door—

She's outside the sauna now? What happened?

"Madison? Madison?" Jennifer is cooing. "It's okay—you're all right. Don't try to get up. Just rest a second."

That's fine. The air out here is blissfully temperate.

"What happened?" The words are slurred, misshapen in her mouth.

"You fainted," Jennifer says breathily, relieved. "You've only been out for about a minute. I dragged you out here. How do you feel? Look at me."

Madison feels... okay. Sluggish, though. Her mouth is dry.

"I'm okay," she mumbles. "Can I have some water?"

The door opens, and Ellie strides in on a roll of even cooler air from the air-conditioned hallway beyond. She's carrying a small cup.

"I saw it on the security camera," she says. "Good first aid work, Jennifer. Sip this, Madison, but only little sips."

Madison takes the cup as Jennifer slowly helps her upright. "Thanks," she says.

"Get your breath," Ellie says, "then join me in the dojo in one hour for your Hard Correction."

Fear shoots electricity along all four of Madison's limbs.

"You're kidding."

"Thirty minutes in the sauna was the task," Ellie says. "Unfortunately, for reasons outside of your control, I grant you, you failed. I have to be consistent, Madison."

"She *fainted*," Jennifer says. But it's weak, as if she's already given up in her defense.

"I fainted," Madison says. "How is that my fault?"

"It's not a discussion, I'm afraid," Ellie says.

Madison searches Ellie's face for any sign of reluctance—they're *close* now, aren't they?—but there is none. She realizes she was foolish to look.

"Jennifer," Ellie says, "well done for taking immediate action in a potential medical emergency."

Madison stops the petulant words before they leave her mouth: *But Jennifer left the sauna too! This isn't fair!* She immediately feels guilty—they've literally just moved past that kind of shit—and then Ellie makes it worse by seeming to read Madison's mind.

"Falling unconscious," Ellie says, "in the middle of a task means you didn't complete the task. Failure to complete *ends* said task for everyone, as with Frankie, and so..."

Ellie gestures to Jennifer, a motion that makes Jennifer go a little pale. Jennifer looks shocked, not realizing that she could have actually been in for a Hard Correction herself.

Would you have still helped if you'd thought about that? Madison wonders, enraged. This is all such *bullshit*.

"If you want to stay here," Ellie says, "then you have to accept your Correction. These are the rules."

"Elite doesn't start until tomorrow!"

"That's right, and you can leave right now if you don't want to do the Hard Correction. But then you don't get to *do* Elite, when you're *this close* to True Strength, when you've been through what you have." Ellie shakes her head sadly. "That's a tragedy I couldn't even begin to describe."

"This isn't fair, Ellie," Madison tries. "I didn't choose to..."

She trails off, furious but impotent. She didn't complete the thirty minutes, and Ellie doesn't compromise.

Jennifer helps Madison to her feet.

"It's up to you," Ellie says, turning away before pausing halfway to the door. "If you like, we can do today's feedback session before the Correction. Might be good to have everything clear in your mind beforehand."

Madison glances at Jennifer, who shrugs almost imperceptibly. "I have to think," Madison says.

"I'll be in my office if you wish to do a short session," Ellie says. She leaves.

Madison sways on the spot.

Jennifer grabs her. "Easy."

"This isn't fair, Jen!" Madison snaps, fear driving her anger. "I can't help it if I faint! I'm going home! Fucking Elite doesn't start until tomorrow and so Ellie can fuck right off!" *But*, she realizes, *if I leave, Jennifer will go through the rest of the course alone.*

"You don't mean that," Jennifer says calmly. "You're angry. I know you're scared, and it's okay."

"I'm not—" Madison stops. Lying would be pointless.

"If you could reach that other side by yourself," Jennifer says, "you wouldn't be here. Out there, no one's coming to save you. Get through this Correction, and you get to be Elite."

"If I can even make it to the end of the Correction." Madison moans bitterly. But she believes it's possible, and to her surprise, a little thrill is creeping in. Is she becoming a masochist or something?

Either way, whatever the Correction is, the Sunset Ceremony was only a warm-up.

This will be her rite of passage.

Chapter Fourteen: Johnny

A Beautiful Day in the Neighborhood

THE BOGGART'S VOICE speaks so closely that Johnny instinctively throws a panicked swipe with the Swiss Army knife. Another lance of pain pierces Johnny's chest. His phone falls to the mattress as his chest heaves, stinging him at the apex of every breath as he scans the darkened hospital room for the creature. It's speaking *inside* his head, almost as clearly as those words pulled from his memories at the airport.

Thick black liquid is pouring slowly down the wall behind Johnny's bed.

Johnny tries to leap away but finds that he suddenly can't move. He watches helplessly as the liquid impossibly lifts away from the wall, moving horizontally as if pouring over an invisible aqueduct, and moves through the air toward his face.

He clamps down on his scream, able to move his mouth at least, to prevent the liquid from going into his throat. It reaches him, and it's terribly cold and heavy, its weight pulling him down onto the bed, his turned-around face smashing into his pillow as the liquid covers the rest of his body like an icy, clinging weighted blanket from his nightmares. Now he screams into the pillow as the liquid moves down past his waist, his groin, his thighs. The sheer cold of the terrible substance makes him break out in shivering gooseflesh, but the immense weight of it holds him tightly in place. He begins to run out of air as the liquid covers his toes. His chest starts to tighten. Each slowing beat becomes a stabbing knife, far worse than the pains in his wounded chest, and he understands that the Boggart is squeezing *his heart*. His thoughts fade, becoming foggy and difficult to comprehend, but his body pumps adrenaline in its last desperate effort to provide Johnny with whatever he needs to stay alive, and he manages to think the truth: *I didn't take them, that wasn't the deal, they put the morphine in me, I didn't take it—*

The terrible squeezing, at least, stops, even as the cold liquid-lead prison cocoons his entire body. There is a long pause.

And yet, the Boggart coos inside his head, *there is this* painkilling *substance in your body right now,* yes!

But *I didn't take it!*

There is another long pause, and then the unspeakable black liquid oozes off Johnny's body in a wave and dumps itself onto the floor.

Johnny sits up, gasping, clutching at his screaming chest and pressing the pillows against the headboard. He pulls his knees up as the Boggart's long, hairy fingers clamber up and grasp the edge of the mattress. It pulls its enormous goat-eyed, porcupine-quill-teeth-filled head up and out and over the bed, its body re-formed—for Johnny knows that black liquid was the Boggart itself—and rises. It spreads its long limbs across the entire room, pressing its hands and feet against the walls. The Boggart watches Johnny, smiling and saying nothing. Johnny can faintly hear Ivan and Bailey yelling questions over the phone, their tinny voices floating up from the device lying on the mattress. The creature, still grinning, nods slowly toward the phone.

"*Johnny!*" Bailey yells. "*Why are you screaming? What's happening?*"

"It's here," Johnny whispers, his eyes not leaving the Boggart's.

"*What did you say? I can't hear you!*"

"Say goodbye to your friends," the Boggart says quietly.

Bailey's phone gasp is audible in the silence.

"What was that?" she says. "That voice... It's there? It's really there?" She sounds near hysterical.

"Yes," Johnny mutters. This might be the last time he ever speaks to Bailey. "I love—"

The Boggart snaps its fingers. The line goes dead.

"I didn't take any painkillers!" Johnny repeats, desperate. Desperation is all he has. He manages to point a finger at the Boggart. "That wasn't the deal! *They put them in me! I didn't take them!*"

Behind the Boggart's wiry form, Johnny sees the door to his room start to open. Someone Johnny can't quite see pauses in the doorway. They let out a faint, dopey-sounding sigh.

"Leave us, yes," the Boggart says without turning.

The door closes again.

The Boggart lowers its face until it's level with Johnny's. The sweetness of its breath pushes sickeningly against his nose. "Were you trying to run away, Johnny?"

"This isn't right," Johnny says breathlessly, ignoring the question as he argues for his life. "Our deal was that I couldn't take painkillers. *Take*, as in make a *conscious choice to ingest*. These painkillers were administered! After I was attacked by one of your lot!"

"Not by Boggart," it says, but then it cocks its head and sniffs the air, a long, slow inhale. "Hmm," it says. "*Hmm.*" It closes its horrible eyes and hangs in the center of the room. It is silent for several minutes, during which Johnny scans the area again for anything better than the key-ring pen knife.

The goat eyes open.

"Very well," it says. "Your fate will be decided by rite of *challenge*, yes."

Challenge? Johnny surmises there is an infinitesimal chance that he could jab the tiny blade into the Boggart's eye. It's probably a less than one percent chance... and then Johnny remembers the Boggart's claim that it cannot be hurt by anything in this world. *This world.*

"This complication on *your* side," it says, "has meant our agreement must conclude, yes." It grins, gleeful and eager. "I choose *challenge*, at sunset. You must return to the house by then. By then you will have passed this substance, and you must be free of interference, Johnny-Mine. Fail to return by sunset, your life is forfeit, yes."

Johnny's breathing slows a fraction. This isn't a reprieve; it's only a stay of execution. But he thought death was already here.

"Do I need to prepare?" Johnny asks.

"No."

"What is the challenge?" But the Boggart is already backing away, still grinning. "The Shallows, then! Am I already in them?"

"Of course," the Boggart says, chuckling.

"But how the hell did I get here? My friends can't remember anything. I was stoned and probably lost a few hours myself. What happened?"

The Boggart continues its dark laughter as its body begins to expand, its eyes and mouth running together as it turns back into its liquid form. "How you arrived in your Shallows," it says, "as flawed as they are, is of no concern to me." It sniffs again, even though it has no nose that Johnny can see, and its features are now melting into tar. "Yes... very flawed. You have seen the cracks, no doubt."

The bollocks talkers. The empty-then-full houses. Yes, Johnny has seen the cracks, as if the Shallows haven't been properly constructed...

"Wait," he says. "You said *my* Shallows. There are more?"

The Boggart's hairy limbs have retracted back into the body now, the head lowered to the floor and spreading outward, disappearing into the liquid blackness of itself as it pours over the linoleum. "Of course," the Boggart says. "Feel for them, if you wish, for they are all around you, yes."

Feel for them? He thinks of the haze rising off him — to where? Rising off to these other Shallows? A memory from the previous, equally insane night returns: He *did* experience a change in perspective, when he had that weird double sight after he managed to mentally latch on to the haze. He remembers half seeing himself from above, a moment forgotten in all the panic and delirium. He looks at the haze now, focuses on it automatically as his mind turns the question over, and then he suddenly has the knack of it and is seeing —

— *seeing himself again from above, sitting in his hospital bed —*

Then that fucking glitch in his brain happens once more, jarring his mind and stealing his focus, and he's back in his own head, gasping.

"Jesus!" he cries. That was his Shallows, not elsewhere, but the sensation was still uncanny, and he was right: The haze *is* a beacon. No, he didn't see the other Shallows, but what he *did* see was the information the haze was sending, like looking at some kind of all-natural security-camera footage.

"The haze," he whispers, amazed. "It *is* a broadcast. It's...sending out what I'm doing."

The disappearing Boggart's laughter sounds as if it were coming from far away.

"Your *adenterrach*?" it says. "Of course. Same as for anyone who comes here looking for their answers, yes. You are not even a little *special,* Johnny-Mine. So many people come to the Shallows, leading their little parties here."

I didn't come here looking for answers, Johnny wants to say. *I didn't mean to come here at all.* He realizes he assumed the haze exists because he's under a deal with the Boggart...but he wasn't *told* this was the case. Yes, he might be announcing his presence to the monstrous world, but that doesn't mean the haze is doing the announcing. A transmission, yes...but not necessarily for the monsters?

"A broadcast...beaming out to where?"

"Into the universe, you simple child," the Boggart says, its voice dripping with scorn. "And received. Used. Your kind do so love your frightening *stories,* yes, your precious *books.* Where do you think they come from, Johnny-Mine, if not the Shallows...and the places below it?"

Stories come from the Shallows, Johnny thinks, amazed. *My actions, my story here, beamed out into the mind of someone else, and used. Can that be true? Can someone be seeing this conversation in their mind, right now, and thinking it's their imagination, writing it out?*

"Until sunset, Johnny Blake," the Boggart says, "when I shall consume you, yes, and leave no sign of that which you were."

With that, the black liquid flows away in a sudden tide. It pours out beneath the door. In a few seconds, it's gone.

Johnny collapses, barely able to believe that he is still alive. He *is* in the Shallows, then. But one of *many*?

Try to see them again. Maybe you can see someone else's Shallows...

Johnny shifts on the bed, heart hammering, head hot. He tries anyway, tries then to find the knack—

And then there he is again, sitting on the bed below, looking down from the haze itself, a view of himself in the Shallows, his *Shallows*—

That glitch again, and he's back in the bed.

"That's *here*, though!" Johnny cries in frustration, slapping at the mattress. Maybe he can't see the other Shallows, then? He just needs information, any fucking fact; *he just doesn't want to die.* But why would people ever choose to come here, he wonders, if it's so fucking dangerous?

Dangerous. The tiepin!

He leaps out of bed, pushing away the resulting pain in his chest, and shakes out the clothes piled on the chair. A tinny *ping* sounds as the tiepin hits the floor. He snatches it up. Someone put it inside his jeans pocket. Johnny thanks the heavens as he gingerly pulls on his clothes, including the T-shirt with its circle of red dots where unspeakable teeth penetrated his skin. He clips the tiepin back onto the T-shirt's neckline, wondering if he can find some tape to double secure the thing in place...

The thought dawns on him: *Bailey. Ivan.*

He grabs his phone, his hand shaking as he wonders what the hell the Boggart's challenge will be. Whatever it is, the game will surely be rigged. But will it? Their bond, as the monster put it, does seem limited by rules of engagement—

No. Johnny shivers as he remembers how confident and gleeful the Boggart sounded about the challenge. The way it relished the theatrical nature of the words *at sunset.* Johnny fears that whatever this challenge may be, it will be beyond him. *So much so,* he thinks, *that you'd better start working on a plan B. Surely getting out of the Shallows will make a big difference.* But how can he without more information? Where is he supposed to get answers?

He realizes he might know.

He puts the call on speaker while he begins to pull on his jeans.

"Johnny!"

"I'm alive. It's gone."

"Jesus! Thank God!" Bailey starts crying.

Johnny hears Ivan's relieved moan in the background.

"That *voice*," Bailey sobs. "Oh my God, that was horrible. This is real, isn't it? This is *real*."

"It is," Johnny says. "And the Boggart confirmed it. We're in the Shallows."

"But..." Bailey sniffs. Clears her throat. "What *are* they?"

"Some kind of... I don't know, alternate version of..." Johnny stops as he realizes that he nearly said *Coventry*, but he has a sneaky suspicion the Shallows may actually be much, much bigger. He got all the way to the airport. Would he have been able to fly all the way to a Shallows version of Bulgaria if he hadn't had to take off the tiepin at security? Were the Shallows as big as the real world entirely? "I think they're a copy of the real world, and, as fucking mental as that sounds, there's apparently more than this one. A lot more. The Boggart said 'your Shallows,' like we came here and this Shallows was made *for* us. So maybe the Shallows is a place that gets made for you on arrival?"

"But why did we come here at all?" Bailey asks.

"Good question," Johnny says, looking at the bottom of the door. He doesn't think the Boggart is coming back, but even so... "And there's something else: It seems like there's something wrong with this Shallows too. 'Flawed,' the Boggart called it. I've seen the flaws myself."

"Oh my God...," Bailey whispers.

Johnny tries to think of something hopeful. "But if we came here," he says, "that has to mean we can get out."

"How?" Bailey asks.

"I don't know," Johnny says. "Maybe those flaws even mean there are more options to find a way." *Cracks*, he thinks. *That's what the Boggart said*. "Listen, I'm going to take a cab back to the airport to get my car, and then I'm going to drive to you guys. It's probably going to take about an hour and a half. But then..." The time crunch. *Crunch*. The word sends a shiver down Johnny's spine. "I have to find a way to get us all out of here before sunset." He doesn't know if leaving the Shallows will make a difference—whether the Boggart's challenge still stands in the real world, if the *deal* even still stands—but right now, it's all he has.

That, and one lead.

"And to do that," Johnny says, "we have to find Mister Kaleb."

Johnny's predicted hour-and-a-half travel time turned out to be woefully optimistic; the helpless wait for a cab ride back to his car and the subsequent interminable drive to Ivan's house took over two and a half hours. The embraces Johnny received at the end of the journey felt like coming up for air.

Now they sit around the table in Ivan's cozy kitchen, the greetings over, but the room is beginning to feel awkward to Johnny. This is a rarity when in the presence of Ivan and Bailey, but Johnny understands why this moment is different. All of them are avoiding discussing the impossible.

But sundown is in seven hours, and now the impossible must be confronted.

Johnny notices Ivan squinting at the air above Johnny's head. One of the Bosnian's ham-hock hands smothers a mug, and his lined, craggy face—the visage of a man who spends as much time as he can outdoors—today looks particularly world-weary. His posture is more slumped than usual, his cinder-block head sitting lower, his perma-stubbled face haunted.

"I don't see this haze," Ivan says.

Johnny isn't surprised. He's the one who apparently came to the Shallows looking for answers, as the Boggart put it. Leading a little party. He's the broken junkie, not family man Ivan or intelligent Bailey; if he came here for answers, then his friends came as backup, or he fucking dragged them down too, same as always. If his haze emanates from him—if he's the focus of the *story* being beamed from him and *out into the fucking universe*—then it makes some sense that he's the only one who can see it.

He sees the worry in Bailey's face as she considers him.

"I'm okay," he says. "For now, at least."

"I know," she says. "But things lately have been... They haven't been right. If something had happened to you, I wouldn't have forgiven myself."

"Hey," Johnny says, surprised. "Don't say that. Anything that's been going wrong with us is *both* of us, and—let's be honest—mostly me."

"I kept thinking about some of the things I've said to you," Bailey says. "Addiction is a disease. It isn't your fault."

"Bailey," he says, "I've put you through the wringer. It's all right."

"Well..." Bailey chuckles nervously. "Hold on to that loving feeling you have for just *one* minute longer, ah... because we have to tell you something."

Her big eyes, always so expressive, make her anxiety clear.

"Tell me what?" Johnny asks Bailey, who hesitates and looks sheepishly at Ivan. "What?" Johnny repeats. "Is it about Kaleb? I thought you couldn't find him." The initial discussion, while Ivan made coffee for every exhausted member of the group, was of Ivan and Bailey's fruitless efforts to find the old man.

Their one lead is cold.

"We went to the bungalow," Ivan says, "once we gave up looking for Kaleb. Don't blame Bailey; it was my idea. I insisted."

Ivan. Always taking care of business, looking after his own. The man to Johnny's fucking *gelding*.

"What?" Johnny cries. "I told you not to!"

"You did," Ivan says.

Johnny nearly continues the admonishment... but instead shakes his head and pats Ivan heavily on the arm.

"Good lad, Johnny," Ivan says, patting Johnny back. "There you go."

"You said the Boggart promised to stay in the attic," Bailey says. "And you said that thing was all about rules. It didn't eat the cops, and *they* went all the way inside the attic. We're against the clock, so we took a calculated risk."

"What did you expect to find?" Johnny sighs, rubbing at his tired eyes.

"I don't know," Bailey says. "Something you missed in all the madness, perhaps? I mean, we didn't find anything, like, particularly weird, apart from your note and your altar or whatever you said it was."

"Did you touch it?" Johnny asks, his head jerking up. He doesn't know why that feels important, but then he knows he's lost inside the Boggart's world of trip wires and deals.

"We didn't touch anything, man," Ivan says soothingly. "We agreed on that before we even went in."

"We didn't *want* to touch anything," Bailey says darkly. "That whole setup... We didn't like it at all, either of us."

"The note felt bad," Ivan says. "Even though the sentence should feel like a positive thing: 'I WILL GET CLEAN.' Still felt wrong. It looked like it was written in a big hurry. Like you were scared or something."

But Johnny has stopped listening. For the briefest moment, Ivan's kitchen disappeared, yet Johnny could hear a voice — *Ivan's* voice — saying the same thing in another place, another time, setting off a chain reaction in his brain.

I WILL GET CLEAN. Ivan saying it. Where and when? It's fleeting, slippery. Already Johnny is back in Ivan's kitchen, and the memory is fading fast.

"Ivan," Johnny says quickly. "Say that again. I need to hear it."

"The sentence should feel like a positive thing—"

"Not that part. The other part."

"I will get clean?"

Those exact words. Coming from Ivan's mouth. But when? Fucking *when*?

Click.

Ivan. Seated at another table. Sandy and David's table. Talking to Johnny.

"Johnny? What is it?"

It's hazy, but the memory is returning: Ivan across from him. Where was Bailey—

Johnny gasps as the scene floods his mind.

You write "I will get clean," something like this. Something to say to the universe that you will beat this disease—

Johnny stands up so fast from the table and is so lost in the vision that he doesn't hear his chair clatter to the floor behind him, doesn't notice the wound in his chest barking in protest.

But you must write the statement to begin our transition over there, Ivan says in Johnny's memory. *Don't worry. You will be safe in the Shallows if you enter properly and are prepared correctly, and you will be. But you mustn't go into the Shallows alone. I mean, not that you can anyway. You don't know how. But I'll come with you, man. The Shallows, the Deep Place—to enter there without a proper guide, or unprepared... Look, there's no nice way to say it. Monsters can—*

Glitch.

The scene garbles in Johnny's mind, becoming inaudible, invisible; Johnny curses that fucking mental record-skip in his brain as the glitch takes the sight away. He was remembering... *Wait...* There's something else returning, a last whisper of recall, enough for Johnny to catch his own past response:

Should Bailey come too—

Glitch. Now it's fully gone.

"Dammit!" Johnny cries aloud, now completely back in Ivan's kitchen, still standing. "Fucking glitch in my head ruined it. I had a memory of something for a second..."

That is it. Ivan, in his own kitchen right now, triggered some kind of connection to a memory...

Bailey and Ivan are frozen in their chairs, staring up at him.

"Holy shit," Johnny whispers. "Ivan, you were there."

"Where?"

"The note," Johnny says. "The one on the table, the altar, all that bullshit."

Bailey stands. "Hey, you're okay..."

"I remembered something," Johnny says breathlessly. "Ivan, you saying that just now... I think you were the one who brought us here."

"How would I do this?"

"You told me about the Shallows," Johnny says. "You came to the house at some point. I guess it would have to be after Sandy and

David left. And you told me to write the note. You said it was how we would start our transition here. You said you would come with me because it's unsafe to go alone or unprepared, and then I brought Bailey along too."

"*Why* would I do this?"

"You don't remember? Try."

"I've never even heard of the Shallows!" Ivan cries. "How would I know this, man? And what would even be the point if we don't remember anything? Coming to a place where houses are empty, people talking nonsense?"

"Johnny," Bailey says, "you said that the note caused your deal with the Boggart. Now you're saying it's the way we got here?"

"Maybe something went wrong *because of* the note," Johnny muses. "It looked like it was written in a hurry, right? Maybe it was written wrong somehow. Like me or Ivan made a mistake." Mistakes. Flaws. *I've seen the flaws.* "The Boggart said this Shallows is faulty, like it's not fully baked." He begins to pace. "Maybe that's why our memories have been fucked since we got here. So if we try and figure this out..."

"I know nothing about this place, man," Ivan says.

"*Now* you don't, but Sandy and David said you did," Johnny says. "In my memory it sounded like the Shallows was something you're normally familiar with. *Think*. Memories seem to be working very fucking differently here. Maybe we can jog your memory like you just jogged mine. I remember you saying 'the Deep Place'—does that ring a bell?"

Ivan shakes his head, looking down. "I don't know. I wish I did."

"It has to be connected to the Shallows," Johnny says. "The Boggart said there was a place below them..."

An idea strikes him. He snatches the paper towels off Ivan's counter and tears off a sheet. "If the note had something to do with bringing us here..." Johnny starts pulling open the kitchen drawers. "Pen, Ivan, I need a pen." He finds one and writes five words on the paper towel in big black letters:

WE WILL LEAVE THE SHALLOWS

He puts it on Ivan's table. "Do you have any candles?"

"No."

Johnny stares at those words, recalling the ones he wrote on the table at the bungalow: **I WILL GET CLEAN**.

The intention is obvious. If Ivan said to go to the Shallows and Johnny and Bailey agreed, then they all came here for a reason.

"Ivan," Johnny says quietly. "What about objectives? It looks pretty clear that me getting clean was our objective, and that you two came with me as guides or something. You even *talked* about guides, Ivan."

"What if," Bailey says, rubbing her eyes, "getting to this Deep Place *was* the objective?"

"But why would I want to go there if, according to Memory Ivan, that's the place that has something to do with more monsters?" Johnny asks. "And bring my friends into that danger too, while I'm at it?" It didn't make sense; if the method of becoming clean was to enter into a deal with a creature that would consume Johnny if he failed... why would Ivan ever propose *that* as a solution?

"Maybe we're in the Deep Place," Bailey says cautiously. "You said the haze coming out of you rises, right?"

"We can't be in the Deep Place," Johnny says. "If the Boggart is telling the truth — and I think it has to, rules et cetera — then we're in the Shallows."

"But did you check where the haze is coming from?" Ivan asks.

"It's coming from *me*."

"Is it?" Bailey says. "If there's a Deep Place — or rather, a place deeper than this — then maybe that's where it's coming from. Maybe it's being channeled *through* you."

"It's not..." Johnny catches himself. He hasn't checked that. Certainly not by using what he's starting to think of as *the knack*, that subtle trick he used at the hospital to see what his haze was broadcasting. He looked up, perhaps, but not down.

He looks at the floor, feeling nervous. There's nothing there.

Do it, he thinks. *Use the knack. Really look.*

He does.

There's nothing —

No. It's coming up from his feet...

From *beneath* his feet. It's difficult to see, but as he focuses-while-not-focusing upon the glassy, smoky haze, he can see that it is indeed rising from the floor. From *beneath* the floor. He takes a step, feeling as if he is standing in the steam rising from a Manhattan manhole cover. The haze moves with him. He is a conduit. His attention moves lower—

—his chest constricts, his jolted wounds creating pain fresh enough to be felt through the morphine's waning influence, and now he can't breathe as an almost unbearable sense of anguish and despair moves through him, the terrible and unavoidable knowledge that—

"No!" Johnny yells as he glitches once more, involuntarily jerked out of the feed from below. This time it was a blessing, snapping him out of that awful mental prison.

"Johnny!" Bailey says, moving toward him, but Johnny holds up a shaking hand to let her know it's okay. "What did you see?" she asks.

"It's what I *felt*," Johnny whispers. "*Fuck*, Bailey, it was so... *sad*. There was so much pain there. Human pain."

"Did it feel like an exit, though?"

"I don't think so." He now knows this much: He does *not* want to go to the Deep Place. That little glimpse just confirmed it. Whatever the Deep Place is, it won't be pleasant. He understands now why only monsters can exist there. "And the exit *has* to be the note. If it was our way in, then a note somehow has to be the way out. It didn't work with the one I wrote just now, but somehow..."

He notices what's missing.

The glass pyramid, the tea-light holder. The laid-out altar.

"I've got it!" he cries. "Sandy said the bungalow is special. We need to put the new note on the kitchen table where everything's set up properly."

"And what if it doesn't work?" Bailey asks.

"Then we go back to the only other lead we have," Johnny says, wiping his forehead. "We have to somehow find Mister Kaleb and make him talk to us; he was scared, but I think he *wanted* to tell me what he knows. Maybe we can convince him?"

Bailey and Ivan exchange a glance.

"We don't have any better options," Johnny says, "and I'm running out of time. I've got until sunset. *Sunset.*"

"We're with you, John-John," Bailey says.

"He told me he lives around there." Johnny pauses. *Did* Mister Kaleb say that? *Technically, I live on the next street over,* Kaleb said. *I have a place here, but I don't really* live *here.* "We'll look for him again on the way back to the bungalow."

"We looked for his house, Johnny," Ivan says softly. "We really did."

"I know you did," Johnny says. He's thinking about the knack, though. "But I wasn't with you."

"Good point," Bailey says. "There's the two other streets to check again, with you this time, one on either side of the bungalow. Even if we found Kaleb and talked to him, we'd easily be done and back at the bungalow before sunset."

"Right," Johnny says, not verbalizing his fears: the idea of Ivan and Bailey getting attacked by monsters too, maybe ending up in deals of their own. The thought of them being somehow subjected to that terrible feeling he experienced when connecting to whatever lies below—the Deep Place, perhaps. He shivers in the warmth of Ivan's kitchen and looks at his seated, worried-looking friends. He doesn't know what they see in his face, but suddenly the pair stand, move close, and embrace him. Johnny bites back his tears as he holds them as tightly as he can.

"Let's...let's get in the car," he says, coughing a little as he releases them, his chest wounds barking quietly at him. The morphine is wearing off. In a few hours, his chest wounds will really hurt. "One of you had better drive."

When he arrived at Ivan's house, sunset was seven hours away. Now it's a little more than six.

Chapter Fifteen: Madison

If You Know What's Good for You

MADISON ENTERS ELLIE'S office to find her sitting behind her desk. She's come for her short feedback session pre–Hard Correction, as instructed, and she's furious.

"Hi," Ellie says.

"Why aren't we in the usual Consulting Room?" Madison demands.

"This is only going to be a short one," Ellie says, not looking up. "I don't like the idea of doing half a session in the proper room. It's important to keep spaces sacred. This room is for anything."

Ellie's office is pretty much a larger version of the feedback room — same roof beams and thick carpet, same armchairs and paint color. The only difference being the added large desk between the chairs and the window; Madison isn't sure if *sacred space* applies when the spaces are pretty much the same. She notices a picture on Ellie's desk. She wonders who the hell it would be a picture of. *Probably a picture of a squat rack,* Madison's mind spits.

"So why, like, do it at all?"

Ellie raises her eyebrows. "I gave you the choice," she says, as Madison slumps into the chair in front of the desk. "You're angry."

"Yes."

"Happens a lot with you."

"Guess so."

"Angry with me or yourself?"

"Both."

"Okay. Why not first tell me why you're angry with me?" Ellie asks.

"You're kidding, right? You have to ask?"

Ellie shrugs.

Madison sits up and points across the desk. "You're making me do my first Hard Correction when I haven't quit anything."

"All right. And you're angry with yourself because?"

"Because I fucking failed!" Madison snaps. "But Little Miss Military 1996 or whatever wouldn't know what that's like these days."

"Of course I do. I told you about my failure," Ellie says, smiling. "Told you about my biggest failure, in fact."

"Hannah?"

"Yes, Hannah Quimby-Beck."

Madison doesn't know what to say. She is angry, but she now isn't fully sure she's right. She glances at the clock. Ellie said this would be a short session. Now that she's here, Madison finds she wants to run down the time. Better that Ellie talks. "How *did* you find out Hannah killed herself?" Madison asks carefully. "Do you stay in touch with your students after the course?" She has been wanting to know the answer to that for a while.

"I'll tell you," Ellie says, "if you tell me about *your* greatest failure. Fair's fair."

"You first," Madison says, thinking she isn't going to tell Ellie a goddamn thing.

Ellie folds her arms on her desk. "After the program, I keep tabs on all my students whenever possible. I do care, you know."

Madison believes her.

"Hannah dropped off the radar for a long time," Ellie continues. "So long that I got in touch with her family around last June. They told me what she'd done."

"Oh," Madison says. "I didn't realize it was that recent."

"I missed the funeral," Ellie says. "That made it a lot worse."

Silence. Somewhere out in the fields there is the sound of a crow's caw.

"Your turn," Ellie says. When Madison doesn't speak, Ellie says calmly, "We had a deal."

Madison leans back in the chair, tipping her head back and staring at the ceiling.

Fuck it.

"My mother wasn't strong enough to leave us. To actually cut the cord. Much easier to live in denial and keep doing damage." She tracks the swirl patterns in the ceiling with her eyes; the memory is coming through, clear and strong. "She could have left in the right way—minimized the damage to my dad on the way out. But no, that was too difficult. Instead, she just carried on doing what she wanted, because that was what mattered."

She sees it now; the sight of the back patio of her family's modest but middle-class home, seen as a nine-year-old Madison ran back from her friend Beth's house down the street. They were supposed to be going swimming later, and Madison had forgotten her swimsuit. Beth's parents were waiting to leave, so Madison had to be fast...

"And she was sloppy," Madison says in Ellie's office, even as the ceiling has now vanished from view, replaced by the sight of the door into her family's house, the memory of seeing her nine-year-old self's hand as it reached for the door's handle, the sound of her mother's voice on the other side, moving back and forth, as Patricia always paced when on the phone.

"*—stupid little hobby means he's away all week, other side of the bloody country,*" Patricia is saying. "*How far away are you now?... Good. Park next door. They're away. Let me just grab a bag.*"

Madison remembers her breath catching in her throat; she didn't know who her mother was talking to, but her father was indeed away all week. She'd never heard her mother sound like that—playful, flirtatious. Then the next words drowned out all doubt that this was very, very wrong:

"*Yeah?*" Madison's mother said with a happy laugh. "*Well, that's because I know you cannot wait to fuck me.*"

The nausea that filled Madison's entire body. Her mother's awful, teenage-girl giggle...

"Isn't it just the worst," Madison says, dragging herself back to the present and looking straight at Ellie, "when your mentors are sloppy?" She waits for a response to the barb. Of course no response comes. "My dad found out," Madison says, sniffing and moving on, moving on, as always. "There was a divorce. Nasty and dragged out. Dad got custody, but I'm pretty sure he only fought for it to spite Mum."

"I'm very sorry to hear that," Ellie says. "But those are your parents' failures, not yours."

"True," Madison says, but her face is suddenly hot. Probably from the sauna. "But my mum..." She fumbles for the words.

Her *parents'* failures.

Her brain begins to lock up. She's suddenly torn, wanting to rebuff Ellie's probing efforts to analyze her but snagging on the implication: that what happened later wasn't her fault, an idea Madison has always rejected ever since—

"Uh—"

This should be easy. Bat it away, as always. The idea is nothing new: *her parents' failures.* Is it because Ellie is the one saying it? So what? Because the one person who is the poster child for not accepting excuses is offering her one?

Tears. Oh no. Oh *no.* Exactly what she came here to bleed out of herself.

Ellie waits.

"My...mother...," Madison says, and then her mouth moves silently. It feels as if a concrete block is lodged in her throat. Her rapidly blinking eyes are becoming wet, and her lips are starting to twitch.

No—

Ellie stands as Madison breaks down into full sobs.

"Wait...wait...," Madison says, holding up her hands, but Ellie ignores her, moving around her desk as Madison's memory drags her into the next, most awful part; her mum opening the door, hiking her bag over one shoulder, the eager smile on her face vanishing as she sees her daughter standing before her. Patricia's mouth stiffens, perhaps trying to decide which is the best tack. Did Madison hear the conversation? And nine-year-old Madison waits, the moment stretching her out like a torture rack, and now more than at any other time she *needs* her mother to make this right, to not fail her. Then Patricia's face goes slack. She hefts her bag higher up on her shoulder, still looking at Madison, then closes the door behind her and brushes past her daughter without another word—

Ellie bends to embrace Madison in the chair. She wraps her wiry arms around Madison's shoulders and draws her head against her hard frame. The hug is stiff, as usual, as if Ellie has always been inexperienced at hugging. Madison is too busy trying to stop her whole body from convulsing to care.

"I knew it the moment I met you. I could see it," Ellie whispers. "She failed you. Mine too. Mine too, Madison."

Madison lets out a wail and melts into the awkward, angled mannequin that is Ellie, something uncertain but poisonous pouring out of her. She remains there for several minutes. After a while, her sobs become sniffles, and Madison finds herself struggling to feel anything at all. *What just happened?*

"I think it's time," Ellie says softly in Madison's ear.

Madison nods, not understanding what she is agreeing to. The room feels unreal and Ellie's voice sounds tinny to her ears.

Ellie withdraws to the other side of the desk, returning to her computer as if nothing has happened.

"I have something to finish here. Take a few minutes to calm down, and I'll see you on the squash court."

"Okay," Madison says, wiping her face with her long sleeves. She feels suddenly alone and embarrassed. Numb. Better to leave quickly and regroup.

The Hard Correction.

Yes. Go.

She stands, and as she does, she sees something through the window she didn't notice on the way in.

Sarah's motorbike is still parked outside.

She opens her mouth to speak but then stops.

"*Just get on your bike,*" Jennifer said, "*and ride it off into the sunset, right now.*"

Madison heard it as British slang: "On yer bike, pal," meaning, "Get out of here." But Jennifer isn't British, and Madison now understands that Jennifer meant an actual bike, thinking Sarah's motorbike was Madison's. Madison's car is parked around the side of the building, out of sight since day one. Why is Sarah's bike still here? She's been gone for two weeks.

Madison is suddenly uneasy.

Your emotions are out of control, she tells herself. *You fainted, you had a breakdown, and you're about to be physically punished. Your adrenaline is sky high.*

Her eyes fall onto the tape dispenser on the corner of Ellie's desk. She remembers a trick a friend taught her at university.

Ellie is absorbed by something on her laptop. Before Madison can think, she is standing and quietly palming the roll of tape off the desk, turning as she does so. Her heart pounds with the excitement of the impromptu theft. If she gets found out, she has the perfect excuse: She was freaking out over her first Hard Correction and her judgment was impaired.

"Ellie," Madison says far too loudly, "can we give it another fifteen minutes? I'd like to go and meditate in my room first."

"Yes," Ellie says, furrowing her brow at something onscreen. "I have to gather the equipment first anyway."

"Thanks," Madison says, walking toward the door and trying to ignore the word *equipment* as she focuses on her plan. *This is pointless,* she thinks. *The bike's still there. So what?* It probably *is* pointless, but after listening to the way Sarah talked about that machine, Madison finds it hard to believe she would just leave her whole way of life behind at No Days Off. *Okay then,* Madison thinks as she approaches the doorway. She's trying to find the edge of the tape with her thumbnail. *What do you think is really happening?*

She doesn't know. But she's thought of a way to find out. As she steps into the hallway, the door opening outward, she gives a fake cough to cover the sound of her nail peeling perhaps an inch-long strip of tape. She lifts it carefully and it makes little noise, certainly not as much as Ellie's heavy and rapid typing. She quietly bites the extended tape free and leans back into the room, grasping the door handle. "See you down there, Ellie," she says, closing the door behind her while keeping the latch depressed with her thumb.

"Okay," Ellie murmurs back, continuing to type something.

Madison presses the tape over the latch, holding the handle down as if she's trying to close the door quietly but really hiding the lack of a latching click.

Lightheaded, either from the excitement or from having fainted, Madison scurries down the hall and waits around the corner. Perhaps a minute later, Ellie exits her office and walks toward the dojo, face dark, looking lost in thought.

What the fuck am I doing?

But she's already tiptoeing back to Ellie's office door and turning the handle. *There's no way this has worked.*

It has. The door swings open, the latch still taped down.

Madison darts around Ellie's desk, feeling exhilarated. Then she remembers the Hard Correction and refocuses on the task. The computer is, as expected, locked.

But the landline isn't.

Madison's own phone is still in the digital safe outside; she could use her passcode to access it but the safe will, she knows, alert Ellie when opened. Taking out her phone would also mean instant dismissal from the course. Madison dials Imani's number on Ellie's landline, worried that there might be some kind of passcode to get an outside line. There isn't.

"Hello?"

"Imani," Madison whispers. "I have to be quick, so don't ask any questions."

"I didn't think our next call was until tomorrow," Imani says, sounding worried. "Are you all right?"

"I'm fine," Madison whispers. The door is still open and she's listening for approaching footsteps. "I think Ellie might be trying to pull her biggest mind game yet."

"So why are you trying to spoil it?" Imani asks. "I thought you were massively into all this—"

"*I don't know,*" Madison snaps, "and I just—Ims, I don't like this one. I might want to leave tomorrow." She's panicking, worrying about Ellie coming back. She tells herself to be quick, concise; she considers telling Imani about the Hard Correction but doesn't. "I need to check what happened to another student who supposedly quit. Can you Google something for me?"

"Okay."

Madison realizes she doesn't know Sarah's surname. What is she even expecting to find? She hasn't thought this through.

"Mads?"

"One sec, one sec." No Sarah, then. But her eye falls on the picture on Ellie's desk. It's of two women and is so blurry that Madison barely recognizes Ellie in it. The low definition of the image makes Madison think it was perhaps taken from far away and then digitally zoomed in to make the subjects larger. The way the two women are posing makes Madison think that the original farther-away picture had a grand vista in the background. Ellie is squatting and her companion is sitting on the ground, both women wearing backpacks and running gear and looking happily exhausted. Each has her arms up and her shoulders turned away from the camera as if to say, *Look at this view,* playfully gesturing like game-show beauties displaying the big prize. The other woman is a slim, willowy brunette wearing glasses. Her long, skinny legs make Madison think of a runway model. The ex? Madison wonders. She doesn't think so. There's a good foot or two of space between them. This isn't a couple posing together. These are friends.

No. Not friends. Teacher and student, working one-on-one, and Madison realizes that she does have the full name of another quitter. One whose initials Ellie keeps on the wall downstairs as a reminder. One whose picture she keeps on her desk.

"Imani," Madison says. "Look up 'Hannah Quimby-Beck suicide.'" She wants to know more about this woman. She wants to know more about this whole fucking course.

"Suicide? Okay," Imani says. "Hold on."

Silence down the line. Silence in the hallway. Madison's pulse races.

"Nope," Imani says. "Nothing—wait, hold on. There's a Facebook page for a Hannah Quimby-Beck. That's not a name that's going to bring up a lot of matching results. Yeah, it's a post from... looks like Hannah's mum. She's asking for help finding her daughter. This Hannah killed herself, then?"

"What's the date?" Madison asks.

"September thirteenth, last year."

Ellie said June. That's quite a difference. But mid-September is still close to the end of summer. Maybe Ellie simply misspoke.

A door downstairs makes a noise. Is someone coming this way? She has what she needs.

"Thanks, Ims. I'll talk to you tomorrow."

She hangs up before Imani can reply and dashes around the desk, her excuse for being in there now seeming very thin indeed as she tries to walk out as casually as she can; sneaking out would only make it look worse. She turns left out of the doorway, expecting to see Ellie looking at her in surprise, but no one's there. She makes her way down the hall, and it seems that whomever she heard opening a door downstairs was on their way to somewhere else. Madison tries to slow her breathing as she walks, but her spinning thoughts only keep her adrenaline high:

Why is Sarah's bike still here? And how could Ellie be so wrong about when she spoke to Hannah's family?

And it suddenly strikes Madison that she didn't see Sarah leave. That, in fact, other than Namrah, who went home due to injury, she didn't see any of the quitters actually leave.

Her hands are shaking.

Don't be fucking stupid, she thinks. *What are you thinking? That Ellie did something to them? You're freaking out—and overblowing everything as a result—because...*

Yes. She's freaking the fuck out because she's about to have a Hard Correction. She's trying to find reasons to get out of it, because that's what she always does. What the *old* Madison always did, and she will no longer be that woman. No Days Off showed her that.

Ellie showed her that.

Madison heads to the squash court.

Fifteen minutes later

The squash court. The phone book. The billy club.

Madison pinches her fingers for all she's worth.

Trust in the process, she tells herself. *Trust in the process.*

The words don't quite land. She glances at the observation-room window in the wall to her right, remembering being in there, safe behind the plexiglass, watching Frankie. She sees herself dimly reflected there; her fifteen-pound weight-loss goal achieved and then slightly lost, purely due to her putting on extra muscle mass. Now there is no one in there, no one left except her and Jennifer, her friend now standing against the opposite wall, fidgeting nervously under the court lights in the high ceiling.

"This will be a real Hard Correction," Ellie says, her voice echoing ominously off the court's white walls. "Not like Frankie's. No tricks here." She bends and picks up one of the phone books and the club. "I am going to place this phone book on the top of your head, and then I am going to hit the phone book with this billy club, hard. I am going to do this four times. It will feel as if your spine is being compressed, and you will most likely fall down. You need to get up again after each hit if you wish to remain and progress to Elite. Any questions?"

"No."

The tension in Madison's neck and back is almost unbearable as she waits for Ellie to begin. As frightened as she is, she wants this. Ellie might have lied about Sarah being a plant, but Sarah confessed it, unbidden. Whatever systems Ellie has in place—even if she's made mistakes—*this is working when nothing else in Madison's life has.* This Hard Correction is required to get to Elite, and she wants to be there.

No. She *needs* to be there.

"Ellie," Jennifer says from the other side of the room, "this sounds like an exercise as well as a punishment."

"Perhaps it is," Ellie says, not looking at Jennifer. "But this is what we're doing."

Ellie steps forward, handing Madison something small and rubbery: a mouthguard. Madison places it between her teeth without question. With her foot, Ellie nudges one of the phone books closer to Madison and stands on it. She places the book she's holding on top of Madison's head.

The book feels heavy and dense; Madison glances down at the book under Ellie's feet and sees that it's brand-new, dated this year. *They still make those things?* Madison's mind spins.

This doesn't feel right, a voice inside her says. *Does it?*

It doesn't. But Madison knows she has to believe—in the process, in Ellie, in herself. She has to. She is *this* close to finishing, achieving.

Ellie's eyes are now level with hers. "This will hurt, and you're going to feel it afterward. But it won't be permanent. Last check: Are you ready, *Serena*?"

The name again. Madison pinches her thumb and forefinger together ever more tightly. This time the vision of Serena is distant and dull in her mind. Fear has sent it far from her.

"Yes," she says softly.

Ellie nods, raises the club.

I believe in the process, Madison tells herself, willing it to be undeniable. *I believe in the process—*

Ellie brings her arm down.

WHAM.

The sound is so loud that Madison hears it all through her body.

The room goes dark as her eyes clamp shut, and she hears a second *wham* as her hip collides painfully with the squash court's hard floor. When she opens her eyes, she sees darkness spackled with flickering mosquitoes of white. Then the pain registers. Sharp and cutting, it does indeed shoot all through her spine. She rolls gently for a moment while she tries to breathe. Her wind is gone, and *shit*, the level of pain lodged in her vertebrae and neck is staggering.

She still can't see. She can hear, though.

"Get up."

The words take a second to make any sense, and then light suddenly fills her eyes, and she can see the ceiling again, but the thought of taking another one of those hits is unfathomable. Something else is in the driver's seat now, though, her body rolling onto all fours. She makes a faint croaking sound as the first thin gasps of air get into her lungs, her breath wet around the mouthguard between her jaws.

"Mads?" Jennifer is calling. "Mads, are you okay?"

Madison pushes the floor with her hands, sways unsteadily to her feet. She's up.

Ellie immediately places the phone book back on top of Madison's head and swings the club—

WHAM.

White specks explode in Madison's eyes as she falls once more, and this time the pain seems to erupt from either end of her spine. Her legs have shot out directly in front of her. She has landed on her tailbone on the utterly unforgiving wooden squash court floor, the two impacts colliding in the center of her back. She has retained her air, and now she screams as she rolls onto her back once more, letting out a series of high-pitched wails.

Jennifer would be back up by now—

"Get up."

She can't. She can't do it to herself. This is her limit.

"I can't."

"Ellie." That's Jennifer. "Ellie, I don't think..."

Madison starts to cry. She's failed.

You didn't, she thinks. *This isn't right—*

No! She thinks, *That's the old you talking. The real you made it to* Elite, *dammit. You're so close...*

"*Serena*. Get up."

Madison's Pavlovian response is to pinch her thumb and forefinger together. The image of Serena Williams swims to the surface, somehow clearer now, *working*—

No, she thinks. *I'm doing this. This is a living nightmare, but* I'm *the one getting up*—

With a slow effort, she rolls back onto her hands and knees as the tears run off her nose and onto the hard floor, pooling on the red strip that marks the court's short line.

"Stop," she hears Jennifer say. "Ellie. *Stop*."

Yes, Madison thinks. *Please. Get this to stop. Stop it* for *me, because, God help me, I will keep going*—

"Madison can stop this anytime she wants, Jennifer," Madison hears Ellie say.

Madison stays on all fours, shaking. In a moment, she will stand. In a moment. In a moment.

"Lean into the pain," Ellie says. "Embrace it."

"She won't quit!" Jennifer says, "Ellie! Ellie, this is too much!"

"You didn't need to come here just to be an athlete," Ellie says to Madison, ignoring Jennifer's protests.

Madison sees Ellie's feet step down off the phone book. "You talk about being a Bad Bitch? You're already a Badder Bitch than ninety percent of the basics walking down the street, Serena. You're here to transform, to cross over, and you're holding back."

Madison looks up at Ellie. Sees four Ellies, the far squash court wall behind Ellie's legs seeming far away, the wooden floor stretching out like a field.

"I've been running this course for years," Ellie says. "I know when someone is holding back from reaching their next level. Let it go. Let it all go."

But how the fuck do I do that? Madison thinks deliriously, getting one knee up. The movement makes her feel nauseous. Her spine feels like it is creaking. She manages to focus the four Ellies back into one, sees the floor at her feet, and the idea of lying down and closing her eyes is an irresistible siren song...

Madison seizes the thought in her mental grip as if catching a bullet. She sees it for the seductive lie it is, knowing what broken, rancid, *weak* thing will live forever should she take the brief, illusory respite of the *quit*.

She puts her hand on her raised knee. Pushes. Stands.

She straightens fully upright, and with the knowledge that *she, Madison, is standing upright,* belief floods her body, certainty in her own strength, in her ability to—

No. No, not *quite*. She needs to state it.

She raises her tear-streaked face and her furious fists.

"Give... give me everything you've fucking got," she says.

Ellie's face is filling Madison's vision again, and Madison sees movement in her peripheral vision: Jennifer, stepping forward from her position by the squash court wall, uncertain, perhaps thinking of intervening. Madison raises a hand in Jennifer's direction to stop her and then lowers her head to allow Ellie better access to her skull. She feels the book's weight on top of her head, and Ellie's arm moves—

WHAM.

There's a third heavy, painful thud, and when Madison opens her eyes again, she thinks she might have lost a few seconds. Was she out? Her spine is filled with fire, and there is a sharp pain in one of her ribs. Did she land on her side? The ceiling lights high above blaze in her vision, too bright, sparkling a little, the sight of them stabbing at her head. She realizes that Jennifer is shouting.

"Ellie! Fucking stop this!"

Madison tries to form thoughts. She can't. The room is turning into a blur of color, the red lines marking the various court sections mingling with the light brown of the wood and turning into mud in Madison's sight. All she has left is to pinch her thumb and forefinger together. That's what she's supposed to do, isn't it? But she thinks she might be hurt, and badly. That isn't supposed to happen, is it? She feels a wash of nausea again, heavier this time, and understands that she's moving.

This is the process… the process…

She's rolling over. She's getting up. She's actually getting up.

Her rib squeals. That landing really hurt it. *Why didn't we use the dojo,* she wonders hazily. *It has mats. This floor is so hard.* But then she understands that's exactly why this space was chosen.

"That's it, Serena," Ellie is saying. "One more and we're done."

"Madison!" Jennifer yells. "You're concussed! *Stay on the fucking floor!*"

"Get up."

Madison clumsily stands, wonders where Ellie has gone, then realizes she has to turn. She does so and nearly falls, and now Ellie is striding forward and Madison has time to think, *Come on,* before Jennifer is suddenly in the center of the squash court too, getting between them and grabbing Ellie's arms.

"No!" Jennifer yells, pushing Ellie back. "She's hurt, really hurt!"

"Let go of me, Jennifer," Ellie says. "You're interfering with Madison's journey."

Her voice is calm, but Madison thinks she hears something frightening and familiar in it now, shooting through every word. Familiar how? Then she has it: This is whatever has been behind that occasional break in Ellie's voice, that *edge,* now brought to the fore.

Madison's fear escalates, but not for herself. For Jennifer.

Jennifer takes a deep breath.

"I can't let you do this, Ellie. This is too much. What's happened to you? This isn't what we—"

"Jennifer—" Ellie interrupts, but then stops herself. Her shoulders straighten. Her voice becomes normal again—or whatever passes for normal with Ellie. "Jennifer, I have to ask you one more time to let go of me."

"Just *listen*—"

"Are you refusing to let go?"

"What? Yes! She's hurt!"

"You're at Elite now," Ellie says, and that edge is back. Madison can hear it, monstrous and deadly. "You understand that things are different."

Ellie suddenly moves like liquid, and her arms are free. She's shrugging Jennifer off and slipping past her, but as Jennifer ducks and tries to grasp Ellie around the waist, Ellie's flailing elbow catches her above the eye. Jennifer staggers back, letting out a guttural grunt.

"*Fuck!*"

No, Madison thinks. She's seen how the unrelenting grind of the course has stretched Jennifer's patience, but Ellie is moving past Jennifer already, focused on Madison.

Jennifer moves in again and grabs Ellie from behind, this time wrapping her arms around Ellie's waist. "Leave her alone!" Jennifer barks, but it's like trying to hold an anaconda as Ellie maneuvers in Jennifer's arms, her face still terrifyingly placid. "Just fucking stop!" Jennifer cries, and now *she* sounds frightened as she realizes she can't keep hold of Ellie. In desperation, she turns her grasp into a bear hug and lifts Ellie off the floor.

Madison tries to take a step toward the pair to stop them both, but her balance goes and her knees give way. Her hands slap onto the wooden floor, breaking her fall before her head hits the merciless deck. She hazily watches the chaos unfold in front of her.

"Absolute last warning, Jennifer," Ellie grunts, not from anger but from effort. She now sounds more clinical than ever. "Let me go. We are at Elite, and I cannot allow anyone to prevent me from doing my work—"

"Just stop this and we'll talk—"

"I asked you three times," Ellie says, before her foot kicks down into Jennifer's knee.

Jennifer cries out, and the pair of them fall, landing awkwardly, but Ellie is already wrapping her arms around one of Jennifer's.

Jennifer stiffens. "Get off!" she screams.

Ellie is finally breathing hard as she begins to do something to Jennifer's arm. It looks like her forehead might have been cut—no, Jennifer's eyebrow was split by Ellie's elbow. That's Jennifer's blood on Ellie.

"Get off!" Jennifer repeats, and now there is raw panic in her voice.

She scoops up Ellie's smaller body and gets to her knees in one powerful but unsteady swaying motion, Ellie still locked on to her arm. Jennifer drops them both back to the floor. Ellie's spine slams against the wood with a dull crack, and Madison hears the air rush out of Ellie's body in a gasped *howuk*, but the smaller woman doesn't let go.

The sound penetrates Madison's stunned mind; that fall could have broken Ellie's back. Madison stumbles forward to intervene as the room pitches sideways, throwing her off-balance. Jennifer looks like she could kill Ellie; her eyes are wild and crazy with the tension and madness and pain of three nonstop weeks spent at her physical and mental limits. Ellie is still trying to do whatever she's doing to Jennifer's one arm with both of hers. Some kind of lock? Her expression looks icily calm compared to Jennifer's hysteria.

"Jennifer!" Madison yells, and now the room tilts the other way, and she can't find the body mechanics she needs to rise. She looks up, helpless, only to see Jennifer's back arch sharply as she lets out a bellow of pain. Ellie is still clinging to Jennifer's arm like a sloth.

"Okay," Ellie gasps. Her hands finally find purchase on Jennifer's biceps. "I'm sorry, Jennifer. *Breathe.*"

She leans back, torquing Jennifer's arm.

Jennifer's eyes look as if they are about to burst from her head, suddenly all too lucid.

"*Stop!*" Jennifer screams, and now there is unbridled terror in the word as it reverberates like a damning chorus off the squash court walls. "*Stop! I DON'T CONSENT! I DON'T CONSENT—*"

There's a horrible dull *pop*, and Jennifer's arm moves in a way it shouldn't. Madison's already nauseous stomach turns over as Jennifer's screams rise from a full-throated bellow to the high-pitched squeal of an injured dog, clutching at her now dislocated shoulder. Her face is gray, her eyes bulging with uncomprehending shock as she tries to take in everything that this injury means.

Madison sees it with her: the pain, the time to heal, if it will heal correctly at all. But her first thought is not about any of these things.

Her first thought is: *I need Jennifer and now she won't be able to finish the course.*

"I'm sorry," Ellie says, her chest heaving. She still hasn't released Jennifer's arm. "But this is a Hard Correction. It's sacred. *Sacred*—"

Jennifer's free arm becomes a blur. Her hand finds the dropped billy club and snatches it off the floor. The swing is wild, a screaming, desperate Jennifer acting in instinctive self-defense, but the club manages to connect perfectly with Ellie's skull.

The *crack* rings out across the room as the skin on Ellie's forehead splits.

Ellie's eyes flash open, wide and staring as her voice is stunned into silence, but her grip doesn't loosen. Jennifer screams and swings the club again, and this time Ellie tries to turn her head away, but it isn't enough. The club collides with her other temple. Does Jennifer know she's hitting Ellie in the head? This blow doesn't draw blood, but almost immediately a lump begins to rise on Ellie's skull. It's all happening so suddenly.

"Jeh," Ellie gasps, her voice slurred, the words a mumbled mess. "Stop, Jeh, stop."

The club connects one more time, the hardest yet, and now Ellie screams—*Ellie* screams—and lets go of Jennifer's arm. She scrabbles up and around and on top of her.

No, Madison thinks. *You shouldn't have clubbed her, Jennifer, not now. Something's wrong.* She catches a glimpse of Ellie's wild eyes, looking as if they are no longer seeing what is in front of her. Blood pours from her eyebrow down her cheek. Whatever was in Ellie's voice is now clear in every stiffened muscle in her body, her face, her lips pulling back from her teeth.

"*Aaah!*" Jennifer screeches, trying to fend Ellie off with one good arm, but the cry is cut off as Ellie, looking like an asylum escapee, drives her elbow into Jennifer's temple, the strike smacking the back of Jennifer's skull against the solid wood floor. The larger woman gasps out an *ufff* of air, her defending arm now falling limp, but already Ellie is bringing her elbow down again into Jennifer's face.

"No!" Ellie screams, her teeth bared, her eyes bulging white. "No! No! No!"

Jennifer is out after the second blow. Ellie doesn't stop. Jennifer's face is turning purple, and her eye is swelling shut. Her head rocks sharply with each blow, and crimson is now beginning to stain her hair; the horror and violence of the blood and blond mingling makes Madison deliriously wonder, *How can this possibly be?* remembering Jennifer waving that same blond hair at Ellie a few days ago and saying, *"So by week three everyone's fucking roots start to come through, right? Not just me,"* and Ellie laughing, civil, pleasant...

How the fuck did we get to this—

"Ellie!" Madison yells, willing her body to come back online, desperate to save her friend. She rises but falls painfully again as Ellie drops two more heavy elbows.

"*No! No! No! No!*"

Ellie's bloody face shows no trace of the calm self-control Madison knows too well; Ellie has become something else. Madison manages to get her limbs to limp-scramble toward the two women, a flopping stop-start motion that is as frustrating as it is slow. The right side of Jennifer's face is swelling, becoming unrecognizable. Just as Madison reaches Ellie, reaches *for* Ellie, the older woman finally stops. She sits astride Jennifer, breathing heavily, looking down at her with increasing confusion.

"Call an ambulance!" Madison screams. "Ellie, you...Oh my God..."

Jennifer isn't breathing.

"Ellie...Oh my God. Ellie, I think...I think you..."

Ellie looks around, her swelling face now a bloody mask.

"Mad'sn?" Ellie says, blinking rapidly and beginning to sit up. "Mad'sn?"

Ellie gets off Jennifer, and Madison drags herself over to her friend, calling her name. She places her hands on Jennifer's still chest, prepares to administer mouth-to-mouth, but a movement catches her eye. She turns to see Ellie standing beside her again, swaying and blinking and holding the phone book.

Oh God, Madison thinks. *I should have left. I should have gone home.*
She feels herself recoil at the idea, even now.
But I'm Elite...
Ellie's chest heaves. She blinks away the blood running into her eyes; she smears it across her brow with her forearm but still looks uncertain as to where she is.

"Serena," she says.

"Ellie," Madison gasps. She weakly begins to compress Jennifer's chest. Jennifer's body doesn't respond even a little. "Oh, Ellie...I think...she's—"

"She's just...'sleep." Ellie frowns, hearing herself.

Madison sees that Ellie is now bleeding from one of her ears.

"She isn't!"

Ellie frowns again and responds by placing the phone book on top of Madison's head.

Madison jerks back to get away, the movement bringing a jolt of pain and dancing light. Ellie's hand follows anyway. Madison wants to be away, anywhere. *Please, God, let me get out of—*

WHAM.

Madison's world disappears into a single thought: *I haven't even crossed over—*

Then she's out.

Chapter Sixteen: Johnny

Welcome to the Dream Lounge

"DOESN'T IT SEEM a little later in the day to you than it should?" Bailey asks. She shifts nervously from foot to foot.

Johnny, Bailey, and Ivan approach the end of the pleasant, urbane street, the first of the two they plan to check. The houses here are ordinary, almost identical to those on the road with Johnny's rental. Johnny's presence — and his use of the knack, his mental side-eye that lets him see what his haze is broadcasting — has made no difference. After knocking on every door and meeting several residents Johnny believes didn't exist the night before, Kaleb has not been found. Johnny didn't fully expect his plan to work. How could he when he barely understands how he uses the knack himself? He's felt nothing at every house. "The sun's, like, lower than it should be already," Bailey says. "Or is it just me?"

Johnny agrees but doesn't say anything. He's been thinking the same thing for a while himself. Time *does* seem to be going too quickly. He didn't leave the hospital that long ago, but already it's past three. Sunset is in less than four hours, yet it was six hours away when they set off to find Kaleb. It surely doesn't feel right. Does time work differently in the Shallows?

"This Kaleb," Bailey says. "He sounds like a Puck."

"A what?"

"Didn't you ever do *A Midsummer Night's Dream* in school?" Bailey says. "Puck's like a mischief-maker." Bailey has become a lot more chatty over the last thirty minutes, Johnny notices. A sure sign, for her, that's she's scared.

"Listen," Johnny says, squeezing Bailey's hand. "I think the Shallows are safe for you both. I was attacked, but I'm involved with the Boggart. It said I would stand out to other...beings, I guess, once I was in a deal. I think you two are okay, so I don't want you to worry about that." He means it, but he's still worried about himself. He can't stop trembling. Time is slipping relentlessly away, and his chest is starting to hurt.

"But we're involved with *you*, Johnny," Bailey says. "So I'm not sure if we're safe at all. And how come the only way into the Shallows seems to be making a deal with the Boggart? I mean, if you came here only to try to get *away* from here, then...what's the point of coming here?"

They're approaching the final four houses, the car parked farther up the street behind them.

"Maybe coming to the Shallows *isn't* the point," Ivan says. "Maybe that's just the first part. Maybe we are really supposed to go to the Deep Place."

"Maybe the Boggart hijacked your note," Bailey mutters.

"How so?" Johnny says, peering at the next house and trying the knack. Nothing. They'll go and knock on the door, but he doesn't expect to get a different result than Ivan and Bailey did.

"Maybe it interpreted it," Ivan says. "Like the note—your *intention*, if we're saying that—sailed out into the universe, but the Boggart 'helpfully obliges' and 'answers' it early, saying, *Okay, intention accepted. You make the change happen or I'll eat you.*"

"No, no," Johnny says. "We made a deal."

"That's my point," Bailey says. "Was the note your deal, or did the Boggart just tell you it was and *then* you agreed with it?"

"Why would I do that?" Johnny asks, looking at the house next door as he heads for the driveway of this one. He uses the knack on it almost absentmindedly as he considers Bailey's idea. "I'm not a—"

He stops walking so suddenly that his chest screams at him almost as loudly as Ivan and Bailey scream.

"Oh my God, Johnny!" Bailey yells. "Do you see that?"

Johnny does, and he is surprised, but not as amazed as his friends. Johnny has now seen more incredible things than this.

An enormous house now stands nearby.

The houses on either side of it are shunted farther apart to make space for it. Number 113.

Then it vanishes, its neighbors instantly snapping back together.

"What did you do?" Ivan begins.

"Hold on," Johnny replies. In his surprise, he stopped using the knack. It's hard to get the vision back, but he manages it. Using the knack is a subtle art, it seems, and not one with which he has had much practice. One moment they are staring at two houses, the next they are staring at three. It suddenly makes sense.

The house is hidden.

"Let's hope he's home," Johnny mutters. "You two stay here."

"Of course not," Bailey hisses. "You don't have the bloody time for your 'I have to fix my own shit' bullshit."

"No way...," Johnny begins, but Bailey steps in front of him, her eyes furious, a look Johnny has seen too many times in recent months...but then she softens, looking as if doing so took great willpower.

"Let's all go together," she says. "Please?"

"Together, Johnny," Ivan says solemnly. "No such thing as—"

"A self-made man," Johnny finishes. "I know." He touches his chest, recalling his usual response to Ivan's favorite phrase: *But no one is coming to save you.*

He doesn't have the time to argue.

They head for Kaleb's house.

It stands before them three stories high. Black wooden beams crisscross its white outer walls. It is clean, the thatched roof looking as if it was only recently laid. The windows are incongruous with the building's period style—Johnny doesn't know enough history to place it; it might be Edwardian or Tudor. Each is made of bright and incredibly ornate stained glass, which would work perhaps if the images contained religious iconography. One is of a Black man holding a microphone—it takes Johnny a moment to recognize that it's James Brown. Another shows an image Johnny knows only from the clip played every time England's sporting history is mentioned on TV: Bobby Moore lifting the 1966 World Cup.

The overall effect is that somebody wanted to make the house *look* old without paying attention to detail. It feels like a house in the Olde Worlde section of some insane theme park. Johnny can't see the lower floors behind the six-foot-high pine fence that surrounds the yard. In the middle of the fence is a gate set with swirling iron detailing.

It all blinks out of sight as they approach. They freeze. It returns, leaves again. Johnny realizes that the flickering is speeding up the closer they get. It feels like the air should be moving, or there should be sound, with such a large, solid structure snapping in and out of existence as the houses on either side hop outward to make way and snap back in to pretend it was never there. Instead there is only silence, as if reality is perfectly happy with either configuration. He listens to his body for a moment. His heart is racing.

"Hold on a second." He closes his eyes and tries to slow his breathing. After a full minute, he opens his eyes once more. The house's presence is steady, at least for now. "Okay," he says. They approach the gate, but as Johnny reaches for its handle, it suddenly vanishes once more along with the rest of the house. He snaps his hand back to his chest, wondering what would have happened had he been holding the gate as it disappeared.

"Breathe, Johnny," Bailey says, her own breath hitching. "Try to relax again. You have time."

"That's what I don't have," Johnny says, trembling with frustration. Using the knack to keep the house in place is like mentally trying to grasp the world's slipperiest bar of soap.

The gate appears in front of him again. Johnny's hand shoots out and grabs the handle, and his entire body tenses as he expects it to disappear before he can turn it, but it doesn't.

"Do you have it?" Bailey asks.

Suddenly Johnny realizes he might be able to keep his friends safely on the outside after all. He twists his wrist and pushes forward so hard, so fast, that he dives past the gate and lets go of the handle.

He hears Bailey and Ivan gasp in surprise before their shouts are cut off.

He trips over his own feet and lands sprawling on some concrete. The pain in his chest explodes. He rolls on the ground, groaning, waiting for the knives in his pectoral muscles to withdraw and wishing to God that he had some—

No. Anything but that.

He opens his eyes to discover that the gate is gone. That's good. Whatever his friends might say, this part, this risk, this *cross* is his to bear. He's the one who dragged them into the Shallows; he has to be the one to fix it. He closes his eyes for a moment as his chest pain recedes. Even with his limited time, God, he can wait for that.

Eventually Johnny sits up, moaning, and sees that the garden path upon which he is sitting still leads to the open gate, but the street beyond has disappeared. In its place is an impossible view. Green hills rise high above an open valley. A distant river winds its way across it, and immense white clouds float across a blue sky.

The sun seems a little low for the time of day there too.

Johnny struggles to his feet, amazed. The glitching isn't happening on this side. He turns toward the house, lying at the end of a short expanse of unnaturally green grass crammed with large topiaries. At the front door, one foot on the step as if he was caught reentering the house, stands Mister Kaleb. He has one hand raised to shield his eyes, casting his face in shadow.

He is dressed in, to Johnny's surprise—it would also be to his amusement if the circumstances were different—a Hugh Hefner–style bathrobe. The hat is gone, revealing a thick thatch of silver hair remarkable for a man of Kaleb's advanced years. More unusual are Kaleb's feet. They are made of polished wood, intricately carved, remarkably lifelike. The robe covers him from the knees up.

Kaleb straightens, as if summoning his composure. He drops his hand, and now Johnny can see his face. The old man is grinning. "Oh," he says. "Hello."

Johnny stares, his chest still afire.

Kaleb sighs. "I had actually decided I was going to come see you, but... well, it'll soon be time for me to go inside, so if you want to talk, you'd better come with me."

"Time for you to go inside?" Johnny asks.

Kaleb shrugs sadly and points to the far corner of the garden. Johnny looks. The grass there is covered by shadow, the sun's rays blocked by the high fence, creating a corner of darkness.

The grass inside it is bulging up in several places.

It looks as if nine or ten enormous moles have been trying to push through. As Johnny watches, the top of a familiar-looking head breaks through the soil.

A bald, red scalp covered in burnt-looking blisters begins to emerge. Johnny knows, if he waits, the face that follows will be crumbling into a churning, turning whirlpool of sand.

Johnny's breath catches and his skin feels as if it has been doused with ice water. He falls back a few steps, his hand moving to his injured chest as he feels again the pain of those unseen razor teeth sinking into it, remembering the agonizing tug deep in his pectoral muscle as a monster of this kind tried to eat his flesh from his bones. Another unspeakable head breaks through the soil. A third pokes its crumbling way out of the ground. Johnny's own head spins from the emerging creatures to Kaleb in the doorway, waiting for the old man's response. Kaleb just watches, his face almost sad. Johnny waits. None of the Needle Monsters fully emerge; the tops of their skulls sit just inches above the surface, nestled between the moving bulges all around them. After a few moments, Johnny's breathing slows, even as he watches them closely, still expecting them to explode free at any moment, imagining their crimson, painful-looking cratered bodies clawing and galloping across the garden toward him—

"They're only in that shadow," Johnny says, breaking himself free of the thought. "Are they waiting for nighttime? For full dark?"

"Come inside," Kaleb says. "I'll explain."

"But the Boggart said they live in the Deep Place," Johnny says, watching the Needle Monsters as he walks toward the house. He flinches as a fourth head breaks the surface. "What are they doing here?" He remembers the tiepin still clipped to his shirt and forces his breathing to slow.

"Come inside," Kaleb repeats.

"My friends are outside," Johnny says. "Are they safer here or where they are?"

"Friends?" Kaleb asks. "So you *do* have an entourage. I thought so. They'll be safer where they are, for now. I'm not sure it would be a good idea for them to come here." He sighs again, looking toward the emerging creatures. "Not if you want to leave here once the shadows are longer, and certainly not after sunset. Getting across the garden would be extremely dangerous. I'll have to meet them another day. Unless your friends have something similar to that." He points at the tiepin.

"Will they be safe from the Boggart?" Johnny asks.

"Should be," he says, his voice low. "A Boggart will make its presence felt around here every now and then, but there *is* only ever one per territory, and according to you, its deal is with you alone. As you've seen, I... *avoid* them for the most part, unless I have to negotiate for something." He gestures toward the shade again. "I've had a lot of practice."

"So you *have* met the Boggart, then?" Johnny asks.

"Several," Kaleb says, his voice suddenly grim. He nods at his wooden legs. "In fact, these are the result of a harsh but successful negotiation with such a creature. Unique circumstances. And a long time ago. A once-in-a-lifetime chance, I'm afraid. They'd never allow it again. Sorry. But I actually used to be a lot taller. Giving me shorter legs is their idea of a joke." He chuckles bitterly. "But I'm alive to tell the tale. That's the main thing."

"I need to get out of the Shallows, Mister Kaleb," Johnny says. "I tried to catch a flight out, but..."

Kaleb is shaking his head, looking almost amused. "Waterton

may be closer to the Shallows than most places, but once you are *in* your Shallows, they are *everywhere*. You can't get out by a boat or a plane or presumably a spaceship. When you enter the Shallows, you enter *your* Shallows. Wherever you go, you are inside them."

"But..." Johnny nearly doesn't ask the question, time being so precious, but curiosity, ever the enemy, prevails. "*Why the fuck do people come here,*" he snaps, "if it's so dangerous?"

Kaleb blinks. "You mean you don't know?"

"No!"

"Hmm. That's surprising. I thought you knew. You don't remember why you came here?"

"This is why I'm asking *you*, Mister Kaleb. Something went wrong, we think. My friends and I, my *entourage*...we can't remember a lot of stuff."

"Oh. You probably didn't come here in the best way, then. Okay." He nods at the gate. "Close that, please. Important. If you want to talk, it has to be inside. I need to shut up shop *right now*. Come on." Kaleb steps back without another word and gestures toward the doorway.

Johnny glances at the open gate, torn, and then runs to close it before sprinting back to the house. He feels guilty, but Ivan and Bailey know where he went, what he is doing. Hopefully they will just wait in the car. Kaleb holds the door for Johnny, casting repeated glances around the doorframe to that horrible, undulating darkness in the corner of the garden.

Johnny takes one last look there himself. "They come here *from* the Deep Place?" he asks.

"Yes," Kaleb says. "There are many such monsters waiting down there. Don't be surprised by its existence, Johnny. Deep down—ironically—humans have always known the Deep Place is there, even if we don't admit it. The knowledge of its existence has been buried in us since our kind first lit a fire against the dark." They step over the threshold and Kaleb shuts the door, locking it in three places.

As he does, Johnny takes in the incredible front hallway. Front *foyer* would be a more accurate term. It is enormous, the size of a ballroom. A grand central staircase curves in from the upper floor, its handrail a dark, shiny mahogany. Enormous oil paintings hang on the walls depicting various scenes: a mountain sunset, a grand cityscape at rush hour. The breathtaking size of this interior is utterly impossible given the dimensions of the building outside.

"Shoes, please," Kaleb says. "Sorry to ask."

Johnny kicks off his Nikes.

"Sorry for keeping the place hidden," Mister Kaleb says. "I really did need to think, and I didn't want you to stumble across the house until I'd decided. I hope you don't mind. This place seems to turn up in everyone's Shallows, in one form or another." Kaleb sounds as if he's changing the subject. He still looks nervous, even inside this supposed sanctuary. "I don't know if it's the unique nature of the place. I'm not exactly seeking out the Boggart to ask. An *unintentional nexus*—that's the best way I can think to... Sorry, I'm spiraling a little. This whole thing is... well." He claps his hands and looks awkwardly around himself—anywhere but at Johnny. "The last conversation I was expecting to have, frankly. I had to be sure of what I wanted to say. I just wanted to be certain you were here when I came out earlier."

"You made all this?" Johnny asks, looking around in wonder not at the opulence but at the skill required to create it. He can barely use the knack to see hidden things, but Kaleb is using it to make—and hide—entire buildings.

"Yes. I've mastered my intention to a great degree, but then I've been here a very long time. Must be getting on two decades, I think."

"Intention? Like willpower?"

"I suppose so, yes. Exercised in the right way, following the right procedures."

Johnny thinks of the note on his kitchen table. "Procedures like... spells?"

"Yes and no," Kaleb says, mulling it over. "It's not as if there's a set of instructions. I've had to just pick up stuff here and there, but I've picked up a lot. The intention is the most important thing. *Then* comes the way you express it. But it's not like in the movies where there's an incantation or specific words. It is the *force* of the intent that matters." He shakes his head and holds out a palm. "I'm not explaining it very well. Give me your hand. When I know what I'm trying to explain, I can pluck a perfect example from your mind, your memory, that will help illustrate it. It'll stand out. I won't need to root around for it. I promise. I call it the Haystack Picker," he says, giving a forced chuckle.

Johnny looks at Kaleb, struck again by the man's small and unusual frame, and then the old, old memory suddenly comes again—

WHAT'S WRONG WITH THAT LITTLE MAN?

Johnny winces. He's thought about that too much in the last twenty-four hours already.

"It's okay," Johnny murmurs, moving on quickly. "I think I get it, and I'm short on time." He wonders how he would describe using the knack. Effort, but not *real* effort. Looking, but trying not to look. "You're real, aren't you, Mister Kaleb? Not a Shallows person. But you don't have the haze," he says, miming something rising off himself with his hands. *Or the* adenterrach, he thinks, *as the Boggart would call it.* Beaming out into the world and carrying the events of his doings in the Shallows, his story. *Hope you're enjoying it if you're seeing all this*, he thinks bitterly. *Whoever you are.*

"I did," Mister Kaleb says. "But my story is over, and my haze is gone. I knew that when I decided to stay here."

"How did you get here?" Johnny asks.

"I'd like to know how *you* got here," Kaleb says, "if you don't remember how. Do you have OCD, anything like that?"

Johnny hesitates before replying. "Yes. Sandy, this lady I met, she said OCD is an attempt to—"

"To *control* the world, Johnny. I have a little OCD myself; it's a big part of the way *I* got here. OCD is trying to shape chaos by imposing your own order on that which has none. In a certain sense, it's logical, even if it's pointless."

"Logical how?"

"People like us," Kaleb says, sounding as if he is choosing his words carefully, "are sensitive to what they consider to be *darker* elements of the world. Elements like, indeed, the Boggart. These people understand, even if they do not know it, that rules and rituals are a way of defending against the darkness, because that darkness *runs on* rules and rituals. These people carry out these rituals subconsciously, automatically. The immense irony is that these rituals are, for the most part, pointless. We're already protected by the nature of our separate planes of existence, at least when we are outside the Shallows. Only the most unfortunate people end up threatened by elements like the Boggart." Kaleb sighs, looking around the foyer. He shakes his head sadly. "All that makes it very easy to wind up in the Shallows. If you're short on time, the full story of how I got here is too long. In a nutshell: I became lost. Very lost. I learned some things I perhaps shouldn't have, didn't understand them fully, and then..." He gestures at their impressive surroundings as if to say, *Here we are.* "To come here not knowing, chaotically—that way is most dangerous by far. To come here ill-prepared or *without a guide coming through with me?* It was bad. Dangerous. I didn't know where I was for a long time. Can you imagine?"

"How do you know all this?"

"I've met a great many people in my years here," Kaleb says. "Picked a lot up. One person even gave me that tiepin, and a lot of good it did me. I also learned a lot during the negotiation that allowed me to make this place. This safe haven." He sounds glad.

"Safe? From the Needle Monsters outside?" Johnny asks. "They can't get in?"

"They can't," Kaleb says. "The outside of the house always looks different depending on whose Shallows are going on around it, but the inside is always a fortress and should stay that way unless—or until—the rules change enough to make my agreement null and void, and any change in the rules apparently takes an extremely long time."

"Have those things been right outside all the time you've lived here?"

"Oh no," Kaleb says earnestly. "They weren't here at all at first. They've been drawing slowly closer over the years. It's only recently that they've worked their way inside the fence. If they ever did somehow make it inside the house..." He mimes putting a gun to his head and pulling the trigger. "Nice and quick. I would have had a good run by that point, that's for sure." He gestures to the stairs. "Let's go up to the Dream Lounge. You need to see it, believe me." He sees the concern on Johnny's face. "You'll love it. And you're safe here."

Johnny knows he is, so much so that, ironically, the feeling of safety is putting him on edge. This isn't just the absence of tension; it's a feeling of *warmth*, as if the shutters have been drawn against the darkness and the fireplace has been lit. The only negative is the pain in his chest now that the morphine is out of his system.

"I have to be back at my house by sunset," Johnny says. "Please, I need information."

Kaleb raises his eyebrows. "Really not long, then. Okay. I had a whole thing lined up, but I'll be brief. I think what I have to say will tell you everything that might benefit you. Fair?"

Johnny takes a deep breath. He doesn't have time for a monologue, but he *does* need to keep Kaleb on track. More than a decade spent alone in this impossible mansion would make anyone long-winded. "Just tell me one thing first," he says. "How do I get out of the Shallows?"

"You don't know that either?" Kaleb asks, surprised. "Oh. That's unexpected. Well, the reason anyone comes here is always the same, Johnny—whether they come here intentionally or by accident—and that reason is also the way out: the Deep Place. It's where the answers always lie. The Shallows are simply the gateway."

"Where the monsters live?"

"Many of them, yes."

"Why would anyone go there?"

Kaleb looks confused. "Johnny, if you enter even the Shallows without a guide—let alone the Deep Place—the monsters will always eventually find you. And the Deep Place is the only exit."

Johnny's hand goes to the tiepin clipped to his T-shirt. He thinks of his guide, Ivan, who can't remember a damn thing.

"Can't I just write another note in front of the same altar?" Johnny asks.

Kaleb scoffs. "Do you think I'd still be here if it were that simple?"

Johnny looks around at Kaleb's finery and understands that it is a golden cage. "Has a human ever survived the Deep Place?" he asks, his voice quiet.

"Oh, of course," Mister Kaleb says. "All the time, in fact."

Johnny breathes out a sigh of relief; Kaleb continues talking and ruins it.

"Those who go in with guides almost always come out intact. You're probably more at risk getting on a plane. But the journey is still extremely unpleasant. It's those *without* guides who rarely come out again. Many of those who manage to return home do so scarred and twisted in such a way that they are unrecognizable and unknowable."

Kaleb tuts. "Actually, we should probably talk about this on the veranda. The Dream Lounge can wait. This way."

Mister Kaleb leads Johnny through a large oak door at the back of the foyer. It opens onto a vast marble terrace that, impossibly, leads onto a deserted beach. There is no sign of the hills and valleys Johnny saw beyond the front gate; here in back, the horizon is all sea.

Kaleb gestures toward a pair of empty loungers. "Let's take a seat."

Johnny does as he's told, listening to the surf rolling in and out and wondering if maybe, just *maybe,* he's dreaming after all.

"I met a traveler once," Kaleb says, sighing again as he settles onto a lounger himself and adjusts his robe. "One of the many, many people passing through, but I'll never forget this one. I leave the house every now and then to take a walk in the daytime. Even for me, being stuck here gets to be a little much. Part of my negotiation was to have two protected nights out each year. I used one of those to come see you the night you arrived, even though the Boggart was an unexpected *interruption.* I'm still not sure about the rules of that, but either way: It was important I see you—"

"Is this important?" Johnny interrupts, trying to stay calm. Time is slipping away, and Kaleb keeps taking tangents.

"The traveler part is," Kaleb says. "He was an old fella, older than me. Wore this brown corduroy suit. Richard, his name was. Said he'd actually come here on purpose. Described himself as 'an escapologist and explorer,' whatever that means. I got the feeling he might have just come for the challenge. I don't know. The man had a lot of answers and wouldn't fully tell me where he got them. I liked him, even if he was a little pompous. I think he said he used to be a lawyer." Kaleb's face becomes serious. "But what he told me about the Deep Place... he was *very* clear about that. Told me *exactly* what it's like. Since then I've learned to *see* what it's like for myself, to see it from here. It took a long while to be able to use my Intention that way, but I have a lot of time on my hands. You've also learned to look beyond a little, haven't you? You must have, to find this place."

"I can see into the Deep Place?" Johnny asks, latching on to the subject he's now most interested in. He's frightened by this news but not surprised; he's already learned to *feel* down into the Deep Place.

"I doubt it, at least so soon," Kaleb says. "It can be learned, though."

"What *does* it look like?"

"Desolate," Kaleb says. "It's different for everyone, but the emotion most felt by the human world is loneliness, and so each version of it is along the same lines, mostly manifesting as..." He pauses for a moment, struggling to find the right words. "Like a desert," he says eventually. "One hundred times wider and more harsh than any found on Earth. It feels like..." Kaleb's eyes grow dark, and when he speaks next his voice has a tone that Johnny has not heard before; more than that, it is as if someone else is speaking at the same time as Kaleb, someone who has been into that terrible land. "Imagine a cold, mournful, vast place," Kaleb says, "where a barbaric and haunting battle once occurred, one that claimed all lives and was so full of unspeakable deeds and pain that it tainted the landscape forever, a poison that bled right down into the very bedrock. Nothing can grow there. All withers. And it must be crossed, crossed, crossed, *moved through,* bearing all that is to be experienced there until the end is reached, if one is to be free. If they can withstand it." Kaleb straightens, blinks slowly, and when he speaks again his voice has returned to normal. "It must be moved through, Johnny," he repeats. "Its other name is the Howling Wastelands, you know." He nods to himself, his face sad and solemn. "It's always so close to us, here in the Shallows. This place is so very *thin*."

"Then it *is* different for each person? Like the Shallows?"

"Much less so than the Shallows, but yes."

"Are there Boggart down there?"

"Goodness, no. The Boggart do not go into the Deep Place. Rules for our protection do not apply there, and if the Boggart were to visit..." Kaleb winces. "The feeding would be a frenzy. There would be open slaughter. The Boggart's sense of fairness will not allow such a thing to happen. There's no sport in that."

"But what's the point of it? The Deep Place?"

"To find what you need, if you can survive it. That's what I was told, anyway. But I decided that I have everything I need right here."

"You don't want to get out?"

Kaleb falls silent for a long time.

"I imagine my sight goes a lot farther than yours, Johnny. I can see only so far into the Deep Place. I don't know if the Howling Wastelands cover all of it or only as far as my vision allows, but they are vast." His hands come up as seems to picture the sheer scale of the Howling Wastelands, perhaps actually seeing them right now. "I often watch them enter, those visitors who go there alone. Once they pass out of my actual sight, I can even track them, like watching someone's location move on a map. They stop for a while. I feel an echo of their pain." Kaleb shudders a little. "And then they start moving again. Then they stop. Start again. Stop. And then their light just...goes out. I feel the Deep Place consume them."

"Always?" Johnny asks, his voice small.

"Rarely—very rarely—they make it all the way across the Howling Wastelands. I do not know what happens in there, but I do know this." He looks Johnny dead in the eye. "It *hurts*. I feel them die. I feel their screams pouring out of there."

"It's truly the only way out?" Johnny asks.

"I'm afraid so."

"Then I need to go there."

Kaleb blinks. "Jesus, *you still want to*? After what I just told you?"

"I don't have a choice."

Kaleb shakes his head. "Bloody *hell*," he mutters. "Well, usually people spend a lot of time here, figure out how to do it—the Shallows normally teaches you at least the bare minimum required—but maybe I can teach you some myself. Save you time." Kaleb seems to consider this for a moment. "Yes," he says, standing up suddenly. "You need to have both options for this to be fair."

"Both options?"

"One thing at a time," Kaleb says, looking out over the beautiful sea. "If I teach you now, you have to promise to come into the Dream Lounge afterward. Just to see it before you decide to go. Deal?" Kaleb hears the word and dismisses it with his hand. "You know what I mean.'"

Johnny sighs. "I don't think I have a choice."

"Stand up," Kaleb says. Johnny does. "Okay. I want you to look beyond, but look *down* when you do it."

"No," Johnny says quickly. "I did that. It was—"

"Awful, I'm sure," Kaleb says. "But that means you're doing it wrong. It's like meditation, when you have your thoughts but let them pass, don't connect with them. Same with this. You don't have to feel anyone else's emotion, whoever's story *down there* is sending up those vibes. That's theirs, not yours."

Kaleb gestures at the ground with a hand. Reluctantly, Johnny looks down and tries the knack.

—*help*—

He mentally recoils.

"It isn't your pain, Johnny," Kaleb says. "Know that and move past it."

Johnny tries again, prepared this time, and when the anguish tries to move into him, he mentally sidesteps. Suddenly he is in contact with it but outside it, like a passive observer. It's still a balancing act, though, as if whatever is washing out of the Deep Place is trying to pull him in, like a tide drawn to the moon. He feels a state of both relaxation and high tension, maintaining a simultaneous awareness and empty mind.

"Good, good," Kaleb says. "Now: the doorway. You may find it useful to picture it as a hole in the — Ah, there you are."

A tearing sound is already filling the air; Johnny has turned back to look at the marble terrace where a hole now begins to shred itself open in the carefully laid floor. The noise is awful, as if someone is running a hair dryer through a distortion pedal and dialing the whole thing up to 11. The slabs stretch apart in thin strands of reality that crisscross the yawning gap like spiderwebs before finally breaking and snapping back to their original edges. Only blackness lies beneath, but something blooms at its center. A grayness.

It looks like drops of faintly glowing liquid — if gray can glow — thrown into a bucket of black water. Johnny watches it spread, utterly present, simply being and letting what he has put into place bear fruit.

He blinks. Something changes.

He's *glitched*.

The hole is gone. The hair dryer from hell stops.

"Shit!" Then it's back... then it isn't, but then if Johnny squints it's kind of *half* there, seen and yet not seen. The dual visual is extremely disorienting. Then the entire hole vanishes and stays that way. Johnny tries over and over, but he can't bring it back.

"Hmm," Kaleb says. "I didn't expect that."

"I have this fucking glitch in my head," Johnny says. "It keeps screwing things up whenever I try to use the knack, you know, to work with this stuff."

But Kaleb is staring at the spot where the hole was a moment ago. "There's something in your mind that's making it happen," he says. "I've seen this a few times. But practice might minimize it, even if it won't stop it." He thinks for a moment. "Did you write a statement or anything like that to come here? Make some kind of offering with it?"

"Yes, but I don't have time to practice — "

"You're resisting something," Kaleb says. "In your mind, even if you don't know what it is. Something at odds with that statement, something working against what you wanted to do. You said you had an altar on this side?"

"At my rental house, where I came through."

"It'll probably be easier there," Kaleb mutters thoughtfully. "Your desire for the Shallows was stated in that now-in-between place, and it will be a powerful spot to open the *next* door. The space in that house will be like a pierced ear, trying to heal over but weakened. That said, once I've shown you what I have inside, maybe you won't even need to try that." Kaleb grins, looking eager as he steps off the sand and onto the marble terrace. He gestures toward his house with its crazy stained-glass windows. "Shall we? We'll be very quick."

Johnny's temple pulses. Dammit, he *knew* the altar was the way out. He figured that out at Ivan's. He has to get back to the bungalow, now, and fast.

"You said you'd at least *look*," Kaleb says, and his voice is suddenly wheedling, petulant. "You'll have enough time to get back. I promise I won't keep you too long. I'll keep an eye on the sun in your Shallows."

Johnny glances back at the gentle waves beyond the beach behind him and follows Kaleb toward the house.

"This literally has to be five minutes," Johnny says. "I'm sorry."

"That's all right, that's all right."

Mister Kaleb leads them inside, across the foyer, and up the immense staircase. The thick carpet runner feels wonderfully soft and luxurious under Johnny's sock-covered feet, and Johnny hears faint jazz music coming from the other side of a closed door upstairs. It has a small brass plaque screwed onto it:

THE DREAM LOUNGE

Kaleb pushes it open. Sound pours out into the hallway: voices raised in conversation; a live band, to Johnny's great surprise. He can smell alcohol, human bodies...but it all somehow smells different from any other bar he's been in. Why?

Then he sees beyond the door.

The room is indeed a lounge, and a large one at that; an oak-and-brass bar runs along one wall, the floor dotted with round tables and thick leather armchairs. The lighting is low but colorful and warm. A massive TV at one end of the room is showing an old movie with the sound off. There is a small stage in one corner upon which a trio of middle-aged men in smart 1920s evening wear are lost in the bliss of the music they're making. The room is perhaps half full of patrons, laughing and talking and drinking, and all of them turn to the door as Kaleb enters. Their faces spark with delight when they see him. Some rise to greet him as he walks into the lounge, but he holds up a hand, smiling.

"My associate and I have some business to attend to," Mister Kaleb says. "We'll be done soon, as he can't stay long."

The people pout playfully. One or two of the women wave at Johnny flirtatiously. Even exhausted, Johnny can't believe what he's seeing. Kaleb leads him to the largest table in the corner. It is, of course, the best seat in the house.

"They're not real, are they?" Johnny asks.

"No."

Johnny doesn't know what to say. He tries to listen to snippets of conversation, but he can't bear it for long; it sounds off somehow, the uncanny valley in sonic form, too much of it in one place. It makes him shiver, and Kaleb sees it.

"You get used to it," Kaleb says, eager. "The way they talk. After a while it almost sounds normal. Sit, sit." He gestures to the large wingback chairs on either side of the table.

When Johnny settles into a chair, he nearly gasps in amazement; it is the most comfortable piece of furniture he has ever sat in.

"Inside this house," Kaleb says, clearly pretending not to notice Johnny's surprise, "my intention is much more potent. I can make what I like, within reason, but it takes a lot of effort and time to generate. There is a great deal of limitation. It's taken many years of practice." He taps his head. "My foundations, shall we say, were never the best. That makes manifesting your intention a lot harder, both here and in the real." He suddenly looks awkward. "Actually, now that I'm showing you this, I'm a little embarrassed. But you still had to see it."

"Why?"

"Because you have to see all your options before making a decision. There are many other rooms. But given that time is against us — I'm keeping an eye on that; don't worry — and the stress of your current situation, I assumed that something fun like this would be of the most interest to a young man like yourself. You like the chair?" Kaleb grins, a knowing smile that Johnny suddenly wants to slap. "It's very comfortable, especially when you really let yourself go. Try it. Relax."

Johnny has no intention of doing anything of the sort, but for the sake of the conversation, he stretches out in the seat as if he's at least trying to settle into it. A sudden soothing washes across his mind: peace, the sense of safety he felt downstairs now multiplied tenfold. His limbs feel pleasant, like warm noodles, and his arms relax on the rests, palms up in supplication to this all-consuming sense of well-being. The pain in his chest remains, but it's as if he can tuck it away inside a little separate box in his mind, objectively aware of it on the mental back burner.

"What...is this...?" Johnny murmurs.

"That's what's here," Kaleb says. "This is how you can live. How do you think I bear it?"

"What..." Johnny's face tries to scowl but manages only the most fleeting of attempts; this feels far too good to get frustrated. *Time*, his mind screams at him faintly from a distant corner of his psyche. *Sunset.* It's right, Johnny knows, but hell, it can wait a minute. Hasn't he earned a little more of this with all he's been through?

"Unfortunately, after your first time, the experience is never quite the same," Kaleb says, shrugging. "Diminishing returns and all that. I've not managed to fix it. But even so, anywhere in the house you settle into? You'll have comfort. The chairs here, the loungers on the veranda, the beds. It's always there. It's a big deal, believe me, even if after a while... well. It keeps me going, at least."

Johnny can't imagine this ever getting old.

All of a sudden, he remembers thinking this same thing about the *last* incredible soothing thing he found. But the chair still feels too good for him to sit up and end it. *Five minutes more. Please.*

"So," Kaleb says, glancing nervously around the room. "Are you interested?"

"In... what?"

Kaleb rubs his chin and settles back, exhales. His expression is sad and longing, and Johnny sees something flash behind his eyes. Wait—was it just his eyes?

Johnny sits up, the chair becoming just a chair once more.

Kaleb breaks into a surprisingly affectionate smile. "As you know, I had to go away and think very hard about what to say to you. Even though I considered this with everyone who's been through here the last few years, I never pulled the trigger. I swore that the next time I would, and then here *you* are! So now I'm making the offer. He spreads his arms and gestures around the room. "You can stay here, Johnny. Avoid the Deep Place altogether. Come live with me."

Jokes? *Fucking jokes, now?* Then Johnny realizes:

"You're being serious."

Kaleb nods, giving a smile that might be a little forced. "Stay with me. Master your intention—I'll teach you. Keep me company. In return, you will know peace. At least, of a kind, and for a good while. Don't you want that? I know you do. I knew it the moment I first met you." He sighs and shakes his head. "I have been very, very lonely, even with my companions. Here you can have almost anything you want, nearly as good as the real thing. Here you'll be safe."

Johnny stares at the smiling old man in the bathrobe, dumbfounded.

"That's *it?*" he says. "That's what you wanted to say?"

Kaleb looks confused. "You'll be *safe,*" he repeats. "At least until the next time the rules change enough for this place to no longer be a haven, and that might never happen at all."

"Even the Boggart can't come here?"

"The agreement is all-binding," Mister Kaleb says. "I can't say it for absolutely certain—I've stayed away from those kind of things as much as possible ever since—but yes. I think even the Boggart can't come here."

"Stay here until when?"

Kaleb just stares at Johnny.

"You mean for the rest of my *life*?"

"Better than being eaten," Kaleb says. "Isn't that what you're trying to avoid? The Boggart do so like to make deals."

Johnny detects a low sound underneath that of the jazz band. It is multifaceted, rumbling, a stop-start chorus of ragged moaning wails. Then it fades out entirely, replaced for a moment by the meandering sounds of the jazz trio before coming back to sit just inside Johnny's awareness.

"What's that?" he asks.

"Our eager visitors outside, I'm afraid," Kaleb sighs. "They sing, you see. It isn't pleasant. We drown it out in here, but sometimes they can be loud."

Johnny listens for a moment to the deeply unsettling sound. He shudders. "I can't stay here, Mister Kaleb. My friends... It's not just me. I somehow brought us all here. I don't even *know* you."

"They can stay too!" Kaleb says, looking confused. "Of course they can. I just didn't want them here while we talked."

"Why would they want to?"

Mister Kaleb shakes his head and leans toward Johnny. The smile is gone, replaced by a look of—to Johnny's great dismay—worry. "I've told you what the alternative is. Is either of your friends a guide?"

Johnny shakes his head. Ivan would be a guide if his memory hadn't been Swiss-cheesed.

"Then please," Kaleb says, his voice low, "let me be a guide for you *here*, son."

Johnny winces a little at the word, but Kaleb rushes on, sounding as if he doesn't want to lose the moment.

"For you," Kaleb says, "I'm not sure it's possible to escape the

Boggart by going through the Deep Place. Even if it's not, being eaten would be perhaps preferable to some of the ends I've witnessed in there."

"Why couldn't we just live out in the Shallows, though?" Johnny says, feeling angry. He's come here for answers, not this. "Live in it like the real world? Yeah, the houses can't seem to make their minds up if they're empty or not and some of the people are vegetables, but not all of them. You said the Shallows are an entire world. There were enough regular people at the airport. Why would we need to hole up in this house for the rest of our lives?"

"The Shallows were never meant to be a haven," Kaleb says. "They're a starting point. Their natural protections break down over time. After a while out there, perhaps maybe a week or two at most, the Needle Monsters, as you call them—and worse creatures than they—would slowly become more and more abundant, would become aware of your friends and try to track them down. You, Johnny, currently stand out more to them since you are bonded to the Boggart, necessitating your token of protection, yes? It was necessary. Soon it will be necessary for your friends too, and they will have no such token. Their only option then will be the Deep Place...or here with me."

An idea suddenly strikes Johnny. How the hell didn't he think of this already? "Come to the Deep Place *with* us! *You* be our guide. You said it yourself: Your intention is strong. You've been here years."

Kaleb shakes his head. "Not only am I old, but also I don't think I can be a guide. Those who come out of the Deep Place with *their* guides come out empowered by their experience. They can now be guides themselves, aid someone else on their journey and keep them safe. I have had no such experience."

"Look at what you can do here," Johnny says. "You can't be telling me that isn't enough to get us through the Deep Place."

"That," Mister Kaleb says sadly, "is exactly what I'm telling you. I never went through it, Johnny. I came here without a guide myself." He looks at his hands. His fingers twitch. It strikes Johnny that if what Kaleb says is true, Ivan has probably been through the Deep Place once with *his* guide. He curses his screwed-up Shallows yet again for wiping all their memories.

"But it might be enough," Johnny says. "You don't know."

Kaleb sighs heavily. "I'm sorry. I thought you knew by now that I'm just not strong enough."

Johnny looks around the room, thoughts tumbling, wanting to stand and leave, but the comfort of the place pins him. He *could* bring Bailey and Ivan inside; wouldn't even this be better than risking the Deep Place without a guide?

Kaleb seems to see Johnny's moment of weakness and leans forward eagerly.

Johnny sees Kaleb's face *shift* ever so slightly.

Not Kaleb's expression—his actual face shivers. Did Johnny imagine it? He doesn't think so. That's twice he thinks he's seen something odd. But even if Kaleb has been using his intention somehow to wear a mask, why would he? And an old man's at that?

"Is everything okay?" Kaleb asks, and this time his tone changes the moment his face flickers, his eager but calm voice revealed to be as false as the face. Kaleb's real voice spoke with intense anxiety. It's brief, but Johnny definitely heard it. Johnny can't make out the blurry details of Kaleb's true face, but he saw enough to recognize the emotion.

Kaleb is beside himself with nerves.

"Who are you really?" Johnny whispers.

Kaleb straightens, caught, and immediately looks perfectly relaxed and jovial. The mask has been pulled back into place.

"You noticed." Kaleb shrugs, smiling as if the discovery means nothing. "How embarrassing! But wouldn't you do the same, if you could? For fun?" He leans back in his chair. "You could learn."

Johnny watches Kaleb closely, but now the disguise fits like a tailored suit. Kaleb is clearly focusing on keeping it steady now that he's been spotted.

"That sounds weird, if I'm honest," Johnny says carefully. "And I don't think *for fun* is the real reason. What is?"

"Oh, come *on* now!"

Johnny sees the blatant denial and thinks of the setting sun. He can't trust Kaleb, and time is running out. Johnny doesn't know if getting out through the Deep Place means he doesn't have to face the Boggart, but dangerous as it may be it's the only way to get Bailey and Ivan out. He stands. "I have to leave."

Kaleb's face flickers again—perhaps he's panicking now, unable to keep things as he wishes—and as it does, those damn words pop into Johnny's head again, the *voice* that has been repeating over and over during the last horrifying twenty-four hours. The voice of someone who should once have been Johnny's guide in another place and time; someone who failed in that role so very badly thanks to the same fury that burns in all six of those words:

WHAT'S WRONG WITH THAT LITTLE MAN?

"I have to *go*," Johnny says, swaying for a moment, his mind struggling to return to the present. "Right now."

"Johnny, Johnny, no matter what, I'm your friend. I promise you, I mean you no harm."

"Thanks for the offer, but I'll pass." Johnny doesn't add the word that wants to follow: *coward*. He also doesn't admit that Mister Kaleb reminds him far too much of himself. Instead, he crosses the Dream Lounge without another word, heading for the door.

"Even if you die down there?" Kaleb asks.

"I wonder," Johnny says, ignoring the question, "if the face thing is really because you can't look at yourself in the mirror."

Johnny is through the Dream Lounge door and at the top of the staircase before he hears wooden footsteps behind him.

"Wait. Wait!"

"Not interested."

"No, take this with you."

Johnny turns, sees Kaleb's shaking hand holding something out to him that catches the light. It's a small, sharp knife.

"I took it off the bar," Kaleb says, looking embarrassed. "It's for lemons. I'd make you something bigger, but even making that knife takes a very long time. It's not for use against the monsters, if you take my meaning."

Johnny doesn't know what to say.

"In case you need it," Kaleb says. His eyes are pools of fear. "I've seen it too many times, Johnny. From afar. People who pray for a quick death down there. You think you won't, but you will wish you took this knife."

Johnny hesitates, then takes the blade before descending the stairs.

It takes him a while to reach the bottom. When he does, he looks over his shoulder; Kaleb is still at the top, hugging himself in his stupid robe. His mouth gapes open, closed, open, closed, his face flickering wildly, the words in his throat held back by his mask. He reaches toward Johnny, but the flickering becomes too much. Kaleb's shoulders drop, and his arm returns to his side, beaten. His face becomes still once more.

"They'll get in eventually," Johnny calls up, his voice trembling. "The Needle Monsters. You said it yourself."

"And there are many, many more of them," Kaleb says, "in the Deep Place. To go there is suicide. Johnny, look at what I'm offering."

But Johnny is lurching out the front door into the light of a sun not long from setting.

"It's suicide!" Kaleb yells as Johnny jogs past the topiaries to the gate. He doesn't look at the moving, shadowy grass in the corner, and by the time he reaches the exit, he's running at a full sprint. "Johnny! Johnny! It's suicide!"

Chapter Seventeen: Madison

Winter Is Leaving

PLASTIC MATERIAL RUSTLES outside, waking Madison.

She opens her eyes, her returning consciousness carrying a heavy, dull pain with it.

What time...

Then she sits up far too quickly, her pulse hammering as the terror of her disastrous Hard Correction slams back into her mind. The pain spikes with movement, and she winces at the too-bright light in the ceiling, her *bedroom* ceiling. She's been moved. Her mouthguard is gone. What woke her? She hears it again. Plastic sheeting flapping outside. She tries to find and focus on the clock, her eyes sweeping past the darkened sky through the window. The sun has gone down. She's still dressed in the training vest, yoga pants, and Nikes she was wearing in the squash court.

Check the door before you do anything, she thinks. *You need to get out of here.*

She manages to get to her feet on the third attempt, her equilibrium not quite yet returned. Lights still dance in her eyes. *A concussion,* her brain hisses as she crosses to the door. *Ellie said there would be no permanent damage. She was wrong, fucking wrong.*

Jennifer! She wasn't breathing when—

Madison staggers to the door, struggling against the room's mild attempts to pitch left and right. She tries the handle, using it to hold herself upright at the same time. The door won't open. It's locked from the outside. The lights in her vision dance more brightly for a moment, and the room starts to spin. Madison has to cling to the handle until it stops.

What now? She has to find Jennifer. Who knew what else Ellie might have—

Jennifer wasn't right about everything, Madison's unhelpful mind whispers. *Ellie's PTSD wasn't a fucking act.*

"Shut up," Madison hisses, and then that rustling comes again from the courtyard below, audible through the windowpane. Whatever plastic sheeting is down there, there's a lot of it. She tries to steady her breathing and her hands as she moves around the bed in the small room, swaying over to the window, nausea washing through her. She realizes that her spine is only aching now rather than screaming, but the sharp pain is still coming from her rib. Dulled some, but still there; it's cracked perhaps, or maybe broken.

Jennifer, Madison thinks.

She must find her friend. She looks down into the yard, sees Sarah's bike still parked beside the gravel turning circle. Ellie's Land Rover is parked on the opposite side.

She also sees Ellie herself.

The woman in charge at No Days Off is laying out a large tarp, lit by the vast corona of the security floodlight. With difficulty, Madison lowers herself to her knees, using the wall for support. She needs to know what's going on, but she doesn't want Ellie to see her. The tarp is perhaps fifteen feet square. Ellie then busies herself finding stones under the nearby bushes to weigh it down before disappearing out of Madison's line of sight.

A few moments later Madison hears the clop of horse's hooves.

Ellie reappears, leading Winter by her bridle, the white horse with its distinctive gray nose crescent obediently following her owner. Ellie walks the horse into the center of the tarp and halts Winter there. The horse gently swishes her tail as Ellie rests her head against the beast's skull, stroking it slowly. The blood has dried on Ellie's face, and Madison can see, even at a distance, that Ellie's forehead is badly swollen. It looks like Ellie has put some kind of dressing over the nasty split in her brow. Her eyes are closed, but Madison's are bursting out of her head, for Ellie's other hand holds a shotgun.

Ellie stops stroking the horse and looks up at Madison's window. Madison doesn't move quickly enough, and Ellie sees her. Their eyes lock. Ellie pumps the shotgun once, in and out.

"No," Madison whispers, understanding that no, she is not going to be okay after all.

Ellie turns and places the barrel against Winter's head. The horse pulls lazily away, but not too violently; she clearly doesn't like the hard metal against her skull and is letting Ellie know, but she trusts that this will only be a temporary situation.

Ellie pulls the trigger.

The bang is so loud it's as if the window has no glass. A thick spray of dark red exits the back of Winter's skull, and the horse drops heavily onto the tarp, landing in an ungracious tangle of jutting-up knees.

Madison slaps her hands over her mouth to catch her scream. Ellie lets out a low moan of despair and slowly drops to the ground, setting the gun down. She collapses against the large body of the pet she just murdered, laying her head on Winter's side.

Madison watches in horrified disbelief but doesn't take her eyes off the shotgun.

Eventually, Ellie gets back to her feet. She picks up one edge of the tarp in her now-bloodied hands and wraps it over the horse. She repeats this with the other side until Winter is covered. She rummages inside her Land Rover for a moment and returns with a roll of duct tape. After a few minutes, the tarp is secured around the horse. Ellie glances up at Madison's window again and then walks out of view. When she returns, it's with a set of chains. By the time Ellie has wrapped them around the dead horse, attached them to her car, and dragged the gruesome package out of sight, Madison decides that she needs to find a weapon immediately.

Many hours pass before Ellie comes to Madison's room. During that time Madison listened to the distant sound of heavy machinery, something totally alien in this peaceful corner of the world. Her nausea has subsided, her equilibrium has improved to a degree, and her clarity of vision has slowly returned. She can see stars through the window, the same window she earlier considered trying to escape through, her fear so intense that she temporarily forgot she was on the second floor of a taller-than-average house. She thought about doing the mattress-out-the-window trick—hang from the ledge and drop down onto the springy surface—but even if she could trust her body to handle that after the Hard Correction, she thinks she would still break a limb. Then she'd really be stuck. The bedroom door is old, thick, and very heavy; at her best, Madison couldn't have broken it down. As damaged as she is, there is no chance.

If she has to defend herself, then at least Ellie is damaged too, and badly by the looks of it. The blows to her head with the club may have been what tipped Ellie over the edge; they have certainly reduced her a degree. But Ellie made short work of Jennifer; Madison isn't anywhere near her friend's size, and Jennifer had trained in jiu-jitsu since her teens. If things are to get physical between Madison and Ellie, even now, Madison knows there will most likely be no contest, especially when the best weapon she's found is a flat iron. The irony of planning to use a beauty device to potentially mangle Ellie's face is not lost on Madison.

She grips it tightly in her fist now as she paces the room, her head pounding, the power cord wrapped tightly around the plates to keep them shut. The plug swings free like a mini ball and chain. The flat iron is a laughable weapon, but it's the only thing she has. She nearly didn't pack it; when the hell would she need to straighten her hair on this course? But she had room in her suitcase and thought she may as well, she might want to look nice at some point, there may be an end-of-course dinner or something. She searches for a better weapon all the same—

She hears footsteps coming along the hallway.

Shit, she thinks. *Here we go, Serena. Get ready. Get ready.*

Her heart rate accelerates, making her buzzing head hurt even more, but her limbs are full of ice. She tries to hold the flat iron casually, as if she were just about to repack it perhaps. Madison thinks that, if she has to, she can land one good blow with it as long as she catches Ellie unawares.

If it comes to that, she reminds herself. *You don't know Ellie's plan.*

No. Ellie looked Madison in the eye and then shot her own horse. Ellie has now entered the realm of extreme violence; this *is* going to come to a fight.

She hears the key turn in the lock. Ellie enters, her gait steadier, and closes the door behind her. The foot of the bed is in between her and Madison, with about three feet of space between it and the wall. It's no barrier, but Ellie will have to move around it to get at Madison, should she decide to. Ellie folds her arms. Her positioning, stance, and body language send a clear message, one of assertion—intended dominance—and Madison knows Ellie doesn't do things like that by accident. The nasty swelling on Ellie's forehead looks fit to burst, and Madison can now see that Ellie's wound is held shut by butterfly strips. Her eyes are narrow, but not out of anger; it looks as if Ellie is having trouble focusing.

Serena, Madison tells herself, pinching her thumb and forefinger together behind her back. She widens her own stance a little and tries to keep the sway of her body to a minimum. She doesn't want Ellie to know how badly she's still hurt.

"Why did you lock me in here, Ellie?" Madison asks. She doesn't dare mention the horse.

"I needed some time to calm down," Ellie says quietly. She has, Madison notices, washed Winter's blood from her hands.

"Uh-huh. Why?"

Ellie takes a long, slow inhale. Holds it. Lets it out. "I think a blind man could see that things got a little out of hand, Madison," she says calmly, her words still a little slurred. "I found the tape on my door, by the way."

Madison tamps down panic. "I'm sorry, Ellie. I wanted to call Imani."

"Why didn't you ask for the iPad?" Ellie says. "I would have let you have an extra call."

"I didn't know if you listened in on the iPad calls," Madison says. Ellie still hasn't seemed to have noticed the flat iron. "I wanted it to be private."

"Why?"

"Because..." She can't think of a lie. "That's private."

"Mm." Ellie looks at the straightener now. Back up at Madison.

"Where's Jennifer?" Madison asks, trying to divert Ellie's attention from her makeshift weapon.

"You know why I created Elite?" Ellie asks, taking a step forward, but she doesn't move around the bed.

Madison stands her ground. She doesn't want Ellie to see her back up, and Ellie would definitely notice. "Where is she?" Madison repeats, her voice low.

"It was because," Ellie continues, speaking uncharacteristically lazily, "I kept having students who could accept their Hard Corrections and reach their physical endurance goals, but they *still* couldn't break through. People like you, with minds so good at finding loopholes, at avoiding difficulty, at self-sabotaging. If a lot of them—if *you*—weren't like that, they wouldn't come here. But when those people still can't get out of their own way, they need to go to a whole other place."

"I don't want to do Elite anymore, Ellie," Madison says. "I'm going home. You said Elite doesn't start until tomorrow, so that means I can still leave."

Ellie takes another slow inhale. Then another. Madison tenses.

"It's tomorrow *now*, Madison," Ellie says eventually, raising her wrist to show Madison her watch. "Past midnight. This is now exactly what you agreed to. You can't go home. You can't quit."

"Everything is different now, Ellie," Madison tries. "The rules don't apply anymore because Jennifer...got hurt. I think I have a fractured rib, and I've almost certainly got a concussion. 'No permanent damage'—

remember?" She bites down on the next sentence, on her building fury, wanting to scream, *You didn't keep to your half of the fucking deal, Ellie.*

"Yes, things have become a little intense, I grant you," Ellie says, nodding sagely.

"Intense?" Madison's shock overcomes her restraint. "Ellie, this has turned into straight-up *abuse.*" She catches herself, but it's too late. The words are out.

"Abuse?" Ellie asks, scowling at the ceiling and swaying a little. "Madison, you signed up for this, signed up for physical punishment. Was I not extremely clear about how intense this would be? You're here for results."

"Intense doesn't mean abuse, Ellie."

"Is it abuse if it works?"

"Isn't that exactly what an abuser says?"

"If that is something that someone says after *doing* something that causes nothing but damage," Ellie babbles, her eyes briefly closing, "then yes. That would be abuse. As with all such things, we shall have to see what the end result is."

Ellie steps sideways into the space between the foot of the bed and the wall, giving herself a clear passage toward Madison.

This time Madison does back up.

"The thing is," Ellie continues, "even at Elite, there are still those who..." She pauses. Blinks a few times, looks down.

"Ellie," Madison says, "listen to yourself. You're not thinking clearly, struggling with your sentences. This has gone way too far. Jennifer needs to go to a hospital. You do too."

"*People,*" Ellie interrupts loudly, screwing up her eyes, "who still wouldn't figure it out even if they were subjected to straight-up torture. So I came up with something a while back, a year or so ago, maybe. Haven't had someone like you since. Haven't had a reason to use it."

"Just let me get Jennifer to a hospital," Madison pleads, "and I'll do anything you want." Tears are coming, not from fear or pain but from seeing what Ellie really is. The sheer, terrible letdown. Madison had believed.

"I needed a way," Ellie says, talking as if to herself, "to make it so you people wouldn't be *able* to use a loophole. Inarguable—"

"Ellie, please," Madison says, putting her hand to her forehead. The effort to stay calm is so great that the room temporarily flashes white. Her voice shakes. "If she's not already dead...her *head*. She might have bleeding on the brain."

"And the whole setup's been sitting there, unused," Ellie continues. "So while you were in here, I went and got it all ready."

Madison tries another tack, holding one placating palm out to Ellie. It wavers in the air like that of a marionette; she keeps the hand holding the flat iron low, not wanting Ellie to notice it. "You're going to have another Hannah Quimby-Beck on your hands, Ellie. I'm sure she's the reason you came up with this thing, right? But that isn't going to make this—"

SMACK.

Madison drops the flat iron in surprise, crying out as the pain in her head screeches. The room swims back into view, and she finds she is staring at the wall. Her head has been turned. This has happened before, she realizes, as she becomes aware of a burning pain in her cheek. It happened a lifetime ago in a park in Coventry.

Ellie has crossed the short distance between them in a nanosecond and slapped Madison.

"Don't ever say that name," Ellie says, stepping back a foot.

Madison blinks back tears of pain.

"I honor that woman," Ellie whispers, holding a trembling finger in Madison's face, "in my own way. She will always have my total respect, and she will have yours too. Her story, however I tell it, is a *tool*, a *means*, and this course...this *course* is all about—"

"The ends justifying the means!" Madison barks, holding her face and backing against the window. Her fury is too much to contain, and it is abundantly clear that she isn't talking her way out of this. Fair enough. There has been some steel forged in her over the last three weeks, after all. She lets Ellie see it. "You're *sloppy*, Ellie, and maybe you weren't in the past, but you are now. I don't want to be here alone with you!" A sense of intense unreality washes over her as she presses her back against the window and suddenly remembers the last time she cowered like this was when her mother was in one of her many rages.

Anger straightens Madison's spine.

"The cops are going to come looking," Madison says, "when Jennifer and I don't show up at home, and Ellie, you're going to prison, and your course, your precious work, it's going to stop. The work will stop! What's more important? Me—one person—crossing over or you helping all those other people you've yet to meet? I failed! Jennifer failed! So just let us..."

Madison trails off as she sees the rage drain from Ellie's face. It's like watching a robot get switched off. Her shoulders droop, her arms hanging by her sides.

"I never, *ever* give up on a student," Ellie says. She cocks her head, looking sad, and holds up a finger. "Especially not you, Madison. I don't think I've ever had a student understand all this the way you have—what it means to truly commit to going beyond, how catastrophic it is to *quit*. I can't let you come this close only to fail. You're graduating, whether you like it or not. That's what it means to be Elite." She shrugs, her brow furrowing sorrowfully. It's the most human Ellie has ever looked. "And you're my friend," she says.

Silence.

Then Ellie lunges.

Madison darts away from the window, but Ellie clambers around behind her back with surprising speed, her arms wrapping around Madison's throat and the back of her head like a vise. They squeeze, taking Madison's air. She thrashes, and the two women fall to the floor. Madison tries to scream as her rib and head flare white-hot and has only a second to panic before her vision darkens and she drops unconscious once more.

PART FOUR

Elite

No pain, no gain.

— *Proverb*

Chapter Eighteen: Johnny

The Deep Place

EVEN THOUGH JOHNNY knows they've been to the bungalow before, he tells Ivan and Bailey to wait in the hall while he checks every room. The Boggart, it seems, is not downstairs. If it's in the attic, there are no sounds coming from above.

Eventually they settle at the kitchen table. Ivan and Bailey anxiously watch the kitchen door, waiting for the Boggart's inevitable climb down from the attic hatch. In their laps lie the objects they collected during a ten-minute diversion to a DIY store: three hand axes. As they left Kaleb's, the sun was already below the rooftops, the horizon turning a dark orange. There's no doubt about it: Time is screwy here, out of sync with time at Kaleb's house. Johnny thought he was in there for thirty minutes at most, but when he came out, he could see how much daylight he'd lost. Bailey and Ivan said he was gone for hours. He told them what Kaleb had told him about the Deep Place. There wasn't much discussion, only grim acceptance. Through the window Johnny can now see that the light is almost gone.

"We don't need another one of those," Johnny says, gesturing to the hastily scrawled note on the kitchen table. It still sits, untouched, in front of Johnny's altar. The tea light has long since burned out. Johnny taps the side of his head. "Just this," he says.

Bailey squints at the note.

"Careful," Johnny says. "Don't touch it. We don't know how all that works."

"Trust me," she says. "I didn't have any desire to touch it before, and I don't now."

"Just be ready," Johnny says. "Kaleb said opening the door would be easier here, and I don't know if things can come through the other way."

"You didn't ask?" Bailey says, gripping the handle of her axe.

"It was all pretty rushed," Johnny says, reddening. The pain in his chest is constant now, and the sky outside is almost fully dark. He's never felt this scared, tired, and trapped in his entire life. But he has work to do. "Are you ready?"

Ivan and Bailey nod, lifting their axes.

"We believe in you, Johnny," Bailey says.

Johnny can see she means it. The light in her eyes breaks his heart. He can only think, *I don't trust myself.*

"Okay—" he begins, but his words cut off as he looks down and uses the knack.

A hole screams instantly into being.

It's bigger than the one he made at Kaleb's house—and created more easily here, Kaleb was right—and Johnny suddenly understands that what he's creating isn't a hole after all.

It's a pit.

"Oh my God," Bailey whispers.

Ivan stands, holding his axe at the ready. Once the pit is fully formed, the screaming stops. It still glitches in and out, less frequently than at Kaleb's, but enough that Johnny isn't sure they can pass through.

"Is it finished?" Bailey asks. "Should it be like that?"

"I don't know," Johnny admits. "I don't think so."

But it isn't fully disappearing either, a ragged hole guttering like an old neon sign as it shifts in and out of perception.

"Wait," Ivan says. He's looking across the kitchen.

Johnny follows his gaze. There's a small bit of what looks like black sock fluff wedged into the corner of the cabinets.

"What's that?" Ivan asks.

Johnny's confused by the question. "You mean the little..."

But he sees that now the fluff isn't as little. It's growing. It's not fluff. It's pooling slowly out of the corner like tar.

It's black liquid that Johnny has seen before.

"Are you doing that?" Ivan asks.

"No," Johnny says, and stands up as straight as he can. "Get on the table."

The two of them do as he says, and Johnny follows. The black substance has slowly spread out from the corner in a large arc several feet wide. Johnny raises his axe, but Ivan stands between him and the growing pool of darkness.

"Ivan," Johnny says, grabbing Ivan's shoulder. He will not let Ivan take care of business for him today, will not be the gelding. It's his job to protect Ivan and Bailey now. "I'm under a deal with it. You're not."

The liquid has stopped spreading. It now covers almost the entire kitchen floor.

"Stay there," Ivan says.

Johnny stops struggling; Ivan is right on the table's edge. If Johnny tries to get past him, he could slip and fall into the liquid below.

Johnny glances out of the window again. The sun has now set.

"Wait," he tells the others. He looks at the flickering pit embedded in the kitchen floorboards. They could all easily jump into it from here, into whatever nightmare the Deep Place is below. The option is in place.

But he needs to hear what's in store for him if he *doesn't* jump. It might not be as bad, after all... but something tells him that it absolutely will be. The pain in his chest is screaming as if he has opened a hole to the Deep Place right in the middle of his body.

They watch as the edges of the liquid draw in and up. The center begins to rise. It sprouts reedy columns that harden and form angular limbs, flexing and separating from the risen pool as reaching fingers and toes splinter into life at each end.

A bulbous black shape gathers at the middle.

The liquid surface sets; it dries instantly and becomes coarse black hair, as if it had never been anything else. The two eyes open in the center. They blink, their pupils those of a goat.

"Oh shit," Bailey whispers, frantic, clutching at Johnny's shoulder. "That's it, isn't it? This is the Boggart. Oh shit." She holds her axe higher, her grip tightening.

"You brought your associates," the Boggart says, opening its blade-filled mouth. "Very well. We talk downstairs this night, yes." Its limbs are spread wide, held stiff against the floor and ceiling. Its head hangs suspended at eye level.

"You can't touch my friends," Johnny says fiercely, before sheepishly adding: "Can you?"

"Why do you believe this?" the Boggart asks. "The..." It sniffs at the air. "*Needle Monsters,* as you call them, can."

"Not yet," Johnny says. "Mister Kaleb told me, he said *they'd* have a couple of weeks before the Shallows' protection started to break down—"

"True," the Boggart says, smiling. "But I am not interested in your friends, Johnny, or your Mister Kaleb. A meal without a deal? Meaningless to a Boggart, yes." It chuckles, low and long.

Johnny is suddenly struck by how darkly gleeful the Boggart is. Old stories flash across his mind: Mercury, Loki...Puck, as Bailey said. The merry magical mischief makers of myth. Were they all glimpses of...this? If so, the stories were way off. There is far more evil than mischief in a Boggart.

Ivan points his axe at the monster's head. "You can't have Johnny," he says. His voice is low. Firm.

"Quiet, Ivan," Johnny murmurs. But a thought strikes him as he remembers the last two people he brought into the Boggart's presence: the cops, Tillsey and Rinton. They became something akin to comatose, albeit while upright; yet here is Ivan making threats and Bailey swearing her head off. His friends aren't at all reacting to the Boggart's presence in the same way the cops did. Johnny glances at the pit in the floor. It's gone—no, it's back, still flickering in and out.

The Boggart notices him looking.

Shit, Johnny thinks.

"I see," it says.

"We're leaving," Bailey says, her voice trembling.

Johnny wants to say *I don't think it's that simple, baby,* as the Boggart raises its thick brow in amusement.

"There is nowhere," the Boggart says, "that you can escape this challenge. Not in all the realms, yes."

Johnny blanches.

"Perhaps it is just as well," the Boggart continues, "that your friends see this." Its hands leave the wall and clap together in a rapid staccato beat. The thick black hairs on its hands muffle the *whack* of its palms: *WHOK-WHOK-WHOK-WHOK.*

"It is time for your challenge," the Boggart says.

"No," Bailey says, her face white, but the Boggart just grins.

"I'm afraid Johnny made a deal, yes."

"Did I?" Johnny cries. "My note, my altar—they were just how I came here to the Shallows, weren't they? But you said that was me making a deal with you!"

The Boggart shrugs coquettishly. "You are in a deal with me *now.* This is what matters. But yes: I was in this territory and felt the strength of your intention. 'I WILL GET CLEAN.' It was pure. You will taste fine, yes." It looks Johnny dead in the eye.

"You can't make deals like that!" Johnny cries, feeling stupid.

"The *ways* to make a deal, Johnny-Mine," the Boggart says, "are many. Intention can be diverted." It cocks its head, pleased. "I told you we were in a deal. You agreed. And so, there *is* a deal, yes."

It snaps its fingers. An image swims impossibly into the air before Johnny, or perhaps it is in his head: a vision of himself in the attic, the Boggart before him, its limbs wrapped around the metal stanchions.

You can only ... consume me, he sees himself say, *if I ever take painkillers again?*

Very good, yes. That is our deal.

But—

Repeat it: That is our deal.

That is our deal.

The image vanishes.

"I don't give a shit what is deal and what is not deal," Ivan says, stress affecting his English again. "Bailey's right: *We're leaving.* All of us."

"This is a good friend," the Boggart says, pointing at Ivan, its voice becoming simpering, mocking. "Defending you, yes. And lucky *friends*; I have prevented them from truly seeing me the way your police associates did." The monster roars with ragged laughter. "For I wish very much," it says, "to hear your *good friends'* thoughts on the truth, yes."

"What do you mean?"

"I am not here to stop you from leaving," the Boggart says. "The only way out of the Shallows is through the Deep Place, whether you pass my challenge or not, yes. *But.*" It raises a long, black, hairy finger and waves it slowly back and forth in the air. "I am deal-bound to tell you the truth of such an exit. And, Johnny-Mine..."

Its feet creep along the walls. Its head glides through the air toward Johnny and his friends on the table, who shuffle back a few inches, avoiding the altar at their feet. Johnny's gaze never leaves the goat eyes sliding toward him, but he does draw Kaleb's knife from his pocket, holding it out along with his axe.

"Once you know what awaits," the Boggart says softly, "you may *wish* to fail the challenge. To fall between my jaws instead of the Deep Place. *Yes.*"

"Don't listen to it, Johnny," Bailey says.

"I know what awaits," Johnny says. "I've felt it. And why the fuck would I want to fail? You *eat* me if I fail."

"But that"—the Boggart smiles—"can at least be swift."

"What is it talking about?" Bailey asks.

The Boggart answers. "The ordeal that is the Deep Place. You say you have felt it, Johnny, but that is like smelling a meal from outside the kitchen!" It sniffs for a second and then makes a snatching motion with its hand, as if plucking something out of the air. "There," it says. "I believe this is yours, yes. *Taste it.*"

It holds out its empty palm and blows on it.

Something invisible washes into Johnny.

The pain in Johnny's chest suddenly feels utterly fresh, jagged, and—worse—it is all over his body, as if he is being bitten everywhere at once. He tries to scream, but he has no breath; his throat is closed by overwhelming fear and grief, the shock of emotion even greater than the physical pain. He slumps against Ivan's back, and Ivan turns to catch him before he falls off the table. The head of Ivan's axe bangs into Johnny's ribs as he curls into a ball, all his muscles clenching. His own axe clatters to the kitchen floor, as does his knife.

The Boggart snaps its fingers, and the sensations disappear. Johnny lets out a gasp of relief, the pain pouring out of him in an awful tsunami... but the second it's gone, he straightens. He must protect his friends if he can.

"Johnny!" Bailey cries.

Johnny faces the Boggart. "Kaleb told me it would be hell down there." He stops, his breath taken by the real pain that still lingers in his chest; whatever just happened has set all his nerve endings ablaze, and *oh God, he wants his pills so badly*. "If that's what it takes to save my friends—"

"I did not finish speaking," the Boggart says. "Down there, yes, your *protection* against the lesser creatures?" It waves a hand. The tie-pin on Johnny's T-shirt disintegrates and floats away like silver confetti. "*Useless*. The substance your healers gave you has now left your system, yes. Your pain from an attack by only *one* denizen of the Deep Place: intense, yes."

Johnny wants to deny it but knows to do so would be pointless; the sweat on his brow and the trembling of his body would only make his answer laughable.

But that's not just from the pain, is it? his brain helpfully whispers. *You know what you want, and badly.*

"And so," the Boggart is saying, as if reading his mind, "your need is even more heightened, yes. Imagine navigating the horrors of the Deep Place—of the Howling Wastelands—with such *need* within you? Without a *guide*?"

Johnny's hands are shaking. The need is already so severe that the room is starting to gray at the edges of his vision. Then he is suddenly thrust aside, colliding with Bailey, who only just manages to keep them both from falling off the table as they helplessly watch Ivan leap toward the Boggart, his axe raised to swing down into the creature's eyes.

"No," the Boggart says.

Ivan is immediately halted by some invisible force. He hangs suspended, his limbs locked in place. Only his head remains animated. He looks around himself in terror.

"Let him go!" Bailey screams.

"Ivan!" Johnny and Bailey lunge forward, pulling at Ivan's limbs, but he is utterly immovable.

"Go through the door, Johnny," Ivan gasps.

"You surely do know, yes," the Boggart says, frowning, "that this *friend* of yours is not real?"

Johnny freezes. More mind games?

"You do not believe me," the Boggart says. "Even though this friend has no *adenterrach* rising from him. Was that not a clue?" It wiggles its fingers through the air in an upward motion. "You came here looking for answers, yes, but you believe you came as a group." It shakes its black head in disdain. "You would each have an *adenterrach* if this was so. All of you, all sending out the story."

"Shut up!" Johnny yells. "Just let him go!"

"Ask him," the Boggart insists, amused. "Which city was his birthplace?"

"He knows!" Johnny cries. "Right, Ivan?"

Ivan blinks. Blinks again. "Zenica," he says eventually. "Zenica."

"His parents?"

"Daris!" Ivan screams. "Merjem!"

The Boggart smirks, impressed.

"You and the real version of this man," it says, "must be *good friends*, yes. Friend of Johnny: Name your *škola*."

Ivan has no answer. The Boggart laughs.

"Your *school*," it says.

"Johnny," Ivan gasps.

"You cannot be expected, Johnny-Mine," the Boggart says, "to know *everything* about your friends."

"Don't listen to it, Ivan," Johnny pleads. "It's mind games—"

"He is *false*," the Boggart says, sounding exasperated. "This friend, in this place, this copy of your world? *He is of this Shallows*, yes, merely better formed because of your knowledge *of* him. He only knows that which you do. Your chaotic journey here has left you remembering so little, yes! Farcical! Delightful!" It closes its eyes, grinning, and sniffs a few times; it suddenly looks horribly pleased with itself. "Here!" It cackles and motions with its hand.

Johnny's view of the kitchen vanishes.

"*Remember,*" the Boggart's disembodied voice says.

The sound of Ivan's and Bailey's frantic breathing fades, replaced by those of a Bluetooth speaker playing Tame Impala in the background. It sits on the counter in what until only recently was Sandy and David's kitchen.

Johnny has been here before.

This is the day he moved in. Yesterday. He is still standing in the same kitchen, but different day, different position. He sees the past version of himself sitting at the table, avoiding the gaze of Past Ivan, who is standing.

No, Present Johnny thinks, trying to claw his way out of this room. He doesn't know why, but he knows he wants to stop this. He can't. He's a passenger here, it seems, lost in the vision that is filling his mind. The memory starts to play with brutal clarity like a horror film before an unwilling child.

On the table between Past Johnny and Past Ivan sits a small pile of OxyContin strips.

His secret stash! Why is it even out, Present Johnny wonders. Sandy and David have just left, and he is feeling okay...but wait. A memory flickers.

He found something in his bag, didn't he? A picture. He found a picture, and the timing of it all—the new house, being here alone, *the reminder of the reason he's really come here in the first place*—is bad.

Really bad.

Everything crashed down, the progress he thought he had made turning out to be false and fragile, and then he just thought, *Fuck it.* He fetched his stash, set it on the table, pretended to agonize over a decision he had already made.

And then Ivan showed up, didn't he? He was wet. It was raining outside...

Then he has it.

Oh...no.

Johnny remembers everything.

―――

Not knowing if he wanted Ivan to stop him or not, he left the pills on the table in full sight, the doublethink of the addict in full control. Ivan saw them, became furious. This is far from the first time they have been in a situation like this together, and Johnny does not blame his friend for his impatience. They have been through the familiar, maddening dance: frustration. Compassion, as always, even after all the times Johnny has pushed Ivan to his limit. And then the final, bittersweet stage: help. To waste another's time for his own pathetic, repeated failings? The shame is indescribable.

Ivan talks — at this point, Ivan has been talking for a while — but it's not the words that hold Johnny utterly captive.

It's Ivan's hand, held aloft as he stares at it. Johnny stares too, because Ivan's hand is glowing with green fire.

Ivan closes his eyes, gives a grunt of effort, and the fire goes out. His hand is untouched. He breathes heavily and looks at Johnny.

"Do you believe me now?" he asks.

"Y-y-yes," Johnny stammers. "Could you always do that?"

"Yes and no," Ivan says, leaning on the table as he catches his breath. "I can only do this trick about once a year. It's an old sign — an incredibly sacred secret — that my family use if we ever need to show we know what we're talking about." He straightens, wincing, his face red from exertion. "Now listen. How you go there is very important." Johnny can see how Ivan is trying to keep calm, but Johnny knows his friend is sick of this. "You must write the statement to begin our

transition over there," Ivan says. "Don't worry. You'll be safe in the Shallows if you enter properly and are prepared correctly, and you will be. But you mustn't go into the Shallows alone. I mean, not that you can anyway. You don't know how. But I'll come with you, man. The Shallows, the Deep Place — to enter these without a proper guide, or unprepared... Look, there's no nice way to say it. Monsters can come. You might not even remember going there unless you go with a guide, or if you've been there before."

"Who was your guide?" Johnny says.

"My grandfather," Ivan says quietly and with great reverence. "He took me there as a child after the war. I needed it, badly. He didn't have much choice. The Shallows and the Deep Place are very secret things. Very few people know, and I shouldn't even be telling anyone outside of blood family. It's only kind of allowed because I own this house, and even then, it's dubious. There's usually a council, a process, nominations. It's only used when things are most hopeless. I am breaking a family oath by telling you — do you understand this? But you are family to me, Johnny, and these circumstances are..." He snaps his fingers, looking frustrated as he searches for the word.

"Dire?" Johnny offers.

Ivan nods. "This. And you must never tell my parents."

"Of course never," Johnny mutters. He can see the seriousness on Ivan's face, even if none of this matters anyway.

Johnny wants to die. He has had enough of fighting everything.

"Going there helped me get over my PTSD, Johnny," Ivan says, "but if I'd gone there without my grandfather? As a kid? I would have been dead, and painfully so. I need to know you know this is no small thing that I'm talking about doing."

"How dangerous is it?"

"There's always a risk, even though you should be safe. It is like getting on a plane to go on holiday. It is extremely unlikely that it will crash. But the risk is there."

"Should Bailey come too?" Johnny asks weakly, trying to sound casual, as if he were thinking only of Bailey. "If you're saying it's safe, I mean, maybe if we told her how important it is..."

The pity that instantly appears in Ivan's expression confirms how pathetic the question is.

Johnny makes a half-hearted attempt to not glance at the picture again. The picture that is lying where it has been tossed on the table.

The picture he found in his suitcase's front pocket when rooting around for his charger. The photo is creased, its corners bent.

Ivan sees the glance.

"You want me to take that?" *he asks carefully.*

Johnny nods.

The photo is reverently scooped up and tucked into Ivan's pocket, the post-rollercoaster photo, taken during a particularly thrilling go-round on the Nemesis and bought at the stand afterward. In it, Johnny and Bailey lean forward into their safety harnesses, clearly exhilarated, their hands clasped together. Both are smiling. This was taken in the early days, before Bailey found out the kind of person the mildly famous musician she managed to bag really is.

They look happy.

"No," *Ivan says,* "I don't think bringing Bailey would be a good idea. I'm sorry, Johnny."

Johnny already knew that would be the answer; it wouldn't be fair of him to ask Bailey anyway, even if this is life or death. It's his life, his death, and the clinging, dragging weight of it has finally been unshackled from around Bailey's waist. For now, it has been lashed across Ivan's back. Johnny thought he was getting better. He thought he was on his way out. But then she told him the truth about himself, and he knew his self-belief had been built on vapor. Soon, he knows, the weight of it will break even Ivan's stamina.

"I told her I was coming to see you about this," *Ivan says, sighing. He doesn't want to say this.* "She does worry, man. She does care."

Johnny's hands go to his head. The horror of discussing Bailey as if she is someone distant, separate, and totally free of him — which she is — is too much to bear.

"I am sorry to do this," *Ivan says, reaching into his other pocket,* "but I must give you this. This is all part of the preparation. You need to have no illusions about the way things are."

He produces a folded piece of paper.

"I haven't read this," *Ivan continues, placing it on the table and sliding it over to Johnny.* "I don't know what it says. But I asked her to be clear."

Johnny picks up the letter as if it were a live grenade. He opens it.

I'll Quit When I'm Dead

Both sides of the page are filled with Bailey's neat, rounded handwriting. Johnny reads, holding one hand over his mouth.

That last section of the letter. That brass-knuckled gut punch:

> I allowed this to go on for way too long, and I have to find out why. No, I think I know why. This whole thing, in fact — you and me — has taught me a lot of things. I'm weak, Johnny. I can't speak for you — I shouldn't have said what I said, and I am sorrier for that than I can ever express. But I have to figure myself out.
>
> I want to be there for you, but I think it will eventually kill me. I'm not strong enough to bear it yet, but even if I were, I shouldn't want to. Not if you won't help yourself. Sometimes trying to save a drowning person means that you get dragged under and die too. The fact that I allowed this to go on this fruitlessly, for this long, is another thing this relationship told me: I don't look after myself either. At all. And that needs to change.
>
> Ivan's going to help you now. I might ask him to help me too. He has a way to help that's different and you need to listen to what he has to say. You aren't alone —

Johnny drops the letter onto the table and snatches up one of the OxyContin strips.

Ivan grabs his wrist. "No."

But Johnny yanks his hand free. Ivan doesn't grab him again. Johnny rocks back and forth in his seat, looking at the painkillers in his hand.

"Don't do this, Johnny," *Ivan says.*

"I can get her back," *Johnny babbles, still looking at the tablets. They can make all this so, so much better, just for now while he needs them, and then he can finally sort his shit out, be who Bailey needs him to be —*

"You can't," *Ivan says solemnly.*

"How do you know?"

Ivan lowers his head. "You just can't. You have a lot of work to do. You're going to heal." He moves to the kitchen counter and tears a paper towel from the roll, then places it in front of his friend. "You are lucky," Ivan says, "that you have just moved into Waterton, into this house. This whole town is thin. Close to the Shallows. Much easier to cross over. There are a lot of places like this in this country. People from my family know all of them, and there may be more that haven't been discovered. It's why they bought this house all those years ago." Ivan takes out a pen. "This is why I wanted you to come here, man," he says. "The Shallows are all about what you intend to do, to be, you know? Look, you write your goals down," he says, giving up on the complicated version. "It's like a statement to the universe or whatever. On either side of the paper."

"Ivan...," Johnny begins.

"Later," Ivan says. "We do this now. I think your two statements should be 'I will get clean'—don't worry about the language; it's the intention that matters, and the universe knows what 'get clean' means because you do. And the other should be..." He pauses. Gently pats Johnny's shoulder. "'I will let Bailey go.'"

Johnny puts his head in his hands.

"It's the holding on," Ivan says, rubbing Johnny's back, "that kept you alive, that brought you back. But now it's killing you. It's keeping you like this. It's keeping you broken. Those goals, the Shallows, the Deep Place...if you do things right..."

"I'll do it." Johnny sniffs, pulling his head from his hands. He looks up at Ivan, red-eyed. "I'll do it. I'll do it."

He takes the pen.

"That's good, Johnny," Ivan says.

Johnny pauses. "What happens next?"

"We light a candle," Ivan says. "Which, thanks to Sandy, we already have right here. She probably knew we were going to do something like this. You put an offering down. Anything will do, any kind of commodity—chocolate, orange juice—and you put the note and your offering in front of the candle." Johnny wonders if the open bag of Werther's Originals that Sandy left on the table will count.

"And?"

"And that's it," Ivan says.

"No magic words or anything?"

"Nope, and certainly none needed in Waterton," Ivan says. "My grandfather always used to say that making a doorway to the Shallows is the universe's rupa u zakonu."

"What does that mean?"

"Loophole," Ivan says. "You need someone here who is on the inside with all this bullshit to make it work properly, or at least someone who has been to the Shallows before. They need to be present. You're not on the inside, Johnny. You couldn't open the doorway alone, but Lucky Johnny has Genius Ivan onboard." Ivan gives a forced looking smile, but Johnny is staring at him in amazement.

"I can't believe all this. Not just the existence of this kind of thing, but there's this whole side of you I never even knew."

Ivan shrugs. "If you had any idea how secret this all is... The council would vote to have me killed for telling you this, because that is the rule." He hisses. Shakes his head. "Let me get my lighter." Ivan disappears into the hallway.

Johnny hears Ivan fishing around in his coat. By the time Ivan returns, Johnny has finished writing his goals. Ivan holds up the lighter. "Are you ready?"

"You mean right now?"

"Yeah," Ivan says, and his eyes fall to the note sitting in front of Johnny. He reaches for it, but Johnny moves first, placing it before the candle. He does it too quickly. He sees Ivan notice. Ivan reaches for the paper again, but Johnny waves Ivan's hand away.

"No, no," Johnny says quietly. "Don't touch it. That's my, my, uh..." He can't finish the sentence because he can't think of a reason Ivan shouldn't touch it. The **I WILL GET CLEAN** side of the paper is face up.

Ivan's brow furrows. He drops the lighter and grabs the paper, turning it over.

The words **I WILL MAKE THINGS AS THEY WERE** stare back at them both.

"What the fuck," Ivan whispers, his face pale.

Then red.

Johnny sees something in his friend's eyes he never has before, and certainly never directed at him.

Fury.

Ivan snatches up the note, balls it in his fist. "Do you have any idea..." Ivan turns away from the table and starts to pace. "Jesus Christ, Johnny, do you know what you nearly did? Do you know what you're fucking around with?"

"I-I can't," *Johnny stammers, reddening himself.* "I can't let her go."

"You have to be clear," *Ivan says.* "What you want has to be clear—"

"You said the language didn't matter—"

"It doesn't!" *Ivan yells.* "But what does 'make things as they were' even mean in your head, Johnny? Tell me right now!"

What does it mean? That he has Bailey back? That he isn't quite as addicted to painkillers anymore? That things would be like they were at the start?

"If you can't fucking tell me immediately," *Ivan says, storming up to the table and leaning over Johnny,* "then you aren't fucking clear!"

"Okay, calm down—"

"Do you know how fucked the Shallows you went into could have been because of this?" *Ivan yells.* "What you could have created? A broken place, Johnny! Somewhere that might fry your mind just by your crossing into it! And dangerous even if you went over with your brain in one piece! A place easy for dark things to—ach!" *Ivan paces a few steps away from the table, storms immediately back.* "Did you think you were being clever? Johnny, do you know what I'm risking for you even telling you about these secrets, the* punishment *that would be—" He slaps his hands to his face, exhales.* "You're an addict. You're scared. You're at your lowest point. Okay. Okay. Okay." *He drops his hands, crosses to the bin, and throws the screwed-up note into it.*

Ivan shakes with anger.

"I need to calm down," *Ivan says, his hands on his hips. He is looking at his feet. Johnny feels a very particular kind of shame: that of the disapproving father. To Johnny, this is unbearable.*

Ivan lowers his face, red for a different reason. "I need to have a clear head if we're going to do this."

"I'm sorry, Ivan," *Johnny says.* "I—"

"I'm going for a drive," *Ivan says.* "I'll be back in half an hour, and we'll go again." *He scoops up the pile of tablet strips.* "I'm taking the pills with me. Okay?"

"Okay."

Ivan holds out his hand for the packet Johnny picked up earlier. Johnny drops it into Ivan's palm without a word. Ivan stuffs the lot into his pocket before sighing and gently cupping the back of Johnny's skull, pressing his forehead to Johnny's.

"We do this together," *Ivan says.* "And we do it properly."

"Okay." *Johnny's hand finds the back of Ivan's head as well, his eyes on the table.*

"I love you," Ivan says.

"I love you too."

Ivan straightens, pauses as if to add something else, then turns and leaves the room. A moment later, Johnny hears the front door open and close.

He sits alone for several minutes. Eventually, he fetches one of the joints that Sandy left behind and lights it with Ivan's lighter. Before he puts the joint to his lips, Johnny looks from the ignited lighter to the candle, and decides to touch the flame to the wick. It's safe, he knows; Ivan said Johnny can't open any doorways by himself.

Then Johnny takes a good long drag on the joint. Then another. It feels good, but nowhere near good enough to take the edge off his terrible, terrible craving. He stands and walks to the bin on empty legs, feeling as if none of this matters anyway. He is ready to die, after all. He never thought he'd be here again. Unaware that he is starting to hum along with the music playing over the speaker, Johnny reaches into the bin and pulls out the paper and stares at it: **I WILL GET CLEAN.** *He turns it over.* **I WILL MAKE THINGS AS THEY WERE.**

The weed is settling heavily into his body. Johnny walks back to the table, hesitates, and drops the paper in front of the lit candle. He doesn't mean anything by it. He's just... having a moment. Playing. Deciding. Ivan will be back soon. He takes another pull on the joint, and, as his eyes focus on the gently dancing flame, his mind starts to count, noting the odd and even numbers at regular points in the rhythm. It's normal for him, so normal he barely notices. Bailey. The whole thing is madness. The flame continues to dance in an unseen breeze.

Ten, eleven, twelve (even) — thirteen, fourteen, fifteen (odd)...

Johnny looks past the candle to the patio doors. To the conservatory on the other side. The dark garden beyond.

Get outside, *his stoned brain whispers.* Get into the green.

Outside in the warm, hazy air, he looks up at the sky and the stars that are starting to emerge. He looks toward the garden's farthest apple tree, tucked almost flush against the back hedge. He staggers over to it, his brain quietly counting all the way. He lets it, running his hand across the trunk's bark as he walks around it, smiling stupidly. As he completes his circle, the air in front of him — between Johnny and the house — ripples as if in a heat haze.

Forty-four, forty-five, forty-six (even) — forty-seven, forty-eight, forty-nine (odd) — fifty, fifty-one, fifty-two (even)...

Johnny staggers back as a ragged circle appears in the air before him.

It's perhaps five feet in diameter. Johnny cannot believe what he is seeing, and yet he must because it's right there. It looks at first as if some unseen hand has simply held up an ephemeral, misshapen Hula-Hoop and Johnny is looking through it. All he sees within the circle is the house on the other side. He approaches carefully. The joint and the impossibility before him make him feel as if he is dreaming. He reaches around the circle and waves his hand up and down on the other side. He can't see his hand. Then everything else he sees through the circle distorts for a moment, futzing in and out of clarity like a broken TV — glitching, even — and Johnny realizes that this is a doorway, one that leads to a house that's identical to his new home.

The note. The candle. The sweets next to it. "You're not on the inside," Ivan said, meaning that Johnny shouldn't have been able to create this portal without Ivan's help. So how has he?

His OCD. Sandy said something about it having an effect in this place, didn't she? Angry, Ivan must have forgotten about Johnny's OCD when he left, or underestimated just how much influence it could have. He turns back to look at the apple tree that he has just walked around; he'd been counting and noting the odds and evens as he did it, his OCD in full flow. Why did he carry out those two actions together?

It was instinct. Pure and simple. Unconsciously performing a ritual in the most literal sense.

His pulse starts to race. He has an opportunity here; Ivan said Johnny couldn't go to the Shallows without him, but it looks like he just proved Ivan wrong.

Ivan also said you could cause a disaster, *he thinks.* Your Shallows could be dangerous. And you're going in unprepared.

He stands for a moment, swaying, looking at the circle before him, and he realizes that he simply has to try to make things as they were. No matter what.

The earth feels as if it's moving beneath his feet.

He can't live without Bailey.

Johnny steps carefully into the circle, managing to avoid touching its edge; he doesn't know if he should, and something tells him he probably shouldn't. Just before his head passes through the portal, Johnny wonders what Ivan will think when he returns. A faint wovvv *sound comes from behind him as he passes completely over. He turns in time to see the portal closing. He thinks hazily about flicking the joint he's still holding back through, but...*

Johnny's consciousness twists sharply around on itself.

He freezes. His muscles lock, and his eyes roll up into his skull. His head falls back on his neck as his mind tries to adjust to the countless infinitesimal pieces of perception that it requires to know where his body is in space. It cannot. Something is wrong here; the assemblage of the world around him is ever so slightly off.

Enough of it clicks into place as his brain shunts things around, making this new reality workable, understandable. Something has to go.

It chooses the path of least resistance, compressing most of Johnny's memory of the last few hours — especially the journey to this new realm, the part that is causing the most confusion — and folds it away somewhere deep and rarely visited. Thus it creates the equilibrium it needs. Johnny is aware that something bad is happening, even if he does not know exactly what it is. Please, *he thinks, his paralyzed mouth unable to move as his mind babbles a futile plea to the universe.* Let me go back, I'm sorry, I shouldn't have done this, *and then his voice returns to him and he uses it to scream in horror:*

"Ivan, help me —"

But it's useless, and he knows it, and now the last of his recent memories are spirited away at speed, locked up deep in his subconscious. Click.

It's done.

Johnny exhales. Christ, *he thinks.* This shit is strong. *His mind has completely wandered. Never mind. It's supposed to. That's what a nice roast does. He takes in the sky.*

The stars are so clear that Johnny swears he can see them twinkling.

Then the stars are suddenly gone, replaced by the kitchen ceiling. The memory vision has ended, and Johnny is back in the present moment.

The Boggart's immense black head is split in the middle by its awful smile. Johnny looks at Present Ivan in horror.

"He didn't come with me," Johnny says to Bailey, stunned.

Bailey.

Oh my God.

"He did not," the Boggart says. It holds its hand out theatrically, palm up, fingers spread wide. "Either way, *this* friend, yes? He is done now."

It snaps its fingers into a closed fist.

Ivan's body dissolves into a glowing white light, just like the tiepin. His eyes are there a nanosecond longer than the rest, widening in surprise before they too are gone, lifted by an unfelt breeze and floating skyward.

"*Ivan!*" Bailey shrieks in horror. "*Ivan! Ivan!*"

She and Johnny grasp at the light, trying uselessly to hold it in place, their fingers finding nothing as what was once Ivan disappears through the ceiling.

"Such *noise*, yes," the Boggart says airily. "For naught: Even this Shallows impostor is already beginning its long return journey to the Whole, Johnny-Mine, the source, the energy behind all, yes."

"*You didn't have to do that!*" Johnny screams, even as understanding lands: *If that wasn't the real Ivan, then the real Ivan is still alive somewhere...*

The rusty bear trap of his other, very real loss snaps tightly shut as Bailey, with terrible timing, grabs his shoulders. She begins to babble that which he already knows.

"That wasn't Ivan," Bailey gasps. "Johnny, that wasn't the real Ivan!"

"Yes, yes," Johnny says, looking at Bailey's eyes, her hair, taking in the scent of her. It's all so perfectly done.

But the real Bailey would not be here either.

She sees it in his face.

"Born in Leicester," she babbles. "Parents were Graham and Felicity."

"It's okay—"

"I did gymnastics as a kid, I represented Leicestershire—"

"Bailey." He takes her by the shoulders too. She feels real. He starts to cry. He can't stop.

"Johnny, listen to me!"

"Here is your challenge." The Boggart speaks authoritatively. Johnny looks toward the monster as it opens its black, hairy fist.

The Boggart is holding eight OxyContin tablets.

Despite everything—despite knowing what taking those tablets will mean—Johnny feels a physical pull, his chest seeming to reach toward the pills. Here is an escape on every level. He can leave all the pain behind in one go. Forever.

The Boggart's perma-grinning face shows just how pleased it is with itself. Its voice suddenly becomes more resonant, more bass, more volume.

"*To cross the Deep Place, the Howling Wastelands,*" the Boggart says, "*can take a human lifetime, and you are without a guide, yes. No painkillers below, Johnny-Mine. Your craving will leave you without resistance to all that will come for you in the Deep Place. How can you overcome this when those not as afflicted as you could not? Do you think your intention is enough?*"

Despite himself, Johnny tries to picture overcoming his addiction, to imagine doing so while enduring great physical suffering. He tries with everything he has. He knows in this moment that this belief is key to his survival. For one brief, shining moment, Johnny feels his body, his skin, start to lift.

And then, right on cue, he glitches. Johnny drops back into the reality of the moment.

He does not have what it takes.

"Or take your medicine," the Boggart says, and its voice has returned to normal. "And know peace before the end, yes. I offer a quick death here, Johnny. In the Deep Place such a thing will not come. No one is coming to save you, and death in the Deep Place is slow indeed."

"That's not true!" Johnny yells, frantically stalling. "What... what about..." In desperation, he tries something he does not believe, going against a lifetime of independence that has sustained him ever since he understood what his father was. "What about *help coming to those who help themselves?*"

"Then help yourself, Johnny." The Boggart grins, holding out the pills. And Johnny knows he is so tired of fighting. Tired of being sad and afraid. Tired of the yearning, just fucking *tired*.

"We're going together, Johnny," Bailey pleads. "You make the portal solid, and we'll go *together!*"

Johnny hangs his head.

"The Ivan that just died," Johnny says, unable to look at her, "didn't know anything about the Shallows because *I* didn't. He only just remembered his parents' names because *I* could." He points at Bailey with a heavy arm. "Those facts you just said about your life? You know them because I know them. I know your life better than I know Ivan's." He touches her cheek. "Neither of you could remember what you were doing the day I went into the Shallows because *I* couldn't remember."

Bailey looks even more horrified than he feels. But he keeps talking. He has to.

"You aren't real, Bailey. You're of the Shallows. You can't come with me."

"That's not true—"

"The real Bailey had to leave," Johnny says, looking toward the impossible glitching hole in the floor. "You're Bailey the way I remember her before all this. You're the Bailey from *the way things were*."

Bailey gasps, seeing the skin on the back of her hands beginning to atomize into a familiar white light. It rises like vapor.

Johnny's head snaps to the Boggart.

"Not of my doing," it says, cocking its head. "But yours, yes."

"I'm not doing this!" Johnny cries. "Help me! Stop it!"

The Boggart simply watches as Bailey continues to stare at her dissipating hands, shaking her head in protest. Johnny doesn't know how to stop this as Bailey looks up in terror. Her pupils disappear as her eyes fill with a white light.

"*Johnny,*" she says, and her voice sounds as if it is coming from very far away. Particles of her clothing, her arms, her hair, all begin to rise now as if drawn from above by a powerful magnet. Johnny's hands grasp her forearms as the pieces of Bailey sift upward between his fingers like floating sand. "Johnny... what's happening..."

He doesn't have an answer; he wants to hold on to her, to keep her with him, but it is as if his knowledge of her fiction has rendered her intangible. Trying to keep her here is like trying to catch water. Bailey

I'll Quit When I'm Dead

looks to the sky, and Johnny sees her perceive something he can't. Her frightened face suddenly wreathes itself in joy. "Johnny!" she gasps. "I see it! I see it! Oh, Johnny, it's..."

"You're returning to the Whole," Johnny says, echoing the Boggart's words as he understands. Then he understands something else: When she is gone, he will be alone again.

Bailey's body ascends, her feet leaving the table, arms stretched to the heavens. Her face is a picture of awe and delight as she returns to her constituent particles, which rise from what's left of her: a Bailey-shaped figure at the bottom of a skyward-bound column of herself. Her dusting feet pass the level of Johnny's chest.

Something inside him reacts. He grabs her with his intention and not his hands, the knack somehow focused to new heights by sheer desperation.

Bailey's ascension halts. She cries out in dismay, the particles of herself freezing in place above her. "Johnny!" she gasps to the heavens. "You would stop me having this?"

"I can't do this alone," he pleads, even as he knows he has no choice. "I'm sorry. I don't know how to do this."

Bailey looks down at him. The light of her eyes almost blinds him. "Please," she says. "Let me go."

It's all that's needed.

Johnny staggers back and *pushes* Bailey skyward with the knack just before it glitches her out of his grasp for the last time. She rises quickly, her dazzlingly bright eyes on his until she disappears through the ceiling and out of sight.

Johnny stares at the void she has left. A stinging snap of that distortion-pedal tearing sound screeches from behind him. He turns to see the pit he has made yawning open, becoming still. The screeching stops. The portal is solid.

"Your challenge, yes," the Boggart says. "Make your choice."

"Instant," Johnny breathes, staring at the hole, his vision almost completely obscured by tears. "If you eat me. You swear on whatever the Boggart swear by that it will be instant."

"I swear it," the Boggart says.

Johnny looks at the Boggart's grin and those long, thin, sharp teeth. He looks at the portal—

Fuck it.

The thought springs out of nowhere, devoid of hope or strength. If anything—Johnny will think about this later when he deeply regrets this decision—it perhaps comes from raw anger at an entire childhood of being bullied, at school and at home. He's exhausted, yes, but he's also *furious* that he's still a victim. All he knows for sure is that his feet are moving, and his legs are leaping, and his body is falling through the air and into the portal. He has time to hear the Boggart roar—Johnny can't tell if it is rage or laughter—and then that ragged, distorted screeching fills Johnny's ears as he falls between the worlds.

The falling sensation abruptly stops, the gravity of two realms intermingling, and when Johnny opens his eyes, he discovers that he is lying on the ground somewhere, alone.

He realizes what he has done.

He takes in the landscape around him. Above him it is night, or at least a jet-black sky devoid of any stars. There is no visible source of light, but somehow there is just enough to see by. Johnny expected to hear wind—he was told of the *Howling* Wastelands after all—but there is none. In fact, there is an uncanny *lack* of any breeze. The background noise of such a vast space is uncommonly flat and muted, like he's standing in the universe's largest recording studio. A desert landscape rises and falls away in all directions, but this is no desert. The ground beneath Johnny is an impossible sea of knurled concrete. A loose scrim of grit and sand lies on top of it.

Johnny is utterly unsurprised to see that the sand is a dark blood red.

There are no landmarks whatsoever on the horizon except for very thin, faint, shining lines rising at random in the far distance. They seem to emanate from unseen sources on the ground, beaming into the blackness above.

It takes Johnny a moment to realize that these are rising haze. *Adenterrachs.*

He looks up, not to see his own *adenterrach* but to search for the portal through which he has just entered. The enormity of his choice hits him almost as hard as the awful craving that ripples throughout his skin. He holds his forearms against his injured chest, allowing himself a moment before he begins his long walk to whichever way is out of here. Before he begins his torment.

Johnny Blake drops his head, bends forward and downward, curling himself over onto all fours. He laces his fingers behind his head and rests his brow and elbows on the sand-covered concrete, rocking silently.

He dropped the knife. It's still in his kitchen, far out of reach.

After a few minutes he begins to scream into the rough surface beneath him with everything he has.

His choice is made, and now there is no turning back.

Chapter Nineteen: Madison

Getting Beneath the Surface

THEY HAVEN'T BEEN driving long, only perhaps a minute or two, but Madison can't check the time. She is crammed in the cargo space of Ellie's Land Rover with a wad of fabric in her mouth and tape over her lips.

It has been difficult to avoid choking; her face is sore and burning where it was dragged across the carpet. She was vaguely aware of her limbs being moved while she lay unconscious, the pain both waking her up and dropping her straight back under. When she did become fully aware once more, she found herself lying on her side with her already stressed spine and fractured rib aching. Her limbs were immobilized, her hands and feet tied and her wrists and ankles then connected by what seemed to be a length of rope that ran all the way along her back. Not the cruelty of a full hog-tie, then—Ellie clearly wanting Madison to at least be vaguely comfortable while still unable to struggle. Testing her bonds turned Madison's rib into a knife anyway. Ellie then pulled her all the way from her room, along the hallway, and down the stairs before loading her onto a furniture dolly; she used that to wheel Madison from the house to the back of the Land Rover.

Any questions Madison tried to ask through her gag were ignored. Ellie was done talking, it seemed. Madison tried to keep calm, telling herself that yes, Ellie might be a lunatic, but she'd always had a strong sense of fairness. Any challenge she had for Madison would be passable. It had to be.

The ride so far has been quiet, slow, and uneven; Madison thinks they might be driving across the fields. Ellie has stopped and stepped out of the vehicle a few times, and then there were the sounds of moving metal — gates opening and closing, Madison thinks — before Ellie returned to the driver's seat and the journey continued.

The Land Rover stops. Madison's jaw aches badly now as she hears the driver's door open and close one more time. There are a few seconds of silence. Then the latch clicks.

There were no footsteps, Madison thinks. *We're on soft land.*

Madison is still on her side, her back to the door, but when it opens, she turns her head, trying to see Ellie. Ellie looks down at Madison for a moment, and then, without a word, she grabs Madison's ankles.

Madison tries to thrash, but the rope connecting her hands and feet becomes taut, and her rib screams in agony. The best she can do is squirm as Ellie leans in and jams her arms beneath Madison's. It's an oddly intimate embrace, Ellie pressing her cheek to Madison's and breathing hard in her ear as she pulls her out of the vehicle.

Madison seizes her moment. She draws back and thrusts her forehead into the bridge of Ellie's nose.

At least that was the plan; she only connects with Ellie's brow, causing Ellie to gasp a little and pull away, hands covering her face.

Madison drops heavily into the tall grass, unable to break her fall with her bound hands. She is badly winded, and her rib barks, but she blocks out the pain — she's become really good at that — and tries to wriggle away. She gets about three feet, gasping and wheezing before Ellie grabs her under her arms again and lifts her torso slightly off the ground, dragging her knees across the grass. She dumps her face down on another flat cart. Whatever Ellie's plan is, she has apparently taken the time to think it through.

Madison, lying on her chest, takes in her nighttime surroundings. They are on a hillside, one high and steep enough that, even from the ground, she can see fields far below. How long past midnight is it? She has no way to know. The sky above is full of stars, and somewhere in the valley are houses, and inside those houses, Madison knows, are people living their lives, too far away, too deeply asleep, to hear her scream even if her gag were removed.

She looks at the Land Rover as Ellie pulls the cart away from it. It's parked at the end of a long set of tire tracks in the grass. There is no road in sight. They are in the middle of nowhere. There is only the sound of the breeze and the cart's trundling wheels.

"Uhhh!" Madison gasps through her fabric gag.

"Can't understand you," Ellie mumbles. She still doesn't sound fully lucid, her words slurring, and that is frightening. "I'll take your gag off in a second. We're nearly there."

Where? Madison bucks and rolls off the cart. She lands on the grass—it is instinct, her will to escape forcing her to try even though she knows it will only pointlessly stall whatever's coming—and the pain in her rib causes her to cry out, the sound a dull *yawk* around her gag. But what she sees silences her like a needle lifted from a record.

A backhoe sits beside a pile of earth. The earth sits next to what looks, from Madison's vantage point, like a freshly dug pit.

Madison screams. Huffing wet breath into the cotton in her mouth, feeling as if she is suffocating, Madison tries to squirm away, but all that does is roll her onto her uninjured side, her arms pinned painfully behind her.

This time Ellie squats down, facing Madison, and gets one arm under her and the other around her before drawing her in tight once more, planting a shoulder in Madison's stomach. Ellie inhales, and with impossible strength she deadlifts Madison as if she were lifting a rolled-up carpet, the pair of them chest-to-chest. Ellie grunts out a little *hup* noise before Madison is jerked farther upward, her torso now falling forward and down as her stomach lands on Ellie's bony, wiry shoulder. Madison's face is now pressed against Ellie's back, and as Madison twists, trying to break free of Ellie's iron grip, her fractured rib finally breaks.

Madison lets out muffled, torn screams into her gag. Ellie's stone-like arms continue to hold Madison in place as she trudges toward the grave. Madison grits her teeth around the wadding in her mouth, trying to bite off her screams, not wanting to give them to Ellie, but *oh God in heaven, it hurts.*

The pit is perhaps only a few feet away now, and Madison can finally, *finally,* hear Ellie breathing hard. Damaged or not, Ellie is still impossibly strong. For once, Madison wishes she were heavier. She tries to thrash, moaning as her rib shifts, but Ellie's grip is a steel band. As Ellie slows, Madison stills; being dropped to the ground would be bad enough... but does Ellie plan to drop her into the pit? Judging by the pile of earth, the pit is at least several feet deep.

Before she can think too hard on that possibility, Ellie squats and lowers Madison backside-first to the ground. The smell of chlorophyll and soil fills her nostrils, the freshly dug pit reeking of earth and mold.

Ellie exhales. "You said to me on the day we met that you would rather die than chicken out ever again. Did you not?"

"*Yeh,*" Madison desperately yawps into her gag. The pit is close. The vertical rails of a ladder stick up over the edge.

"But you asked to *quit* now that we're at Elite, Madison," Ellie says. She sounds so terribly disappointed. "You asked to quit when you knew you couldn't. Do you understand what a capitulation that is? You need to have nowhere—*nowhere*—to run. I know your fears, Madison. You are going to face them, and you are going to devour them. You're going in there to learn. You need to spend some time somewhere with zero way out."

"*Nuh! Nuh! Nuh!*"

Ellie steps between Madison and the pit. She leans forward and grabs the backs of Madison's bound arms, then, walking backward, hauls her closer to the edge. Madison's knees drag across the grass and packed earth and she can't see past Ellie's legs, can't see how far the fall will be. *Oh shit, how far is the fall...*

Ellie halts and steps aside.

"I told you," Ellie grunts, "how important finding True Strength is. The most important thing you can do in your life. I don't like doing this at all, Madison. But I realize that the only way you personally stand a chance is to go into a deep place. This is for you."

Madison looks down into the pit.

It takes her glitching brain several horrified seconds to make sense of what she sees at the bottom. It is too much, *too much, this can't be happening, this isn't real.*

At the bottom of a six-foot drop lies the tarp-wrapped body of Winter. The plastic has ripped away from the horse's head; the distinct gray crescent is still intact, but there is a ragged hole in the animal's skull.

That alone—the sight of that magnificent, ruined animal lying there dead—would have been enough. But it's what's on top of Winter's body that short-circuits any hope Madison had of staying calm, of keeping a cool head, of outsmarting Ellie and finding a way to escape her.

It's a wooden coffin.

Madison screams.

"Give me a minute," Ellie says as though she can't hear the muffled sounds of terror coming from behind Madison's gag. She sways and sits suddenly, like she *needs* to sit down. "Have to breathe."

Madison, too, has to breathe. She stops screaming and tries to pull oxygen in through her nostrils. It's not enough. She's hyperventilating. She's close to blacking out. *Calm down, panicking is the worst thing you can do, as long as you're up here and that coffin is down there, you still have a—*

"Horse graves," Ellie says. "People around here need them dug all the time, so I knew my digging up here wouldn't raise unwanted questions...but that meant I needed a dead horse. A while back, when I was first thinking up this particular protocol, it was horse graves that gave me the idea." She gestures weakly at the pit. "Of course I couldn't have people see me driving a rented backhoe up the hillside and then later see me riding Winter around. And Winter, my girl...she was getting old. Eating a lot less. You might have thought she was impressive when you saw her, but you should have seen her before...the muscle mass, my goodness. But she'd lost a lot of it. She didn't like to stand as much. Sleeping more. The vet said she might live another year. But then I needed to escalate things with you, and...well. Killing Winter would mean I would lose an extra year with her, but the cost to you—to the rest of your *life*—

if I didn't use Winter's death to set this up? I couldn't fail you like that, Madison. And Winter was so tired already." Ellie sniffs, shaking her head before scooting over to Madison. Madison tears her eyes away from the pit to look at her. Ellie is smiling sadly, and Madison thinks that half of Ellie's face looks a little slack.

"I told you," Ellie says, "by whatever means necessary. Including sacrifice."

But did you really have to make that sacrifice? Madison thinks, though she knows by now that Ellie's logic has not only taken a holiday but also permanently emigrated. Madison stares into the pit again. She doesn't want to look at Winter, but it's better than looking at the coffin. *Sacrifice?* Is that what Ellie thought this was? Had she shot her beloved horse because she couldn't stand to see it being weak?

She lowered you down to the edge of the pit first, Madison desperately thinks. *She didn't just drop you down there. That means she thinks a fall from this height is too much. That means she really doesn't intend to kill you. She wants you to have a chance.*

She understands then what Ellie's test will be... but also remembers how unhinged and *sloppy* Ellie has become. Her death is perhaps certain after all.

"Yes, you would rather die than chicken out," Ellie says, moving behind Madison.

Madison braces herself—Ellie could still decide to just kick her into the pit and be done with it, but Madison knows that if Ellie is talking, she wants Madison to be able to listen, not rolling in pain from a fall. Sure enough, Ellie is wrapping a rope around Madison's chest. "This is what it truly means to face your fears," Ellie says. "It doesn't mean bravely going after a new career or allowing yourself to start dating after a bad breakup." She comes back into view and tears the tape from Madison's mouth so fast that Madison doesn't have time to react. Then Ellie yanks the rag from between her teeth.

As soon as Madison has full lungs, she screams.

"Yes," Ellie says, solemn and deadly serious. "Screaming is exactly what it means. It means getting deep in the weeds—in the box—and screaming until you have no screams left."

"Ellie, stop!" Madison barks. "Do you understand that I am going to die if you put me in there? You are killing me if you do this!"

Her words are cut off by a sharp slap across the back of Madison's skull. The darkness briefly flashes white.

"Listen," Ellie hisses.

Madison suddenly hears it: the *real* rage inside Ellie, slipping out for only a second. The kind that is so fierce it must be buried extra deep, like a reactor core... and where, in responsible people, it can be harnessed safely, fueling and empowering. Ellie's definition of responsibility, however, is unique, and Ellie is very angry indeed. Madison listens, but her ringing head refocuses her bulging eyes on the coffin.

The burning shed from Madison's nightmares would be a stately home by comparison.

"Inside the coffin," Ellie says, "there are two oxygen tanks with masks. They take up a lot of room, but I'm sure you'd rather have them. If you keep calm and breathe slowly, you should be fine. Digging you out by hand, once the dirt has settled, will take at least six hours — coincidentally, that's the average time in which the air inside a coffin runs out if the occupant doesn't have an oxygen mask."

She's going to put you in there —

"And I will not start digging until dawn," Ellie says.

"This isn't part of the system, Ellie!" Madison screams. "You've gone too far! This is supposed to be about... about choice! The strength to keep choosing to say yes! You're taking that away, forcing me to do something..."

Even in her terror she can't finish the sentence. That *is* what this has all been about: being *forced* to find strength through extreme methods.

"There it is," Ellie says, and holding the rope she has just tied around Madison's chest, she begins to lower Madison into the earth.

Chapter Twenty: Johnny

The End

TIME PASSES IN the Deep Place.

Eventually, Johnny gets to his feet.

That horrible red sand grinds underfoot against the rough concrete floor.

His craving is now all-consuming, and the knowledge that there can be no abating it is—

Bailey, he thinks. *Bailey.*

The memories seem to rise from the scrim of red sand itself, as if his feet stirring the silicate below are dredging up everything he has been fleeing. This is going to be far, far worse than he feared. As Kaleb said: suicide.

A Needle Monster crawls slowly over the top of the nearest concrete rise.

Its hardened, burnt-crimson face is down, sniffing the sand, jittering back and forth as if sensing for something. Its hands and toes grip the concrete so tightly that they look capable of scaling a vertical surface, lending the creature the air of a giant, charred red spider. Its body twitches and judders horribly at regular intervals, the tight, uneven muscles in its black scarred back pulsing and twitching unnaturally at different points, as if being electrocuted from within.

Its whole form is *frantic*, terribly eager. It stops as it crests the low peak. It falls still for a second; then its whole body twitches violently as if it has detected a scent, and the monster begins to gallop down the slope on all fours, moving toward Johnny with astonishing speed.

Johnny straightens. He has no physical strength to fight this beast. He barely survived the encounter at the airport. He remembers again that creature's attempts to rip his muscle from his body with its teeth, its preferred method of dismemberment, and how his own endurance then was far higher than it is now.

This will be a drawn-out, tearing death, his many past sufferings pulled from his soul in the process, and it will hurt.

He instinctively tries to use the knack with a knee-jerk instant of fear-driven, half-formed intention: the vague, unspecific thought of *STOP*.

It works, to a degree.

The Needle Monster stumbles, its momentum so great that it slides a few feet as it falls, but then it is instantly back up and galloping once more.

Hope stirs in Johnny's stomach—*he can affect them*—but it dies as Johnny desperately tries to build on it, to form a clearer image in his head of what he wants to do to the creature. He's blocked by unlocked memories that keep crashing in. The Boggart has opened the floodgates, it seems, or maybe that's the Deep Place at work, and now here is an image of Ivan in the new house and *Ivan is dead*—*no he isn't; that was Shallows Ivan and*—

The monster is now close enough for Johnny to hear its red, charred fingers and toes slipping and gripping on the sheen of red sand on top of the concrete. *Break*, he thinks at it frantically, *die*, and yes, he feels the clear intention start to form, it's *working*, and he tries to send it into the monster.

His cursed brain glitches again, the knack slipping from his mind's struggling grasp, and he has time to blink dumbly in shock before the Needle Monster leaves the ground in a mighty leap. Johnny sees a flash of its crumbling, churning quicksand face before it lands heavily upon him, its weight knocking him flat and sending a screaming pain through his injured chest. He hits the concrete, the wind knocked from him. The monster wraps its arms and legs hungrily around him in a familiar and sickening embrace. Johnny's arms are tightly immobilized against his sides.

No, Johnny thinks, but it's too late. The monster presses its unspeakable face against Johnny's chest, and this time the pain comes even before the teeth, as if the monster knows there is no need to latch on first; its prey is already helpless.

The needle pierces Johnny's chest. Another memory comes, and this time it is not a vague, distant sound like that at the airport, no piercing recall of *WHAT'S WRONG WITH THAT LITTLE MAN?* He is in the Deep Place now; memories abound, but this memory — drawn out by the needle that protrudes from the monster's sand face — is dragged *through* Johnny's brain, snagging as it comes. He experiences it so clearly and overwhelmingly that his addiction feels like a case of indigestion —

—*he's smashed a glass on the floor, let it slip carelessly from his hand mid-argument. Everyone at the party turns to look, shocked, and ironically the realization that he doesn't care — even at an industry event like this, even when all the music bigwigs are now staring their way — breaks the spell of his anger. This isn't who he is —*

This isn't the bad part, he knows. That's when —

—*he looks at Bailey and sees the rage in her has turned into tears, and he knows he has finally shattered something irreplaceable, and it isn't just the glass. She thought he did it on purpose, that he smashed it deliberately, perhaps to frighten her, and so when she rises to top his perceived anger, the words she uses are a rapier blade in his heart.* "The only reason you're in this mess," *she says, her voice shaking,* "is —"

His intention in the Deep Place explodes out of his chest, his frantic desire manifesting into his current reality, that of being *away* from his mind. The blast hits the Needle Monster and pushes it, breaks it. It flies away and rolls through the sand, leaving a long trail. It tries to right itself to charge again, but now its right arm and left leg are snapped and hanging loose. The two intact limbs scrabble hungrily as the monster tries to make its way back to Johnny. The twin fears of returning to that memory, of being *in* it, and of being here, facing this unspeakable horror's attack, focus Johnny's knack to laser accuracy. He moans and pours all his intention over the creature with everything he has.

The Needle Monster bucks and arches as its body crumples and crinkles, twisting under the sheer force of Johnny's intention. It dies, bent and curled and angled like a spider's corpse, but Johnny feels no victory as he exhales, gasping. These are only his first steps in the Deep Place; drawing himself upright to overcome his foe took a Herculean effort. He looks at the broken-puppet body, not even knowing how these creatures work, what they get out of this. Is it the pain of the memories they draw out? The meat of their victims flavored by adrenaline and cortisol? He is aware of a steady, low rustling; it quickly rises to a cacophonous, moaning wail that he recognizes. Wearily, he raises his head.

Several more Needle Monsters are crawling into sight. Five of them: three are close, two in the middle distance. The craving in every fiber of his being is, to his surprise, lessened slightly by his anger, and at an unlikely source: injustice.

He wasn't supposed to be alone like this.

He straightens with great effort, grinding his teeth in a grimace so intense it is almost comical, even as his mind whispers, *Lie down and let this end. It will hurt, but it will finally end.*

But how long would it take to get out? *What would be waiting on the other side?* He scans the bleak landscape. Perhaps the real Ivan will appear and come to his aid. But there are only the monsters. He isn't surprised; no one is coming to save him. The only person who *can* help him — as it has always been — is himself. And as always, it will not be enough.

But if no one is coming to save him, he will not go out on his back.

"I swear to fucking God...," Johnny begins, pointing at the nearest approaching horror, but then doesn't finish his sentence; instead he simply charges toward the nearest Needle Monster.

It rears up, and Johnny tries to seize it from afar, to crush it with his intention before he even gets there, but it doesn't work. He is exhausted, and the creature is too far away. As he closes the gap between them, it is suddenly easier to define where the creature is in space, to grasp it with his mind... but he can't find purchase. He tries to refocus, but now the monster is too *close,* its grotesque red visage trembling and grunting toward Johnny's face. His mind recoils; the creature slips through his intention, and then it is upon him. Immediately it presses the churning quicksand of its face against Johnny's neck. Its hidden teeth begin to bite. Johnny roars and wraps his arms around the monster to hold it tightly to him. The press of his body against the monster's creates an intense awareness of where his intention ends and where the monster begins. Now he clutches at the creature with his mind *and* his arms, feeling the monster stiffen as it understands something is wrong. Its needle burrows into his neck, and Johnny lets it happen, even as the piercing pain ignites inside his flesh, because now his intention is even more connected. He bellows, crushing the monster as the memory is sucked free—

Bailey, from an even earlier time, or rather her lap; he can't meet her gaze. She's trying to get him to open up about his family, just as she once did about hers. And for her that wasn't just difficult—it was the hardest thing she could do. She did it for him. But now, he can't return the favor. He stumbles over his words. It's embarrassing. When he finally looks up, he expects to see disgust, or judgment perhaps. Instead, what he sees there is love. She strokes the side of his face. "Thank you for trying; I know you'll tell me when you're ready," she says, before adding: "I'm never going to let you go—"

The loss is so intense that Johnny stops breathing, the crushing in his chest becoming literal as he gasps and finds that the monster pressed against him is dead. He has killed it. He pushes it off him, crying out as its teeth and its needle pull free of his flesh, but then something hammers into his side, and it is another one of them, biting down, and this time Johnny immediately pulls it to him, into him, knowing this is both his only chance and an immense risk as he grips with intention and limbs and the needle begins to spear him—

Glitch.

No!

But it's too late, the cursed glitch in his head interfering with his oh-so-tenuous grasp of the knack and fumbling his grip on the Needle

Monster, on everything he tries to do, but the needle is piercing him, dragging another barbed memory through him—

His father. Before the beating. The disgust *in his face, the acid words that burned away a piece of young Johnny's soul.*

WHAT'S WRONG WITH THAT LITTLE MAN?

Johnny's intention blasts the Needle Monster back a foot, tearing his skin as it goes, but Johnny now knows the only way he can beat them is to let them come close. *Oh God,* the creatures pounce, bite, needle, and here it is—

A gathering of some kind at an unfamiliar house. The children are playing in the back garden; Johnny is one of them, perhaps eight or nine years old. The adults are indoors, talking and relaxing. A new visitor comes, walking down the side of the house to enter through the back door into the dining room where the parents are sitting—

Johnny screams in the Deep Place, for this is the worst, the absolute worst. He can't—

—this visitor is familiar enough with the family who lives here, friends enough with the family, to enter through the back door.

It is a little person.

He is a man, dressed in a smart suit and sporting an impressive moustache. Johnny has never seen a little person before.

"Hi, kids," the man says politely, smiling and raising a hand before he heads into the house.

"Ooh!" Johnny cries, already giddy from an hour or so of rambunctious play. He points at the newcomer.

"What's wrong with that little man?"

Some of the other kids laugh, some don't—perhaps the kids who already know this visitor. The little person just smiles a sad smile and enters the house. Johnny continues playing.

Later, Johnny goes inside to get a drink.

He passes through the room where the adults are seated around a table, and as he does, he feels the conversation stop. The little person's eyes look away from

Johnny. Johnny feels uncomfortable but knows it can't be anything to do with him; perhaps the adults have fallen out. All he knows is that the silence is unpleasant and oppressive, and he wants to be out of there very quickly. He gets his drink, leaves, and spends another hour or two with the other children before going home, even if he isn't quite as carefree as he was before. He knows something is wrong—

Johnny has to kill the creature, has to end this, and the white-hot pain from the creature's bite is overwhelming, but Johnny knows that he must draw the monster in close, tight, to crush it, even though that will mean *being even more in the memory*. But Adult Johnny tightens his trembling arms around the monster latched on to his ribs, babbling, *No, no, no,* even as he becomes aware of a third closing in, and as its needle buries deep—

Young Johnny is in his bedroom. His dad hasn't said a word on the way home, and Johnny's attempts to converse are met with one-word answers. His mother drove, his father in the passenger seat. Johnny can smell the beer rising from his dad's body. Johnny's dad had said he wasn't going to drink today.

At home, Johnny is sent to his bedroom. His dad's face is a dark high-blood-pressure red, his lips set tight. Confused, Johnny does as he is told, knowing that to argue would be a bad idea even if he desperately wants to know what he has done.

From upstairs, he hears the raised voices below. They reach a crescendo as Johnny thinks, Please don't let it happen again, *but his silent prayers are of course ignored. He hears it: the distinct, harsh smack of a slap, followed by several heavy thuds. He hears the muffled sounds of his mother's crying followed by the ominous pounding of his father's footsteps coming up the stairs, and Johnny knows that the warm-up is over. His bedroom door flies open, and his dad steps into the room, breathing hard.*

"Now you," he says, swaying a little. "You..."

His dad looks out the window and takes a few deep breaths. Johnny can see the veins pulsing in his father's neck and forehead.

"You stupid, obnoxious little shit."

"What—" Johnny manages to squeak, never getting to add the did I do? *because his dad is screwing up his face into a look of such total disgust that Johnny cannot believe this is his father, or that his father is aiming so much revulsion at him.*

"Ooh!" his father screeches, quoting his son, his voice twisted into a high,

wheedling, mocking tone that pierces Johnny to the core of his soul. "WHAT'S WRONG WITH THAT LITTLE MAN?"

It is a harsher savaging than any he has ever experienced on the playground, coming from his own father in his family home. It cattle-brands the knowledge into Johnny's bones that he is indeed a stupid, obnoxious little shit.

"I'm sorr—"

"Do you have any idea," his father says, "how embarrassing you were? That's my son saying that, that's my family!"

He slams the bedroom door, and now Johnny can see that his father is carrying two things: a phone book and a rolling pin.

One end of the rolling pin has a fresh red mark.

"Stand up," his dad says—

The third Needle Monster fastens onto Johnny's leg, Johnny seeing the top of its black-and-red crusted head as this time it bites through his jeans. Its teeth break his skin and lodge in his flesh. Johnny is crushing the monster on his shoulder but cannot complete the kill; his mind keeps glitching, interfering with his dual focus, and now the physical pain is too much. He cannot get his mind right; Johnny understands that he is going to die.

The thought is soothing, even if—as the Boggart said—the means of the final journey into death are terrifying and painful. It will at least soon be over.

But he promised himself he would fight to the end.

"Help," he hears himself quietly gasp as he tries to get a handle on the Needle Monster eating his leg. He manages it, pulling the heavy creature close, and he has a second for another breath before he goes about his desperate work. Johnny fills his lungs to cry out with all he has, and this time it is a bellow.

"HELP!"

He knows, of course, that no one is coming to save him, and then the sand nearby is blasted into the air as something else arrives, its presence pushing out in front of it as it bursts into existence, and Johnny knows that it is more monstrous attackers.

But it isn't. It's Mister Kaleb.

The old man dives forward, his hat flying off behind him, but that isn't the only thing he's trailing. The mask Kaleb so carefully wore in the Dream Lounge is already bleeding away from his true, weeping and bellowing face, a layer rapidly dissolving into nothing as he leaps across Johnny and *through* the two Needle Monsters. They are ripped painfully away, but they instantly latch on to Kaleb, who is already wrapping them close and crushing them the way Johnny did. Kaleb's intention is clearly stronger; the Needle Monsters die instantly. Johnny wants to call out as he sees the face beneath Kaleb's mask. He can't; the pain of his injuries has taken his breath. He rolls for a moment, trying to sit up, watching in amazement as Kaleb gasps and drops the corpses. The old man — for even his true face is old, perhaps because Kaleb has only limited control over the glamour — puts one hand over his eyes. He extends the other and moves to help a speechless and bleeding Johnny up.

"Don't look at me," Kaleb says, his voice wet and ragged. "I can't use my intention for everything at once. I can't keep the..." He gives up, dropping the hand from his face and lowering his head, still avoiding Johnny's gaze. "Couldn't find you," Kaleb says breathlessly, his speech trembling, tears streaking his cheeks. "I tried to follow you but couldn't — when you called out, it was like a beacon —"

Johnny looks from the extended hand to the real face of the frail man before him. He tries to see the terrifying fury and power that once resided there throughout his childhood. He can't. All he sees is a broken, ashamed, and lonely old man. He nearly feels a stab of pity, and yet he resists taking Kaleb's hand. This man, his crime... Johnny can't even speak.

Kaleb looks up, his red and wet eyes pleading. "Please, son."

It's not a general term of endearment.

"You've been in the Shallows all this time?" Johnny croaks. "Hiding?"

"I told you when we talked on the street," his father replies, sighing heavily and shrugging sadly. "I said it. That you of all people were the *last* person I expected to see here." Kaleb looks away, unable to hold his son's gaze.

His extended hand drops.

Before Johnny can respond, the concrete around Kaleb's feet cracks. Needle Monsters begin to claw up through the ground.

"Shit," Kaleb murmurs, moving in front of Johnny. "Stay back." Johnny crawls a few feet backward. The concrete continues to crack like a frozen lake; perhaps ten or twelve Needle Monsters clamber out of the depths. "Stay back!" Kaleb barks again, rushing to the first monster that frees itself from the concrete and rugby-tackling it.

On his feet now, Johnny ignores his father's command, limping in as quickly as he can. The creature is already dying in Kaleb's grasp, but then another attacks and latches on to Kaleb's leg. Kaleb's eyes roll back in his head as the monster's needle digs into his flesh, but he still manages to kill the creature. By the time Johnny reaches his father, five Needle Monsters are dead, but five more are swarming Kaleb and dragging him to the concrete. Kaleb has disappeared beneath the mass of red, scarred assailants pinning him down. Johnny climbs painfully onto the nearest back and wraps his arm around the monster, holding it tight; its spine snaps under his intention. Johnny falls backward, dragging the dead Needle Monster with him, dropping it to the concrete as he immediately lurches up and staggers to his father once more.

It can't be for this, Johnny thinks. *He can't die for nothing—it's too cruel even for him—*

Kaleb's bloodied face is now visible. His eyes are wide and frightened. He screws them up for a moment, grunts, and the monster on his arm suddenly arches sharply. It dies. Mister Kaleb coughs up blood.

"I've got nothing left, Johnny," he gasps. "I told you. I'm old." He tries to catch a breath, and there is the sound of blood bubbling in his throat.

"Dad," Johnny cries, saying the word before he can stop himself. "Hold on, hold on—" He jumps onto the back of the nearest creature and tries in vain to focus his intention on it. The sight of his father's dying face—the panic it induces in Johnny's brain—means Johnny's mind is glitching, spinning and snapping like a cornered animal.

It's too late. Mister Kaleb is breathing his last.

"Dad! Dad!"

Kaleb's eyes grow wide. "Oh my God," he says quietly. "Oh my God. Johnny." He blinks.

"Wait!" Johnny cries pointlessly as he tries to stop what is happening. He *tries. Glitch. Glitch.* He can't focus his intention, can't narrow it like sunlight through a magnifying glass. "Fucking *work!*" he screams at himself.

"Please forgive me," Mister Kaleb slurs. "I'm sorry. I should have come with you. I'm sorry. I'm sorry."

His hand grips Johnny's. Johnny grips back, and something happens: Kaleb's mind connects with Johnny's just like he said it could — the *Haystack Picker* — finding the freshest memory there. Johnny feels it happen, his father's grasp tightening against his own as Kaleb sees the remnants of the memory the Needle Monster drew forth.

The horror and guilt are shining in Kaleb's dying eyes as he sees his past self standing in Johnny's childhood bedroom. Sees his past self holding the phone book. The rolling pin.

"Oh Johnny—"

The Needle Monsters fall on Kaleb's body like a pack of hyenas feasting on a carcass, but he manages to look directly at Johnny, desperate to communicate one final message.

"Please, forgive me—"

The message is clear. It reaches into Johnny's very bones.

"Be free of me," Kaleb says.

His hand goes limp as something deep in Johnny's brain goes *click*. The glitching stops.

Johnny feels the blood in his scalp move as a great sense of soothing washes through him.

The creatures are suddenly easier to seize with his mind. One is already turning away from Kaleb's dead body and leaping toward Johnny. Johnny lunges forward himself. The creature's compact, muscled weight takes his wind as they slam into each other. Johnny lands on top, already breaking the creature's spine with his intention. It gets a good bite out of his arm before it dies, those horrible sharp teeth leaving circular marks in his skin, but Johnny has killed it *quick*.

With no time to comprehend what just happened, Johnny moans

as he stands, every part of him burning. Two Needle Monsters rise from his father's body and charge. Johnny, exhausted, pushes one of them with his intention, just to throw it off its rhythm; it works far better than he hoped. It stumbles, drops, and skids into the other's path, its thrashing limbs snagging and entangling those of its comrade, causing both to tumble across the ground in a mess of blistered skin and sand. Johnny throws himself onto them, and they buck underneath him. *There they are*, and he has only a second before they bite and chew—

He mentally flinches, expecting a glitch to derail his intention to crush them both.

It doesn't happen. Johnny's intention flows out of him as clearly as a song.

The Needle Monsters' bodies crackle and snap beneath him. He grits his teeth against the pain as he rolls away, the bleeding holes and open wounds in his body beseeching him to lie still. He does for a moment, then realizes his father's body lies only a few feet away. He sits up, sees what remains of Mister Kaleb, and wishes he hadn't. He turns and vomits onto the sandy concrete.

Johnny stays on all fours, turning away from the contents of his stomach, feeling the addiction in him that is stronger than any thirst he's ever known. He is alone, and even if he were to make it out of the Howling Wastelands, on the other side there is only his addiction and no Bailey. He wonders if he can use his intention to break his own neck.

But something is different. There is now something new in him. Some very recently installed ground floor. It's only small, and very far away, but it's *there*. Something strong and quiet beneath the eye of the storm.

His intention goes to work on his wounds. He shivers as he understands what has happened. All his injuries have stopped bleeding. They are still there, the angry nerve endings barking and scratching, but at least he can keep from bleeding to death. Johnny pauses. He isn't imagining it.

The craving. He couldn't soothe it before, but maybe now he—

He cries out, the slight—*ever-so-slight*—satiating of his addiction such an internal relief that he rocks back onto his heels, his head coming up too fast. He closes his eyes, trying to restore his equilibrium.

He doesn't know how long it will take to cross the Howling Wastelands. Even if he can use the knack to find the way, he knows there will be a great many monsters to battle.

But he thinks—he *thinks*—he might be able to make it.

This is not a feeling he has ever truly known.

Johnny slowly gets to his feet. Already he can hear more Needle Monsters approaching. He begins to turn in a circle, feeling now with his intention for any hint as to which way to go. *There*, a faint sense of direction. It's not rock solid, but it will do. He thinks he can find his way as he goes, even if he can't tell how far he must travel.

I'll find out, Johnny thinks.

He takes his first shaky steps as the scratching, searching sounds of other, unseen monsters on the horizon grow louder.

Chapter Twenty-One: Madison

The End

MADISON GAGS, TRYING not to think about why the bottom of the pit is so uneven. She doesn't want to think about how they're on top of Winter's body. About how Ellie buried her horse under just enough dirt to keep the coffin relatively level and prevent it from tipping over.

Madison sees the back end of the coffin now and — horribly — the close-up sight of Winter's partially buried and unwrapped head. Ellie *wanted* Madison to see the dead horse. She wanted Madison to know *just how much she was prepared to sacrifice.*

Madison gags again. She won't give Ellie the satisfaction.

Ellie cuts the rope that was digging painfully into Madison's chest and armpits, carefully moving it free as if she is trying to avoid unnecessary friction burns on Madison's skin. *Crazy, crazy bitch,* Madison thinks. Ellie raps her knuckles on the coffin's lid, considering it. The sound is dull and deep, the wood hard and thick. It looks unused, clean. Then she moves back to Madison.

"I can't even imagine how scared you are right now," Ellie says, planting her feet on either side of Madison where she lies chest down in the mud. The dark walls of the pit rise up all around her, their top edges out of Madison's sight. "But I cannot let you live the rest of your life as you are. You must truly become Serena. Down here, you'll have no choice."

Suddenly the tension in Madison's lower back and shoulders is relieved; Ellie has cut the long rope binding Madison's feet to her hands. She still isn't fully free; the ropes around her wrists and ankles are still tightly in place. She pulls herself to her knees and sees Ellie scurrying up the ladder. The high mud walls make Madison feel for one crazy moment as if she is inside the small end of a giant telescope, peering at the moon and stars of another galaxy.

Ellie clears the top of the pit and pulls the ladder up. She drops it behind herself, out of Madison's reach.

"Sit up," Ellie calls down. She is a silhouette against the stars. "Pull your hands under your butt and along the backs of your legs."

Madison does, her breath coming in short pants.

"If you want, you can use this to cut the remaining ropes, but it shouldn't be necessary." Ellie's silhouette tosses down a small object that lands next to Madison with a light thud. It is a knife. "If I were you, I'd get inside the coffin as quickly as possible. You can cut the ropes later if you want to, but the earth is coming down now."

"Ellie!" Madison yells. She uses the coffin to pull herself to her bound feet, gasping away the jabbing punch of her broken rib. The pit is deeper than she thought, perhaps nine feet. Easily outside the limits of Madison's standing reach, and just outside of her ability to jump and pull herself up by her fingertips even if she weren't severely injured. She thinks desperately about trying to somehow climb out with her feet and hands still bound, but then Ellie confirms Madison's doubts.

"It's only so you can make yourself more comfortable," Ellie says, and Madison doesn't know if it's from the exhaustion on top of the concussion, but Ellie is slurring. "Trust me: You're not climbing out. Even if your limbs were fully free, I don't think you would be able to get out of a hole this deep *too* easily. You'd do it eventually — you're resourceful and strong, Hannah — but it would take you a while."

Hannah, Madison thinks. *Oh, Ellie.*

"Bound as you are," Ellie is saying, "you'd have no chance. By the time that crappy knife cuts through those ropes, this hole will have been filled."

Ellie begins to back away.

"Wait!" Madison yells, but already she is diving back to the mud to snatch up the knife.

"This is what I don't understand about people today," Ellie says, her voice sad as her silhouette sways in the moonlight. "None of you — *none* of you — seem to understand what 'no matter what' means anymore." She points at the coffin. "Get in. You don't want to be standing around in there when the earth comes down." She backs fully out of Madison's sight.

"Ellie!" Madison yells. Frantically, she feels around the edges of the lid, the stabbing sensation in her concussed head almost as bad as the one in her broken rib. She gets her fingers underneath the coffin lid and lifts. In the darkness, it's hard to see inside the box. She slides the lid away but not off the box, creating a narrow opening through which she looks inside.

Where are the oxygen tanks?

"I. Believe. In. You," Ellie calls; she sounds farther away now, her voice barely audible. Madison slaps her bound hands uselessly around the coffin's unforgiving interior to pointlessly triple-check what she already knows.

There are no oxygen tanks and masks inside the coffin.

Madison emits a shredded scream that tears apart any illusions of what she thought she had become.

"Ellie! There are no oxygen tanks!" Madison screams. "Ellie! There are! No! Tanks! How can you do this? I believed in *you*!"

There is only the sound of the wind.

Then the sound of the backhoe coughing to life.

"Oh God, oh God, oh Jesus, help me," Madison babbles tearfully as she heaves her body into the coffin, careful not to tip the lid all the way off. Is she really going to do this? It's certain death, no matter how much air she can conserve. If Ellie won't start digging until dawn, and even then it will take six hours to get her out—

Dirt shivers down the walls of the pit as the backhoe approaches. Ellie was telling the truth. Madison knows she will not be able to climb out of this pit before the giant pile of earth becomes a tsunami of soil that will bury her. Breathing hard—something she knows she must stop doing immediately—she gasps with pain as she sits down in the coffin, her body spasming with adrenaline. She slides the lid over her as she lies on her back, using her knees and bound hands to maneuver it fully into place.

The sounds from above aren't muffled enough, though; the seal isn't right. Sobbing, Madison jiggles the lid around, desperately trying to line it up. Finally, it drops home, flush, the ceiling of her tomb settling only inches from her face as her claustrophobia kicks into overdrive. Her breathing is fast, wheezing, *gasping*, everything it mustn't be as she hears several tons of soil beginning to move.

Then it starts to crash into the pit.

The change in sound and air pressure is immediate. At first the falling earth is a roar, even inside the coffin. It crescendos to a drum-roll-esque clatter as it hits the lid, reminding Madison of being inside a car at a car wash. That sound quickly becomes flat and muffled. A thick layer of dirt has already piled up on the coffin lid, and more is coming fast. The sense of *closeness* inside the coffin becomes unbearable as Madison understands that she is already buried under enough weight to prevent her from lifting the lid and escaping. She opens her mouth to scream, then snaps her lips shut—she needs the air; *there are no tanks*. But then sheer terror overcomes her, and she screeches in the dark like an injured cat.

The noise outside is growing faint as the earth creates a soundproof barrier. She feels the rumbling of the backhoe through the ground—a distant, constant wave.

It's mind games somehow, Madison thinks desperately. *Even Ellie wouldn't go this far.*

She pushes the lid. There isn't even the slightest amount of give.

The muffled rumbling of the backhoe and the diminishing sound of the falling dirt continues. Madison's hands feel at either side of her for the knife. She finds it. She manages to get the blade between her wrists and begins to saw frantically, needing a task to focus her mind, to stop thinking and keep panic and terror at bay. If she doesn't, she knows she is dead.

You're dead anyway, she thinks. *You could fucking meditate from now until tomorrow night, if you were capable, staying calm the whole time, and you would still run out of air.*

It's the only chance she has. She just has to stay calm. No—more than that.

She has to be Serena.

"Serena," Madison whispers, pinching her thumb and forefinger together around the knife's plastic handle. Then she realizes that saying anything at all is using up air she cannot spare. *Serena,* she thinks, but it doesn't even begin to penetrate the fear in her mind. She stops cutting. She must calm down or she will die.

Serena, she thinks. *Serena.*

She settles. It's only a small improvement, but the fact that it has worked even a little is something.

You're not *Serena, though, are you?* a voice in her head says. It sounds flat, reserved, and without malice. It is only speaking the truth, and it makes Madison's flesh break out in goose bumps. *You never really were. You just thought you were.*

"No!" Madison sobs, using up precious air to deny what she always knew, deep down, was true. "*Serena!*" She yells it now, air be damned, crying and punching desperately at the coffin's lid, re-bloodying her still-healing knuckles. "*Serena! Serena! I'm Serena! I'm a Bad! Fucking! Bi*—" She can't complete the sentence; it's too ridiculous. It's all been too ridiculous. All she's done is brutalize herself at the whims of a madwoman for three weeks. How does that make her a bad *anything* to be proud of?

The rumbling of the backhoe moves away and then stops. After a few more seconds, there is only the sound of Madison's sniffling breathing.

She has to slow it. *Now,* or she will suffocate, and even if she manages to slow her breathing, her death will almost certainly be agonizing.

Panic seizes her then, true panic. Madison begins to kick two-footed at the coffin's lid, screaming into the darkness as she bangs her fists against wood that is covered by tons of impenetrable soil.

"*I'm Serena!*" she bellows, her screams turning the pain in her head into a chain saw. She knows she's using up her oxygen but is too lost in her panic to care. "*I'm Serena! I'm Serena! I'm Serena!*"

But she isn't.

Above her, Ellie's Land Rover drives away.

Madison's mind's eye sees the vehicle's tires rolling across the grass, its engine and the cool nighttime breeze the only sounds up there in the moonlit field now. She pictures that same breeze skittering loose dirt across a freshly filled pit. Then it settles, and the field is still once more.

Silence, unaffected even by the sound of Madison screaming and screaming away the last of her air.

Review

Chapter Twenty-Two

Outstanding in Their Field

"Is it anyone we know?" Reg Eccles asks.

He and Brandon stare at each other for a moment; the early morning sun continues to rise as the sound of police conversation drifts over from the taped-off crime scene. Inside the tape, investigators work around a freshly dug-up pit.

Brandon looks confused by the question.

Reg Eccles is confused by Brandon's confusion. It's a simple question. He's beginning to regret this morning's walk. This is exactly the kind of weirdness his wife worried about when they moved to the Vermont countryside. Brandon bends and scratches Emma's ear while looking at Reg with an expression as uncertain as the sunlight under which they are standing. The silence is punctured by the police at the crime scene suddenly bursting into laughter.

Gallows humor, Reg imagines, is a constant part of their job.

"The police, you mean?" Brandon asks. "Are the police anyone we know?"

"No, no," Reg interrupts, embarrassed. "I asked if there was a dead body; you said there was a coffin. I mean, was it someone local?"

"Oh shit, no, sorry," Brandon says, shaking his head. "It was the way you asked. I was being facetious. I suppose I'm just... It's goddamn *weird*, Reg. No, not a local, just a coffin."

"I thought you said there *was* a dead body."

"A horse, Reg. I was being... Look, I'm a little shocked. Sorry. Someone killed and buried a *horse* along with a coffin. I mean, it's the fact that the coffin was in there too that got the cops interested—"

"They put the horse in a coffin?" Reg asks, thinking, *How big is the fucking coffin?*

"No," Brandon says, tutting, annoyed with himself. "The horse is just... in the ground as well." He leans closer to Reg, glancing at the cops before adding in a conspiratorial tone:

"The coffin was empty."

The night before

Madison jerks and smashes her hands up against the coffin's lid as she again comes back to consciousness. It is the seventh time this has happened. She has repeatedly fainted in raw panic. The last two times were the worst, with her remembering instantly where she is and what's happening: She's in the coffin, already the air inside the box is hot and thin, and she can't stop breathing heavy and fast even though she knows it will kill her.

Hyperventilating—the worst thing she could be doing—she looks at the glowing hands of her watch in the darkness, her own hands shaking as if she were being electrocuted. It's 2:40 a.m. Madison has been in here just under two hours, and already her air feels like it's running out. She has been screaming for nearly all that time. Even if she somehow manages to survive the six hours Ellie said she would, that won't be enough. Ellie won't even *start* digging until dawn.

I'm buried alive and I'm dying—

Panic. Hyperventilation. Killing her that much faster.

She faints once more.

"Can you state your name for us, please, miss?"

The child does as she's asked. She is terrified. Everyone in the courtroom is staring at her, and even though that means only a handful of people, it's plenty. She looks to her father, who looks back at her and nods imperceptibly, encouraging. The child doesn't look at her mother. She can't.

She is nine years old.

She doesn't know why they're even doing this. She knows neither of them want her; Lizzie, perhaps, but not her. Even at nine, she understands that her parents are doing this purely to spite each other. The child watched Lizzie answering the questions put to her by her father's lawyer — obedient to a fault, Daddy's golden girl as ever — telling the well-prepared horror stories of their mother's alcoholism. The girl watched with a growing sense of dread; she would of course do anything for her father too, is about to do the same as Lizzie, in fact, but knows she will never get the same look from her father that Lizzie got to bathe in.

She finally brings herself to glance at her mother's face across the courtroom; will she see any reason there not to tell the fabrications her father has prepped? Any kind of yearning in her mother's face to make this right, perhaps a look at the girl that shows any regret, or perhaps displaying a desire to win this battle that went beyond the token, outraged resistance to the father getting his way? She doesn't see it; the mother never looks her way.

Then the moment of terror comes: the questioning by her mother's lawyer, a tall and officious-looking man, but she has also been well prepared for what he will ask her. That doesn't stop the sweat running down the girl's forehead, the sensation that her spine has turned to slime and started to drain into a pool in her gut. She looks her mother's way again, and here, even when the child is the focus of the courtroom, her mother's gaze is locked on the judge. Something leaves the girl then, something quietly giving way to a dull, awful acceptance that she has known to be true for a long time.

She speaks to the court. She gives the speech her father made her thoroughly rehearse.

The child wets herself on the stand.

Of course she does. It was to be expected, surely, as she knows — thanks to her mother's regular furious rants — that she is weak, that her father is weak, that her greatest failing is her weakness. Weak little babies wet themselves, don't they?

She can't believe it's happening, hardly even noticing at first before the damp sensation spreads down her leg. She feels as if she's going to faint when she realizes; she knows everyone will notice when she stands up, and she bursts into genuine tears at the thought. This saves her a little, all eyes on her pained face as the judge tells her she can go back to her seat, but she knows everyone can still see. Something inside her forms a knot as she walks, now avoiding her mother's gaze once more. Her wet clothing rubs against her skin. She hopes no one notices. The twisting and tightening within her mind is like that of a valve being shut off, closing a bulkhead inside her soul and drying her tears, if not her underwear.

She is unaware that the tightening is permanent.

Her father wins custody. The child will never understand why he fought so hard — why he prepped his children's testimonies so thoroughly to go along with the proof of his wife's infidelity — for he will kill himself within a year and a half of this, leaving the child parentless. She will go to live with her aunt on her father's side. She and her mother will never speak after that day in court.

Four years later, when the girl is thirteen, her mother will die of cancer.

Her aunt and uncle carefully give her the news. She didn't even visit her mother in hospital.

She tells everyone she's fine. She's been fine ever since that day on the stand. Even when she finds herself inexplicably crying in the middle of geography class and asks to leave the room, she's fine.

She hurries to the bathroom. An older girl is already in there, who spots the teen as she heads into a stall. The older girl asks the teen if she is okay; the teen says yes, trying to hide her tears. She locks the door and commands herself to get it together.

Don't cry for her, *she thinks.* Don't. She was a cheater and a liar—

That's when it hits her. The lie that's been told for so long went from being a source of shame to something the teen truly believes.

Her mother never was *an alcoholic, was she? That's what her father made her say, what he made her rehearse. Her mother was a cheater and a liar but never actually an alcoholic.*

But the daughter stood up in court and lied... *just like her mother.*

Which means she's weak like her mother. She is a rancid shell, just like her parents.

Suddenly the stall is like a box, its tiny walls pressing in as she struggles to breathe, knowing that she is her mother's daughter, her father's daughter, her family name a curse, and she begs for that twisting to come once more, to close off whatever this new feeling is.

She suddenly understands exactly how to do it. The blessing she was given at birth that will allow *her to do it.*

With the revelation comes relief. One simple reversal would be all it takes, and she understands now that her wish has been fulfilled; she isn't a liar, she can't be a liar, because that's what the people from that other *family are. It isn't a perfect solution; even reversed, her name will still be close enough to the one that followed her around for years, branding her as* Burn Girl *as clearly as the mark on her leg, always leading to a variation of* "Aren't you the Burn Girl who was set on fire in a shed or something?" *But now, at least, she can finally say,* "No. That's the other person. See? My family name is different. That *can't* be me."

The tears stop.

She doesn't think about the consequences. All that matters now is that the feeling has stopped. She straightens, grabs tissue from the dispenser. Dries her eyes. Blows her nose. She exits the stall.

The older girl is still standing there, the dust-mote-filled sunlight all around her as it streams through the dirty windows of the school bathroom.

"You sure you're okay?" she says, looking concerned.

"Yeah."

The older girl doesn't look convinced. "What's your name?" she asks, trying to be friendly and not knowing that the timing of the question is perfect. A sign, surely, that the universe approves. One simple reversal, *the teen thinks,* that's all it takes. She can be someone else from this day forward.

Her first and last names are both first *names.*

What a gift. She can switch them — a simple twist — and forever be changed.

She pauses, wondering if this change will be a wall between herself and anyone she lets get close; perhaps, then, she can make an exception for those people who truly know her, an inner circle allowed to use her true, shameful name. Yes; a secret bond between her and the people who won't judge her for living under a name she was never given...

None of that matters right now. She feels strangely light, as if she were hollow, and tells herself this is a good thing.

She holds out her hand and tells the older girl her new turned-around name, trying it on for the first time.

It fits like a suit of armor.

"I'm Madison Bailey," she says.

Madison awakes screaming, punching and kicking at the lid of the coffin, hearing her rapid breathing and knowing simultaneously that she is burning up precious oxygen and that it won't make any difference. She is going to die in this box. Her parents, her fucking parents, their weakness led her to this, their poison made her desperate, made her crazy with need. They made her ashamed of her own name, ashamed to be a liar like them...

You could take it back.

She continues to punch and kick because, as always, the motion, the anger, means she doesn't have to engage with the impossible thought, and if she can't be Serena—

"*I'm not Bailey Madison anymore either!*" she sobs in the darkness beneath the world. "*Don't make me be her! Bailey Madison is a fucking... a fucking...*"

You were a child.

The response in her head is spoken in a voice that is clear and unfamiliar.

Her punches stop.

"She's a... I'm a liar."

Her hands go to her face as she realizes that, even if Ellie's method was so terribly, terribly wrong, the woman almost had a point. Knowing oneself before the end *is* beyond important.

If not Serena—

"I'm..."

She almost can't say it.

"I am Bailey Madison," she sobs through her fingers. "*I am Bailey Madison.*"

She bawls inside the box now, the kind of soul cry that comes only when valves deep inside untwist.

Something floods through her system, bringing with it acceptance here at her end.

Breathe slowly, the voice says, and Bailey Madison wonders if it is the last of Madison Bailey — her shield, her cocoon, her assistance through the world — imparting one last gift. *You might make it.*

I can't, Bailey Madison thinks. *And it won't make any difference.*

It might, the voice says, and when it adds the next four words, they somehow have the power of which they have previously been bled dry.

You can do it.

Her fists unclench. Her hands open. This is fucking pointless. But. But.

But what else is she going to do?

Bailey Madison's next breath is still ragged and trembling, but it is at least a little slower; her exhale is slower still.

Over the next five minutes, her breathing has halved in speed. Over the next fifteen, it is a third of the frantic, gasping mess that it was before. She doesn't look at her watch. It won't help. All there is to do is sit with her body.

Bailey Madison's existence over the next hour is like a waveform, rising to near panic and then slowly returning to a state of highly strung equilibrium. She doesn't know how effective she is being against her dwindling air supply's attempts to kill her — whether she has staved off the inevitable for a few hours or a few minutes — but she thinks she does okay. She lies so still that, if it weren't for her slow continuing breath, she might wonder if this is death already, if Bailey Madison has been somehow lucky enough to not notice the peaceful moment of her passing.

It means that — just as she begins to find that whatever is being drawn into her lungs is no longer enough — she is still alive by the time she hears the scratching sound.

Her awareness is so ragged and delirious by now that it takes a while to register, coming seconds after the revelation that she's still alive, if only just. Her breaths barely take in any oxygen at all now. She's been in the box for several hours, and her air was already running low long before she started checking the time. She should have been dead three times over, *would* have been if she hadn't managed to stop panicking and slow her respiration.

The scraping again, and this time it has to be someone digging.

Bailey Madison gasps in the darkness. She can't dare to believe.

She slaps her hands against the inside of the coffin's lid, instantly torn by the dilemma of using up her remaining air to scream, *I'm here*, but she's suddenly *so close* to getting out. The digger is getting closer, and quickly too, despite the slow and labored rests between scoops — pausing and scooping, pausing and scooping. The earth must still be relatively loose. She looks at her watch in disbelief, its glowing hands blurry and hard to see: 4:35 a.m. Madison tries to wet her lips with her dry tongue, seeing that it's still over an hour away from dawn. Has Ellie come to her senses and dug her up early? Or is it a morning walker, someone who saw something suspicious? It's possible. Madison's lungs are struggling to work even a little, her entire body tensing with the unbearable closeness of both her salvation and her death.

An hour passes. It's almost worse than waiting to die. A sense of delirium fills every cell of Madison's body as she begins to slowly suffocate. She keeps blinking herself awake, worried that she will never wake again. How long were they digging before Madison even heard them?

"Madison," a muffled voice calls. "Madison, I'm coming!"

"*Yes! I'm here! Get me out! Please—*"

She slaps her hands over her mouth and frantically waits as the scratching gets closer and closer. She's still too frightened to believe that she might be getting out, even at the sound of a shovel scraping only inches from her face. The digging person moans, and that only confirms their identity. The shovel *clumps* against the lid. Madison rams her palms against the inside of the wood with all her remaining strength, the coiled spring of tension that her body has become finally unleashed as she screams, no longer conserving air, and there is a moment of awful resistance as the lid doesn't move, and then there is a *croak* of soil, and a crack of air appears all around and above her.

The lid is moving upward as a sweaty, agonized Jennifer, her face purple, swollen, and unrecognizable, is falling back against the pit's wall. Her left arm is tied in a loose sling made from what looks like a sweater. Her mangled face is twisted in pain; she's clearly popped her shoulder back into place. She holds the lid back with her leg as Madison sits up, gulping in precious oxygen, wanting to clamber up and out of the pit right away but physically unable to yet. She paws at Jennifer's mud-covered foot, slapping at it to tell her, *Thank you, oh God, thank you,* because she's incapable of speech.

"Holy shit," Jennifer says. She winces again, pain carved all over her face, but leans forward and pats Madison's hand right back. "Holy shit."

"Water," Madison gasps as she sits forward and saws Ellie's dull knife across the rope still binding her ankles.

Jennifer shakes her head, grimacing. "Don't have any." She steps down into the coffin and, once the rope is severed, reaches down with her good arm to help Madison up. Both women now stand in the wooden box like it's some kind of subterranean life raft. She tries to slip her arm under Madison's shoulders, but Madison stops her.

"Arm," she croaks. "Your arm. I'm okay."

Jennifer doesn't protest and turns toward the ladder — Ellie's ladder, Madison sees, placed back in the pit.

Madison's joints screech. She shouts as she jars her broken rib, but the pain is brief and somehow distant, the endorphins released by her resurrection making the stabbing sensation seem like a sound coming from another room.

"Ellie," she says.

Jennifer shakes her head and points up. "Crashed her Rover into the gate," she grunts. "I followed the sound of her horn all the way from the house. Her head was on the steering wheel. She was totally out. I think she blacked—" She moans suddenly, cradling her bound arm. "Blacked out at the wheel," she continues. "I searched the Rover for you — found the shovel and the ladder and a bunch of rope. Followed the fucking tracks. No keys in the backhoe. Couldn't risk using it anyway, might crush you—"

"Ellie's in the car?" Madison croaks. "Now?"

Jennifer nods. "I used the rope to tie her hands before I came looking for you. I'd have locked her in the back to be doubly sure, but I couldn't lift her. Don't think I could stop her now if she caught up to me." She catches herself, snorts bitterly. "Couldn't stop her *before*. But she'll find a way out of those knots. We have to go, Mads, now."

There are fresh tears in Madison's eyes now, but they are no longer tears of joy and relief. She watches Jennifer for a moment, unsure she can climb the ladder yet. She needs to breathe more. She's too lightheaded to risk falling back into the pit.

"Come on," Jennifer urges.

But Madison remains standing still. The surprise and gratitude have passed. They have been replaced by anger.

"Let me guess," Madison croaks. "We better run before Ellie comes, right?"

"What?" Jennifer says. "Yes! Come on!"

Madison nods sadly.

"Yeah. I figured that if I did get out of here—" Madison coughs and tries to wet her dry mouth and throat with as much saliva as she can. "That there'd be something like this," she continues, staring at Jennifer and shaking her head. "It *is* absolutely amazing, what you've done. But as soon as I saw it was you who dug me out, it confirmed everything."

Silence.

Madison clears her parched throat again and waits. Jennifer still doesn't respond.

"'Crazy solutions.'" Madison scoffs. "That's what Ellie said, the day I met her. 'No matter what.' How the fuck did I hear that and still come here? Knowing Ellie would always take the extreme option?" Madison looks up at the stars she thought she'd never see again. "When I wasn't screaming away all my fucking air, the thinking got intense. Clear. I kept thinking about all the stuff Ellie was babbling on about. The pain of the quit, the pain of the quit. How a person would do anything to take it back. But really what she meant is that someone would only do anything to take it back once they'd fully drunk all of Ellie's Kool-Aid. Once they'd been through weeks of extreme exhaustion and stress, their minds stretched to the breaking point and fully ready to believe, to 'buy in,' as you put it. I don't think many people make it that far, but you definitely did."

Jennifer stares at Madison in the darkness.

"I just kept thinking about the photo I saw on Ellie's desk," Madison says. "Why was my mind so snagged on a picture of a tall, skinny brunette in glasses? But an idea occurred to me that just *couldn't* be true... and I kept thinking about what Ellie said about broken bones."

"Madison—"

"Ellie's whole near-death, Bosnian war-zone revelation," Madison says, "that led her to this whole 'pain is the way to strength' obsession. Maybe fully breaking your arm was a step too far, though, and a mere dislocation was the compromise." She points at Jennifer's injured arm. "She wanted me to believe she's crazy enough to legitimately bury me alive, right? She wanted me so scared that I'd go into true survival mode and *finally fucking cross over.* And what better way to demonstrate how she'd finally snapped... than to pop out a student's arm? But she needed someone who would be *zellie* enough to let their arm be dislocated. For Elite to work she had to sow all those little doubts about herself, all the way through: *Uh-oh! Is Ellie dangerous?* The other little details too, like getting Sarah to leave her bike here, to make me think Ellie'd done something to her. *Dangerous.* Except, the problem is—in true sloppy Ellie style—she actually *is* dangerous, and doesn't even fucking know it."

Jennifer says nothing.

"Even after seeing your picture," Madison says, "I probably wouldn't have put two and two together if you'd kept an eye on your fucking roots. It's a month-long course. You made a joke out of it, but I think that's because you knew we'd notice after three weeks, right? *Jennifer?*"

Jennifer shifts on the spot, trying to bluster. Madison holds up a hand to cut her off.

"Or should I call you Hannah?" Madison says.

"You're... you're crazy..."

Madison shakes her head. "The only reason I'm not clawing your eyes out right now—you were an accomplice to *burying me a-fucking-live*—is because I'm so fucked I can barely stand—"

"*That wasn't part of the plan!*" Jennifer says. "I had no idea she'd do this! She'd talked about the coffin and oxygen tanks in the past, but that was just an *idea*. I didn't know she'd actually had it built!"

"Listen to yourself! Christ! Jen...*Hannah*...what happened to you?"

"You don't understand," Jennifer says quietly. "You never..." It clearly torments her to even say the word. "You never *quit*."

Madison stares at the big woman in amazement, thinking of Jennifer's arm popping out of its socket. Could she herself ever go that far if she *did* quit...

Madison notices the amount of earth around them, or notably, the lack of it. There is earth piled up around them where Jennifer has dug, certainly, but nowhere near enough for her to have cleared out the depth of the pit that Ellie supposedly filled back in.

"Fuck...," Madison breathes, amazed. "I guess I was supposed to be so relieved and desperate once out that I wouldn't notice the amount of earth that's been dug up? Ellie didn't fill the hole all the way in, did she? Just enough for me to hear it come down and muffle sound. But *hey*, you still moved a fair bit of earth with one arm in a sling. Impressive. That had to hurt like hell. But you're a lot stronger than you used to be, right?" She sneers. "So skinny in that photo."

"I *had* to get strong," Jennifer whispers. "I had no choice, if I wanted to come back." Jennifer's eyes grow wider, her tears catching the dim light of the stars. "Ellie's right about the pain of the quit, Madison. It's a living hell. But I would do *anything* to come back, even if I knew completing the course this time wouldn't be enough for Ellie. *I had to prove how badly I wanted it.*"

Her hand goes to her strapped-up shoulder, and Madison knows Jennifer is telling the truth about that at least; this woman really would do anything. She's proved it. Madison wonders if she sounded the same as Jennifer less than twenty-four hours ago. She had many revelations down in the depths, but not in the way Ellie envisioned.

"Was Frankie a plant too?" Madison asks.

"No! The chair collapsing with Frankie was a mistake. Ellie never made mistakes like that in the past! I wasn't supposed to hurt Ellie either, but she was going to do permanent damage to you! I had to really stop her, I could see you were concussed, *and that's not what this course is supposed to be*!" She starts to cry. "I agreed to the dislocation. That's different. The other students aren't supposed to be damaged." Her shoulders drop. "It's all changed now. Madison, look what she did to my *face*." She sniffs back tears of betrayal. "She wasn't supposed to do that. Maybe if I hadn't hit her with the club..." She shakes her head. "I was supposed to spread doubt about her, but I ended up meaning it. Those little tics of hers aren't an act. I don't know what happened to her. She's been different for a while, getting worse. But I still believed! I still wanted to go beyond." She sniffs again. "And for you! The dislocation was supposed to make you scared of her, that you would believe she'd hurt you! She was supposed to spend a day pushing you to your absolute limits, right? Like death's door limits, acting crazier than ever! Then I was gonna come to get you to escape, we were gonna run miles across the fields at night, I was supposed to collapse and you'd have to carry me for miles — it... it was a whole thing, *and you'd make it* because you'd think you were running for your life!"

Jennifer's eyes shine in the dark for a moment. She seems to see what she's describing.

"Then Ellie would be there at the end," she says, "she'd explain everything... and then we'd *both* graduate."

The light dies in Jennifer's eyes as her face collapses.

"But when she started concussing you on the squash court... I... I was supposed to try and stop her. She said you'd be fine, but you weren't, so I *really* had to jump in... then she grabbed my arm and I immediately knew what she was going to do. Having a limb dislocated... agreeing to it... that was supposed to be the moment when I finally became bulletproof. Became *other*." She starts to cry. "*But I still tried to stop it.* I couldn't help it. And then she *did* it, and other than the pain I felt... nothing. Just nothing. No euphoria. I *knew* it would hurt — that was the point — but with that pain came the realization that *this was fucking pointless.*" Jennifer's words come as sobs now. "She didn't even move me from the squash court. I woke up there. I had to find you and get out of here now that Ellie's totally lost it. For *real,* she's lost it."

"Oh, she has!" Madison yells. "Guess what the crazy bitch forgot to put in the coffin?!"

The horror on Jennifer's face is immediate and genuine. "Not the tanks—"

"*Yeah,*" Madison says. "Your genius mentor just genuinely buried me alive for this little Elite moonshot of a deception."

"But you must have been in there for hours. How did you stay alive this long?"

A distant car alarm bleats into life.

"Fuck," Jennifer spits. She limps the few feet toward the ladder. "Knew that lethal bitch would know how to get out of that shitty knot. Come on." When Madison doesn't move, Jennifer points up with her good hand. "You hear that alarm? She's *loose* and she's *on her way*! You have to trust me!"

Madison's lip starts to tremble. *Dammit.* She wants Jennifer to be telling the truth so badly. Jennifer straightens, taking a deep breath. "I don't care about graduating," she says. "I..." Her mouth works silently for a few seconds, preparing. "I quit," Jennifer says.

Even now, the word goes through Madison like an electric shock.

"*I quit,*" Jennifer says. "Again."

Jennifer's face is that of a scolded child. The car alarm continues to screech somewhere in the distance, the obnoxious sound of it pouring into the pit.

"Do you believe me now?" Jennifer says. "I'm sorry. I'm so sorry, Madison."

The idea of slapping Jennifer and not stopping flashes through Madison's brain. Instead, she takes Jennifer gently by the shoulders. Jennifer is another victim of Ellie's madness, and at a crossroads between fury and compassion, Madison chooses the latter, knowing it isn't the same as forgiveness.

"You dug me up with one good arm after being beaten to unconsciousness," Madison says softly. "You tracked me down and saved my life. It's the most superhuman effort I've ever seen."

Jennifer wipes her face with her good arm.

"I'd say you graduated," Madison says, "but that's for you to decide, and no one else."

Jennifer just nods.

"Let's just get out of here," Madison says. "We need to get help." She means getting Jennifer to a hospital, and urgently. She realizes that, should they survive, *help* for both of them will mean seeing a very fucking good therapist.

She does agree with Jennifer on one thing: They want to be out of here before Ellie arrives. Jennifer's dislocated shoulder, Madison's broken rib and a likely concussion.... Ellie is breaking her own precious, precious rules left and right, and that truly *does* mean anything is on the table. They are at the whim of a delirious and highly dangerous woman.

Jennifer lunges for the ladder, but her foot slips in the loose dirt. She stumbles, her weight slamming onto her reset shoulder. Her scream is shrill and deafening in the confined space.

"Jen," Madison gasps.

But Jennifer is moving aside, pulling Madison toward the ladder.

"No," Madison says, resisting again, the word scratchy and raw in her throat. "You go!"

Jennifer waves her off, her face a crush of agony and frustration. "Think I'm...passing out. Don't want to fall on..."

Jennifer's face goes slack, her eyes rolling up in her head as her body becomes limp. She drops silently forward and Madison catches her, Jennifer's chest landing against Madison's shoulder. Madison nearly collapses onto her back under Jennifer's dead weight. The broken rib screeches. She wraps her arms around Jennifer's broad back, trying to get her feet into a braced stance so she can push Jennifer upright. Jennifer's much larger body keeps coming. "Oh, you heavy fucking...," Madison grunts. For a moment she wonders if this is all part of it, but Jennifer's weight is dead in a way that only the unconscious possess. This is real, and Madison can't leave her behind. Ellie has finally cracked, the severe head trauma from Jennifer's beating shutting down whatever remaining governors the woman has on her mania. She can't leave Jennifer in here. What might Ellie do if she finds out Jennifer has also gone against the program?

That's the problem with getting really good at being resilient, Madison thinks. She takes a desperate breath, spits a hissed curse, and grits her teeth as she manages to bend at the waist and slide her shoulder down to Jennifer's stomach. *It makes it a fuck of a lot harder to know when you should actually stop.*

She wraps her arms around the backs of Jennifer's legs and straightens, screaming, as she lifts Jennifer in the world's worst fireman's carry. If Jennifer's shoulder pops out again, they'll just have to deal with that later. Jennifer's unconscious torso hangs down Madison's back, her weight pressing Madison's neck so far sideways that it feels as if it might break. Madison knows Jennifer might slip off if her arm isn't secured in place, but she barely has her as it is and there isn't time to wrestle limbs into position. Madison is hurt, Jennifer is *heavy*, and Madison has to get up the ladder before her own body gives out under Jennifer's weight. She has to climb, and fast.

Madison lets go with one arm, tightening the other around both of Jennifer's legs, and grips the ladder's nearest rung with her free hand, the pain in her rib making her focus unassailable, and she bellows her way up the nine steps, grabbing one-handed at the next rung every time her feet have successfully moved up. Each upward push to the next rung feels as if she is dragging the world up by her broken rib. When she reaches the top, she flop-rolls Jennifer onto the grass, sobbing and moaning with relief beside a large mound of excavated earth. The sky is a dark blue now—light, but only just. Madison is aboveground, that's all that matters, and even if Ellie will soon be upon them, she can take a minute to breathe. Each expansion of her lungs now feels like a stabbing blade.

"That wasn't the same," Ellie's slurred voice says, "as carrying her across miles of fields. But for a graduation task, I'd say it's more than satisfactory."

Madison rolls onto her good side, her rib still screaming, and scoots backward as quickly as she can. Ellie stands on the opposite edge of the pit. Her arms are behind her back, her usual pose, but now she sways a little in the breeze. She even takes a staggering step to correct her stance.

"I didn't do it," Madison gasps, "to *graduate*."

"Of course."

"How long have you been standing there?" Madison groans.

"Look at what Jennifer's done," Ellie says, ignoring the question and gesturing at the piles of earth in the pit. "Second time's the charm. She got back up off the mat. Years in the making." Ellie's voice hitches a little as she speaks, and Madison wonders: *Is Ellie emotional?* "I'm so proud of you both."

"A week early too," Madison spits. "What superstar students."

"I think the coffin thing is more than enough to shave a week off, Serena," Ellie says, smiling. "And what Jennifer has been through is more than enough to do the same, regardless of anything she might have said. Graduates. *Elite* graduates." She takes a deep breath, smiling contentedly.

We decide! Madison wants to scream. *We decide!*

But she doesn't. Ellie is still very dangerous, and Madison's rib is broken.

"Hannah, you mean," Madison says instead, trying to keep the grimace out of her expression as she rolls Jennifer onto her back.

"True," Ellie says, unfazed. "We were lucky that her name is so unique. Means it was easy for you to find the fake info we planted on the internet. Google 'Hannah Quimby-Beck.' You won't find another one."

"How did you know I'd get online?" Madison says, backing away a little and hoping Ellie doesn't notice. She tries to see where the gate is in case she needs to run; when she turns back to Ellie, she keeps Jennifer in her peripheral vision, watching for signs of her stirring back to consciousness. Ellie might be *saying* they've graduated, but what Ellie says and what she does, Madison now knows extremely well, can be two different things.

"I didn't." Ellie shrugs. "I saw you take the tape and guessed why, but that was fine."

"Are her fucking initials always up on the dining room wall?" Madison asks.

"No," Ellie says. "Usually, they're those of someone else who quit. Someone always asks what they mean, and I get to explain the devastating impact of the quit. But this time I figured it wouldn't hurt to use Hannah's when she's sitting right there with maybe second thoughts about what's coming. And I meant it: She really was my greatest failure. No one has ever been as destroyed by the quit as she was."

Madison can believe it. "And the picture on the desk?"

Ellie looks genuinely confused for a moment.

"Oh," she says eventually. "You saw that?"

Sloppy, Madison thinks, unsurprised, but the memory of Ellie's office triggers another question. "Sarah's bike?" Madison asks.

"I would have actually directed you there if you hadn't noticed," Ellie says. "The way you tensed up when you saw it out my office window told me that wouldn't be necessary, though. None of this is essential, but as you can see, it all helps." Her shrug makes her sway for a second, forcing another correcting stumble-step. "You still went through with the Hard Correction regardless."

"*I believed in you*," Madison spits. "You made me gaslight *myself*."

Ellie nods sadly. She begins to walk around the grave, her gait unsteady and slow. Madison circles away from her. "Were we ever friends, Ellie?" she asks, unable to help herself.

Ellie, of course, answers the question with a question. "What do you think?"

"Friends don't bury each other alive."

"What if someone is burying their friend alive for their own benefit?" Ellie has reached Jennifer.

"I'm pretty sure that's abuse," Madison says, stopping herself before adding *you crazy bitch*.

Ellie crouches down to check on Jennifer. Madison stiffens, but Ellie's investigation looks genuine. Her face shows concern.

"I'm pretty sure you received what you signed up for," Ellie says. She looks at Madison and sighs. "I just don't get it, Serena. I guess I'm a dinosaur. People say they want something, and then when they get it but it's not exactly how they imagined it, or it's harder than they thought, they don't like it." She shrugs again, but the movement makes her put her hand to her head. She lets out a soft moan. "But if they actually follow the system like they should, they'll find out it *works*."

Madison bites back a bitter laugh, turns it into a cough. "You're hurt, Ellie. Badly. Jennifer too." She doesn't elaborate; she doesn't want to antagonize Ellie, but she needs her to realize that they all need to get to a hospital.

"Jennifer fought back," Ellie says, "and with a weapon. She wasn't supposed to. As you know, intention and application can vary wildly. I can't blame her for that."

"I think," Madison says, "that you have a much worse concussion than I do. I have a broken fucking rib." She can't help it. She looks at Ellie's swollen head and the heartbreak is just too much. "I wasn't supposed to have any permanent damage, Ellie!" Madison cries. "That was our deal!"

"*I* think," Ellie says thoughtfully, as Jennifer begins to stir, "that I might have to change that part of the pledge. Like I said, the course is always evolving."

Madison understands that if she were to leave Jennifer behind, she could run right now. Ellie is distracted, and Madison thinks she'll get a good head start, even with her broken rib. But Ellie could run far faster before, effortlessly so. Is she faster still, now that she's hurt? And Madison can't leave Jennifer; her mentally and physically damaged friend is helpless. Besides, Madison's fury at the arrogance of this impossible woman anchors her to the spot.

"So even when it comes to a pledge," Madison says, keeping her voice steady and low, "the ends still justify the means? What if I'd died, Ellie? What if I'd *died*?"

"I told you," Ellie says, brushing Jennifer's hair from her forehead, "there were oxygen tanks in the coffin."

"There were no oxygen tanks."

Ellie blinks. Looks up.

"If I hadn't been able to get myself under control," Madison says, "and Jennifer hadn't got here early, I would be dead."

"There are tanks," Ellie says. "Just not ones you can see. That part was a lie. I had two of them installed when I had the box made. It has a false bottom. I turned them on before I went to get you. Just enough air comes through a little tube in the..." She holds her head.

"You're in a position of trust." Madison says, unable to stop herself. "You took advantage of Jennifer's desperation to prove herself and made her agree to have a fucking limb dislocated. What kind of a mentor does that?"

Again, Ellie looks confused. "I didn't make her agree to anything. Jennifer *asked* for that. We'd agreed beforehand that I wouldn't stop no matter what. This is something *I*, at least, hold sacred. Yes, she changed her mind at the last minute, but I was prepared for that possibility—"

"Jennifer *asked* and you agreed?" Madison says, horrified. "You're supposed to be a leader, not an enabler! She wouldn't even *want* her arm dislocated if you hadn't fucked up her head! Take some goddamn responsibility!"

"That's *all* I do," Ellie says.

She doesn't get it, Madison thinks in amazement. *She really, absolutely doesn't get it.*

Jennifer groans, sitting up. Ellie moves to help her, but Jennifer shakes her head, grimacing as she pushes her painful way to her feet.

"Sweetheart, do you need anything?" Ellie asks her.

Jennifer shakes her head again and wordlessly walks around to where Madison stands on the opposite side of the pit.

Ellie cocks her head. "You know, Madison, you could have a free hit on me, if you want to. Right in the face. It's only fair. I have taken a liberty with you, even if I do still see it as being within the remit of my mandate for your course."

"Grow up," Madison says, even though the idea is sorely tempting.

"I'm serious," Ellie says, holding up both hands. "I make no apologies for giving you what you needed, but you should be allowed to reciprocate."

"I don't care about fucking punches," Madison says, "but if you're the prophet you seem to think you are — if you're as *disciplined* — you'll take what I have to say instead. Right?"

"If that's what you need," Ellie says. "Criticisms I receive are often justified."

"You're too busy being proud of how *adaptive* you are," Madison says, "to realize that you're not actually adapting where it counts. You *can't*. People like Jennifer get destroyed, and the only answer you have is to keep doing the same thing? Didn't suffer enough, so suffer some more. That's all you know, and it makes you wildly irresponsible. The end will always justify the means, right?"

Ellie just smiles, beatific. Madison has to look away, her gaze falling on Jennifer; the big woman is looking down, crying. Her heart, Madison understands, is even more broken. Everything Madison is saying is continuing the undoing of Jennifer's faith in Ellie, in the system.

"But what an end," Ellie says. "You got exactly what you wanted. Look at you, carrying a one-hundred-sixty-two-pound woman on your back as you climb a ladder, and you did it with a broken rib. The Marines would be proud. You finally did it. You're finally Serena."

Ellie's smile turns into a grin, and the pride there fills Madison with disgust.

"You think this was a success?" Madison says. "You think I've come out of there...what, fixed? I'm supposed to be Serena now?"

"True Strength." Ellie beams.

Madison stares at her for a second and then bursts into hysterical laughter.

She bellows so hard that she drops down to one knee, the pain from her rib making the laughter a torture, and *that* strikes her as funny, so she laughs even harder, which hurts even more. Jennifer stands awkwardly next to her, avoiding Ellie's curious gaze.

"Oh, *Ellie*," Madison gasps. "I'm not. I'm not Serena at all. I learned two things down there, and neither was whatever the hell you expected me to figure out." She grunts as she gets back to her feet. "One of them is just how fucked up I truly am to have even come to something like this in the first place."

Ellie's face becomes blank, and Madison wonders if, apart from her expression of grief for her dead horse, this is as close to crestfallen as Ellie looks.

"Serena—" Ellie checks herself. "Madison—"

"Wrong both times, you fucking lunatic." Madison's laughter dries up as Jennifer staggers a small step backward, her bruised and swollen face a cautionary tale of what Madison so nearly could have become.

"I'm okay," Jennifer says, clearly not okay.

"Do you want to get out of here?" Madison asks her friend quietly. If Jennifer wants help, then Madison will provide it, but only if Jennifer is willing. She learned from bitter experience that this is the only way such assistance works.

Jennifer glances at Ellie, then nods.

"My name's Bailey," Madison whispers, slipping an arm behind Jennifer's waist.

Jennifer just nods again, tears running off her nose.

Birdsong is slowly creeping into the sounds of the early morning breeze, wafting around the three women standing by the open pit: a would-be mentor and her two badly injured students. Madison looks to the gate in the rising morning light. Now that she can see better, she knows which way to run if they must, but she doesn't think it will come to that.

"We're leaving, Ellie," she says.

"Of course," Ellie says. "You graduated."

"Whatever you say." But she still has a question to ask. "You seem pretty proud of that contraption down there. You said you had it ready for a long time, ready for when it was needed."

"I did."

"Hidden oxygen tank system, all that, yes? When did you last test it?"

Ellie doesn't answer immediately; the pause goes on for a long time. "This last stage of your course," Ellie says eventually, "was called relatively on the fly. I have faith in the people who made it for me."

"*When did you last test it?*"

No answer.

"Ellie, I couldn't breathe down there. I was running out of air. You fucked up, big time."

"You were panicking," Ellie says.

"I slowed my breathing down, and I still started to run out of air. It didn't work correctly."

"As you wish."

"The *other* thing I figured out down there," Madison says, "is that your only answer to the question of what I needed was for me to be run literally into the ground. You're supposed to be helping the people who *don't* have what it takes, but all you know is how to grind people into powder. What about the people who need more than that? What other methods do you actually have?"

Ellie looks at Madison with an expression that under normal circumstances would ignite a spiral of rage, but Madison's protesting brain — already feeling as if it were about to burst from all the screaming — sends sparkles of white dancing across her vision.

Ellie is looking at Madison with pity.

"You are right in one respect," Ellie says. "It seems I can't help you." She shrugs. "This is a learning experience for me."

"We're going to a hospital," Madison says. "We're going to the house, and I'm getting my car keys." If Ellie tries to stop her, Madison decides, she will take a running jump at her and aim a kick at her head. It's her best option. Ellie is concussed, and more importantly, she's short enough for Madison to pull it off.

"Go with my blessing," Ellie says, her gracious smile so maddening that for the rest of her life Madison will remember this moment.

She will often regret not taking Ellie up on her offer of a free hit.

Such regret is always fleeting. In those moments Madison will remember the brutal intention that flooded her whole body — *to kick a concussed woman in the skull* — and she will shake her head and go on with her day. Regret will slowly turn to satisfaction that she instead simply said:

"We don't need it."

She tries to spit, but her mouth is too dry. Walking slowly, leaning on each other, Madison and Jennifer leave Ellie beside the pit and the ladder. The two women make their aching, limping way back toward the house, following the scars left in the mud.

Chapter Twenty-Three

IF YOU WERE to ever ask Johnny how long it took him to cross the Deep Place—in its manifestation as the Howling Wastelands—he would say that it felt like five to six months, but even he wouldn't claim that was correct. There was never anything to eat, so surely he would have starved long before then. Time is, he knows, unusual in the Shallows, and no doubt even more so in the Deep Place; without any rising and setting of the sun to track the passage of days, he could only tell you what it felt like to him.

He collected many new scars along the way. By the time he left, most of his marks were shadows of the gaping wounds they once were.

Eventually, Johnny walked back into the world.

Johnny rises to his feet, shaky but unhurt; the blessed, blessed return trip through the final portal was messy to say the least, a tumbling fall back to reality rather than a heroic final step. He uses the wall to stand. He is once again in the bungalow's kitchen. He is home.

The first thing he does is charge to the sink and blast cold water directly into his mouth. He slurps it greedily, not knowing how long he has gone without clean water.

The only water to be found in the Deep Place tasted brackish and dirty, and Johnny drank only the absolute minimum of it. He came across it in small pools that had been filled only God knew how—it was as much of a mystery as the Deep Place having light but no stars or moon in the blackness above—and he had no way to filter out the damned red grit. He sometimes wondered if what he was drinking was Needle Monster piss. Amazingly, as disgusting as it tasted, it never made him sick. If anything, it was slightly rejuvenating, but Johnny was still careful not to drink too much.

He staggers away from the sink, feeling nauseous but noting the darkness through the window. It's nighttime. He is still hungry beyond all reckoning, but he needs to know something first. Even so, he pauses as he passes by the hallway mirror; he runs his hand over his thick beard, seeing it for the first time. His hair is considerably longer too. His clothes are torn to tatters, their original colors faded and bloodstained. He nearly tears them off so he can see how many scars he has and how bad they are, but thinks better of it. He needs to do this one step at a time or he will go mad. Besides, his intention was used to heal a great many of his wounds at the point of their creation; perhaps they won't be so bad. He turns away from the mirror and continues to the bedroom, already noticing the change in the rules here from those of the Deep Place. Thinking of his scars reminds him of the limits of his intention here in the Real. A wound in the Deep Place would be at best an intense, short-lived pain and at worst a healed but nasty scar. Here in the Real, such a thing could mean bleeding to death.

But I'm home, he thinks. *I'm fucking* home.

Yet he still needs to know.

He enters the bedroom and grabs his laptop; he can't trust the phone in his pocket to be accurate about time and date. It came through the Deep Place with him, after all. He opens the laptop and enters his password, his eyes already on the corner of his screen.

It's the same date—the same night—he left for the Shallows, perhaps maybe an hour later. The real Ivan will be returning soon, as promised.

He doesn't know what he expected to find, but he is relieved and unsurprised at the same time. He pulls out his phone to see if it gives the same details. It does. Johnny unlocks the device and texts Ivan:

> I'm sorry. You're a wonderful friend and I love you. I know you said you'd come back shortly but please come and see me tomorrow night instead and we'll talk about everything. I'm fine, don't worry.

He puts his phone in airplane mode and looks at the bed in front of him, so wonderfully soft—*softness*, a ludicrous idea in a world of concrete, red sand, and blackness—and very nearly dives onto it, but there is now the other thing he needs to do before anything else. He spots his suitcase on the floor and opens it, rooting for the zip pocket on its interior wall. His other emergency stash is still there: eight blister packs of painkillers.

Ivan didn't know about these.

Johnny doesn't give any part of his mind a chance to interfere. He snatches all the packets and heads toward the bathroom. His breathing is rapid, his body responding with adrenaline as it knows what is coming.

He kicks open the bathroom door, nearly dropping the packets from his shaking hands. He darts to the toilet, placing the packets on the counter beside it. He immediately selects one and thumbs the tablets out into his palm. He repeats the process with the next packet, and the next. By the time he has emptied three of the eight blister packs, his palm is full of pills. He holds them for a moment, feeling their insignificant—yet utterly significant—weight.

He turns his hand over and drops the entire pile into the open toilet bowl.

He stares at them for a moment, seeing the tiny avalanche sitting submerged on the porcelain. He breathes faster as he snatches up the rest of the packs and empties them all directly into the bowl, and by the time the last pill pops free of its pack, Johnny is sobbing. He slams his hand onto the flush lever. He watches as the water swirls the tablets up from the bottom like an addict's snow globe. Then it all drains away with remarkable speed, and Johnny gasps as the disappearing water carries his tablets out of sight, leaving him with nothing but a fist full of empty blister packs. He drops them into the wastebasket and staggers back against the wall, his hands over his eyes. He stands there for a moment as tears of relief pour down his cheeks.

Once he calms down, he becomes aware of how much he wants to shower, to shave — but he realizes there is another, far more important thing that must be taken care of first.

The fridge is calling. *Hollering.*

Johnny is so excited he begins to laugh as he staggers to the kitchen. By the time he reaches the fridge, he is letting out animal bellows of victory.

Some time later, scarcely able to believe the intensity of the pleasure he has just experienced, a full-to-bursting Johnny heads back to the bathroom. He knows he will perhaps pay a price for gorging himself, but he doesn't give a damn. It will have been worth it. He stands at the mirror and trims his beard into something he actually quite likes; he decides that it will stay. Then he removes his bloodied, ragged clothes and turns on the shower. Johnny steps under the showerhead, chuckling to himself as the hot water runs gloriously down his back. It's the greatest shower of his entire life. The chuckles almost turn into tears, so moved is he by the feeling of being cleansed, but he breathes slowly, and the smile — the grin — makes its way back onto his face.

Once finished, he throws his ruined clothes in the trash and moves to the bedroom to fetch his bathrobe and hears the front door being unlocked. Ivan. Johnny knew that sending the text saying come tomorrow instead was a long shot. His friend would never leave him alone knowing how close Johnny had come to relapsing.

"Johnny?" Ivan's voice calls from the hallway. "I just got your text, but now I'm already on the street anyway and I'm thinking, *Hey, I simply have to see my friend Johnny, what a guy, love this guy, wow.*"

Johnny smiles, drying himself quickly. Ivan, already trying to fix the sour mood from earlier, trying to make peace even as he barges in to save the day. This time, however, Johnny more than welcomes it.

"Just a second," he calls, finding his bathrobe and pulling it on.

Johnny opens the bedroom door, and Ivan's grin — he's pleased at his own joke — vanishes as he takes in the beard that wasn't there when he left, the visible freshly healed wound that travels almost elegantly down Johnny's neck and disappears under the collar of his bathrobe. Johnny smiles faintly and beckons Ivan to follow him into the bathroom, where he points wordlessly at the empty blister packs lying in the trash. Ivan stares at them and then turns to Johnny, his hands beginning to shake as they rise to his friend's face. His fingers touch Johnny's beard, the sides of his head.

"You... you went alone."

"Yes," Johnny says, nodding, holding Ivan's forearms and smiling sadly.

Ivan starts to cry. He shakes his head and draws Johnny to him. "I let you go alone."

The two men embrace in the tiny bathroom, Johnny resting his head against his friend's shoulder. "No," Johnny says, beginning to laugh quietly. "You were with me. You were with me, man."

They go to the kitchen and talk.

Ivan asks a thousand questions, and Johnny answers all that he can; he leaves out, however, the parts with the Boggart. He is too tired to go into such detail, and he knows that Ivan will grill him endlessly on this subject. Johnny will answer those questions too, but not today. It would take far too long, and eventually Johnny has to politely tell his friend that he simply must sleep. Now fed and showered, he feels a deliciously intense sleepiness creep into his body.

Ivan agrees immediately, apologizing for the hundredth time, Johnny countering with his own intense gratitude for Ivan's gift. Ivan demands that Johnny promise to come to Ivan's parents' house for dinner, and Johnny happily concedes. They embrace once more on the doorstep before Ivan leaves, now shaking his own head and chuckling in wide-eyed disbelief.

"Johnny, man," he says, looking his friend up and down. "I can't believe... *man*. You did it. Hey, you know Sandy called me, just before I got here? She said she didn't have your number and asked me to pass a message on."

Johnny leans against the doorway, his arms folded. "Go on."

"Something David wanted to tell you," Ivan says. "He said there's something for you in the attic."

Johnny's almost surprised. Almost.

"Okay."

"David is special, as you probably know," Ivan adds. "He knows things." He eyes Johnny for a moment, trying not to look suspicious. "You know what she's talking about, Johnny?"

"Yeah," Johnny says, smiling. "And it's okay."

Ivan shrugs. "She sounded calm. She said David said *you agreed with her*. That she knew you would."

"About?"

"That this is a *good house*."

Johnny grins. "Be a lot fucking better when I've had some sleep."

"Not even here a whole day," Ivan says, "and this is how he treats his guests. His *landlord* even." He grins and heads down the path.

Johnny watches him go and then closes the front door, smiling himself.

He falls onto that heavenly bed. He slept in the Deep Place whenever he was at the point of exhaustion, but such naps could never be anything more than brief. He always had to be alert. The monsters would close in while he slept.

Here in the Real, he has no such concerns, even without being able to physically manifest his intention. Here, such creatures can't manifest themselves, and Johnny has long since overcome his terror of the unknown. Besides, Johnny is now very familiar with his monsters. He has faced them many times, and though they are no less dangerous, he now thinks of them as a lion tamer thinks of his big cats: never to be underestimated; always to be shown respect and kept under control.

But there's something in the attic…

That will have to wait. He knows the rules; indeed, there is only one that matters, and he isn't breaking it. He wanted to take off his bathrobe, but with his wonderfully full belly, he doesn't have time to undress or even to get under the covers before he is unconscious.

He sleeps until three the next afternoon.

Johnny does not wake in all that time or cry out in fear or have bad dreams; he does not have any dreams at all, in fact. Johnny Blake sleeps like the dead. When he wakes, he pulls aside the curtain above the bed. Glorious sunshine blazes in, and Johnny lies on his back for a while, reveling in both the daylight and the unbridled comfort of the mattress.

But things must be finalized, he knows, before he can truly start getting his head around what he has been through.

Get his head around it? Somehow, he feels like he already has. The thoughts of the Shallows and the Deep Place are of course incredible things, but Johnny discovers he feels the same way about them as he does about the knowledge that he will one day die.

Impossible reality. Sometimes one must just shrug and say *yes*.

He gets up from the bed and puts on some clean clothes. Rummages in his suitcase until he finds his travel flashlight. Then he walks down a hallway full of autumn sunlight, shining through the frosted glass of the front door.

The pole to open the attic hatch lies on the hallway floor.

Johnny picks it up and raises it to the catch, unhooking it. He takes a deep breath and pulls. The hatch swings open.

There is nothing on the other side except a familiar square of darkness, but Johnny isn't hugely surprised. *In* the attic was the message. He must go up.

He hooks the ladder's base with the pole and pulls it down to the hallway floor. He calmly hangs the pole back on its hook before placing his foot on the bottom rung and looking up through the hatch again. It looks like a window into the Deep Place through which he has only just fought. Johnny calls out to it, his voice clear and loud:

"I'm coming up."

He begins to climb, his grip on the ladder's rungs firm, his upward steps sure-footed. He carefully pokes his head through the hatch, but not too carefully; here, he knows, the monsters need to be allowed to get you, and he has learned the hard way. He turns on the flashlight and shines it around the darkened space, peering beyond the framework of metal stanchions. The attic is empty of anything except the regular, expected clutter. No Boggart.

He does not, of course, do anything as foolish as to doubt that his experience was real, to even slightly believe that it was all some kind of impossible hallucination. He has the scars to prove it. But he does want to know what was supposed to be in the attic for him. Did David just get it wrong? He shines the flashlight into the attic's eaves, trying to see anything unusual—

There's something lying on top of the pile of boxes that was once the Boggart's nest.

It looks to be about the size of a serving tray and colored a dark green. Johnny climbs the rest of the way into the attic and clambers around the metal jungle before him until he reaches the boxes. The item appears to be some kind of large, thick leaf, only not one of any plant Johnny has ever seen before. The closest thing it resembles would be a rubber plant leaf, but this is at least three times the size of any in Johnny's experience, and almost rectangular in shape. Embossed on it is a series of tiny, angular patterns laid out in neat lines, colored brown; Johnny realizes that these have been burned into the leaf's smooth and shiny surface. They could almost be letters, were they written in any alphabet that Johnny could recognize, but as he looks at them he discovers that he can understand what they say. His brain is making sense of them even if the language is coming across as garbled. There are large gaps in his actual understanding of the text, but the meaning of the words—the *intention*—is as clear as the light from Johnny's flashlight, and he knows that is of course what matters:

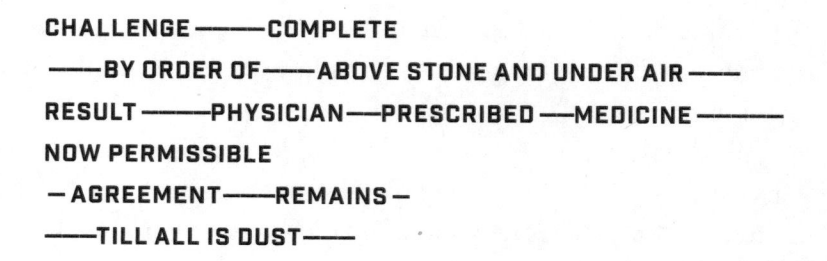

CHALLENGE ———COMPLETE
———BY ORDER OF———ABOVE STONE AND UNDER AIR———
RESULT ———PHYSICIAN—PRESCRIBED —MEDICINE ———
NOW PERMISSIBLE
— AGREEMENT———REMAINS —
———TILL ALL IS DUST———

"I understand," Johnny says.

Something gently crackles in the air around him. The leaf in his hands instantly begins to dry out, becoming thinner, crisper, its color changing from green to brown. Within seconds it has crumbled into a dark powder, falling in a drift around Johnny's feet.

"Okay," Johnny says quietly. He is almost disappointed that the Boggart isn't here. He has a question, one that he isn't sure Ivan will be able to answer. Ivan and Bailey in the Shallows were facsimiles of his friends; yes, part of the Whole, as the Boggart said, and therefore real in themselves, while not the actual people they were supposed to be.

But the Mister Kaleb he met in the Shallows—Martin Blake—was that the real version of his father?

There are no answers to that here. At least the real versions of his Ivan and Bailey are fine...

The faint sting comes as he realizes that she is fine *without him*, the girl who once told him—and later, Ivan—of the secret name only shared with people she trusts deeply. *"You can call me Bailey, if you like."* The memory of that precious sentence would have once been crippling; now, Johnny notes, it's only sad. He'll be okay. Johnny takes in the musty smell of the loft space and thinks: *What now?* As he returns to the ladder and begins to descend, the answer comes to him:

One step at a time.

He wonders what the first step might be. The world seems so impossibly huge now that he knows this new policy—*one step at a time*—is the right way to go. He has already lived the impossible, but to adjust, to function in this world, will be another vast undertaking. He's ready to try.

He moves idly into the bedroom, seeing his portable audio interface and MIDI controller nestled at the bottom of his suitcase. He could get them set up, tweak some old music projects. That would be a start.

But not the right start, perhaps.

There's another possible beginning; there is, despite David's message, maybe one more conversation to be had.

He considers getting his phone and making *that* call. Yes, he's changed beyond recognition, certainly, but has she? Time, for him, has been a lot longer. And would she even want to hear from him?

He shakes his head, realizing he shouldn't even think about having this on his radar right now. He walks back into the hallway, knowing he can of course call any day (*tomorrow—no, geez*), and today is far too beautiful to spend indoors. Even through the frosted glass, he can see how incredibly blue the sky is. The air will be clear.

He should be under it all.

Johnny fetches his other boots from his suitcase—the pair that came through the Deep Place are worn away to almost nothing—and puts them on. He's halfway out the door before he remembers his phone. He nearly leaves it where it is but decides against that. *Headphones too,* he thinks with a smile. Today requires music.

Johnny Blake steps outside and goes for a walk.

Chapter Twenty-Four

BAILEY STARES AT her novel's final line. She likes it; something about it moved her, and that's a good sign in her book. *For* her book. She wants to go straight back to the start and begin the third draft, but she's already let it take too much time away from her studies. She dropped out once, and that was bad enough. There's no way she's going to let herself be kicked out of university.

She closes her laptop, thinking that she should at least do something to mark the completion of this revision. It feels like enough of a different book to justify it. This version, including the notes she made during her time at No Days Off and filtered through her memories of that whole experience, is something new. There's a bottle of prosecco in the fridge that her flatmate, Penny, won at the Student Union, and Penny doesn't even like prosecco. She won't miss it.

She heads to the apartment's kitchenette and opens the fridge; the journey doesn't take long. The apartment is a small two bedroom, its seventies-wallpapered living room seeming larger than it is thanks to the french doors set in the wall, leading to the Juliet balcony beyond. Bailey and Penny furnished the place over several happy weekend trips to local thrift stores. While the resulting style of their home runs the gamut from art deco to mock Elizabethan, Bailey couldn't love the chaos more if she tried. Inside the fridge lie two slices of leftover pizza, sitting on a side plate wedged onto the overstuffed second shelf.

Prosecco and pizza. The perfect cheat meal.

She gets a glass, heads back to the threadbare sofa, and plonks herself down. She's breaking the diet deal with Imani, but that's okay; it's a special occasion, and besides, it certainly won't stop her grinding out more chin-ups than anyone else in the gym later.

Nothing ever does.

She pauses mid-bite, catching the thought. That overconfidence. She has to keep an eye on that. She lived with Ellie Fellowes for three weeks. She knows where that kind of thinking leads.

But she did make you into a machine—

"*I* made me a machine," she says out loud to the silent kitchen, and catches *that*. What's wrong with her today? Must be finally finishing that damn redraft. "It doesn't matter," she says, exhaling. She looks at her watch. Two hours to her Emerging Markets lecture, thirty minutes to her Zoom call with her therapist. Shit. She forgot. As much as she'd love an excuse to *not* do therapy, she and Jennifer made a deal: therapy every week, twice a week. For her part, Bailey still has enough inheritance money to afford that, and she has stuck to it.

She lifts the glass of prosecco to her lips and considers taking "It doesn't matter" a step further. She raises the glass into the air, the toast ready in her mind. She could say it. No one would hear. Part of her thinks it's deserved: *To Ellie,* she could say. *Who did her best, such as it was.*

But then she doesn't say it after all. She downs the entire glass in one swallow instead, coughing a little, the fizz reminding her of a bizarre ceremony in a garden at sunset.

Bailey has not seen Kelly at the gym since leaving the hospital after the hell that was No Days Off. Bailey's concussion wasn't minor, but eventually they decided it was safe for her to go home—even if the bright lights stuck around for weeks. Her rib has long since healed. She's messaged Kelly several times on Facebook but eventually found herself unfriended. She managed to get investigating Detective Munsen to admit that they had formally questioned Kelly, which at least explained Kelly's absence from the gym and Bailey's online ostracization. Bailey would love, love, *love* to compare notes with the woman.

She very much doubts that Kelly went to Elite, or even that Kelly's experience on Heavy reached the extremes that Bailey's did. Kelly's review, Bailey thinks, would not have been quite so gushing if that were the case.

Bailey's phone buzzes again. She clears the call—it's Imani—but this time sends a picture of her meal along with the text:

> Can't talk now, just finished the second draft. See you lataaah

Imani writes back:

> Good job! Now maybe you can finally tell me that other story you have, eh? No pressure no pressure no pressure

Bailey chuckles, but the half joke is getting a little annoying. She's going to have to sit Imani down and kindly make it clear that she will not be talking about No Days Off anytime soon. The therapy sessions—dragging hell out of her from the feet up—are bad enough. She might have had revelations in that place, but they were of her own making, not Ellie's. As her therapist says: "Insight comes quickly. Change comes slowly." Throw in the trauma of being buried alive, and Bailey thinks that change will indeed take a long time.

But for now, she's changed enough, even though she knows—hell, she can admit it, as Ellie taught—she can always do better.

She goes to take another sip and realizes that—of course!—she should make another toast, this time to the subject of her book. She hadn't meant to put the character version of him through so much hell—not even a little bit. The idea started from her fervent wish that he could be helped, her own insipid, cowardly way of making up for the devastating things she said. But the story seemed to write itself, as if she were simply a willing conduit. With that, the thought comes:

If you really are sorry, you'll text him, or call him, and tell him.

She agrees. Her reluctance isn't because she's scared. Not anymore, at least. She doesn't know if it will make things worse for him.

He's probably forgotten all about her anyway; why would he want her messaging him now, even if it's to say how sorry she is? And his issues mingling with hers just made the whole thing so fucking *unhealthy*.

It wouldn't just be a call to say that, though, would it?

It wouldn't, and that's what scares her. She's spent so much time with this fictional version of him, this managing-his-recovery version of him. It wouldn't be fair to put that image onto a living, breathing person and expect them to live up to it. So why, with all this extremely hard-earned fucking willpower that she now supposedly has in spades, does her hand keep going to her phone?

Because you're different now, a voice inside her whispers. *Aren't you?* The voice isn't keening or deceptive. It's heavy with truth. *Because maybe you aren't someone who loses herself in someone else anymore. Because maybe you're someone who would leave in the right way if you needed to.*

She shivers the thought away, draining her glass. The book—she's marking the occasion, right? That's important right now. *Be present...*

She stands up, her pizza finished. She looks at her watch again: twenty-five minutes to therapy. She looks through the french doors. Outside, the sun is shining. She could make it to the big oak tree in the park and be back in plenty of time. It wouldn't even require a brisk pace. Her mind wanders as she looks for her keys.

She shakes that thought away too as she heads for the door. Another glance at the weather through the window makes her think maybe she'll be a little late for therapy today. She can do a slightly shorter session for a change. Today is special. This needs to be a celebratory stroll. She pauses for a moment, listening to her mind's usual resistance, these words light but deceptively poisonous:

This is the start of the slippery slope. You're cutting corners.

She hears it, lets it pass. She knows the difference between the two voices now and reminds herself that she decides what is and isn't allowed. She takes a breath, lets it out. Smiles. She opens the door just as her phone starts to ring again in her pocket. *Imani, Jesus,* she thinks.

She sees the screen. It isn't Imani calling.

For a moment she stares at it in shock. The timing is just too weird. She pauses, staring at the phone as it continues to ring, her heart accelerating as she knows soon the ringing will stop. Would she actually have the nerve to call back if she doesn't answer in time?

Then she understands that she would.

She takes a deep breath and raises her hand to answer the call, turning away from the door. It closes behind her, but the loud click in the quiet hallway brings her to her senses. Of *course* she's not staying indoors, regardless of the phone call. She planned to walk to the oak tree in the park, and that's what she's going to do. She opens the door again, steps into the sunshine, and answers her phone.

"Hi, Johnny," she says. She's smiling.

Bailey Madison goes for a walk.

Afterword

MY SINCERE THANKS to you for reading this novel. Here's where I think the idea for Madison's story came from:

About ten years ago I read the memoir *Angry White Pyjamas* by Robert Twigger. It describes how he, as a newbie to martial arts, embarked on the notoriously brutal yearlong Tokyo riot police aikido course. He was a regular, untrained guy, but somehow he endured endless sessions of exercises that involved things like endlessly pivoting on his knees on the mats until his knees bled... then going back the next day to do the same thing, making his fresh scabs tear open all over again. Students would tape wads of tissue paper inside the knees of their *gi* to help with the pain, but often the tissue would just become soaked with blood and disintegrate. Still, the students kept going.

When I began reading the book, I thought, *Hell yeah, I'm gonna do this too. Forge myself like steel.* As I read on and came to descriptions of sessions that would continue until students passed out or vomited (and need I remind you of the bloody kneecaps?!), I thought, *Hell no, I'll just eat a sandwich instead.* Surely it was perfectly reasonable to not want to put myself through such torment? It's not chickening out when the punishment is so intense, is it? But where is the reasonable

Afterword

cutoff for acceptable discomfort when embarking on a lofty goal? And what do you do when you want to become strong but lack the strength required to begin? Robert Twigger managed it—managed to keep going back to the dojo every day, knowing what was coming. By his own confession, he wasn't a tough guy. He was, in fact, a poet who taught English.

Something else weird happened as I was reading it; about halfway through I realized that I'd heard of this book before. My late dad had read it many years earlier when it was released. The fact that we'd both happened to pick up the same book nearly twenty years apart (I'd completely forgotten about it in the interim) perhaps lent the experience some more weight in my mind: again, it stuck with me. Why did we *both* choose the same book? What about it appealed to each of us? My dad was already a hardworking guy who endured long alternating day/night shifts weekly. What did he see in the story, then? I can't speculate for him, but for me, the appeal definitely stems from my own lifelong frustration with procrastination; the idea of countering it with total immersion, driven by a leader who *won't let you quit*, surrounded by peers all endorsing the same madness in pursuit of a goal; hopefully coming out the other end transformed. But would whatever you gained stick? Would you keep that iron? All of these thoughts were the seeds for *I'll Quit When I'm Dead*, and they germinated for some time.

I could never quite figure out what story the beats would be; I knew the premise, but the full details eluded me. Eventually, once I started working on what was *The Boggart's Biographer* (the initial structure was very different, hence the title), it suddenly hit me that this new story held all the missing pieces of Madison's, and I loved the idea of telling the two together.

Ivan, incidentally, is very loosely based on my dear friend of several decades, the writer and actor Mirsad Solakovic. If you want to hear an *unbelievable* true story, check out the fourteen-minute video *How I Survived Being Tortured at 13* on YouTube. It has nearly three million views.

If you enjoyed the hints of the world the Boggart is a part of,

Afterword

that's all explored a little further in my recent novel *You See the Monster*. I think you'll get a kick out of that one: *How do you convince the entire world that monsters are real... when your life depends on it?* And if you fancy something to really sink into, why not try my (Audible Book of the Year–nominated, *ahem*) Stone Man series? It's four books long—ah hell, I have a whole back catalogue; check it out at the front of this book, fill your boots! Eh? *Eh?*

Finally, if you *really* enjoyed this book, please do one of two things: visit lukesmitherd.com and sign up for the fabulous "Spam-Free Book Release Newsletter" so you never miss a book announcement (emails go out only when there's significant news) and even get a free short story or two, *or*, please leave a star rating on your site of choice. (Smart option: Do both!) For writers—those of us wishing to reach a wider audience—those ratings are beyond priceless. Readers who have followed my indie career are well used to the now-traditional star-rating-begging letter in the post-book afterword. But those days are of course done; I'm now being published by freakin' *Mulholland,* and serious, credible publishers like these guys don't take kindly to my old ways of cajoling, threatening, resorting to tears, and... well, if you know, you know. So none of that* here. I'm a classy author now.

Thank you very much for reading my work. I've always enjoyed connecting with readers, so do please drop me a line and let me know your thoughts on the book. Hopefully I'll see you for the next one.

Stay Hungry, folks.

Luke Smitherd
Los Angeles
February 7, 2025

---

* We'll talk.

Acknowledgments

THANK YOU TO this book's champions:

The amazing Kristin Nelson of Nelson Literary Agency, who backed this book from the jump, got it into fighting shape, and never let it quit.

The sensational Liv Ryan at Mulholland, who then took this book and made it drop and give her infinity...all while keeping the regimen fun. Thank you for being a delight to work with, and for making this book into the Revenge Body version of itself.

There is no such thing as a self-made man. *Huge thanks also to:*

The OG, Sam Boyce. No Sam, no book.

My manager, the great Ryan Lewis.

Barnett Brettler, not only for his immeasurable help with my career (for being a sounding board for just about every book from *Kill Someone* onward) but also for being a kind and loyal friend.

Peter Robinson for reading everything.

Clare Gozdawa for helping keep the ship steady.

Of course, above all...Oxley. X ☺

And, finally, to the Baddest Bitches in existence: every single reader who ever left a review, posted about my work, sent a kind email

Acknowledgments

of support, or did all of the above and (best of all) also bullied friends, loved ones, and vulnerable neighbors into reading my stuff. This book probably wouldn't be here without you. You kept an indie writer going, and from the bottom of your Second Favorite Author's heart: *thank you.*

About the Author

LUKE SMITHERD is the author of *The Stone Man* (shortlisted for Audible Book of the Year 2015) and its sequels as well as several other novels. A former singer and guitarist, he now writes full time, hosts the comedy music-discussion show *Cracker Juice*, and performs around Los Angeles as a stand-up comic. He divides his time between the United States and the United Kingdom.

RAISING READERS
Books Build Bright Futures

Thank you for reading this book and for being a reader of books in general. As an author, I am so grateful to share being part of a community of readers with you, and I hope you will join me in passing our love of books on to the next generation of readers.

Did you know that reading for enjoyment is the single biggest predictor of a child's future happiness and success?

More than family circumstances, parents' educational background, or income, reading impacts a child's future academic performance, emotional well-being, communication skills, economic security, ambition, and happiness.

Studies show that kids reading for enjoyment in the US is in rapid decline:

- In 2012, 53% of 9-year-olds read almost every day. Just 10 years later, in 2022, the number had fallen to 39%.
- In 2012, 27% of 13-year-olds read for fun daily. By 2023, that number was just 14%.

Together, we can commit to **Raising Readers** and change this trend. How?

- Read to children in your life daily.
- Model reading as a fun activity.
- Reduce screen time.
- Start a family, school, or community book club.
- Visit bookstores and libraries regularly.
- Listen to audiobooks.
- Read the book before you see the movie.
- Encourage your child to read aloud to a pet or stuffed animal.
- Give books as gifts.
- Donate books to families and communities in need.

Books build bright futures, and **Raising Readers** is our shared responsibility.

For more information, visit **JoinRaisingReaders.com**

Sources: National Endowment for the Arts, National Assessment of Educational Progress, WorldBookDay.org, Nielsen BookData's 2023 "Understanding the Children's Book Consumer"